AUSTI[illegible]
READER

The Austin Clarke Reader

Toronto

Exile Editions
1996

Dedicated
to my cousins
Lorraine, Authier, and Douglas Luke

This edition is published by Exile Editions Limited,
20 Dale Avenue, Toronto, Ontario, Canada M4W 1K4

Sales Distribution:
General Distribution Services
30 Lesmill Road
Don Mills, ON
M3B 2T6
1-800-387-0172

Layout and Design by *MICHAEL P. CALLAGHAN*
Composed and Typeset at *MOONS OF JUPITER, TORONTO*
Printed and Bound by *AMPERSAND PRINTING, GUELPH*
Author's Photograph by *ROB ALLEN*
Cover by *S. W. HAYTER*

The publisher wishes to acknowledge the assistance toward publication of the Canada Council and the Ontario Arts Council.

ISBN 1-55096-035-0

Contents

"Tom Say . . . ": A Preface

Rinaldo Walcott

Austin "Tom" Clarke. That is how I know him. When I was only eleven years old Tom Clarke, as many in Barbados call him, crashed into my small world. Tom Clarke had returned "home" for a stint as the administrator of the Caribbean Broadcasting Corporation, the television station in Barbados. He hoped to Barbadianize the station. It is the return of Tom Clarke and his aborted cultural contribution that first made him known to me. His time at the CBC would be immortalized in the calypso "Tom Say," by Sir Don and fictionalized in his novel, *The Prime Minister.* Tom Clarke had nonetheless left an indelible mark on his native soil. I have since learned a lot from Tom Clarke's return "home."

For the migrant, the exile, the refugee, the impossibility of returning "home" is only equal to the impossibility of never arriving in the new place. This dilemma of *can't return* and *never arriving* is both literally and symbolically what might be said to characterize Austin Clarke's body of written works, both fiction and non-fiction. The tensions between *can't return* and *never arriving* are not necessarily negative tensions. In fact, I want to insist that the tensions are wholly productive ones. Located between *can't return* and *never arriving* is the space of the in-between. From that space the occupant can relay to us insights that we might otherwise miss. This in-between space offers us the perspective of the radical unfinished project of emancipation and the desire for a true and sustaining liberty. For example, Austin Clarke's political satire published in the Barbadian tabloid, *The Nation,* is an exercise in writing from an in-between space. His columns highlighted the contradictions, tensions and the new (im)possibilities of the post-independent nation. Clarke's commentaries also spoke to what another important Caribbean writer, George Lamming, termed "the pleasures of exile."

It is to Canada, that I want to suggest that Clarke's in-between position has been most insightful and challenging. His works, set in Canada, use the in-between space as a way to allow readers access to a world and a gaze, from another position which is instructive for the nation. Clarke brings the Caribbean (most often Barbados) and Canada together in ways that are not contrived, but in ways that are mutually interrogative of both. The interrogation is achieved through a question of the incomplete project of migration and its attendant woes. The questioning is couched in an ethical stance clearly focused on what it means to be Human. However, Clarke does not propose in his works a liberal humanist project, with a desire to jettison all difference in the name of some universal criteria for belonging. On the contrary, Clarke explores our humanity so that we might better make sense of the incompleteness of the human project when it is only conceived within the parameters of attaining material possessions, the effects of racism and other cultural practices which produce a number of different kinds of exile. These exiles are no different from the exile of leaving one's home.

It is in the use of language that Clarke most firmly brings Canadian and Caribbean together. His characters move between different registers of English, using vernaculars which reference their class, gender, race and other personal and collective qualities. His uncompromising use of Caribbean language-sounds in his work speaks to the importance of challenging conceptions of who belongs. This use of language by Clarke, rewrites the sound and tonality of Canada, implanting a Caribbean presence here as constitutive of who and what Canada is. But language also signals exile, for it is the language and in this case the claiming of English, not just as a (m)other tongue, but also as another tongue, which brings the issues of *can't return* and *never arriving* to a boil. For language signals that five hundred year exile from Africa, as it simultaneously signals the same five hundred year attempt to arrive in the Americas. Thus, in the final analysis, language, reduced to its basic denominator — accents, matter in this country.

Place and blackness collide in Austin Clarke's work to register the deep and profound ambivalences that black people experience in the American hemisphere. Issues of place are even more intensified in the context of nations. But place and blackness are the signal most defining moments for black diasporic peoples. The peoples whom Clarke makes the focus of his art and other works were forged in the prism of exile — and exile is all they know. But in knowing exile, they know how to make demands of nations (even if those demands are some times just for motor cars and big houses) and therefore insist upon having their presence acknowledged. Making demands of Canada is what Clarke and the characters in his fiction do. Those demands insist that Canada become a place where arrival is possible and evident. Clarke, then, is our most lyrical blues geographer, as he tells us stories of pain and triumph. His characters occupy Toronto, that is Canada, like it belongs to them. This is important because it is from the location of residence that political demands and actions might be possible. Taking up space by black people is a crucial part of insisting upon the possibility of arrival, for it is only when the possibility of arrival is evident that black people would have achieved all their rights as human beings in this part of the world.

Austin Clarke's characters make us laugh, cry, get angry and want to celebrate, because his crafting of them populates them with the desires and lacks that we all so easily recognize, but find difficult to articulate — he does the articulating for us. Collected in this book is some of the work which speaks to our humanity, as it asks us to account for how we understand what it means to be Human. Clarke is one of the most imporant Canadian writers because his art challenges us to move beyond the too easy platitudes of us/them, to venture into the much more uncertain and murky terrain of the Self, which requires that we understand our implication and complicity with injustice. Thus, Clarke requires us to think and act on what we can do about injustice.

Austin Clarke — All Our Possibilities : A Foreword

Dionne Brand

There is something distinctly Canadian about trying to focus on an identity or a place which would describe where we live and who we are. The public commentary about this dilemma fills air waves and libraries. Someone always claims to know what that identity means, what its parameters are, and what its symbols. And no sooner are the words out of their mouths than they bounce into thin air and question again. They reveal the emptiness of claiming as well as the arbitrary terror of ownership. Canadian identity is always being claimed by whatever wave of immigration preceded another, using the wavy and tenuous line of two hundred or so years ago as its first marker. Perhaps it is the true origins of this country which make this identity always contested, which make it impossible for anyone other than First Nations peoples to truly claim it, and, perhaps merely landing here, two hundred years ago or two decades ago or two years ago doesn't matter, despite the presumption of displacement and the brutality of conquest. That knowledge attaches itself to the psyche, the knowledge of long before, the knowledge of inherent right, the knowledge of the settler who cannot ever know the ground as birthplace and inherits instead a restlessness, an unsettling feeling which always needs a heavy hand to confirm, which always needs a piece of paper, a showy object of some kind, an edict to legitimise itself, and a host of laws, bills, enactments, re-enactments and gestures to lay claim. And all those things may succeed — and have — in hiding the intangible, the ungraspable, and in the process they've wiped out certain ways of seeing, but into them has crept the intangible, the ungraspable, which is why no one can say with certainty who they are and can only say it with the force of a state. Yet what is truly there, who we truly are, is actually much more interesting, much more breathtaking, than the project of domination and legitimising going on at all levels in the society, including that of the national literature.

I used to see Austin Clarke walking across Bathurst street when I first came to Toronto in the early seventies. I was working at Spear Magazine just across from the Home Services Association. I was learning to be a poet and learning how to put together and paste up a magazine. I was nineteen or so, I was learning a lot of things. Mostly how to write the short rhetorical line of poetry with all its political cut. I didn't have a sense of the national literature, or of Clarke being an important part of it. This was merely an indiscernible landscape vast enough and indistinct enough to imagine the place I wanted to be. Somewhere revolutionary, somewhere where all the maps of the land I was interested in drew in as if they were one place, and it wasn't called Canada. I could imagine my hand drawing in North America, Africa, South America and the Caribbean as one would grab a sheet from the middle so that these continents and the archipelago touched each other and there were no distances or philosophies inbetween. No need to clarify where I was because where I was was just a cipher for where I wanted to be. So, Clarke with his stories about the small, delicate lives of Black migrants to this country, marking his outline of this territory through their thoughts, apprehensions, anxieties and self derision; Clarke mapping this landscape called Canada or more specifically Toronto through their sojourns in kitchens, offices, hairdressing shops, race tracks, through their longing, envy, conviction and love; Clarke was just a figure crossing a street with his pipe and his languages, shielding himself from a community that thought writing perhaps unimportant, mining his observations and sightings of our lives as we lived it and seeing long before us how it fit.

It is not that the national literature doesn't tolerate other observations but it tolerates them only at the level of the newcomer without a past, or with an awful enough past as to make the acknowledged superficial goods of this society desirable and life saving. The subliteratures or 'immigrant' or 'ethnic' literatures are required to denounce their past wholly or reveal some atrocity which will place Canada in the position of rescuer. What these literatures are required to do is constantly 'refer' to Canada and refer to their own difference as anomalous. Anomalous, not challenging or equal to 'Canadian experience.' One can say then that these literatures are only allowed one book. The same book, from its different ethnicities; versions of a Canadian myth of the perpetual newcomer / outsider. Versions which help in the project of shaping the elusive Canadian identity by pointing to its difference from it. Which reminds me of a workshop I once did at CBC television for writers of color. There were ten or so of us in the workshop, all with different stories, of course, but by the time we were done learning the structure of a half-hour drama — what must happen in each ten minutes — the emotions which must be summoned and the resolution which must be had; by the time we had learned the bible of the series — No Controversy being its main tenet — we all ended up with the same story, of course — the static frame of the newcomer or the unenlightened or the backward who learns by the end of the drama how to be a Canadian. What Clarke does and has always done in his work is resist this stultifying requirement. His characters resist appearing only at the beck of this national need and they appear, in their conscious and unconscious, possessed of other occupations. What Clarke explores are the possibilities beyond this "stuck-in-time" consciousness within the national psyche. And that is why his work is highly important and crucial to any assessment of Canadian literature since the fifties. Clarke suggests a rhythm to explode this aspect of the national consciousness into its dynamic pieces, into all its circumlocutions, so that we find ourselves in his work standing in a landscape not only engendered by domination but by all the ambiguity and nuance, variation and interconnectedness which really exist.

In the coming decades his offering to the national literature, his subversion of the national literature, will be read with gratitude by writers who find themselves facing the call to resist or have their spirits perish in the opacity of the dominating identity. It will be read by those writers who resist subliteratures as they resist sub-lives. I am extremely grateful for his works and recognise in them that insistence that the landscape layer all of our possibilities, admit all of our origins, see our lives as changing and dynamic and claim nothing that we cannot or need not hold.

Stories

Leaving This Island Place

The faces at the grilled windows of the parish almshouse were looking out, on this hot Saturday afternoon, on a world of grey flannel and cricket and cream shirts, a different world, as they had looked every afternoon from the long imprisonment of the wards. Something in those faces told me they were all going to die in the almshouse. Standing on the cricket field I searched for the face of my father. I knew he would never live to see the sun of day again.

It is not cricket, it is leaving the island that makes me think about my father. I am leaving the island. And as I walk across the green playing field and onto the driveway of the almshouse, its walkway speckled with spots of tar and white pebbles, and walk right up to the white spotless front of the building, I know it is too late now to think of saving him. It is too late to become involved with this dying man.

In the open verandah I can see the men, looking half-alive and half-dead, lying on the smudged canvas cots that were once white and cream as the cricketers' clothes airing themselves. They have played, perhaps, in too many muddy tournaments, and are now soiled. But I am leaving. But I know before I leave there is some powerful tug which pulls me into this almshouse, grabbing me, almost swallowing me, to make me enter these doors and slap me flat on the sore-back canvas cot beside a man in dying health. But I am leaving.

"You wasn't coming to visit this poor man, this father o' yourn?" It is Miss Brewster, the head nurse. She knew my father and she knew me. And she knew that I played cricket every Saturday on the field across the world from the almshouse. She is old and haggard. And she looks as if she has looked once too often on the face of death; and now she herself resembles a half-dead, dried-out flying fish, wrapped in the greaseproof paper of her nurse's uniform. "That man having fits and convulsions by the hour! Every day he asking for you. All the time, day in and day out. And you is such a poor-great high school educated bastard that you now acting too *proud* to come in here because it is a almshouse and not a *private ward*, to see your own father! And you didn't even have the presence o' mind to bring along a orange, not even one, or a banana for that man, *your father!*

She was now leading me through a long dark hallway through rows of men on their sides, and some on their backs, lying like soldiers on a battlefield. They all looked at me as if I was dying. I tried to avoid their eyes and I looked instead at their bones and the long fingernails and toenails, the thermometers of their long idle illness. The matted hair and the smell of men overdue for the bedpan: men too weary now to raise themselves to pass water even in a lonely gutter. They were dying slowly and surely, for the almshouse was crowded and it did not allow its patients to die too quickly. I passed them, miles out of my mind: the rotting clothes and sores, men of all colors, all ages, dressed like women in long blue sailcloth-hard shirts that dropped right down to the scales on their toothpick legs. One face smiled at me, and I wondered whether the smile meant welcome.

"Wait here!" It was Miss Brewster again who had spoken. She opened the door of a room and pushed me inside as you would push a small boy into the headmaster's office for a caning; and straightway the smell of stale urine and of sweat and feces whipped me in the face. When the door closed behind me I was alone with the dead, with the smells of the almshouse.

I am frightened. But I am leaving. I find myself thinking about the trimmed sandwiches and the whiskey-and-sodas waiting for me at the farewell party in honor of my leaving. Something inside me is saying I should pay some respect in my thoughts for this man, this dying man. I opened my eyes and thought of Cynthia. I thought of her beautiful face beside my father's face. And I tried to hold her face in the hands of my mind and I squeezed it close to me and kept myself alive with the living outside world of cricket and cheers and "tea in the pavilion." There is death in this room and I am inside it. And Cynthia's voice is saying to me, Run run run! back through the smells, through the fallen lines of the men, through the front door and out into the green sunlight of the afternoon and the cricket and shouts; out into the applause.

"That's he laying-down there. Your father," the voice said. It was Miss Brewster. She too must have felt the power of death in the room, for she spoke in a whisper.

This is my father: more real than the occasional boundary hit by the cricket bat and the cheers that came with the boundary only. The two large eyeballs in the sunset of this room are my father.

"Boy?" It was the skeleton talking. I am leaving. He held out a hand to touch me. Dirt was under his fingernails like black moons. I saw the hand. A dead hand, dirty hand, a hand of quarter-moons of dirt under the claws of its nails. ("You want to know something, son?" My godmother told me long ago. "I'll tell you something. That man that your mother tell you to call your father he isn't your father, in truth. Your mother put the blame of your birth on him because once upon a time, long long time ago in this island, that man was a man.")

I do not touch the hand. I am leaving this place.

And then the words, distant and meaningless from this departure of love because they came too late, began to turn the room on a side. Words and words and words. He must have talked this way each time he heard a door open or shut; or a footstep. " . . . is a good thing you going away, son, a good thing. I hear you going away and that is a good thing . . . because I am going away . . . from this place . . . Miss Brewster, she . . . but I am sorry . . . cannot go with you . . . " (Did my mother hate this man so much to drive him here? Did she drive him to such a stick of love that it broke his heart; and made him do foolish things with his young life on the village green of cricket near his house that made him the playful enemy of Barrabas the policeman, whose delight, my godmother told me, was to drag my father, the captain of the village team, away drunk from victory and pleasure, to throw him into the crowded jail, to make him slip on the cold floor fast as a new cricket pitch with vomit . . . ("And it was then, my child, after all those times in the jail, that your father contract that sickness which nobody in this village don't call by name. It is so horrible a sickness.") . . . and I remember now that even before this time I was told by my mother that my father's name was not to be mentioned in her house which her husband made for me as my stepfather. And she kept her word. For eighteen years. For eighteen years, his name was never mentioned; so he had died before this present visit. And there was not even a spasm of a reminiscence of his name. He was dead before this. But sometimes I would risk the lash of her hand and visit him, in his small shack on the fringe of Rudders Pasture where he lived out the riotous twenty-four years of middle life. ("Your mother never loved that bastard," my godmother said.) But I loved him, in a way. I loved him when he was rich enough to give me two shillings for a visit, for each visit. And although my mother had said he had come "from no family at-all, at-all," had had "no background," yet to me in those laughing days he held a family circle of compassion in his heart. I see him now, lying somewhere on a cot, and I know I am leaving this island. In those days of cricket when I visited him, I visited him in his house: the pin-up girls of the screen, white and naked; and the photographs of black women he had taken with a box camera (because "Your father is some kind o' genius, but in this island we call him a blasted madman, but he may be a real genius"), black women always dressed in their Sunday-best after church, dressed in too much clothes, and above them all, above all those pin-ups and photographs, the photographs of me, caught running in a record time, torn from the island's newspapers. And there was one of me he had framed, when I passed my examinations at Harrison College. And once, because in those days he was my best admirer, I gave him a silver cup which I had won for winning a race in a speed which no boy had done in twenty-five years, at the same school, in the history of the school. And all those women on the walls, and some in real life, looking at me, and whispering under their breath so I might barely hear it, "That's his *son*!"; and some looking at me as if I had entered their bedroom of love at the wrong moment of hectic ecstasy; and he, like a child caught stealing, would hang his father's head in shame and apologize for them in a whisper, and would beg the women in a loud voice, "You don't see I am with my son? You can't behave yourself in his presence?" And once, standing in his house alone, when he went to buy a sugar cake for me, I was looking at the photograph of a naked woman on the wall and my eyes became full of mists and I saw coming out of the rainwater of vision my mother's face, and her neck and her shoulders and her breasts and her navel. And I shut my eyes tight, tight, tight, and ran into him returning with the sugar cake and ran screaming from his house. That was my last visit. This is my first visit after that. And I am leaving this island place.

After that last visit I gave myself headaches wondering if my mother had gone to his shack before she found herself big and heavy with the burden of me in her womb. ("Child, you have no idea what he do to that poor pretty girl, your mother, that she hates his guts even to this day!") . . . And the days at Harrison College when the absence of his surname on my report card would remind me in the eyes of my classmates that I might be the best cricketer and the best runner. But that I was, after all, among this cream of best blood and brains, only a bas —) " . . . this island is only a place, one place," his voice was saying. "The only saving thing is to escape." He was a pile of very old rags thrown around a stunted tree. Then he was talking again, in a new way. "Son, do not leave before you get somebody to say a prayer for me . . . somebody like Sister Christopher from the Nazarene Church . . . "

But Sister Christopher is dead. Dead and gone five years now, "When she was shouting at the Lord one night at a revival", my godmother said.

"She's dead."

"Dead?"

"Five years."

"But couldn' you still ask her to come, ask Miss Christo, Sister Christopher to come . . . "

There is no point listening to a dying man talk. I am going to leave. No point telling him that Sister Christopher is alive, because he is beyond that, beyond praying for, since he is going to die and he never was a Catholic. And I am going to leave. For I cannot forget the grey flannel and the cream of the cricket field just because he is dying, and the sharp smell of the massage and the cheers of the men and women at the tape, which I have now made a part of my life. And the Saturday afternoon matinees with the wealthy middle-class girls from Queen's College, wealthy in looks and wealthy in books, with their boyfriends the growing-up leaders of the island. Forget all that? And forget the starched white shirt and the blue-and-gold Harrison College tie? Forget all this because a man is dying and because he tells you he is going to die?

Perhaps I should forget them. They form a part of the accident of my life, a life which — if there were any logic in life — ought to have been spent in the gutters round the Bath Corner, or in some foreign white woman's rose garden, or fielding tennis balls in the Garrison Savannah Tennis Club, where those who played tennis could be bad tennis players but had to be white.

Let him die. I am leaving this island place. And let him die with his claim on my life. And let the claim be nailed in the coffin, which the poor authorities for the poor will authorize out of plain dealboard, without a minister or a prayer. And forget Sister Christopher who prefers to testify and shout on God; and call somebody else, perhaps, more in keeping with the grey flannel and the cream of the cricket field and Saturday afternoon walks in the park and matinees at the Empire Theatre. Call a canon. Call a canon to bury a pauper, call a canon to bury a pauper, ha-ha-haaaa! . . .

Throughout the laughter and the farewell speeches and the drinks that afternoon, all I did hear was the slamming of many heavy oak doors of the rectory when I went to ask the canon to bury the pauper. And I tried to prevent the slamming from telling me what it was telling me: that I was out of place here, that I belonged with the beginning in the almshouse. Each giggle, each toast, each rattle of drunken ice cubes in the whirling glass pointed a finger back to the almshouse. "Man, you not drinking?" a wealthy girl said. "Man, what's wrong with you, at all?" And someone else was saying, "Have any of you remember Freddie?" But Briggs said, "Remember that bitch? The fellar with the girl with the biggest bubbies in the whole Caribbean? And who uses to . . . man, Marcus! Marcus, I calling you! Godblummuh, Marcus, we come here to drink rum and you mean to tell me that you selling we *water*, instead o' rum?" And Joan Warton said, "But wait, look this lucky bastard though, saying he going up in Canada to university! Boy, you real lucky, in truth. I hear though that up there they possess some real inferior low-class rum that they does mix with water. Yak-yak-yak! From now on you'd be drinking Canadian rum-water, so stop playing the arse and drink this Bajan rum, man. We paying for this, yuh know!" I was leaving. I was thinking of tomorrow, and I was climbing the BOAC gang-plank on the plane bound for Canada, for hope, for school, for glory; and the sea and the distance had already eased the pain of conscience; and there was already much sea between me and the cause of conscience . . .

And when the party was over, Cynthia was with me on the sands of Gravesend Beach. And the beach was full of moonlight and love. There was laughter too; and the laughter of crabs scrambling among dead leaves and skeletons of other crabs caught unawares by someone running into the sea. And there was a tourist ship in the outer harbor. "Write! write, write, write, write me everyday of the week, every week of the year, and tell me what Canada is like, and think of me always, and don't forget to say nice things in your letters, and pray for me every night. And write poems, love poems like the ones you write in the college magazine; and when you write don't send the letters to the Rectory, because father would, well . . . send them to Auntie's address. You understand? You know how ministers and canons behave and think. I have to tell father, I have to tell him I love you, and that we are getting married when you graduate. And I shall tell him about us . . . when you leave tomorrow." Watching the sea and the moonlight on the sea; and watching to see if the sea was laughing; and the scarecrows of masts on the fishing boats now lifeless and boastless, taking a breather from the depths and the deaths of fishing; and the large incongruous luxury liner drunk-full of tourists. And all the time Cynthia chatting and chattering, " . . . but we should have got married, even secretly and eloped somewhere, even to Trinidad, or even to Tobago. Father won't've known, and won't've liked it, but we would've been married . . . Oh hell, man! This island stifles me, and I wish I was leaving with you. Sometimes I feel like a crab in a crab hole with a pile o' sand in front . . . "

"Remember how we used to build sandcastles on bank holidays?"

"And on Sundays, far far up the beach where nobody came . . . "

"Cynthia?"

"Darling?"

"My Old Man, my Old Man is dying right now . . . "

"You're too philosophical! Anyhow, where? Are you kidding? I didn't even know you had an Old Man." And she laughs.

"I was at the almshouse this afternoon, before the party."

"Is he really in the almshouse?"

"St. Michael's almshouse, near . . . "

"You must be joking. You *must* be joking!" She turned her back to me, and her face to the sea. "You aren't pulling my leg, eh?" she said. And before I could tell her more about my father, who he was, how kind a man he was, she was walking from me and we were in her father's Jaguar and speeding away from the beach.

And it is the next day, mid-morning, and I am sitting in the Seawell Airport terminal, waiting to be called to board the plane. I am leaving. My father, is he dead yet? A newspaper is lying on a bench without a man, or woman. Something advises me to look in the obituary column and see if . . . But my mother had said, as she packed my valises, making sure that the fried fish was in my briefcase which Cynthia had bought for me as a going-away present, my mother had said, "Look, boy, leave the dead to live with the blasted dead, do! Leave the dead in this damn islan' place!"

And I am thinking now of Cynthia who promised ("I promise, I promise, I promise. Man, you think I going let you leave this place, *leave Barbados*? and I not going be there at the airport?") to come to wave good-bye, to take a photograph waving goodbye from the terminal and the plane, to get her photograph taken for the social column waving good-bye at the airport, to kiss, to say good-bye and promise return in English, and say *"au revoir"* in French because she was the best student in French at Queen's College.

A man looks at the newspaper, and takes it up, and gives it to a man loaded-down as a new-traveller for a souvenir of the island. And the friend wraps two large bottles of Goddards Gold Braid rum in it, smuggling the rum and the newspaper out of the island, in memory of the island. And I know I will never find out how he died. Now there are only the fear and the tears and the handshakes of other people's saying good-bye and the weeping of departure. "Come back real soon again, man!" a fat, sweating man says. "And next time I going take you to some places that going make your head *curl*! Man, I intend to show you the whole islan', and give you some dolphin steaks that is more bigger than the ones we eat down in Nelson Street with the whores last night!" An old woman, who was crying, was saying good-bye to a younger woman who could have been her daughter, or her daughter-in-law, or her niece. "Don't take long to return back, child! Do not tarry too long. Come back again soon . . . and don't forget that you was borned right here, 'pon this rock, 'pon this island. This is a good decent island, so return back as soon as you get yuh learning, come back again soon, child . . . "

The plane is ready now. And Cynthia is not coming through the car park in her father's Jaguar. She has not come; she has not come as she promised. And I am leaving the island.

Below me on the ground are the ants of people, standing at an angle, near the terminal. And I can see the architect-models of houses and buildings, and the beautiful quiltwork patches of land under the plough . . . and then there is the sea, and the sea, and then the sea.

1971

THEY HEARD A RINGING OF BELLS

"What is them I hearing?" Estelle asked, looking up at the skies.

"Them is bells, darling," Ironhorse said.

"It is a man up there playing 'pon them bells," Sagaboy explained. "They is bells that you and me, and Ironhorse Henry hearing play so nice."

"Bells playing hymns? God bless my eyesight! Boy, this Canada is a damn great country, in truth!" she exclaimed.

"It don't have nothing like this back in them islands, eh, old man?" Ironhorse said, really teasing Sagaboy, who was a Trinidadian.

"Well, let the three o' we sit down right here 'pon this piece o' grass, and listen to that man up there in the skies playing them bells." And they did what Sagaboy suggested. They sat on the grass, in front of the tower which seemed to become more powerful and mysterious with each ring of the bells that resounded in the hearts of these three West Indians. Estelle spread her dress around her like an umbrella. Sagaboy and Ironhorse Henry took off their jackets, and without offering her one of them they sat down. Estelle was sitting on the bare grass. But the grass wasn't cold.

The bells were ringing hymns. And the voice of the bells swept a tide of freshness through Estelle's heart, and washed out the heaviness of deportation that had been lingering there. The immigration department had given her one week to leave the country.

Looking up at the bells, she said, "I am too glad the Lord open up this door, boy! Imagine me, nuh, imagine me up in this big-able country. I can't imagine it is really me, Estelle, sitting down here! I sitting down here, this bright Sunday afternoon, listening to some damn man up there, saying he playing hymns on bells! Well well well, what the hell's next? Who would have think that I would ever live to see a thing so nice? I can't believe my ears at all, at all. It is the wonders o' God, boy, the wonders of the good God, cause I poor as a bird's arse and I am still up here in Canada. And I *know* that a good time can't happen to any and every man, saving that man stand in possession of money. If he have a piece of change in his pockets, he could get in a plane, God! and he could be taken to the ends of this earth, *swoosh!* in the twinkling of an eye! Man, I barely had time to swallow a mouthful o' hot-water tea back in Barbados, before, bram! I wasn't in a different place. And now, look me ! . . . I am up in this big-able Canada. From a little little village somewhere behind God back I come up here, and now enjoying a little goodness o' life. Little good living that only the white people and the rich black people back home does enjoy. And now, ha-dai! the thing turn round, boy! It turn round as good as a cent. This is what I calls *living*. This is the way *every* black person should live! Look, I putting my hand 'pon a blade of grass . . . look, Henry, look Saga, man, this blade of grass is the selfsame grass as what I left back in Barbados. The said grass that I now sitting down 'pon, the same grass, man; but only *different.* And it is different only becausing it situated in a different place. A different, but a more better, more advance place than where I come from; and because o' this I am telling you now, this blessed Sunday afternoon, that I glad glad as hell that life still circulating through this body o' mine."

Neither Ironhorse Henry nor Sagaboy could find words of comment for this waterfall of feeling. Ironhorse had not heard anything like it since he left Barbados, more years ago than he cared to remember. But as Estelle talked he had watched her; and, with her, he had listened to the bells singing in his heart. And there he found a deep love for her. A love so great that he could not find words to express it. But he knew he had to remain silent; that he might never get the opportunity to tell it to her. She was Sagaboy's woman. And she was going to be deported next week. There she was, so near to him now; in a few days, so far away; and he could do nothing, nothing except wish that something would happen to his good friend Sagaboy, that he would cough his guts through his mouth, that he would die from the tuberculosis that rackled in his chest like stones in a can. And Sagaboy, sitting on the other side of Estelle, remained very quiet as if he was in a dream. Then, it seemed, the bubble of his dream burst, and he tugged at a blade of grass near his feet, and exploded, "It ain't no wonders of no blasted God, woman! You have just start to live like you should have been living from the day you born. But instead, you been spending your lifetime down in Barbados, the same way as your forefathers and foremothers been spending it . . . in the kiss-me-arse canefield, and in slavery. Down there you didn't have food to eat, nor proper clothes to put on your back, and you didn't comprehend the piece o' histries involve in that kinda life, till one morning, bright and early, Satan get in your behind, and you look round, and bram! your eyes see that topsy-turvy world down there, and you turned round and look at yourself, and you didn't see nothing but rags and lice and filth and misery and the blasted British. And what happen? Revolutions run up inside your head, child, and you start to put two and two together. And you say, be-Christ, it ain't true, pardner, that is not true, at all! So what happen next? You pull up stakes and run abroad. You come up here in a more progressive country, but you still going exist in a worser life than what you was accustomed to back home. Look, every one o' we, you, me, Ironhorse here, we get so damn tired, we get so damn vexed . . . you down there in Barbados, and I in Trinidad, and brisk-brisk! it is pulling out, for so! Setting sail. Pawning things that we never own and possess, borrowing and thiefing, and we sail for Canada. It have millions o' men and women from the islands who set sail already for Britain. And that situation is a funny funny piece o' histries, too. I sits down in my bed over on Spadina Avenue, and I laugh hard hard as hell, hee-hee-hee! at all them people who say we shouldn't make Great Britain more blacker than she is or was, in the first Elizabethan era. And all the time I does be laughing, I does be thinking of long long ago when the Queen o' Britain send all them convicts and whores and swivilitic men and women overseas, to *fluck-up* and populate the islands! Well, darling, now the tables turn round, because this is the *second* Elizabethan era! And it is the islands who sending black people, *all kinds*, the good and the bad, the godly and the ungodly, and we intend to fuck-up the good old Mother Country like rass, as my Jamaican friend would say. Man, I hear if you look round in Britain this afternoon you swear to God that you ain't in Britain no longer, but that you back in the islands. Black people? Oh rass !" And straightway, he broke into the popular calypso, 'Yankees Gone And Sparrow Take Over Now.'

"God, that boy does talk as if he have a mouthful o' honey inside his mouth," Ironhorse said, appreciatively.

"Sagaboy, you talking the truth. You have just talk a piece o' truth . . . you call it histries, but I haven't heard nobody talk it that way, yet!" Estelle said, agreeing.

And then they stopped talking, and listened. The bells were ringing. You could see how the bells changed the tense expression on Estelle's face, an expression which emigration had placed there; and how they brought fear, a fear for the wondrous works of God, in its place. And looking more closely, you could see a primitive beauty painted on the sharp cheekbones and on the large mouth which gave her the haughtiness of a black princess.

"What hymn that is, what hymn he playing there?" she asked. "Ain't that hymn name 'The Day Thou Gavest Lord Is Ending'? Ain't it that said hymn? The selfsame tune, Henry, the same tune, Sagaboy. And that is the very-same song they took my father, God rest his soul, to the grave with! You should have seen him when they pull him outta the sea, drown, and with the water in his body, making him big like a whale, and still looking powerful and strong as he use to be when he was living and in the flesh. Lord! and when they come and tell me that my father *dead*, oh God, Henry, Sagaboy, I cry and I cry till I couldn't find water to cry with no more. And the people in the neighborhood come and look in at the oval hole in the top o' the mahogany coffin when the undertaker-man had bring him home. And the whole village bow down their heads in respects o' the dead, in Pappy behalfs, 'cause my father was a man who had lots o' respects in the whole entire village and in the districts round our village. And the old women in our village bow down their heads low low low, and say, 'Thank God that at least He make a good dead outta Nathan. Nathan look nice as a dead. God go with thee, son,' they say. And when they say that, all the men with their big bass voices start up singing this very hymn that you and me hearing coming outta that tall towerthing. And Lord! water come to everybody's eye. The weeping and the crying and the singing. When they was weeping all that weeping, I had a funny feeling that they wasn't weeping only for my father, but for all the fathers that was ever killed by the cruel hands of the waves in the sea. And then they start filing past the coffin, singing; and the women were wringing their hands, like they was ringing out clothes, earlier that very-same day . . . God! I think I seeing it now, clear clear before my two eyes, as I listen to the magic and poetry coming outta that bell up there, this Sunday afternoon. And to think, just think that the first time I going to call back all this to mind is now that I have escape from that blasted past-tense village in Barbados to come up here, in Canada. Man, it is a long long time ago now, 'cause my father dead, when he dead, he left me a little girl in pigtails."

The bells were ringing still, ringing loud and clear in the quiet Toronto afternoon. Estelle's voice broke down, and she started to hum along with the carillonneur. It was a clear voice, a soft voice. A voice like a stream of crystal water fighting to reach the sea.

"A lot o' salt water separating me from the place where my father drown. And I still remember it to this day," she went on. "I even remember the dress I wear, which was the said white dress that my half-sister Bernice wore when she got baptize in the Church o' the Nazarene. A white sharkskin piece o' material that Mammy had bought at a sale. And when we reach Westbury Cemetery, shadows was walking through the evergreen trees, round the graveyard. And a man come, a big, fat, ugly black man dressed down in black, come and put dirt on top o' the coffin, and then he pull off the silver things that was screwed-on to the coffin, and as quick as a fly he push them inside his pocket; and then sudden so, like how you see dusk does fall outta the skies and nobody don't know, sudden so, that same man drop my father contained in that coffin-box in the hole, and Lord! I couldn't see my father's face no more. Such a mighty screeling went up, such a terrible crying escape from the women that you would have thought the heavens was collapsing, and it weren't just a poor fisherman that was taken to his resting place under a sandbox tree. And I remember that the people in the village was so poor, most of them, that only a handful could afford to rent a motor car from Johnson's Stables to follow my father in. Most of the men had to follow on bicycles, and some even had to carry their women and their wives on the bicycle bars." She paused for a while, it seemed, to permit the bells to return the sadness of the funeral to her mind, and stir up the memories lurking there. She went on, "I can see his face now. I can see Pappy face before my two eyes right now. And I swear then, as I take the oath now, I swear blind that he wasn't dead in truth, 'cause I thought I could see his lips move, or did want to move and open, and whisper something to me from the grave. And I sorry sorry that up till now I don't know, and I can't imagine what the hell it was Pappy wanted to leave with me in the way of wisdom or advice, as he parted from me in the quick. I am the onliest living soul who see the dead attempt to talk. The only one who see that happen. And because o' that, I swear blind that they put my father to rest before his time was up. You understand what I mean? What I mean to affirm and state is this: down there in that damn island, the people don't have no lot o' respect, and a undertaker-man could make a mistake like nothing and put a person in a coffin and nail up that coffin and lower him in a grave be-Christ, before that dead-man is really a dead-man, before he stop breathing. Because them undertakers is really sharks and barracudas. Once they *suspect* that you will soon be a dead-man, that you are in a poor state o' health, that you are passing away, and they know they stand to get a few coppers for burying you, well, boy, they rushes like bloody-hell and they would *kill* you and turn you into a dead person if they think you ain't deading fast enough. Some stupid old women say it is a good thing, becausing God did love Pappy, and that is why He take my only father to His grave. But I don't believe that. Even now, at my age, I still don't think that God could say He is in love with a man, and then turn round and put His hand 'pon that man, strangulate him, and drop him dead, and in the quick, and still say He love him? Standing up by that grave that evening I hold up my two hands, high high in the air, and I screamed so bloody hard that they get frightened and they had was to drag me, still screaming and twirling 'pon the ground, mind you, to a motor car, and administer smelling salts to my nose to revive me and pacify me. 'cause , don't matter how rough and cruel a father treats you, boy, a father is a father. That happen long long ago. Long ago, the Good Lord lift up my poor father up in the heavens with Him. And that is my testimony to the two o' you, as I sitting down here betwixt the two o' you, this bright Sunday evening in Toronto Canada, hearing this hymn, this selfsame tune that carried Nathan Sobers, my father, to his grave in Westbury Cemetery. Ain't you hearing that same hymn, 'The Day Thou Gavest?'"

"I hearing it, Estelle, darling, I hearing it like anything," Sagaboy said, in a whisper, as if his voice had left his body and was now distant, far off, lost in the sea of time. Estelle's words had taken him back to his family and his home, tucked away out of memory in Trinidad; and they had made him think of the recent death of his Karen, his wife from Germany.

"Ain't it strange, ain't it wondrous strange how a person remembers things that happen so long ago? And ain't it strange too, how a simple thing like a bell in a tower could cause that same person to travel miles and miles in memory . . . "

"Strange!" Sagaboy told her. Still, his voice was far away across the ocean, miles away from the grass and the tower and the university campus where they were sitting and from the invisible hand of the carillonneur playing hymns on his bells. And then the bells stopped ringing; and then the three of them became bored with time resting so heavily on them, for they could think of nothing to do, or say, now that the bells had stopped ringing.

All you can hear now is the heavy breathing from Sagaboy, as he chews on a match stick. Henry begins to chew a match stick too. Suddenly he stops chewing, and offers a cigarette to Sagaboy, and to Estelle.

"Back home, I won't be seen dead with one o' these in my mouth, and on a Sunday, to boot!" she said. "What is one man's medicine is a next man's poison."

"You in Canada now, darling, you not back home," Ironhorse Henry reminded her. And with that, the conversation died; and the stillness and the sterility of a Toronto Sunday returned. Estelle blew smoke through her nostrils and her mouth at the same time, looking at the cigarette as if it was a bomb, and shaking her head, and muttering again about one man's medicine being another man's poison. Sagaboy started to cough. Ironhorse Henry looked up at the tower to avoid looking into Estelle's eyes. Sagaboy got up from them, and went aside to cough freely and to spit. He could hardly control his breathing as the coughing racked his body in two, like a hairpin. A lump came up in his throat. The lump tickled him so much that he almost laughed, that he had to shut his eyes. Water began to spring from his eyes as the lump came nearer to his mouth. Then, as if playing a game with him, it went back down deeper. Sagaboy coughed and coughed, and when he did manage to spit . . . "*Blood!* Is blood I see?" But he wiped his feet on it, and hid the evidence from himself, and from Ironhorse Henry and from Estelle, who did not even look behind them while he was coughing.

Estelle broke the heaviness of the evening with a rasp-like noise of her teeth, and emphasized it by shaking her head from side to side, in despair. "Ain't no fairness in this damn world, you know that?" And when Ironhorse Henry had no comment, she added, "Now, look at me. I been here now, how much weeks? Four weeks going 'pon five, waiting and waiting 'pon them bastards at the immigration office, to give me a chance so's I could make a better woman outta myself. And you think they would give me a chance?"

"Your chance going come, love," Sagaboy said, returning to join them; and knowing, of course, that her chance would never come.

"I been hearing that tune since I was a little girl in pigtails. I know a man who waited his chance cause everybody was always telling him his chance going come. And you know how old that man was when his chance come?" She paused for effect; and then she said, "On his blasted death-bed! And they burst out laughing. It was a tense, joyless, clench-teeth laugh. "I am getting more and more older every day, sweetheart. I don't have time to wait. That is old slave talk. Wait, wait, wait. If the greedy wait, hot going cool! If you patient, God going bring you through in the name o' the Lord. If a enemy hit you in your face, on the right hand side, you must then turn 'round and present him with the other side o' your fisiogomy, and let him lick-in that too. Christ Almighty, I telling you now that if I could just get one *little* chance, one little opportunity to work as a domestic servant in this place, be-Jesus Christ, I not waiting. I not waiting, nor praying, nor faltering. Not Estelle."

"This is a white man country, woman," Sagaboy teased her. "You want to cause a race riot?"

"I see eye-to-eye with Estelle," Ironhorse Henry said, in a manner which he hoped Estelle would understand, and in a tone of voice which implied more than was said. "Me and you view this situation in the same fashion. It is a shame that only a certain class o' individual could get through the doors o' immigration, and a next class o' people can't even squeeze through, at all!" He cleared his throat while they pondered on his words. He spat, neatly and accurately, on a cigarette box about ten feet away. "Now, you take them Eyetalians. Them is people!"

"How they get into this discussion?" Sagaboy wanted to know.

"Now, take them Eyetalians," Ironhorse continued, "them Eyetalians, man, you does see them Eyetalians coming into this country be-Christ, as if Canada is in Rome and not in Northamerica, and . . . "

"And why the hell you don't turn into a Neyetalian, then? Why you don't learn to talk in the Eyetalian tongue, and become a Neyetalian?"

"I not arguing nor affirming that it have anything particularly wrong with not being a Neyetalian," Ironhorse Henry explained, "and I not saying that as a Westindian man, I am better off, or worse off. All I affirming is that every day you look round in this city . . . now, you take the corner o' College and Spadina where you live! Man, when I first land up in Toronto, you didn't see ten Eyetalians at that corner. Now? All you seeing is Eyetalians Eyetalians and be-Christ, more Eyetalians. You in *Italy* now, old man, you aren't no longer in Toronto."

"God, but I like them Eyctalians too bad, though!" Estelle said. "I like to see them talking and holding up their two hand up in the air, and laughing and crying and shouting for blue-murder as they talks . . . brabba-rabbabrabba-rabba-seenioreeta! God have given that tribe a very pretty tongue and a real sweet language. And I like to see how the women does dress-down in black, from head to toenail, and still manage to look so womanish, in a positive kind o' way, as if a woman was create to always look that way, and in that manner and fashion o' dressing, in order to be a lady. I am only a part-time citizen o' Canada, but I have never see *one* Canadian woman look as if she was glad to be a woman. She want to be a *man*! You understand what I mean? Them Canadian women, particularly the old ones, with their false hair and their false teet' and rimless glasses, Jesus Christ, they don't look as if they is really women at all. And they certainly don't behave as if they is mothers, neither! Everybody always looking as if she come outta a fashion book that gone outta print in the last century."

"Child, don't let nobody hear you say these things! Shut up your mouth tight tight, 'cause you not born here. Don't criticize the same people that going put bread in your mouth. Keep your tail betwixt thy legs, and live and let the blasted white people live, too. That is my philosophy of the histries o' man." It was Sagaboy cautioning her, with great excitement in his manner. And this brought out a tiny rackling in his chest. It became louder and noisier until he had to cough. But the more he coughed, the more the rackling in his chest continued. He got up from them again, and went behind the small building where he could be at ease to untie the knots in his chest, until the bulldozers there smashed up the eruption inside him. And as the cough was about to break and calm down, a lump wormed its way up to his mouth. Afraid to spit it out, he closed his eyes and swallowed hard. But the moment it hit bottom, the coughing and rackling blew up again, like a storm. The lump returned to his mouth, and he closed his eyes and spat. He moved swiftly away from the spot because he did not want to look at it. Once he did turn and try to look down, but the memory of the previous shock made him move away fast; and he rejoined his friends. But before he could return, and while his guts were erupting, Ironhorse Henry had placed his hand on the fat of Estelle's legs, soft as a feather in a breeze; and he had looked into her eyes, and for a moment, one moment, had expressed the pain that was in his heart.

"I love you bad as arse," he told her, from the bottom of his heart.

"Look, man, behave yourself, do," she said, and then laughed away his profession of love. All this happened while Sagaboy was coughing; and all the time, Ironhorse Henry wished he would drop down dead.

"You find it getting chilly here?" Sagaboy asked them.

"You have consumption, or TB, or something?" Ironhorse asked. He glanced at Estelle to see if she was as revolted as he. And when he saw that she was not, he added, "You gotta be careful with that fresh-cold, man."

"Oh, little coughing can't harm him," she said, putting a pin in Ironhorse's balloon of love.

And then they heard the bells again, loud this time, as if the man in the tower wanted to drown out their voices. They did not recognize the tune that the bells were playing now. And for a long time they sat, silently, arguing in their minds that they did know the tune, but listening all the time to the magic in the hands that tolled the bells so beautifully. They listened, wondering how a man could receive such power of beauty, such sweetness, such purity from his hands, and put them into bells . . . bells that were made to call people to church, to toll them to the sides of graves, to drop flowers on the coffin of a friend, or a lover, or a father.

"Jesus Christ, listen. Listen to the poetry in that damn bell, though!" Ironhorse said, raising his head to catch the smallest note, the softest ting. "That man playing that bell like how great Gort used to caress his tenor pan in the steel band, back in the old days. Too blasted sweet. Man, listen to that damn bell."

"What you say this place name?" Estelle asked.

"The campus," Sagaboy told her.

"I got to come back here, again, some time soon, and hear some more o' these white people bell-music."

"You know something? I just realize that Sunday evening is the same all over the blasted world. We sitting down here in Canada, 'pon the grass, and it is the same thing as when we was little boys back home, sitting down in a place we used to call The Hill," Ironhorse said. Poetry also was coming with his reminiscences. "Every man should sit down on a hill at least once in his lifetime, on a Sunday afternoon or evening, preferably alone, and look at the sea, and think about the past and the present and the future, and learn how to know himself. You gotta be yourself, alone, sitting down 'pon that hill of time, with the sun sinking behind your back and the moon rising in your face, both at one and the same time, before you is man enough to come to me and affirm that you really know yourself."

"I remember that feeling, old man," Sagaboy said, as if he was really experiencing it again, right in their presence. "I remember that emotion. I remember, how every Sunday night back home, we used to sit down on a hill called Brittons Hill. Me and the rest o' the boys, sitting down 'pon that damn hill, like if we was in a upstairs house looking down in the sea. And the same feeling, like I was lost, you know, like I wasn't worth nothing, like how sometimes the same feeling does overpower me in that blasted five-dollars-a-week rat-trap I lives in, on Spadina, right here in this kiss-me-arse advance country . . . " He took a beaten-up, half-smoked cigarette from his pocket and put a match to its black tip. " . . . and the birds chirping. You know something? I have never see *one* blasted bird in this place yet, and I now remember that, for the first time! Back home, the birds chirping nice songs and then they run off to sleep. And the trees, trees all round where we was sitting down, trees dress-up in a more greener coat o' green than this grass. And then a funny thing would happen. Just at that moment before shadow and darkness take them up in their hands as if they was little children put to bed, be-Christ, they would turn more *greener* still! We would be sitting down in the midst of the evening dusk and shadows, thinking 'bout what and what we was going to be when we grow up to be big strong men. And if on that particular Sunday we did have a nice feed, like split-pea rice and fry pork, or something nice and heavy in the bowels, well, pardner, everybody want to be something, or somebody great and powerful. Like a doctor, or a police commissioner, or even a plantation manager. And you don't know that one evening, I must have been so blasted full o' black-eye peas and rice that I say I wanted to be the *governor o' the whole blasted West Indies*. Be-Christ, if that ain't dreaming, tell me what is? But one boy, Lester Theophillis Bynoe, all he wanted to be, with a full-belly or no full-belly, was a hangman. And you know something? Be-Christ, that is what he turned out to be! He is the biggest, the blackest, and the best hangman in the whole Caribbean! But if things wasn't so great, kitchen-wise or food-wise, or if our mothers had give us a regular stiff cut-arse with a window stick or with a piece o' bamboo, well, everybody want to jump on a boat and become sailors and buccaneers. And always, after we finish wishing and dreaming, you could hear the church bells from St. Barnabas Church, miles and miles of sugar canes away, over the fields, coming right up to your two earholes. Church bells, old man, *ding-dong-ding-dong*! . . . " His coughing aborted his reverie, and it shook him like a huckster shaking a coconut to see if there is any water inside. Ironhorse Henry rushed to him, and held him around the waist; and Estelle became very alarmed as Ironhorse Henry beat the coughing man's chest to dislodge the thorns of pain that were inside him. And Ironhorse took out his own handkerchief, and gave it to Sagaboy to put to his mouth. "Let we go home," he said, when the heaving permitted him to form a word. "That damn bell ring till it give me a headache. And it chilly as hell here, too."

And they walked hurriedly away from the campus. Shadows were running slow races across the front lawns, and across the large circle of green grass in front of a large gray building. The bells kept ringing for a while, and then they stopped. And then Estelle pushed her arms through both their arms, through Sagaboy's, on her left, and Ironhorse Henry's, on her right, and like this they walked on in the darkness of the bells.

1971

A Wedding In Toronto

"A police coming in a man's house, and at a wedding reception to boot! and breaking up a party? Merely because some old can't-sleep bitch next door or down-below can't find a man or something? What kind o' place, what sort o' country is this? It never happened in Barbados and it never could. Imagine a police in Barbados coming into a man's house, during a party, and a wedding party at that, to tell that man he is making too much noise! Man, that policeman's arse would be so stiff with lashes he would never do that again! A police coming into a man's apartment, and breaking up a wedding reception because some old bitch who can't sleep, complained?" Boysie never got over the shock of seeing the policeman at the door, standing like a monument to something, with an untranslatable expression on his face, with one hand resting perhaps absent-mindedly on the holster of his gun, and the other raised and caught in the slow-motion paralysis of knocking on the apartment door again. It was a loud, firm knock of authority. The wedding guests were, at that time, in the middle of speeches; and Boysie, who was the master of ceremonies, had been saying some amusing things about marriage. It was at the point when he was saying, *Ecce homo,* over and over again (using his best stentorian, oratorical Barbadian dialect), exhorting them, as: "La-dies and gentlemen! Ladies and gentlemen too! Greetings and salutations, because on this most auspicious of evenings, on the aurora of long and felicitous matrimony, I say to you, to you, ladies and gentlemen, I say, *ecce homo,* behold the man! *ecce homo,* here I stand!" (Freeness, dressed to kill in a three-piece suit; Matthew Woods, spic and span; Estelle, beautiful as a virgin, as a star; and many other West Indians crammed into the happy apartment, screamed for joy when Boysie began this speech, his fifth for the afternoon's festivities. Each wedding guest, including Agatha the bride, and Henry the bridegroom, had made a speech. Some had made two speeches. Boysie had made his first about an hour after the wedding party returned to the apartment. It was five o'clock then. Now, after many toasts and speeches and eats and drinks, Boysie was captivating his audience again. The time was midnight. The guests liked it, and they bawled and told Boysie they liked it. Henry, sober and married; Agatha turning red, and flushed, and happy, and drunk as Dots, Boysie's wife, held her head back and exposed the silver cavities filled with silver, and said, "I could have another wedding reception like this tomorrow! One like this every month!") "I say to you, ladies and gentlemen, I say, *ecce homo,* behold the man! *ecce homo,* here I stand! Here I stand, ladies and gentlemen, with a glass of drink in my hand, wherewithal for to mitigate the aridity of my thirst. And as I have arisen from my esteemed seat this fifth time, and as I have quoth to you, *bon swarr* my dear Agaffa, goodevening Henry, you lucky old Bajan bastard!" And it was here, in the roar of acceptance by each person in the room when they held their glasses up, and Boysie's glass was held right there, at the correct angle, that the knock brutalized the apartment. Its suddenness made them notice it. But they had no suspicions. Boysie said, with his glass still raised, "Perhaps, ladies and gentlemen, it is some poor suppliant wanting warmth of this nocturnal congregation." And he moved away towards the door, his drink still in his hand, to invite the person inside to partake of the hospitality. Bernice went over to Agatha to fix the veil on her dress and therefore, fortunately, blocked her view of the police officer at the door standing with his hand on his holster. Boysie didn't lose his aplomb. The police officer was very polite to him. "Break it up soon, buddy. It's past midnight. The neighbors're complaining about the noise."

Boysie was going to offer the officer a drink, but he changed his mind.

"Don't let me get another report that you're making noise, eh? Break it up soon, buddy."

Boysie did not move from the door until the officer of the law walked back to the elevator; and he did not move until he saw him get into it; and Dots, who had put a record on the machine the moment she heard the officer's voice, was now standing beside Boysie, like a real wife, supportingly.

"And the poor girl's enjoying herself so much! And on her wedding day? Jesus Christ, these people is savages, man. They're damn uncivilized! You mean to tell me, on the girl's wedding day?" Boysie put his arm round Dots' new, shiny, almost bare shoulder, and he squeezed her a little bit, and said, "We going party till that son-of-a-bitch come back!" Boysie left her, and went to Bernice and whispered in her ear, "The po-lice!" Bernice suddenly got tense. "But only me and Dots, and now you, know 'bout it. So keep it dark. Keep it dark." Bernice relaxed because of this confidence. "We got to go on. How the hell could we ask the people to leave? How would Agaffa feel? How would Henry feel, on his wedding night to boot?"

So Boysie and Dots and Bernice made certain not to let Agatha and Henry feel the tension that had begun to creep into the party. It was impossible to recapture the gaiety and the enjoyment that was in the room before the policeman knocked on the door. Dots would have had the guests leave immediately after one more respectable drink; she would have insisted upon it, because she had just moved into the apartment building and she wanted to live quietly, and also because Agatha and Henry had to go on their honeymoon, to Niagara Falls. But Boysie said no, "This is a wedding. Not any old damn party with beatniks." And he left Dots standing there arguing the wisdom of his suggestion with Bernice, and he went to the record player, and looked through the pile of calypso records. (This record player had arrived from Eaton's department store two hours before the wedding reception began, delivered on a hire-purchase, the monthly payments of which were fifty-five dollars and twenty-five cents and which Dots did not know how she would meet; but the sound was high and loud and high-fidelity and stereophonic too, and the beauty and the loudness of the sound allayed their fears of having the machine repossessed. "Man, let we play the thing for today then, and enjoy it, and then see what happen, man!" And Boysie agreed to that, although before Dots said so, he had already agreed in his mind to keep the record player.) Boysie now selected a calypso by the Mighty Sparrow, 'Shanty Town People,' in which Sparrow was complaining of having to move out of his comfortable apartment in Trinidad, because people from the slums had encroached on his location on the hill. The music raged, as the spirits in the guests and in the drinks raged. Estelle was beautiful in her wedding-party dress. She was thinking of how very close she herself had come to marriage. And more than once, during the hectic afternoon and night, she wondered where the hell her man, Sam Burrmann, was at this happy time. But she soon put him out of her mind; and she devoted all her body and energy to Matthew Woods, who shook his body in time in dance as if he was in some mad trance. *Sunday morning, they fighting, they drinking, they beating pan . . . send for the police, still the bacchanal won't cease.* It was a royal time. It was an ironic time to have a calypso reproduce the exact conditions of a party at which the police had come. And judging by the hour hand, it was Sunday morning too! But no one cared for Toronto, or the police, or the neighbors: this was a wedding, and as Dots said, "A person can only get married one time. Even if he divorce and marry a second time, the second time don't seem to be like the first time! So the first time is the time!" Boysie was dancing with her. Brigitte, a German immigrant working as a domestic, had held on to Freeness the whole day, probably by design; probably by the suggestion of Boysie (whose woman she was; Boysie who now in the castle of skin and pride, in his briar patch of host and wedding-giver, had no time for outside-women); and Bernice was dancing with a man who nobody knew, who nobody invited, but who was treated with the same courtesy and hospitality as the bridegroom, or as if he was the bride's father. Agatha's father hadn't arrived yet. Agatha's mother hadn't arrived yet. Agatha's friends, Agatha's many friends from the university, and her lawyer-friend (all of whom had been sent invitations — that was Boysie's personal gift to the couple) hadn't arrived yet. It had been a sorrowful sight at the church, when it was found out that no one was sitting on the bride's side as witness and evidence. Dots quickly saw the situation developing, and quickly saw the embarrassment it would cause Agatha when she arrived sweet and young, virginal and white in her long dress, to glance over the wide expanse of the desert of her friends. And Dots ushered and re-ushered half of the church over to Agatha's side. When the organ roared and snorted through the Wedding March, everybody was laughing, even Agatha. Reverend Markham was happy. It was his first inter-racial wedding ceremony. The choir was in good voice, loud when it was supposed to be loud, soft when the organist breathed with the organ and whispered that the choir should be like a piano, pianissimo. But when they were in the office signing away their lives and their promises to one another, Dots stood like a mother-hen on the top steps of the church, directing the people (those who didn't have cars) to cars and warning the photographer who had arrived late, "Look here! don't take the whole day, hear? We have things waiting at the wedding reception." And after that she whispered in Bernice's ears, "It's a shame, a great burning shame that that bastard, Agatha's father, thinks he is too great and too proud to come and witness his own daughter on her wedding day. A person does only have one wedding day in her life and that bastard didn't even come. He did not come."

"And the mother ain't turned up yet, neither."

"Bernice, gal, you are seeing and witnessing the ways o' white people. They would kill their own flesh-and-blood just to prove a blasted point."

"It is sad, though."

Estelle had overheard, and she said, "They love one another, though. Henry and Agatha. And they won't be living at the parents."

"Still's a blasted shame!"

And now, at the reception, nobody apparently tired after so many hours of eating and drinking and dancing with the problems of 'Shanty Town People' being reproduced for them by the visit of the policeman and by the record itself, these West Indians and two white women, Brigitte and Agatha ("She's a Wessindian now, gal! We adopt Agatha now that her own people and her parents let her down. Godblummuh, we is one people who don't reject nobody through color prejudice.") . . . *I tired and I disgust . . . big Sunday evening, they cussing, they fighting, they gambling, they beating pan and bup-bup!-iron bolt, and stone pelting, send for the police, still the bacchanal won't cease* . . . There were fifty persons invited to the reception. There were fifty persons in the two-bedroom apartment from five o'clock. There are fifty-one persons (with the uninvited man) in the apartment now, at one-thirty Sunday morning. Boysie has his arms in the air and is dancing as if his body has been seized by some voodoo, or St. Vitus dance mood; Dots has thrown one brocaded expensive slipper somewhere in a corner, and she is jumping up. The record, a favorite with everybody in the room, is put on again. It is put on three times, four times, five times, six times; and Boysie says on the seventh time, "Man, play that thing one more time, do, man!" And it is put on the eighth time . . . *and big Sunday morning, they cussing they fighting they gambling; they beating pan and bup-bup!-iron bolt and stone pelting, send for the police, still the bacchanal won't cease, so they violent so they fast, they better go back to their mansion on the Labasse* . . . A smudge of fatigue and sweat walked imperceptibly from under Estelle's hairy armpits. Bernice noticed it; and she took Estelle into Dots' bedroom and rubbed some of Dots' underarm deodorant, "Ban", on the story-telling odor. Estelle smiles, and dashes back out to dance. Agatha, with the first signs of marriedhood and possessiveness, sits and watches Henry dance with a very thin, tight, tense and at the same time, sexy black woman, holding him like a leech in heat; and Agatha continues to watch as if she is comparing her body with the black woman's body in the bedroom of her mind; she watches the woman's hips as they do things with the rhythm of the calypso which she herself, legal and wedded to Henry for better and for worse, knows she cannot do, cannot ever learn to do in this way. Some men are in the kitchen, eating, as they have been doing since five o'clock. ("Boysie!" one of them said, about six o' clock, "we intend to eat every fucking thing in your apartment, boy! So, relax.") There is a big argument going on about cricket. None of these men has seen a cricket Test match in five years, not since they left their homes in the islands. But they are now arguing about Sir Frank Worrell, and the cover drive he made off Alec Bedser at Lords in 1950, many many years ago. One man says, "Be-Christ, them English-people think they could play cricket! Be-Jesuschrist, they can't play no cricket in truth! They *playing* they great. But godblummuh! when Sir Frank leaned into that out-swinger from Bedser, and Sir Frank make a little thing, *so!* be-Christ, it went to the fucking boundary like lightning for four! Right offa Worrell wrist!" And another man smiled, took a sip of his whiskey and said, "And all o' wunnuh in here know that Worrell have more wrist-work in his strokes than Boysie in there have stones in his underwears!" And like a contagion, everybody in the kitchen bawled and poured himself another, larger drink. The record is changed. Sparrow is talking about his boyhood. The men dropped their glasses and ran for the women sitting around the room. They reached out their hands and lifted the dripping, shining, shiningly-dressed, rouged-and-perfume-smelling tired ladies off their chairs. Boysie is dancing with Dots, as if they are lovers: close. His brilliantined head, which had sweated for hours, four hours under his stocking-top, is sleeked down and shining; and Dots' hairdo, done amidst pain and time, talk and gossip in Azan's Beauty World the previous Thursday, when the shop was noisy and filled with domestics and talk about "I hear Enid sleeping with a Jew-man. You hear so, too?" and the waiting was long for those without an appointment, and for those with an appointment. "The girl we meet one day in the subway, that girl wearing the mini, the midi maxi whatever the hell you calls it! anyhow, she

I talking about. She gone and get sheself in trouble. *Pregnunt!"* Dots had listened and had held her peace; and then someone said, Dots had never seen this woman in the parlor before, "This rich-rich Jewish girl I hear is marrieding some Bajan man or other, and somebody tell me his name is Henrysomething, or the other, but Christ! to imagine that I been here so blasted long and nobody, not even a Jew-man hasn't asked me a question. I must be getting old, and looking it, too!" And then they all laughed. Except Dots. *Now, I am a rebel, I seeking my revenge any kind o' way, I'm a devil. I don't laugh, I don't smile I don't play . . .* Boysie is not smiling. He doesn't smile when he is dancing. He is holding Dots so close that he can feel something stiffening in his trousers legs: but she is his wife and he her husband . . . *Anytime we meet, man-to-man, it's blood and sand!* (Estelle thinks back to the time not long ago when Bernice and Dots, Boysie and Henry visited her in the small room she lived in on Bedford Road, when they found her hungry and depressed, delirious with fever and thoughts about Sam Burrmann, a Jewish lawyer who left her after she told him she was pregnant for him, and she thinks about it now, dancing with the man nobody invited, the man who told her he is some kind of agent selling some product which Estelle does not understand, thinking of this man dancing with her so close, touching the child in her womb put there by another man. And she thinks of Bernice. "What a life, what a hard life these West Indians live in this place!" And she thinks of what her life might be. There is a man standing beside her, watching her face, but not caring for her thoughts because he wants her to have one thought on her mind, tonight after the reception. He is the man nobody invited. He is standing in front of her now like a threat, like a challenge. ("Henry married, Boysie married, every-other bitch in here have a husband . . . I wonder if . . . ") The man wants to dance with this "prettiest lady in this place." The compliment is sincere, and Estelle makes herself prettier by doing something to her face and her lips, saliva on them now, and she stands up just as Sparrow says, *They treat me like a savage, of me they take advantage; when I young and growing up in town, all o' them bad-johns used to knock me down . . .* A tear is crawling like perspiration down Estelle's face. The man does not notice. He has his mind on other parts of her body.

It was then that the second knocking was heard on the apartment door. Boysie went to the door. The same policeman, plus another one, were standing there. "I told ya," the first policeman said. There was no anger in his voice. He seemed rather peeved that someone had called to report noise in the apartment; he seemed as if he had been taken away from something he was doing, something he enjoyed doing; as a man who had been roused from a poker game would look; as if he had been disturbed from the pants of some woman, somewhere down in the jungle of apartments nearby. Boysie knew what to do.

The guests began leaving right away. Everybody except those who were staying for the night, those who lived there: Boysie and Dots, Bernice and Estelle. Henry looked at the policemen and said things in his heart which if they were audible would have given him a beating and then a long jail term. Agatha began to cry. She was still wearing her wedding gown; Henry was in his formal morning suit; he and she still in the clothes that began their new life together. The policemen waited until every one of the guests left. As Agatha walked beside Henry along the long corridor, as if she was still walking that interminable aisle up the mile to face the altar and the cross and the Maker stretched out on a cross and Reverend Markham, women with curlers in their hair peeped through open doors; and just as the policemen passed them and went down into the half-awake apartment building, in the elevator going out, one of the white ladies, in a torn pink nightgown which showed the blackness between her thighs vaguely, hissed, "Bitch! Trash!" and slammed her apartment door. The others, among the onlooking guard of honor and dishonor, shook their heads and did not slam their doors: but nobody knew what they were saying in their hearts behind their closed doors. In the confusion, in all the disappointment and crying (Dots and Bernice and Estelle remained sitting on the large new couch, crying for Agatha's sake; and Agatha herself had left in tears, and had touched each of their cheeks with the tears of her kisses as she tried to smile goodbye), the record player was still commenting: *They treat me like a savage . . . they treat me like a savage . . . they treat me like a savage . . . they treat me like a savage . . . they treat me like a savage* . . . and before Estelle got up to take it off, she thought again of the strange man who nobody invited who had asked her to dance just at that point; and it seemed very long ago that her happiness happened. Now, Boysie was walking back along the quiet corridor, alone.

1971

An Easter Carol

Suddenly, I could hear my mother's voice bombarding the small room in which I slept. "Get up get up get up! boy, you too lazy! you think the morning waiting on you? Get up and get! the sun almost half-way up in the sky, and you in there, still sleeping? This is Easter morning! Blessed Easter. The Lord rise-up outta Hell long long time, so you get up, too! . . . and don't forget to clean out the pig pens and the sheep pens, 'cause yesterday morning you didn't clean the pig pens proper, and you left back all my precious milk inside them sheeps' breasts. Come boy! Half the morning gone already! So get up!"

She had hardly taken a breath in all this time. I listened to the beautiful mountains and valleys of her surging voice; and I laughed inside my heart. I was already awake. I had been awake for about three hours. I could not sleep. For all night I could smell the fresh delicious smells seeping under my door from the kitchen: the roasted pork, the great cakes, the sponges, the bananas, the golden apples, the rum and the sweet drinks; and the new coats of varnish and polish and paint on a ancient furniture in our house. This was Easter in our house. Everything was cleansed. Even the pigs were a clean, white, resurrection coat of freshness; and the front of the house was sprinkled with white marl, because there was never any snow in our village. Everything new, was clean, was virginal. My new clothes had been bought months before; and my mother had pressed them many times over, and had hooked them on a hanger onto a nail, high in the heavens of the ceiling in her bedroom where they could be seen, but not touched. And every chance I got, I would watch them: the seams in the gray-flannel trousers, keener than a new Gillette, the sea-island cotton shirt, pressed without a wrinkle or blemish, and rich and creamy as milk from our sheep; my cork hat, white as snow (although no one in Barbados had ever seen snow, except in pictures in a book, or on the foreign Christmas cards which trickled into the village from America and England), and stiff with Blanca; and my shoes, like two mounds of pitch, black, and shining Lord Lord Lord! like nobody's business. And the tie. Mother never trusted her fingers to tie my tie, and never trusted mine neither. So I always wore ties ready tied, and with an elastic band round the neck. All my ties had a thick savage stripe in them. This was my Easter outfit: new and clean, from my underwear out.

I would be wearing it to church this morning, at five o'clock: my first day as a choirboy of the Cathedral. No achievement of mine in my eight years had had so great an effect upon my mother. Not even when, at seven I had successfully fought off five girls, all sisters, with a thick piece of sugar cane; not even when I won the long distance race at the church outing; not even when she and my stepfather came home tired as dogs from the fields, one afternoon, to find that I had cooked a meal for them (a meal which I wanted to stand out as a single landmark of my love), and which they interpreted as a boast, with the result that I cooked their meals every day since then . . .

"Jesus Christ, boy! you heard me say morning here? well, get up!" And then I heard her opening the window of her bedroom, and talking to the darkness outside. "Lavignia, Lavignia? You sleeping too? What time that clock o' yourn saying, darling? This blasted boychild I have in here still sleeping, thinking that the morning waiting 'pon him . . . the sun all up in the skies already! What time it saying? . . . thanks." And she closed the window with a bang, and suddenly I could hear Lavignia's voice no more. And the barking of the dogs stopped; and the cackling of the hens ceased, as if someone had shot them dead.

I searched around in the semi-darkness for my home-clothes: the ragged cap, now too old for me to remember its original color or shape; next, the shirt, patched expertly in many places and looking like the quilted robe of Joseph; and then, the trousers, my stepfather's which were never reduced to fit me, and which warbled about my legs like an old man's underwear, wet in the sea. And then I rolled the crocus bags and the straw mattress from the floor, took them under my arms and went into the back yard to hand them over to the sun, to dry. I had wet my bed again. It was the kind of wetting I did not wish my mother to see, since it might have terrified her to think that I was growing up. But she found it out, nevertheless. "You pissing pissing pissing! Looka boy, you don't know you too old to be pissing? You not shamed?" I was glad it was only three o'clock; that none of the girls in the village was awake; that nobody could hear her reproaching me for this behavior. There must have been something about this morning, this Easter morning, which held her silent and crippled in awe. For she did not strike me with the backhand slap which she had perfected with such habit and such speed and accuracy that it landed, always in the same fat spot of my face.

Again, the pigs and the sheep were on my mother's side: they had filled their pens with mountains of their droppings. And all the time I was cleaning the pens and washing the pigs I wondered if it was like this in Bethlehem, in that stable where Christ was born; if that stable smelled half as dirty as this; if God had purposely made that the birthplace of Our Savior, in order to remind him, always, to be humble. Or if it was to give him a inferiority complex. And I was glad I was not born in a stable. The pigs smelled evil. After the pigs, the sheep. Rank rank rank sheep, whose perfume would have taken a soap factory of scrubbing to wipe off. And then I began to think of my first day in the Cathedral's choir: the morning when Christ was supposed to have come out of grave somewhere in a country so far from my little village and I was going to walk up the aisle of the beautiful church, up to the sacred chancel, and send my voice prancing all over the church, in a solo, in praise of Easter. And all the boys in my village and in the choir would envy me. Particularly Henry, who was only my substitute and who . . . "Them pigs clean yet? You tending to the sheeps? Yesterday morning the sheeps had *my* milk left back in *their* bubbies! And you forget to sweep the yard? Boy, you think you is a man, because you is this big Cathedral choirboy? But lemme tell you something. Your backside ain't so big that I can't put a proper tarring in it, this bright blessed Easter morning, eh!" I could feel the sting of the whip in the threat of her voice. And I knew she meant it. So I hurried through my work, making sure that in my eagerness to wear the rich linen ruff, the crimson cassock and the pearly white surplice, I did not become inefficient. The sun pretended it was going to come up above the tops of the sugar canes. But when I paused and waited for it, it changed its mind, and continued to give only a golden glow over the entire village. My work was done. And I bounded into the house.

"You don't intend to bathe? You intends to go into the people church smelling like a pig pen? Looka boy, get outta my eyesight, and go to the Stand Pipe, and get a clean bucket o' fresh water and cleanse yourself with, you hear?" Who would argue with a woman like this? Who would *dare*?

Across the pitchlake stretch of the road the canes were grumbling and shaking their fists in my face. I imagined monsters coming out of them. Only last week a man had been lambasted by the *Man* in the canes. My head was swollen with monsters coming at me. I heard a rustling in the canes. And I dropped the bucket. And when I stopped running, I was beside our paling. My dog, Rover, came panting at my side: again, he had frightened me. And I wanted to kick him dead. But I only kicked him once; and was glad that he could not talk. Holding on to his collar, I went back across the road to recapture my bucket and get the water. A few malicious windows with heads in them, and kerosene lamps beside the heads, were open. And I walked in the valley of the shadow of the canes this time (my guardian angel-dog beside me!), so they could not see me.

"I thought you wasn't coming back!" my mother shouted. "It is four o'clock. You not riding that bicycle outta this house today, bright Easter morning. You *walking* to church, 'cause I slaved and slaved on them clothes o' yourn, and no damn bicycle seat and bicycle seat ain't going to mash-up my labor, you hear me?"' It meant walking two miles, two miles of canes, two miles of *Men* in the canes. In all that distance I would pass only ten houses until I approached the Square in which the Cathedral was built. I would pass only ten street lamps, which seemed to have been burning since the day the island was discovered, and which were never repaired, and seemed ready to go out any minute. I would be alone all that time, all that terrible distance, with only the brightly lit church in my heart and the rich beautiful music in my ears. "You not riding that bicycle outta this house today." No passenger buses ran in my part of the island on Easter morning. At least, not at five o'clock. And the villagers were so poor that only one family was rich enough to own a broken-down car. But that family was not a church-going Christian-minded family, and I could not hope for a lift. I was the only one in my village that belonged to the Church of England. My mother was brought up in this church, and had recently started to attend the Church of the Nazarene because she felt its services were more like a part of her life, were more emotional, more exciting, more tragic and more happy: something like that holy day when "them twelve mens gathered up in that room upstairs, and talked in twelve different complete language and dialect, Christ, like nobody's business!" There, she could stand up in her large congregation, and open her heart to God, and to them, and tell the whole world that yesterday,

God stepped in and Satan stepped out, Amen! and she was brought through, pretty and clean. There, she could testify how God helped her *when she didn't know where the hell she could get six cents from to buy flour and lard oil to make "bakes" for her child from.* There, she could clap her hands and stomp her feet till the floorboards creaked with emotion, and jump up in the air and praise God. And for all that, feel as if God was indeed listening. But in the Church of England she was regimented to a sit-and-stand exercise of dull, religious drilling. And she always complained to Lavignia that she did not understand one word of what the parson was talking about. He used words that simple, common, poor people could not understand. And never, never "have I see anybody stand up in the Church o' England, and say, Amen, Hallelulia, to God!" It was such a strange church to her.

My mother then began the careful ceremony of dressing me. My hair was ripped by the horse-comb, which, this morning, seemed too fine-toothed to plough the tough roots of my rebellious hair. And each time the plough stuck, my mother cursed and said she didn't understand why the hell I couldn't have good black people's hair like everybody else. After the combing came the greasing. My hair would shine like the stars in the heavens. Then the talcum powder under my arms, and the Bay Rum to make me smell "nice and proper." And the new silk vest, with the price tag still on it. And then the underwear. And all these things she dressed me in, suspicious always that I would destroy them. At eight years of age, she did not think that I was fit to dress myself on an Easter morning, to venture into the powerful Church of England's God. On went the three-quarter gray stockings, with a rim of blue and black. When I reached under the bed for my shoes, I heard her warning voice breaking my eardrums: "No no no! You is not mashing-up them shoes! You are putting on them shoes, *last* thing! I want them shoes to return back inside this house without *one* bruise, you hear me, boy? If I see a mark on them, *one* mark, well God help you!" And she meant it. I had suffered because of this, many times before. And all I was guilty of was that I had walked in them. But she had examined the shoes, and had decided that I had not walked in them "properly." This time she would take no chances.

My shirt was the next piece of vestment in this robing. I was made to stand like a piece of wallaba tree trunk, not breathing, while she threaded the shirt through my arms and buttoned every button herself. I could smell the richness of the cotton, and feel its warmth on my washed body. The ready-tied tie went on next. And then the trousers. Carefully I put one leg through, and then the other, making sure not to touch the trousers themselves. She pushed the shirt gently into my trousers, and snapped the buckle. Only my shoes remained! But I knew what to expect. For weeks she had made me drill about the house, walking on old newspapers so that the soles would not be soiled, stretching the shoes which she always bought too small. I could never understand why. And even although she insisted that my feet were too big for my size, that "big shoes don't look nice 'pon a small boy's foot," I couldn't really imagine she would purposely force me into these undersized shoes just for the sake of her belief.

But I inhaled deeply. I rested my hand on her shoulder as she commanded me, balanced myself on one leg, and got ready for the punishment and torture. The shoe was too small. But that was not the point. It looked nice! My toes went in. I could feel a savage sting against my instep. The heel refused to go in. And as I touched the back of the shoe, to see what would happen, my mother shrieked, "Good Christ, boy! don't step on the back o' the shoe! You want to throw my money down the drain? You are mashing it up. And suppose I have to take them back . . . " But I knew she would never take them back. Intransigence would never permit her pride the blow of taking them even to Woody, the shoemaker across the road, for a stretching. I would have to make my feet get smaller. "Come come, eat this little food." I pulled a chair from the table and was preparing to sit down, when I heard her voice again, "Good Jesus Christ! boy, I didn't tell you to sit down and eat! Not in them trousers that I slaved and slaved so hard over to press and make look nice for you, like if you is somebody decent. *Stand up!* Stand up and eat. It can't kill yuh, it can't kill yuh!" And so I had to stand up and eat the *little food*: about two pints of green tea, warm and thick and rich with sheep's milk; a loaf of bread as big as a house, and a wedge of roasted pork, enough for two persons; and a banana. My mother believed in bananas. They "make your skin nice and smooth," she would say. I soon felt the heavy load in my belly; and I felt good. I would wear *any* shoe now. Even a size seven instead of a ten. "Come come!" she said, "belch! Belch! You belch good and proper, whilst you home, 'cause I don't want to hear that you belch-out, or break wind, in the white people church, or in the public road, like if you don't have no manners, hear?" And I granted her her belch. A smothered, respectable belch, which although it did not satisfy her yet made her say nothing, since it assured her that I had already belched at home.

Now, the shoes! My hand was resting on her fat shoulders. I was balancing all my weight on my left foot. My right foot was said to be slightly larger than my left foot —although she never told me why. I knew the shoe would never fit. But I was not such a fool as to tell her. "Put yuh weight on your instep, boy, do! Don't put all yuh weight on the whole shoe, 'cause the shoe won't go on then." Exasperated, she grabbed my foot and forced it into the pincers of the shoe, while I remained silent, and in agony. "Hold there! don't move!" she commanded. And she left me. Coming back with the large pot spoon which we used as a shoe horn, she said, "Push! Push hard! But don't mash-down the instep. Push hard, boy, like you have life!" The more I pushed, the smaller the shoe became. My face changed from black, to blue, to purple. Still my judgment warned me not to comment on my pain, and certainly not on the smallness of the shoe. She would never believe. "Push! You pushing, or you standing up there with your face like some ram-goat own?" At last, through some miracle, the foot went in. Never to come out again! Lord have mercy, I prayed in my heart, as the pain whizzed through my body. And when the other shoe was rammed on, I was sweating. The perspiration was changing my sea-island cotton shirt into plastic. And she noticed it, and wanted to know *why* I was sweating. "You intend to sweat-up this clean shirt that I just put-on on your back, boy?" And I tried hard to stop sweating; tried very hard, as if to stop it I had only to turn off a faucet. "Walk off and lemme see how the shoes look on your foot, boy!" I held my breath, pushed my chest out, and asked God for strength. The shoes crucified me. I would never be able to walk on the smooth marble in the Cathedral. But I wanted to be at church this Easter morning. This was *my* Easter morning.

"Okay! You ready now." And she dusted my handkerchief with some Evening in Paris perfume, tucked it into my shirt breast pocket, and secured it with a gold-colored, small safety pin, which I was permitted to wear only to funerals and weddings. "Now, turn round and let me see you. Christ! boy, you look real good!

You look just like the son o' the man at the Plantation. Just like a little doctor. Now, I want you to grow up fast, and be a doctor, hear?" And I knew that if I did not answer, yes, she would want to know why. "Yes," I said, wishing that I was already grown up and was thousands of miles from there. She looked at me again and again, and then she took me into her bedroom, and showed me my reflection in the life-sized looking glass. Back in the living room, the white, sparkling-white, Blanca-cleaned cork hat with the green undersides was clamped on my head. I was now ready for the Easter world!

"Since you not riding that bicycle outta here, this blessed Easter morning, I am going to give you twelve cent to put in your pocket. Now, *walk* down. I want you to look fresh when you enter that Cathedral church. Now, seeing that it is Easter, and you have friends, you must buy a penny in sweets . . . no, you better buy lozengers to make your breath smell nice; and a pack o' sweeties . . . for every child like sweeties, and you ain't no different. And keep the rest of the change for bus fare *back* home. You could afford to climb in a crowded bus, *after* church. It don't matter then if your trousers crease-up a trifle. Now, come back inside this house looking tidy. Not as if you went through a pig mouth, you hear me?" She put the twelve-cent piece into my hand, as if it was the last part of her fortune, and which I was to cherish for the rest of my life. I looked up at her, so large, so beautiful, so lovely, and so black—a mysterious queen or something, from Africa, with her hair braided neatly and long; with her old white dress which she washed three times a week, clutching to the feminine twists and turns of her full body. She looked at me, and she looked at my thoughts; and she smiled. She drew me close, close to her breasts and her rolling soft stomach, where I could feel the love and the blood pumping through her body. And she kissed me on each cheek and said, in a voice that came from the bottom of her heart and her belly, "I praises the Lord that I didn't throw you in no blasted dry-well when your father left me pregnunt with you, seven eight years ago in this terrible world with not even a half-cent to buy milk with. God bless yuh, son. I proud o' you!"

I was ready to go now. Outside the morning was glorious. The sun had eventually decided to come up. And I could see its rays setting the tops of the canes on fire with a golden flame. And the dogs and the chickens and the small children were quarreling for their breakfast. My own breakfast felt good and heavy and safe in my bowels. "When you go 'cross the road, and you see Jonesie, say Goodmorning. Say Good morning to Stella. And to Lavignia. I am going to call Lavignia now and let she see how nice you look." And she moved from me and went into her bedroom, and called out for Lavignia.

"Why you don't let me say my prayers to God in peace this blasted morning, eh, Mistress Carlton? I here on my knees, before God, asking Him who the hell He intends to send to lend me a shilling to buy milk with this Easter morning?"

"He coming out now," my mother said, with pride.

"Who? God?"

"The bridegroom coming! Come outside, and see how he look."

And Lavignia, apparently convinced that her prayers would be in vain, left her spiritual complaining and came out in front of her house to see me *dressed like a little doctor.*

"Oh Christ, Mistress Carlton! This boy-child o' yourn look first-class! Boy, you should be grateful you have such a nice mother. I hopes to Christ you don't intend to forget this mother o' yourn when you come to be a man, eh? Cause if you do, the birds o' vengeance going pick out your *blasted eyes*!"

And I had to answer Lavignia with as much respect as I would have answered my mother, and say, "No, please Miss Lavignia. I won't never forget my mother."

"Good," she concluded, and adjusted my tie, although it was already adjusted properly. "Now, you go on down in the name o' the Lord, and sing that solo like if you is a angel. Mistress Carlton, wait, you give this boy some fresh crispy biscuits to help out with the voice? Biscuits good for the voice. If you don't have fresh ones, I have some. Come, boy, take these biscuits. They does do wonders for yuh voice. Eat them whilst you's singing, and the people in that Cathedral church going to think that you is Michael, the Arch-angel!"

I took the biscuits and mumbled on them, all the way down the road with the canes bordering it, mumbling mumbling, trying to take my mind off the torment of the shoes and the threat of the canes. But the canes moaned and the shoes burned. I walked in the middle of the creaking road, forcing my mind from my present predicament and focusing it on the musty-smelling Changing

Room in the loft of the Cathedral. I could see the ruffs sparkling white. I could smell the starch in them; and they were ironed so many times by Henry's mother that they shone, and when you ran your fingers over them they were as smooth as glass. And the crimson robe. And the white linen surplice, all made to fit me, all mine, so long as I remained with an unbroken voice in the choir of this heavenly Cathedral. And I could see myself coming down the steps from the Changing Room with the other choristers, and standing at the entrance of the church while the Lord Bishop and his assistants waited for a few late worshippers to settle in their seats. And in my mind I could see the faces of that vast congregation: almost half the population of the island, who came to the Cathedral in droves whenever the Bishop was preaching. Some came to church as they would, every Sunday, because they liked church: others, because they liked the resplendent robes, with the hoods of the universities of the ministers—all colors under the sun; so pretty and so impressive and so learned. And more than once I myself wanted to become a minister in God's Church of England, to swish my long flowing robes, and adjust my hood and hat and large, ruby-Cyclops ring every second of the service; and pour communion wine at the rails; and mumble those few important indistinguishable words, while the sinners knelt before me, and prayed to *me*, and asked *me* forgiveness because they could not see God, nor talk to Him, unless they had first asked *me* forgiveness, and recognized *me* as His right-hand man. Now, I was walking up the aisle in my mind . . . so long and so smooth, with its marble shining from the long underpaid hours of scrubbing by the Cathedral sexton, my voice warbling; and the men and women at the ends of the pews nearest the choir nodding their heads, and complimenting. How they would raise their heads from their unmelodic hymn books, and nod, and turn slightly with their eyes to locate the voice; and I, seeing them, would raise my voice a little bit higher, a little bit sweeter, until the organ seemed silent and voiceless, as the dumb man who opened his mouth and sang aloud his soundless praise to God, every Sunday, at Matins. And then my solo. The old heads would be nodding, and smiling, because they could not applaud in God's presence, in God's church. And the organist, like a spy, glowering at me through his motor car mirror above the organ keys, anticipating a wrong key, or a blunder . . . and Henry, envious with praise. And then, when it is all finished, the choir, and the Lord Bishop, and the ministers walking down the whipped, chastised church, with the congregation dumb and washed-out by the sermon and the presence in the church of Christ's body come from the dead . . . rejoicing, because this is Easter. And then the Benediction said by the Bishop, and the sign of the cross which he always made as if he was chasing flies from his face; and the limp people kneeling, to say a last something, a word or two, in thanks, to God.

I passed the first street lamp and continued into the desolate black morning, cramped by the thick, unsympathetic fields of canes which refused to let the sun through to keep me company. On and on, in perpetual misery from my shoes. At last I had to give in. I took them off. I tied the laces together. I strung the shoes around my neck. I pushed the stockings into my pockets. My feet were so numb they felt they had disappeared in sea water. And then I ran, hurrying to the Cathedral before the street became too crowded, before I could be seen, and detected, and laughed at. But nothing happened all the way. I reached the vicinity of the Cathedral: the tall tombstones like diminutive skyscrapers, and the trees in the graveyard of the church, and the black birds playing hide-and-seek from tree to tree, and the houses coming alive . . . and finally, the Cathedral itself, facing me like my mother, unapproving. I would have to put my shoes and stockings on before I could cross the threshold of the West Portico. But I had to find some place to sit down first.

The bells were ringing now. I looked up to see them and they filled my heart with joy. And I yearned to be in the choir, in the chancel, singing my solo.

The congregation was arriving. From where I stood, outside the church wall, I could see women dressed in the white of angels, white hats, white shoes, as if they were proud to be part of this great resurrection morning, as if they had remained new brides, new virgins, all their lives. They were standing in the West Portico, waiting for the service to begin, waiting for their friends and enemies to see their new clothes, waiting for the men to pass and whisper little controversial words for their ears. And most of the men in the black of the funeral, wearing their suits of long-ago black, which fitted them like coats of armor, and walking stiff and proud in the morning sunlight spinning through the lazy leaves—they hovered around the North Portico, talking about the Test

Match which ended in a draw. I could see Henry, my arch enemy, standing near them, and with him were some of the boys in the choir. I lingered near the tall wall that kept the Cathedral hearing-distance away from the fish-cries and the whore-cries of the near-by Market and the street of floating women. How was I to get into the church yard and sit on a tombstone and put my shoes on my feet again?

The organ began to rant and swell, breathing its powerful cruel chords into the ears of the disinterested congregation. Everything was fresh. Everything was new. The organ was breathing now like a monster. Somebody important was arriving. From where I stood, looking over the tip of the wall, over the tops of the short croton trees, and over the head of the white angel, silent and stationary in polished marble, I could barely make out the roosters sitting on the helmets of the Governor of the island and his party. The Lord Bishop, with his robes fluttering like the Union Jack in the breeze, came out to meet him at the North Portico. I could see the Prime Minister of the island, and some of his ministers standing uncomfortable in their official clothes; and the lords and ladies of the island, all untitled, but all rich and white, coming to this Cathedral, old as Christopher Columbus, so early in the morning. And they all seemed half asleep to me. As they disappeared into the church, I threw my shoes over the church wall and jumped behind them, onto the soft dew in the grass, near a dead sailor who slept in a tomb. It said he was an "ensign."

They were coming towards me now, coming up the aisle, as I peered through the West Window. The important people, and the choir. I saw Henry grinning into the pages of his hymn book. I saw the choir pass the multitude of people of all colors: the black, the brown, the light-skinned, the light-brown, and approach the front pews of the church, where the Governor and the white people and the rich black people always sat. I was fighting with my shoes. And as they filed into their seats and into their stalls, all that was left was the wide white aisle, like a swath of a canefield, running straight out into the road, through the East Gate. There was a beggar-man standing in the silhouette of the Gate, in the road, drinking from a small paper bag, with which he was conducting as the music romped and played. I was fighting with my shoes. And all the time my tears were falling on the clear freshly ironed cotton shirt, and into the shoes, as I tried in vain to get them back on my feet. And when I looked up and the film of sadness dropped with the tears and I could see, I saw Henry step into the middle of the aisle in the chancel, and my heart broke. And straightaway saw my mother, standing at the entrance of the gate waiting; waiting to examine my shoes.

1971

A Funeral

It was about a hundred degrees in the shade. It was about four o'clock in the afternoon. Clothes was sticking to your back. And the road was full o' people going home from work.

The long black hearse, build in the days when they was coaches, when coaches was drawn by two sweating horses, was now without horses, and had-in a six horse-power engine. The island's biggest, the leading undertaker, or duppy-agent, was driving the hearse.

It was a solemn afternoon. A final journey. And the hearse was decorated with white flowers and mauve flowers, and there was other flowers drawn-in, in white delicate paint, all over the glass panels of the hearse.

The hearse was moving slow slow over the road, like if it was a fat, sad slug. Like a dew wirrum.

All the roads in the capital was really crowded. Jampacked with people. Men and women going home from work, and men who was just strolling, being as how they was unemploy, had slacken-off their pace, and stop, just to watch. Some o' them stop their bicycles, with one foot on the ground for balance. All them-so watched and waited until the procession pass them.

Rain had-fall the night before. And first thing in the morning. So the road was clean. The air was clean and humid. The road wasn't clean because o' the road-sweepers or the garbage-men, 'cause they was on strike. Um was clean mainly because of the torrents o' rain that had-fall.

Yuh couldn't pass at all. Um was impossible to pass. So the people decide to wait. People who had to wait and who decide to become mourners on the spot, and the other people who had nothing better to do, all them-so join-in in the procession.

"What a lovely funeral!" a' old woman say. And straight-off she make the sign of the Cross. Two times on her chest. "Incidentally, who dead?"

"A gravedigger," a man say.

"I hope they have one leff-back for *his* sake," the old woman say.

And you couldn't hear anything more she say, and if she did-intend to say anything else, anyhow, the crowd overpowered her words. And soon she herself was lost in the procession.

The Member of Parlment for Sin-James East was there among the mourners who was walking. He was dress in the same formal suit that he had-on when he was first elected an M.P., at his inauguration, ten years ago. Beside him was Seabert the tailor. Seabert was wearing a new formal black suit, a twin off the pattern that the M.P. was wearing. But being as how Seabert was a tailor, he put on some pretty, glamorous touches on the suit, to make him and the suit look more pretty. The suit that Seabert was wearing had come from the same piece o'material he had promise to sell to Sarge.

And behind the M.P. was Sarge, official in police black, with brass and silver criss-crossing his chest and back. Then Nathan, a friend of the dead man, in a black suit that had turn mauve through age and mothballs. And already Nathan was sweating-up the suit under the armpits.

The Guvvament had organize some real strict public relations to go along with the funeral. The man that was in the coffin was a Guvvament supporter. The Guvvament had decide to make the funeral an effective funeral and a politically beneficial funeral to boot.

Every Cabinet minister was present. The Prime Minister himself was leading the double-line o' dignitaries. He had the Guvvament pass a' ordnance saying that all people at the funeral, especially the officials, was to get outta their cars or hop-off their bicycles about half-mile to a mile from the Main Gate o' the Cemetery and *walk* on their two feet slow slow through the streets.

"That way," the Prime Minister had-say at the executive meeting that morning, "we will be killing two birds with one rock-stone. We will be showing *pure* grief. In public. And also our concern for the *small*-man."

They all laugh-out hard hard when the Prime Minister say so.

"Be-Christ!" he went on, laughing himself, more louder than any of the Cabinet ministers. "Be-Christ, I don't even want to remind any o'wunnuh in here, none o'you. I don't want to have to remind none o'you. I don't want to say um more than one time. This party is the party of the small-man. It is a small-man party. And if any o'you here present this morning, particularly one or two who I hear want to tek-over power from me and be Prime Minister, even before I resign or dead like Lionel . . . Well, lemme tell you bastards something now. If any one o'you in here now, don't understand why we *walking* that last mile on foot behind Lionel coffin, that stupid bitch who couldn't do nothing more profitable than slam a domino . . . Well, well ask the present M.P. for Westbury North, then! Ask *him*. Ask him 'bout the problems we getting down there near the Cemetery. We getting more political licks in the Cemetery constituency than what John dream 'bout. So! This is a political funeral. Lionel will be buried *politically*. Hence! We walking that last mile, outta *pure* politics, on foot! And be-Christ, when they drop Lionel coffin in that hole after we walk-through Westbury North and the Cemetery constituency, I want each and every one o' you sons o' bitches here present to start crying. You hear me? *Weep!* Bawl-out with sorrow. Cry like shite! My political experience tell me that there going-be more votes swinging to our man in that constituency than what John write 'bout!"

So the Prime Minister was walking at the head o' the Cabinet, followed by other party officials plus a detachment of the police force, walking slow slow through the heat and humidity that you could almost cut with a knife, it was so damn hot.

And the moment they come into view, the people went wild and start screeling.

"Skipper! Skipper! Skipper!"

Once or twice the Prime Minister give a nudge to the M.P. for Westbury North, and whisper something outta the corner of his mouth, the left-hand corner, with a cynical, sly smile covering his face.

"What I tell you, man?"

The M.P. for Westbury North say, "Remind me, Skipper, to give you a report of a rumor I hear from a friend, who hear it from a reliable confidential source. It 'bout the two fellows in the party who planning to overthrow you, and . . . "

"We going-break their arse!"

"Lash-their-arse-at-the-polls!" the people screel out.

The Prime Minister then take off his rimless spectacles offa his face, and smile and mop his brown face, and smile some more with the people.

"Skipper! Skipper! Skipper!"

The Prime Minister skin was high brown. Like a piece o' polished leather. He was tall tall. Like a' athlete. And had a handsome body. The people who know and people who don't really know say that he does-sleep in the beds o' more married women than what

John could count or what anybody dare to 'numerate and tally. He does-move like a dancer. And today, he move like one. Like a limbo-dancer. Like a cat on ashes through the thickness o' the crowd, through the thickness o' the smells and bodyodors of the crowd.

He smelled the bodies o' the crowd. He smelled the perspiration dripping down from them, the odors, the sweat, the perfumes and the rum-smells. The crowd was too close for comfort and for the Prime Minister's aristocratic sense o' things. He didn't like smells. He didn't like them being so close.

Sometimes, working late at night in his office or driving home from the residence of one of his ministers who was overseas on Guvvament business, he would get sad, sad even to the point o' depression when he compare his life o' graciousness, champagne and strawberries, Epsom Darby and night life at Cambridge University to the poor-arse country with people who smell, who had no hope, who indulge in crime, a country with financial problems, when he could be cocking-up his two feet still, in Hampstead or in Piccadilly Circus. The budget o' the country was never balance since he became Prime Minister. The budget could never be balance.

But now he remembered where he was, so he merely jerk his nostril in disgust. The smell of the people disappear. And immediately after, he start to smile.

"Lick-in their arse at the polls, Skipper! Mash-them-up! Paint their arse black-and-blue on voting day, Skipper!" the people went on shouting, falling in love with their leader.

He put back on his spectacles on his face, and he look more younger and more powerful than when he wasn't wearing glasses.

All like now-so, the procession reach round the last corner before entering in the Main Gate o' the Cemetery. There was a sidewalk in this part of the walk. So the crowd grow more louder, more longer and more larger. Space, or the lack o' space, now turn into tension and quarreling. And the smell o' the poor people plus the smell o' the Mayflower trees overhanging the Cemetery, and the bougainvillea vines that was crawling over some neglected graves, these smells was mixed up and was turn into a real strong nauseating sensation.

"You walking with your gun?" the Prime Minister say to the M.P. for Westbury North in a whisper, outta the corner of his mouth. The left-hand corner. "I like I don't like this crowd, yuh. I don't like these people. And I know blasted-well that these bitches don't like me. You have-on your gun on your holster? Just in case?"

"But, Skipper, you *knows* me! You knows full-well that I sleeps with my *wompuh* in my hand! How you mean?"

"Well, I feel better, then."

The Main Gate was so close that it look as if it had feet and was coming to meet them. They was people like peas, like sand, in the procession all like now-so. So they had to force and push themselves through the narrow iron gates as if they was catching a passenger bus that was the last bus for the night. It take 'bout a' hour to a' hour and-a-half before all the official mourners plus the police plus the security guards plus all the people who had-join the cortege could squeeze through the Main Gate.

The Guvvament had-tell the Cemetery Board and the grave-diggers that was off-duty to come to work, and that the minute after the last person who look like a real mourner step through the Gate, that to close the blasted Gate.

And this happen like clock-work. Pretty pretty this directive of the Guvvament was directed. This Guvvament was a real efficient guvvament. Everything work. Political murders; firings from guvvament posts; the hiring o' girl friends, kip-misses and chossels to high guvvament positions; the slot-machines whiching the people branded "one-hand-bandits"; plus the thiefing and mispropriation o' guvvament funds, all these things-so work like if the Mafia was running the country and not ordinary, common politicians. Every-fucking-thing work. Most unlike the things that the previous Guvvament did-try to do; and *that* Guvvament was a democratic Guvvament.

The Prime Minister had personally ordered some members of his Security Force to pose as mourners and walk in the middle of the crowd. He didn't want to take no chances with the people. So one hundred of the roughest, one hundred of the most loyal members of the Security Force was assign to this funeral.

Reporters and cameramen from the radio station and from the three newspapers was all over the place. The Guvvament had-plan to put the funeral on the radio news that night as the first item. Naturally, the Prime Minister would be on the front pages of all three morning newspapers.

So when enough of the people had-reach the grave, the Dean, dress like damnation in black, from head to foot, black covering his black body, and with his tortoise-shell spectacles shining in the dying light whiching was fighting its way to come through the large, thick leaves of the almond trees shimmering all round the grave-side, then and only then did the very-rendable Dean begin the Order of the Burial of the Dead.

At seven o'clock the morning before, the Prime Minister had-telephone the Lord Bishop of the country to tell him that he want *he*, His Lordship, to officiate. In addition to the very-rendable Dean. But the Lord Bishop, who wasn't sick, said in a weak voice, "Excellency, I sorry sorry, sir. I have a migraine that killing me, Excellency. As you know from the last time you see me, I been under doctor's care. For two weeks now, going 'pon three. And I even had to cancel all my church app'intments, and . . . and . . . "

The Lord Bishop was a secret supporter of the opposition party.

But before he could complete his excuses and apologies and entreaties, the Prime Minister had slam-down the telephone a long time. "I waiting on His Lordship. He may know about Sodom-and-Gomorrah, but I have a file on his arse concerning sodomy-and-Gomorrah. I waiting on that son of a bitch!"

So they had to settle for the Dean only.

But the Dean did-already behaving as if he did-already the Lord Bishop of the country. And one night he utter a wish 'bout his amibition loud enough and in the wellchosen hearing o' some Cabinet ministers, who laughed-out and remind him whilst laughing that the Lord Bishop was not even born in the country, so anything could happen one o' these dark nights.

And the night that Lionel's murder was annouce on the radio news, the Dean say to his wife, "But why it couldn't be the Bishop? Instead o' that fool, Lionel?"

Lionel had-get stabbed during a' argument over a game o' dominoes. The fellow who stab-heem say that Lionel had-hide the "key" card, the very card he did-need to beat Lionel and win the tournament. But the Bishop, as far as the Dean did-know, didn't play dominoes!

Lionel, before he dead, was also the Deputy Head grave-digger at the Westbury Cemetery. The very-rendable Dean really like big, pretty ceremonies. Officials receptions, pompous gatherings, military parades and social events did-always bring out the best in his civilize nature and properness, and proprieties concerning food. And at all these functions, he uses to behave as if he was already His Lordship.

So on this solemn occasion, he begin to use a voice that was really suited and fitable to the somberness and the sadness of the hot afternoon. And not even the stickiness of his surplice and the stickiness in the weather did-bother or take away from his standing and stature, dress-off as he was, like damnation, in heavy, long black.

He start speaking 'bout love. 'bout family. 'bout the family of love. 'bout the family of the people. 'bout the family of politicians. 'bout politics and 'bout power.

The last thing he mention was the dead. Poor Lionel laying-down in front o' him in a mahogany coffin! But the Dean was talking real sweet when he mention something whiching he called "the politics o' love."

The Prime Minister had-already know what the Dean did-intend to say in the eulogy. Um was the Prime Minister himself who had-tell the Dean what to say. They did-discuss it in detail over some rum-and-sodas, and from the notes whiching the Prime Minister had-write and had-take to the Dean office.

Now the real poetry start to roll-off the Dean mouth:

"I am the resurrection and the life, saith the Lord: he that believeth in me, though he were dead, yet shall he live . . . "

The Dean tongue move-over the words and make them sound real pretty, like pure honey. He had a real Oxford accent, too. But the play-play English accent wasn't strong enough still to muzzle the broad, flat flavor of his native speech.

"The Dean could preach *too-sweet*." the M.P. for Sin-James say to Seabert, the tailor, in Seabert's ear.

Seabert had recently join the Party, and did-seeking a seat in the constituency where he and Nathan was living.

"Too sweet, in truth!" the M.P. say.

"Like a new zipper in a pair o' new khaki pants!" Seabert say.

"Like Frere-Pilgrim cane-juice!" the M.P. say. "With a drop o' rum in it!"

Seabert start to smile, so overpowered he was by the prospect o' power.

"Sweet for days!" he say.

And at this point, the Prime Minister tek-out his handkerchief from outta his breast pocket, tek-off his rimless spectacles and start to wipe his two eyes. He then hold-down his head and give everybody the impression, by the posture o' sadness, that he was serious. All the people see him doing so. A cameraman see him. And caught him. And thinking that the Prime Minister was weeping for the dead, he pop-off a flash in the Prime Minister face.

The flash from the camera light up the total immediate surroundings. It would make a real nice front-page picture, the Prime Minister say.

"I know that my Redeemer liveth, and that he shall stand . . ."

Right then, all o' Lionel family start to cry. His woman, from who he had two children and with who he uses to live, she start-on 'pon one loud crying. His next woman, from who he had one son and with who he didn't used to live, she, too, was crying. His three sisters, one of who had come in from Brooklyn, New York; his mother; and his father; the members of the Darrells Road Domino Players Team, all o' them dress-off in black, with handkerchiefs jutting out outta their pocket, handkerchiefs mek-outta white dots on black silk squares, Jesus Christ, *everybody* start crying now.

But the most loudest, the most body-wrenching crying that was crying did-come from the woman with who Lionel did-live and from who he had the two children. She burst in a' earth-rendering weeping. She raise up her two hands high high high up in the air and bawl for blue murder. She raise she voice when the Dean did-emphasizing the part of the Scriptures, namely about "my Redeemer liveth." And she lower-down her lamentations when he reach the words, "The Lord giveth and the Lord tekketh away." Her voice overtake all the other voices. Her voice reach right up to the tops o' the almond trees and the casuarina trees in the pit of her sadness when the Dean reach "blessed be the name of the Lord." Her voice was clearer, was higher and was more unsettling than even the shimmering, dying light from the setting sun shining on the coconut and casuarina trees surrounding the grave, the people and the grave-yard.

Seabert, as a tailor and man o' letters, recognize the part of the Scriptures that the text was tek-from. "Joab," he say, "chapter one, verse twenty-one."

The M.P. from Sin-James, for who Lionel had-work in the last campaign, see a cameraman pointing his lens in his direction and he start to wipe-off his sweating face with a blue and white polka-dot handkerchief. And start to weep like shite. The flash from the bulb explode like a big big fire-fly before the M.P. could move-'way his handkerchief from covering up his whole face.

"Man that is born of woman hath but a short time to live . . ."

O Lord! Who tell the Dean to say so? Who tell the Very-rendable to utter them words?

Lionel woman jump up in the air. She throw her long silk blue dress high high over her two thighs. She raised um up in a gesture o'grief. And in the gesture, she showoff two of the sweetest, juiciest, prettiest and most luscious pairs o' legs. And the two eyes of the M.P. from Sin-James rested on them. Some other men look, too, yuh. And they liked what they saw. But in the present circumstances, they put it outta their minds, for the time being. As man! 'cause they understood.

They did-understand that Lionel, alas, born as he was, of woman, no longer had all o' this beautiful, nice, black flesh inside his hand to grasp and hold-on 'pon, to hold-on 'pon and slam as he like, as he uses to slam a domino in a big tournament game . . . "The Lord giveth and the Lord tekketh away, boy!" And she, a woman, pretty pretty pretty, and with some class; with good body and better body-line and more better thighs, was now left, poor soul, with only the sting of his death to comfort she.

And the M.P. from Sin-James East start thinking 'bout slamming, 'bout slamming a dom, as they uses to call the game that brought-on Lionel death. And the two eyes of the same M.P. was stick-on 'pon the woman legs, and he couldn't concentrate no more on the sadness of the moment. So he move over a little and rested a comforting hand 'pon the shoulder of the grieving woman. He feel the softness of her neck. And she stiffen-up, like if his hand was a stinging bee.

And she bawl-out again. And the Dean was to pause in his reading of the Order of the Burial of the Dead.

Soon after this, they start to sing a hymn. The hymn come from *Hymns Ancient & Modern*, the book they does-use in the Cathedral and in all Anglican churches. Hymn 477. Hymn 477 is a hymn whiching no old woman in the whole country would ever go-sleep at dusk without singing to herself.

The day thou gavest, Lord, is ended,
The darkness falls at thy behest.

"Remind me," the Prime Minister say, talking to his aide, the M.P. for Westbury North, all the time the people was singing, "remind me to call in the union boss of the Harbor Workers Union and the leader of the Garbage Collectors Union and get the two o' them to brek-up these blasted strikes. They strangulating the people. First thing when we get back to the office, hear?" He wiped the booby outta his two eyes. "Sarge here?" he ask his aide, who was wiping the booby outta his two eyes, too. "Sarge at this funeral?" His aide nod to say that Sarge here. "I want a tail put-on 'pon Sarge. Yuh can't trust nobody these days. Not even the police."

The singing was going-on all the time the weeping and the lamenting was punctuating the singing. And the last puctuation mark come when, in the end, the thick, black soil start hitting the top of the mahogany coffin that was polish to a high-brown sheen.

The undertaker, or duppy-agent, who was a member of the Party and the largest and most expensive duppyagent in the country, this undertaker tek-off all the silverpainted handles and other decorations from offa the coffin, just as they was about to lower Lionel in that deep, dark crevice.

Four politicians and the two grave-diggers on duty slipped Lionel coffin down gently gently, with the help of three leather straps that was so big that they could have fit a giant waist.

The mold start to pound on the shiny mahogany box. The men heard the pounding and start thinking of Lionel in the flesh and how he uses to pound a "key" card. As the mould fall, less louder now that the crevice in the ground was fulling up, as Lionel coffin was getting cover up, the screeling and the wailing start-up more louder. And when the coffin was hidden and conceal by the crumbly mold and the Dean say, "Ashes to ashes," the screeling and crying come to a' end.

It was strange how it come to a' end. Like if the end came and nobody didn't know nor notice it. All like now-so, all you could hear was a moaning from the family. A sound like a painful, almost stifled groan cause by a toothache. One or two white handkerchiefs was tek out by politicians, and placed at their two eyes, in respect. The women in Lionel's life moved from side to side in a slow slow rhythm o' sadness.

"We must set-up a television station soon," the Prime Minister say to his aide in a whisper. "State-own. And state-control, of course! All this nice feeling and emotion this afternoon, all this grass-root sentimentalism should be captured by a colored television camera. It would make such lovely, nice news!"

Standing round them, the cameramen was clicking their shutters tekking pictures and mekking noise like ducks and drakes chattering in a yard full o' chickens.

"I want to have a word with Lionel woman right after the funeral. Send-round my official car for she when she get home from the Cemetery. As man!"

The choirs from the Cathedral, who had-march at the head of the procession, even in front o' the Prime Minister and the Cabinet, start up now to sing the hymn, whiching if it wasn't sung, nobody would believe there was a real funeral. It was a hymn whiching if it was not sung, nobody would believe that anybody dead or that a dead was buried.

Abide with Me.

"Hymn number twenty-seven," the Dean say. "Hymn twenty-seven. Two-seven."

Man, 'Abide with Me' was a more popular song than 'God Save the Queen.'

The men who was singing bass and them who was playing they could touch the alto-parts, these men start to make poetry with the parts. They was singing as if they was competing with themselves and with the choristers. And they was singing loud loud to drown-out the voices of the poor choir-boys. 'cause they had already had-in some strong liquors and didn't really know the tenor-part or the alto-part too good. But um was pure improvisation and imagination that make them sing-so.

They was singing this burial hymn as if they was singing um at a wedding. So 'Abide with Me' become, by the way they was singing it and by the way they was improvising the parts, like a national Sunday anthem.

But all the people in the country did-know that the men had good reason and cause to sing it so. Things was expensive. Crime was high high. Unemployment was more higher. So the men had good reason to sing it. Without no reservation at all. Man, they lift-up their voices, right up to the top o' the almond trees and the casuarina trees and the coconut trees and the bougainvillea, and shake-up the earth itself with their deep, sad challenge.

Shine through the gloom, and point me to the skies;
Heaven's morning breaks, and earth's vain shadows flee:
In life . . .

And when they get to "*in life,*" the people make a pause, they paused, as if their own own lives, the lives they been leading under this Guvvamment's regime, was itself in question. As if it was a strangle-hold the Guvvament had-grapple round their neck. 'cause everybody did-know from their own circumstances that in the midst o' life, they was also in the midst o' death.

And when they reach *"in death"* in the hymn, they paused a next time. This pause was like if they was expressing in a gradual lowering-down the sadness that was in their very voices.

Oh Lord! When the hymn reach *"O Lord,"* man, you woudda think that all the people in this whirl was shouting-out, compelling, telling and calling-on 'pon God to lissen. Lissen, man, God. Jesus Christ, at least lissen to we . . . *"abide with me."*

"The minute the news broadcast on the radio tonight," the Prime Minister say, "the minute they broadcast this funeral — bram! — we calling elections! Political savvy and funerals, boy! Politics is like a *nice* funeral. Yuh does-cry like shite over the coffin, and half-hour later yuh does-fire some liquors at the wake. Political savvy and funerals, boy! And this is one o' the *loveliest* funerals in the history of this country! We calling elections."

"We send-off Lionel, God bless his soul," the M.P. for Westbury North say, "to his final resting place this afternoon with one o' the loveliest funerals for the year, in the history o' this political party. And Lionel was only a common, half-ig'rant party supporter. A blasted yard-fowl. But as you say, Skipper. Political savvy and funerals. So we had to send-he-off with a lovely funeral. And with such a pretty song, 'Abide with Me.'"

When the M.P. for Westbury North was saying this, um was only one hour after the funeral done. All the people at the Cemetery didn't even get home yet then. But the Prime Minister had already gone in Lionel's home, or former home, with Lionel woman. He had just return to his official car after spending some time with she. It was a dark night. A dog was growling as if somebody dead, or as the old people uses to say, as if the dog seeing duppies and spirits and deads. Um was Lionel's dog, too. Spot. The dog was growling. And already the elections was in full swing.

The M.P. from Westbury North, who had-drive the car on this mission for the Prime Minister, start to sing:

A-bide with me, O Lord, a-bide with me.

The Prime Minister wipe his face and his two hands with a white handkerchief. He pass the handkerchief over his lips. And he then wipe-off each finger clean clean clean. And then he throw the handkerchief into the black gutter. The car was park beside the gutter. And the dog was laying-down beside the gutter, beside the car. Because the dog had-come to greet the Prime Minister.

"And that blasted coffin cost the Party one thousand dollars. One thousand dollar bills for a blasted coffin, for a blasted political yard-fowl! But we intend to get-umback, though," the Prime Minister say after he spit in the gutter.

"Lionel leff-back any propery?" the M.P. say.

"He leff-back his woman, though!" the Prime Minister say. "He dead, and leff-she-back." And then he laugh.

"As man!" the M.P. say.

"We send-off Lionel as if he was a Prime Minister himself!" the Prime Minister say. "With a lovely funeral!" He spit again, in the gutter. "How you fix for tomorrow night? You could bring me back here?"

"As man!"

And then the Prime Minister sit down on the plush leather o' the back seat of the large black car with the M.P. at the wheel, and he start to hum:

Shine through the gloom, and point me to the skies; Heaven's morning breaks . . .

And for days afterwards, the people who had-live near the Cemetery and them who had-attend the funeral as witnesses to its size and everybody connected to the Guvvament they all say, "What a lovely funeral they give Lionel!"

And more than anything else, more even than the voice of the Dean, the people remember the singing of 'Abide with Me.' And especially one thing they remember, whiching was the way the choirs sing it and rendered it and how the people did-sing the very last line, in the very last verse.

In life, in death, O Lord, abide with me.

1974

CANADIAN EXPERIENCE

He passed in front of the oval-shaped looking glass in the hallway on his way out to go to a job interview, his first in five years. His eyes and their reflection made four. He stood looking at himself, laughing, and seeing only a part of his body in the punishing reflection the glass threw back at him. He was cut off at the neck. He laughed again. This time, at the morbidness of his own thoughts. The knot of his tie was shiny with grease. He did not like himself. He was not dressed the way he had hoped to appear, and his image was incorrect. This made him stop laughing.

So he went back upstairs to his rented room on the second floor at the rear of the rooming house. His room was beside the bathroom used by the two other tenants on that floor, and the actress on the third. He wanted to inspect his hair in the better light in the bathroom. But before he reached it, he heard the spikes of a woman's heels clambering down the rear staircase; and as he listened, they landed on the muffling linoleum in the hallway; and before he could move, the bathroom door was shut. He was not laughing now. It was the actress. She was between parts, without money, and she spent more time in the bathroom when she was waiting for auditions than on her parts after she was called.

He unlocked his door and left it slightly open, to wait his turn. He wanted the actress to know he was next in line, but he didn't want her to feel she was welcome. She liked to talk, and talk bad things about her friends, her father and her step-mother, and laugh about her career, for hours.

He had to change his clothes. He thought of what else he had to wear. Suddenly, he heard the heavy downpour of the shower as the water began to rain. So he closed his door.

The heavy ticking of the cheap clock became very loud now. It was the only one he could afford, and he had bought it in Honest Ed's bargain basement nearby. He had got it mainly for its alarm, not for its accuracy of time, which he had to check against the chimes of a rock-and-roll radio station. And he listened to this station against his better musical taste whenever he wanted to be punctual, which was not often. For he had been between jobs a long time.

This morning he had to be punctual. He was going to a job interview. It was on Bay Street in the business district of banks, brokerages and corporations. For all the time he had lived in Toronto, this district had frightened him. He tried to pacify his fear of it now by laughing at himself.

The job he was hoping to get was with a bank. He knew nothing about banks. He was always uncomfortable and impatient whenever he had to go into one. The most he had ever withdrawn was twenty dollars. The most money he had ever deposited at one time was fifteen dollars.

For three months now he had been walking the seven blocks from his rooming house on Major Street to the reference library on Asquith Avenue to sit in the reading room, to watch the women and to peruse the classified advertisements in the pages of the three daily newspapers, searching for a job. The *Star* contained about ten pages of advertisements which the paper called "Employment Opportunities." He was looking for a job, but he was still able to laugh at his plight. The *Sun* had three pages. Sometimes he would see the same "employment opportunities" in this newspaper as in the *Star's* pages, and he would laugh at their stupidity of duplication. He needed a job. And the *Globe & Mail,* which he heard was the best newspaper in the country, carried three pages. He did not like the *Globe & Mail.* There was no laughing matter about its print, which was too small. And it dealt with subjects beyond his understanding and interest, and even if he could smother a laugh about that, he found its small print bad for his deteriorating eyesight; and this made him depressed and bitter. Besides, the "positions" which the *Globe & Mail* advertised were for executives, executive directors, industrial engineers, administrators and managers of quality assurance. He did not know what they meant. But he knew he wanted a job. Any job. His clothes had been in the cleaners for three months. And his diet, which had never been balanced, was becoming even more topsy-turvy with each succeeding month of joblessness.

It was, however, with an irony he himself could not fathom, but about which he smiled, that in the very pages of the *Globe & Mail,* he had seen the advertisement of the position for which he was promised an interview this Monday morning at ten.

His noisy clock, with a silver-painted bell on it — and white face and black luminous numerals of the Roman kind — said it was nine o'clock. His room was still dark.

The *Globe & Mail's* ad read:

> We require an energetic junior executive to take a responsible position in our bank. The successful candidate must have a university degree in business or in finance, or the equivalent in business experience. Salary and benefits to be discussed at interview. Reply to the 14th floor, 198 Bay Street.

He was a man past thirty. But he could not, even at his age, argue about taking this "junior position," because his desperate circumstances were forcing this stern necessity upon him. Junior or senior, he had to take it. And when he got it, he knew it would not be a laughing matter. Necessity would make him bitter, but thankful.

He had only to remember his old refrigerator, which took up one-eighth of the floor space in his room, and which hissed and stuttered whenever he turned on his electric hot plate. The refrigerator contained a box of baking soda, which the talkative actress had told him would kill the smells of food; and on the top shelf, cold water in a half-gallon bottle that had once been full of grapefruit juice; a half-pint carton of homogenized milk, now going bad; his last wieners from Canada Packers, like three children's joyless penises; six hard slices of white bread in soft, sweating plastic wrapping from Wonder Bread, which was printed below the blonde-haired child who persisted in smiling on the package. And three bottles of Molson's beer. In these circumstances of diving subsistence, he knew he had nothing to lose — and nothing to laugh about — concerning the "junior position."

He did not come to this country to attend university. Experience of the world, and his former life at home in Barbados were his only secondary education. He had come here against his father's bitter wishes. But he was not unschooled. He had attended the St. Matthias' Elementary School for Boys, Barbados. *For Boys,* he wanted to remember to impress upon his prospective employers, since he was not a believer in the North American practice of having boys going to school with girls. He was a staunch supporter of the British system of public school education. And even though the St. Matthias' Elementary School for Boys was not, in fact, a public school, it was, nevertheless, a school that was public.

He laughed at his own cleverness of nuance and logic. Besides, no one in Toronto would know the difference. Toronto has Upper Canada College for boys, Trinity College School for boys,

Bishop Strachan School for girls and Havergal College for girls. Boys with boys. And girls with girls. His logic was so acerbic and sharp, he was already laughing as he heard himself telling them that St. Matthias' Elementary School for Boys was a . . .

But he stopped himself in the tracks of his hilarity: "I had-better leave out the elementary part and just tell them *St Matthias' School for Boys."* It was a satisfactory and imaginative rendering of the facts. Bay Street, if not the whole of Canada, he had discovered in his time here, was filled with people of imagination. The actress had been telling him that imagination is something called a euphemism for lies.

But he couldn't take the risk of failure. Failure would breed cynicism. Instead, he had said on his application that he was educated at Harrison College, "a very prestigious college for men in Barbados, and founded in 1783, which produced the leading brains of the leading leaders in books and banking, of the entire West Indies." Had he twisted the facts a little too much? Laughter and reassurance about the imaginative men on Bay Street, liars, as the actress called them, and who became quick millionaires, told him he had not stepped off into fraud. Not yet.

In spite of his lack of formal education, he still considered himself well read. Newspapers, magazines, the *Star* newspaper and *Time* magazine did not escape his daily and weekly scrutiny, even long after he had fallen upon the debris of the country's unemployed, in decrepitude. "Decrepitude" was the word he always used to the actress when they talked about their lives, to make her laugh about the apparently irreconcilable differences between her and her own society, and also to impress her that he was not a fool. He had heard the word first on television. And he listened to C.B.C. radio and short-wave broadcasts of the B.B.C. world service, and watched four television news broadcasts each night: two Canadian and two from America. And he never missed *Sixty Minutes* from New York. Except for the three times, consecutive Sundays, when he had lain flat on his back, fed off the public welfare system, on a public ward in the Toronto General Hospital "under observation" for high blood pressure.

"Pressure in my arse!" he told the actress who visited him every day, as he explained his illness.

In the eight years he had spent in this country, he had lain low for the first five, as a non-landed immigrant, in and out of low-paying jobs given specifically to non-landed immigrants, and all the time waiting for amnesty. One year he worked distributing handbills, most of which, because of boredom, he threw into garbage pails when no one was looking, and laughed, until one cold afternoon in February when his supervisor, who did not trust immigrants, carried out a telephone check behind his back, only to discover that none of the householders on the fifteen streets he had been assigned to had ever heard of or had ever seen the brochures advertising *Pete's Pizza Palace, free delivery.* After that mirthless firing, there were three months during which he labored as a janitor for the Toronto Board of Education — incidentally, his closest touch with higher learning; two months at Eaton's as a night-shift cleaner; then two months at Simpson's as an assistant shipping clerk until the last job, five years ago, held along with Italians, Greeks and Portuguese, cleaning the offices of First Canadian Place, a building with at least fifty floors, made of glass, near Bay Street, where he was heading this morning.

He laughed to himself as he thought of his former circumstances. For he was ready for bigger things. The murmuring refrigerator could not, within reason, be any emptier.

So with the bathroom next door still occupied, he looked at himself, at the way he was dressed. It was nine-fifteen now. His bladder was full. Whenever he had important things on his mind, his bladder filled itself easily, and more unusually heavy, and it made him tense.

He wished the pink shirt was cleaner. He wished the dark brown suit was a black one. He should not wear a yellow tie, but no other ties he had would match the clothes on his back. And he knew through instinct and not through Canadian experience that a job of this importance, "junior executive" in a bank, had to be applied for by a man dressed formally in black.

Laughter, his father had told him many times, a smile at the right moment, melts a woman with even the meanest temperament. He tried this philosophy now, and his attitude changed for the better. He put more Vaseline on his hair to make the part on the left side keener, for he had dressed in the dark. And now that the autumn light was coming through the single glass pane, which he could not reach even standing on a chair and from which he could never see the sidewalk, he could see that the shirt he had thought was slightly soiled was dirty.

The morning was getting older, the time of his appointment was getting closer, the hands of the bargain-basement clock were now at nine thirty-five, and he had only twenty-five minutes left to go; and he had to go badly but couldn't, because the actress was still inside the bathroom, singing a popular song. He could hear the water hitting against the bathtub and could imagine her body soaked in the hot beads of the shower, and he could see the red-faced ugly blackheads painted red, at the bottom of her spine. He had asked her once what they were, and she had told him "cold sores." He thought they had something to do with winter, that they came out in winter. He laughed each time she told him "cold sores." He could see them now, because he had seen them once before. Yesterday, too, for thirty-five minutes counted by his loud, inaccurate, cheap alarm clock, he had heard the torrents of the shower as she washed herself in preparation for an audition.

He had nothing to do now but wait. The shower stopped like a tropical downpour and with a suddenness that jolted him. He opened his door. He listened. Mist floated out of the bathroom door, and he brushed through it as if he were a man seeking passage through thick, white underbrush. And as he got inside and could barely see his way to the toilet bowl, there she was, with one leg on the cover of the bowl, which she had painted black, bending down, wiping the smell of the soap from between her legs and then the red, rough dots of bruises on the bottom of her spine, which she insisted were cold sores. When she named them first, he thought she had said "cold stores." He could understand that. "Cold stores," "cold storage" — it was enough to make him laugh.

"Oh, it's you."

He could not move. He did not answer. He could not retreat.

"Close the door and come in."

The mist came back, thick and sudden as fog swallowing him, debilitating him, blinding him, and he lost his vision. But he could see the lines of four ribs on each side of her body, and her spinal cord that ran clear as a *wemm,* with the dozen or so cold sores, fresh as the evidence from a recent lash.

"I have an audition in an hour, so I'm washing myself clean. You never know what directors're going to ask you to do."

He retreated to his room and closed the door. No mist or even warm sores could confuse him now; and he inspected the clothes he was dressed in, unable to change them, and worried about his interview, refusing all the time to think of the naked actress, and ignored her knocking on his door. Whenever he refused to answer her, she would leave a note on his door in her scratchy, left-handed scrawl.

But this time, when he re-opened his door to leave, she was standing there, and he passed her, wrapped in the large Holiday Inn towel she had brought from Sherbrooke and which barely covered the red sores at the bottom of her spine. The two small nipples of her dropped breasts were left bare to his undesiring eyes.

"You're too black to wear brown," she said. He passed her as if she had herpes. "If you don't mind me saying so," she shouted at his back, which moved away from her down the stairs.

This time he did not look at himself in the oval-shaped looking glass in the hall. He just walked out of the house. He wished it was for the last time.

The people at the bus stop are standing like sentries, silent and sullen. They look so sleepy he thinks it could be six o'clock. But a clock in the bank beside the bus stop says ten minutes to ten. He hurries the crowded bus on, with the urging of his anxiety.

The only sound that comes from the larger group of people going down into the subway is the hurrying pounding of heels on the clean, granite steps and the rubbing of hands on the squeaking rails, polished like chrome. More people are coming up out of the subway at greater speed as if they are fleeing the smell of something unwholesome. He can smell only the fumes of the trains. And he wonders if it is his imagination. For he knows that the trains run on electricity. It must be the smell of dust, then. Or the people. Or the perfumes.

He watches a woman's hand as it wipes sleep and excretia from the corners of her eyes. He thinks of the actress, who cleans her face this way.

But it is still September, his month of laughter along the crowded sidewalks, amongst the fallen turning leaves. And the furious memory of growing grass, quicker than the pulse was in summer, is still in the air. There are no lamb's wool, no slaughtered seals, no furs, no coats yet to cover the monotony of women's movement, which he sees like the singlemindedness of sheep, one behind the leader, in single file downwards into the subway and in double file upwards.

He boards a crowded subway car and stands among the sardines of silent, serious people. Where he is, with both hands on a pole, he is surrounded by men dressed in gray and black. Some are darker and richer than others. Some of the women too, are dressed in gray; some better made and better built than others. All the men in this car hold briefcases, either on their laps or between their shoes. And the women carry at least two bags, from one of which they occasionally take small balls of Kleenex.

He has just swayed farther from the steadying pole for moving balance as the train turns, and is standing over a woman cleaning her eyes and her nose with a red fingernail. And, immediately, as his eyes and hers meet, she drops her eyes into the pages of a thick paperback book, as if her turned eyes would obliterate her act.

The second bag he sees some women carrying is larger than a handbag, large enough, he thinks, for rolls of toilet paper and paper towels. The men do not read: they watch the women's legs. And they look over their shoulders, between their shoulders and down into their braless bodies, and their eyes touch the pages of the novels the women are reading; and not certain of the enlightenment and pleasure to be got from this rapid-transit fleeting education, the men reluctantly allow their eyes to wander back to the pages of the *Globe & Mail,* which seem to hold no interest for them. Their eyes roam over the puny print of the stock market quotations, the box scores of the Blue Jays baseball team and the results at Woodbine Race Track.

If his own luck had been really luck — and something to laugh about — the actress told him once, he could win thousands of dollars on a two-dollar bet, as easy as one, two, three. When she told him, "One to win, two to come second and three to come third," he laughed, thinking she was memorizing lines of a play she was auditioning for.

He had been living with so little luck in his life — three months with no money and no hope of any — that he could afford to dream and to laugh as he dreamed, and fill his empty pockets with imagined wealth.

A man beside him shakes out the pages of the *Globe & Mail* to the racing results: "and in the fifth race yesterday at Woodbine, the first three horses to come in, 1, 2 and 3, paid $15,595.03 . . . "

The jerk of the train stopping pushes him against the metal pole and awakens him from his dreaming. When the doors open, he is at his stop.

The air is cool. He can feel his shirt like wet silk against his body. He pulls the lapels of his jacket together to make himself feel warmer. The sun shines blindingly, but weak, on the tall office buildings that surround him. He is walking in their shadow, as if he is walking in a valley back in Barbados. The buildings look like steel. One facing him, built almost entirely out of glass, shimmers like gold. Its reflection of his body tears him into strides and splatters his suit against four glass panels, and makes him disjointed. It is the building he is going to enter.

The elevator is crowded. The passengers are all looking up at the changing numbers of the floors. He looks up, too. He can hear no breathing. A man shifts his weight from one black alligator shoe to the next. A woman changes her brown leather handbag and her other, larger bag, made of blue parachute material, from her right arm to her left. He reads *Bijoux,* which is printed on it. There is only the humming of the elevator; then the sound of the doors opening; then feet on the polished floor outside; the sound of the doors closing; a deep breath like a sigh of relief or of anticipation for the next floor; then the humming of the next ascent and then silence. The elevator stops on the fourteenth floor. There is no thirteenth. He is at the front, near the door, when it opens. Five men and women are beside and behind him. Facing him are glass and chrome and fresh flowers and Persian rugs and women dressed expensively and stylishly in black, with necklaces of pearls. And chewing gum. It is quiet in the office. Deathly quiet. So he stands his ground.

BANK is written on the glass.

"Getting off?" a man beside him asks.

He stands his ground.

The door closes, and he goes up with the five of them and finds himself, gradually, floor by floor, alone, as they slip out one by one. The elevator takes him to the top. The door does not open. And when it starts its descent, he is feeling braver. He remembers the new vigor he felt at the end of three hours with wax and mops and vacuum cleaners with Italians, Greeks and Portuguese, going down the elevator. He will ride it to the bottom.

No one enters, even though it stops two times in quick succession. And then it stops once more, and the door opens, and he is facing the same office with BANK written on the glass, cheerless and frightening, and seeing the same chrome, the rugs and the black and pearls of the women. Just as he moves to step out, the closing door, cut into half, and like two large black hands, comes at him. He gets out of the way just as the blue eyes of one of the women approaching the elevator door to see what he wanted are fixed upon him. Those blue eyes are like ice-water; his are brown and laughing.

" . . . this stop, sir?" is all he gets to hear of the woman's flat voice before the two black palms, like a shutter, have taken her eyes from his view and her words from his hearing.

"And you didn't even go into the office?"

"I couldn't do it."

"Sometimes when I'm auditioning, I get scared and get butterflies."

"There was so much wealth!"

"Are you a communist? I wish I had money, money and more money. All I think about is money. But here I am in this damn rooming house with a broken shower curtain and a leaky bathtub, trying to be an artist, an actress. Do you think I'll be a dedicated actress because I live in all this shit? When last have I had steak? And a glass of red wine? Or you?

"I have some wieners."

"Wieners, for Chrissakes!"

Her flat voice and icy manner killed the kindness in his suggestion.

"The people on the subway looked so educated, like everybody was a university graduate. And not one person, man or woman, asked me if I needed directions."

"For Chrissakes! How would they know you don't have Canadian experience?"

"They looked on me and at me and through me, right through me. I was a piece of glass."

"Must have been your brown suit."

"Everybody else was in gray and black."

"I hope I get this part. Just to get my hands on some money and rent a decent place. But what can I do? I even get tired taking showers in a bathroom where the water leaks through the curtain. My whole life is like a shower curtain. That leaks. Oh, the landlady was here. Fifteen minutes after you left. She tells me you have to give up your room on Friday. So I tell her not to worry, that you got a job today. And you didn't even go into the office! She wants you to pay two months this month. But you didn't even face the people!"

"With all that glass and steel and chrome?"

"Do you want me to tell her you're not in? You could always slip out without paying the rent, you know. I've done it lots of times. In Sherbrooke and in Rosedale. God, I nearly broke my ass racing down the metal fire escape, carrying my box of French- Canadian plays. Everybody skips out on landlords. Try it. She'll never find you in Toronto! The one in Rosedale hasn't found me yet. And here I am, desperate to be an actress and get the money to move back to Rosedale . . . "

"When she's coming back?"

"Seven . "

"She coming in three hours? Are you saying four o'clock, too?"

"You *could* come to my room. I don't have to do the audition. I can skip it. There's a small restaurant on Church Street where a lot of television and radio types eat, and I'm thinking of applying for a waitress job there. It's an artistic restaurant. I'll even slip you a meal if I get the job."

"She said she's coming back at seven?"

"My room is open to you, as I say. Be free. Feel free. Don't you want to be free? Where could you go, anyhow?"

In his hands is a glass with a pattern on it that advertises peanut butter. It has dried specks like old saliva round the mouth. He passes his fingers round the mouth of the glass, cleaning it; and when it looks clean and is cloudy from his hand-prints, he pours the first of the three Molson's into it. He sits on his bed. There is no chair in the room. Only his television set, which he sits on when he is not watching *Sixty Minutes* or the American news. His dangling feet can barely touch the floor. On the floor is linoleum, with a floral pattern. "Rose of Sharon," the actress had told him. "I was a whiz in botany at Jarvis Collegiate."

The sun is brighter now. He can smile in this sun and think of home. He is getting warmer, too. A shaft of dust plays within the arrow of September light that comes through the window. It lands at his feet. The light and the particles of dust on the bright leather of his shoes attract his attention for a moment only. He smiles in that moment. And in that moment, his past life fills his heart and shakes his body like a spasm, like a blast of cold air. His attention then strays to the things around him, his possessions, prized so fondly before, and which now seem to be mere encumbrances: the valise he brought from Barbados and carried through so many changes of address in Toronto; heavier always in winter when he changed rooms, when he carried it late at night on his shoulder, although each time that he moved he had accumulated no more possessions; the two Christmas cards which the actress mailed to him, even though she had been living in the same house, placed open like two tents and which he keeps on top of a wooden kitchen cupboard, used now as his dressing table. *To George, at Xmas* is written in ball-point, in red, on each, in capital letters; and an unframed color photograph taken in Barbados, and fading now, showing him with his father and mother and two younger brothers and three sisters: eight, healthy, well-fed Barbadians, squinting because the sun is in their eyes, standing like proprietors in front of a well-preserved plantation house made of coral stone, covered in vines so thick that their spongy greenness strangles the windows and the doors. The name of this house in Barbados is *Edgehill House.* His present residence has no name. It is on a street named Major. It is a rooming house, similar in size, in build and in dirt to the other houses on the street.

He drains the beer from the peanut-butter glass and refills it. He throws the last bottle into the plastic garbage pail, and the rattle of glass and tin is like a drunken cackle. Inside the garbage pail are the classified pages from the *Globe & Mail,* some shrivelled lettuce leaves, an empty milk carton and the caps of beer bottles. He thinks of the woman in the bank's office, dressed in black, with the blue eyes. He thinks of the flowers and the glass in that office and of flowers more violent in color, growing in wild profusion, untended, round *Edgehill House,* where he was born in a smiling field of comfortable pasture land.

His father never worked for anyone in his whole life, never had to leave the two hundred and eighty acres of green sugar cane and corn to dirty his hands for anyone's money.

"Work on this blasted plantation, boy. Put your hands in the most stinking dirt and cow-dung on this plantation, and it is a hundred times more nobler than working at the most senior position in a country where you wasn't born!"

His father said that almost every day, and more often when his father heard he was leaving for Canada.

"You call yourself a son o' mine? You, a son o' mine? With all this property that I leaving-back for you? You come telling me you going to Canada as a' immigrant? To be a stranger? Where Canada is? What is Canada? They have a Church o' England up there? Canada is no place for you, man. The son of a Barbadian plantation owner? This land was in our family before Canada was even discovered by the blasted Eskimos and the red Indians. Seventeen-something. A.D.! In the year of our Lord, *anno domini.* Who do they worship up there? And you come telling me that you going up there, seeking advancement as a' immigrant? In Canada? Your fortune and your future is *right here!* In this soil. In this mud. In this dirt. 'pon these two hundred and eighty-something acres o' cane and corn!"

It is six-thirty now. Thirty minutes before the landlady is to arrive. He locks his door. He stands outside in front of it, like a man who has forgotten something inside. There is a red thumb-tack on the door. The actress pins it there whenever she leaves messages that she thinks require urgent replies. Whenever there's a thumb-tack on his door, he thinks of the red cold sores on her back, and it makes him laugh. He does not know why: he just laughs.

He climbs the stairs to go to her room. He can see a red thumb-tack on her door, even before he reaches it. It is similar to the one he has left behind on his own door. She has written his name in red capital letters on a folded piece of lined white paper. He pulls the paper from the tack.

I got the waitress job at the restarant. He smiles when he sees she has spelled "restaurant" without a "u". She has signed it, *Pat.*

He did not throw away the balled-up message, even hours afterwards, in all the walking he did that night, until he was standing on the platform of the subway at the Spadina station where he is now.

He looks to his right and then to his left, and there is no one in sight. Across from him, across the clean cement that is divided by a black river of hard dirty steel, are two large billboards. One advocates "pigging-out," and the other tells women about "Light Days, Tampax." Suddenly, into the frame of these two boards riveted to two steel pillars comes the lone passenger, who stands and waits to take the train going in the other direction.

He does not know why he is in this station and why he has entered on the side for southbound trains.

South is the office building with the glass and the flowers and the women dressed in black and BANK written on the glass. South is Bay Street where no one walks after the Italians and the Greeks and the Portuguese have cleaned the offices and have left to take the subway north to College Street. South is nothing. South is the lake and blackness and cold water that smells of dead fish and screaming children's voices in the short summer, and machines and boats and grease.

The balled-up note from Pat, written on its soiled paper, smelling of the ointment she uses for her cold sores, was in his fist when he first reached this spot where he is standing now. He is standing in the center of the platform, the same distance from the left end as from the right.

A rumble grows louder. Chains and machinery, iron touching iron, steel rubbing steel, the sound of the approaching train. He can never tell at the first sound of this familiar rumbling, out of a darkened tube, whether it is coming from his left or from his right. He always has to wait longer for the greater roar. Or if it is night-time, watch for the first glare on the tracks.

He thinks the roar is coming from the southbound lines. He feels more at ease for a moment, and braver, and he even laughs, although he doesn't know why. The man on the other side stares at him from his seat on the brown leather, between the two advertising boards, and the man remains querulous with his staring until the train moves northwards.

He is alone again. And more at ease. He moves to the end of the platform, nearest the tube through which the train will emerge, to a spot where he could see it clearly. He wants no surprises. He wants to see it the moment it appears out of the blackness. The blackness that is like the South and the lake. And he wants no one else to see him. He wants to be alone, just as he was alone in the descending elevator in the office building.

How comfortable and safe and brave he had felt travelling and laughing and falling so fast and so free, through the bowels of that glassed-in building!

He hears the rumble. He hears the sound of steel or iron — metal anyhow; and the low screech of the train trying to emerge out of the darkened, curved tube.

He thinks of Pat. So he throws the balled-up note onto the tracks. And that act is her being thrown out of his life, along with her red-corpuscled sores. He sees the note fall. But does not hear it reach the surface of the black river of hard dirty steel below him. He does not hear it reach the tracks. He cannot gauge any distance now. Cannot gauge any face. The paper is very light. Almost without weight. Definitely without purpose and love.

But the train is here. Its lights reflect onto the tracks which now are shining and getting wider as the ugly red engine, like her sores, approaches. He knows that the train is as long as the platform, half of which he has already paced off. The train is here. And just as its lights begin to blind him, he makes his own eyes pierce through that weaker brightness and fixes them on the driver, dressed in a light-brown uniform. He sees the driver's face, the driver's happy eyes and his relief that this is his last trip; and he himself laughs to an empty platform and station that are not listening, and he steps off the platform, just having seen his own eyes, and the driver's, makes four.

1975

A SHORT DRIVE

This Saturday afternoon at three, with the first real light, and the first cleansed skies washed so blue after the rains, there was a constant breeze and upon the breeze came the coolness and the strong smell of patchouli and summer flowers. It was tantalizing as the smell of saltiness and of fresh fish brought out of the sea on a beach in Barbados. Gwen was a woman with a touch of this saltiness on her breath. And the woman back in Toronto, on Lascelles Boulevard, she too carried a trace of the smell; but her real smell was of Lavender.

Calvin sat nobly and like an emperor, stiff, with the pride of new ownership, behind the steering wheel reduced to the size of a toy wheel against his imposing size, of the Volkswagen which he had just bought, "hot", he said, for seventy-five dollars. He called it his "Nazzi bug". And he too looked clean, as the skies. His skin, on his arms up to his elbow; his neck, right into the V of the black dashiki; his legs from below the knee and down to his toes, all this flesh was "oiled, Jack," he said. He had shampooed his round-shaped Afro, and it was glistening although he had used Duke Greaseless Hairdressing for Men. He had given me some, but my hair did not accept the same shine as his. He looked clean. And he looked like a choice piece of pork seasoned and ready for the greased pan and the oven. He would not like this comparison. But I have to say he looked clean.

His legs were thin and had no calf. This was the first time I had seen Calvin dressed in anything but gray-green plaid trousers and blue blazer. Today, he was in cut-down jeans, which gave me the first glimpse of his legs. I could not believe his long stories over beer in frosted mugs and Polish sausages, about playing running back for the college football team. The black dashiki with its V-neck and sleeves trimmed in black, red and green, tempered somewhat the informality of his casual dress.

"Pass the paper bag. Glove compartment. Take a sip, brother," he said, holding the steering wheel with his left hand, and a Salem in the other. "And keep your motherfucking head, *down*. In case the *man*."

The puttering VW rollicked over the gravel road at a slow pace. Its dashboard was cluttered with additional things which

Calvin had installed. Cassette tape deck *and* 8-track tape deck; FM-AM radio and a short-wave radio, a contraption which looked like a walkie-talkie and two clocks. One he said gave the time in the North-East, and the other the time of the South, of the city of Birmingham, Alabama where we were, and had been together since the beginning of the summer semester. Looking at this dashboard, I was reminded of the glimpse of the cockpit of the plane in which I had travelled two months earlier from Toronto to teach the summer course, in which Calvin was an auditor. I had never heard that term before. But Calvin was my student. And as the lonely heavy southern nights spun themselves out into greater monotony, he became my guide to where the action is, and almost my friend. The noisy VW moved slowly over the rutted road, and I could see in the distance the sights and substance and large properties, the grace and the southern architecture in the residential exclusive district we were passing on our right hand. We were driving so slow that I thought it was a mistake, that Calvin lived in this district, and that we would turn into one of the magnificent gates, any minute now. One of these mansions I had passed, in the dark last night, searching in vain for Gwen's apartment. I now could see the structure I had mistaken for the house. It is a white painted gazebo with Grecian pillars. And in the gazebo is a child's swing and a white-painted iron chair and iron table. There is no child, in the swing.

"Ripple?" Calvin said, after a large gulp, and wiping away the evidence with the hand that held the Salem, just in case. "This is the real shit." Last night, at the bar with the frosted beer mugs and huge Polish sausages, Calvin ordered two gigantic T-bone steaks and two bottles of Mommesin red wine, both of which I paid for. This Ripple wine which cut into my throat like a razor blade dipped in molasses, must have been a ritualistic thing to go with his cut-down jeans and the dashiki. Or it might have been cul tural. I took a second swig at the bottle hardly concealed in the brown paperbag, and squeezed my eyes shut, and shook my head. "This be the real shit," he said, disagreeing with my reaction.

On our left hand, I was passing men, slow as in a shutter speed to afford even the whiz of movement, men bent almost in the shape of hairpins, doubled-up, close to the grass which was so green it looked blue; and from the short distance I was, these men resembled gigantic mushrooms painted onto the sprawling lawns, and wearing broad-brimmed hats necessary to protect them against the brutality of the sun, and the exhaustion that the humidity seemed to sap from their bodies. I could see them move their hands as if they were playing with the grass, but at the completion of each piston-like action, the effort in their movements appearing slowed-down by the encompassing grandeur of the afternoon, when this act of slashing the blades of grass was completed, a shower of grass lifted itself on impact, a blade of steel flashed like lightning, and the grass was scattered harmlessly over the lawn.

"Mexicans," Calvin said, as if he didn't like Mexicans, and with some bitterness; and as if he was pronouncing a sentence not only on them, but also upon their labor.

They were soaked to their backs; and their shapeless clothes made them look Indian to me. But the formlessness of their shirts and pants was, to me, the designer's label and trademark of hard labor. They could have been Chinese standing up to their ankles in water and growing rice.

"Amerrikah! Home of the motherfucking *free,* Jack!" Calvin said. "This South's shaped my personality, and this university's fucked it up, with the result that I don't know *who* I am. I was happier in Atlanta on 'Fayette Street in the black area." I did not know what he was talking about. I was admiring the Mexicans. They looked now like figures in a tableau, painted against the bluegrass lawns; and the manner in which they had thrown out the commercial proficiency of the power mower and the precision of mechanization by the bare power of their hands, made me deaf to Calvin's protestations. And it seemed that they were showing the superiority of their knowledge about nature and things and their own past, in this temporary but scorching menialness of labor; and expressing their own protest, as Calvin was with words, with the violence of their muscular arms.

Calvin was now slouched behind the steering wheel as if the Ripple had suddenly changed the composition of the blood in his veins. His right arm was extended so that his fingers just touched the steering wheel, as if he wanted no closer association with it. As if he was despising the wheel the VW, along with the statement he had just made about rejection. "What the fuck am I getting a college education for? And writing academic papers on Reductionism, for?" I still did not understand what he was talking about. But he brought the VW to an uncertain stop. We were under a tree. Calvin had told me the name of this tree. They were all over the South; and they cluttered the path through a woods to the building on the campus where convocations were held. The first time Calvin told me the name of this tree, he told me about a woman named Billie Holiday. I did not know whom he was talking about: but he started to sing the words of a song, 'Strange Fruit'; and we were inhaling the sweet smell of the magnolia trees and the wind was unforgiving in bringing the strong southern smell to our nostrils. I would have trouble remembering the name of the woman who sang this song and more often the title of the song slipped my memory. But I remembered one line, only one line of the song about Southern trees. *Blood on the leaves, and blood at the root.* Calvin had sung the entire song from memory. His voice was off-key. But that afternoon, I looked up into the thick branches of the trees under which we were walking to the place which served beer in frosted glasses and huge Polish sausages, and only the raindrops accumulated on the leaves after the downpour dropped into my face. And now, this afternoon, the VW stopped uncertainly because he had never accumulated the thirty dollars to fix the brakes, we were stopped under a tree.

"What kind of tree is that? I don't think we have these trees in Toronto."

"The size, or the name?" Calvin asked.

The mouth of the Ripple bottle was in his mouth. A little of the wine escaped his lips, and it ran slowly down into his beard, but I could still see the rich color of red, like blood.

"The name."

"Poplar. This be a poplar tree."

We were shaded by the tree. And I was beginning to feel great relief from the humidity which embraced me like a tight-fitting shirt.

Southern trees bear strange fruit.

Calvin's voice had not improved in the month I had first heard it. I smiled at his rendition.

Black bodies hanging in the Southern breeze.

We remained in the shade, and I could feel the breeze, making my body cool as if I was being dipped slowly into sea water. I was comfortable. But Calvin was not: sadness appeared in his eyes. His lips formed themselves into a sneer. He moved his body, and the bottle of Ripple became heavy and caused the seat and the leather to cry out. The leather in the seats of the VW were the most valuable features of the old rumbling automobile. He moved his body in the small space we shared, and I could smell his perspiration, and his breath laden with the menthol from the Salems, and the sickening sweetness of the Ripple.

"Dualism, my brother," he said. He leaned over, took the bottle from me, and drained it dry. "What the fuck? I've seen the ass-whuppings in Selma, Bamma, Little Rock."

The breeze stopped. The languor of the afternoon was heavy, and we were once more lumbering over the road which turned to hard, dried, uncared-for dirt. It was sad. The sadness was like the sudden fall of dust under the low-hanging trees, when the scent of magnolia rises like shimmering zzz's you see, if you kneel down, rising from a hot tarred road.

"What do you want to be, then? What do you want to make of your life, if not a scholar?"

"Miles!"

"Away from Birmingham?"

"Miles Davis!"

I did not know what to say to this; and so, Calvin continued to let his feelings and fantasies come out of his thin body, and the coming out made him large, and grand and strong as the running back he always boasted he was when he played for his col lege football team.

"As Barry White says, bro', *let the music play.* Let the music play on. Let the motherfucking music *play,* Jack! I be Miles. I am Miles. Or, I am Coltrane. Trane. I am Otis. I'm Nina Simone. And I am 'Retha! And I am on a stage at the biggest theater in the South, but not the Opry, and *thousands* are out there in the dark screaming my name. My toon. My voice. My riffs. My trumpet. My tenor horn. It's the same fucking thing, Jack. Let the music *play."*

The smell of Calvin's Salem's, the old odor that had settled inside the VW, filled my nostrils; and with these smells, was the smell of clothes that are wet, and drying in the back seat. I could also smell the oiliness of southern-fried chicken from Chicken Box Number Two. We had eaten chicken many times in the VW, as if we were still suffering from that segregation of accommodation, although it was our manner of checking out the beautiful women coming out of the women's residence in their pink shorts, and white shorts, and blue shorts. Perhaps, we had left some uneaten boxes in the back seat.

We were by ourselves, on this road of dried mud, in a field that was growing something I could not recognize. Corn came to my mind, as this place was in the same part of geography as that island where I came from; so corn came naturally to my mind; but there was not the lusciousness in the endless spread of green that made me feel we were adrift on the sea; we were alone, although far to the right I could see the smudged whiteness of the pillars and other parts of the architecture from colonial times; and on our right, not with that distance, some small houses, and from them sentinels of rising white smoke that turned blue as it reached high above our heads. And still the sun was shining.

And then in the distance, like the call of my mother's voice, miles away, but only a few yards from the make-shift cricket pitch we had gouged out of our own mud to play the game, my mother's voice calling me home for dinner; rice cooked with few split peas because there was a War on, and served with salt fish from the Grand Banks of Newfoundland, thin and flat and full of bones, but transformed by the improvised wisdom in these things by my mother, and soaked in lard oil, tangy from the cheap Australian butter it was said we imported from Australia, to us in a commonwealth of nations, friends; and tomatoes picked from our backyard; that welcoming call, that wrenched me from my friends and playmates, disappointed that I had not hit the ball for six, or four, or even a single in the hot, hot-competing afternoon. So, did this sound come to me, unanchored in this vastness of living thriving green, in the rickety VW with a stranger, drinking Ripple concealed in a brown paper bag, from the eyes of the sheriff.

In the blue-white distance I heard the heavy rumbling of a train. A freight train. I followed the train as it wriggled its way like a worm through the greenness on the land, as it moved like a large worm, and in my mind, through the history its approach was unravelling and through the myths of trains; men on the run travelled on them; men fleeing women and wives and child-payment hid on them; and men in chains and those who escaped from chain-gangs, were placed on them. And the best blues were written about them. The rumbling of this train, like the rumbling of that train in the cowboy movies of the Old West, seemed interminable as a toothache that comes at sunset and that lasts throughout the groaning night, like a string pulled by a magician from the palm of one hand, like the worm you pull from the soft late grass-covered ground and does not end, and that makes you late to go fishing. I heard a siren. Or a whistle? There were so many sirens I was hearing this summer in Birmingham because of civil rights and fights with sheriffs, that I mistook the name of the sound. I heard a siren. The siren ended the train.

"Police cruiser?" I asked Calvin. "Or ambulance?"

"In this neighborhood, could be either. Both. Chitlins and hogmaws. One goes with the other."

"Cops coming through the grass?" I still did not know what was planted in the growing vastness surrounding me.

Calvin lit another Salem. The VW was immediately filled with smoke. This lasted for one moment. Then, it was filled with a tingling, sweet and bitter smell. It was not the Salem that Calvin had lighted. It was not a Salem. But he filled his lungs with the smoke, and then shot two unbroken, thin and fierce jets of white from his nostrils, making him look in that moment, like a walrus; speaking through smoke and coughing at the same time as if his thinness meant tuberculosis, and with his breath held, and he said, "What can we in the South do, with this dualism-thing? Before it fucks us up?"

"Education could never be so destructive."

"Spoken like a true West Indian who knows nothing about the South, and Amerrikah."

"Education is freedom."

"Spoken like a man who's never lived in Birmingham, or in any city in the South!"

"You need education."

"We need a black thang. We don't need no education, brother. A black thang. And a black conclusion."

"And what about your seminar on Reductionism?"

"Shit! Can you see me discussing that at my mother's Sunday dinner table? She be calling the cops thinking this nigger's crazy!"

The VW became quiet, and filled with the strange smoke. The words Calvin was using were larger than the capacity of the small "bug", too bulging with the possibility of explosion and violence. I went back to the Mexicans on the lawns. I began to have the sensation of being rocked from side to side. But it could have been the vibration of the freight train, which had not yet come to its end from within the tunnel created by the endless fields of growing things. Looking outside through the steam of smoke from Calvin's fag I saw cement and concrete and paper blowing along the narrow sidewalks and into the street. The light here was harsh. There were no flowers. There were no poplar trees. The trees were stubby, but they did not shade the blinding, shimmering waves that came off the surface of the sidewalk. I wished, at that moment, that I was back in Toronto among the red brick, the dirty red brick and cobblestones, passing shops that sold the *New York Times* and the *Times Literary Supplement,* and that sold Condor and Erinmore pipe tobacco and French cigarettes and French leathers or "letters", I never knew which was the proper term, things I was accustomed to, and knew how to handle, among the buildings that were not so imposing and the short streets. Space there was more manageable. I wished for the softness of streets shaded by small trees, and lined with cars many of which belonged to students and were broken into; with garbage pails of green and other wrecks; and I wanted the softness of the northern seductive and betraying nights; and to be amongst the unthreateningness of broken-down homes with cloth at their windows and with unpainted boards nailed across the windows and the doors, derelicts from the nights of rioting in the cities in the North, Detroit, New York, Washington, D.C., and Toronto.

Calvin must have been buried in similar thoughts of wanting to be elsewhere, must have come to a conclusion of similar importance, or to some agreeable compromise with his thoughts about education, for he straightened his back, and the vigor and youth of his years came back into his body. His eyes were bright again; and the whiteness in them shone. The dashiki he was wearing made him look noble and like an emperor, stiff and with the pride of knowing where he was.

"This is the very last time I be laying this paranoid shit on you, brother. You are my guest here in this city. I am a Southerner, and we Southerners're hospitable people. I'm gonna show y'all some real Southern shit now, y'all!"

He had lighted a Salem before he had spoken. He was the kind of man who could not make a serious statement before he had first lighted a Salem. Smoke streamed through his nostrils, and he looked like a walrus again.

"I'm an Amerrikan. This is my mother-fucking country."

"You were born here, man."

"I'm a Southerner. So, let's have some Ripple. Let's drink this shit."

It was a long road. There were no street lights. Dust swirled round the tires of the VW, as it pierced its single weak headlamp through the oncoming darkness. "If the man don't get me for this Ripple, he sure's shit gonna get me for this light!" The moon was a dark sliver of lead, far off to the right. Calvin was still in his cut-down jeans and dashiki. But I had changed. I was in white. White Levis and a white dashiki, bought from the Soul Brother Store. When I went into the store, dark and musty and smelling of old cigars, the owner greeted me, "Brother, come in, brother!" He charged me twenty dollars more than the price I had seen on the same clothes in two other white stores on the same integrated street. But I did not divulge this to Calvin.

"Lay it on me, brother!" Calvin had said in admiration and in approval, when he picked me up.

"Be cool, man," I had told him, trying hard to be cool.

"Gwen's opened your nose!"

"Shee-it!" I said, hoping it came out right, and, heavy, and properly Southern.

"Shit!" Calvin said. His speech was like a crisp bullet in my chest.

Now, driving along this road, in the middle, there was no dividing line, and if there was, we could not see it; in the swirling flour of this thin road, cramped in the VW, with the smell of smoke, a trace of leather, and the acrid and sweet languor from the fumes of Ripple, making less speed than the rattle of the muffler suggested, and hitting stones in the middle of the road, the two of us, rebellious and drunk in our joy, like escaped prisoners; but I, like a man redeemed, Gwen had said, when I was at the door like a gentleman, "Shee-it, you ain't leaving here to walk those dark streets, at this hour, man. This is the South," saying it with a pronounced West Indian accent; we were screaming and hollering as if we were both born in the ecstasy of mad Southern Saturday nights, in Birmingham.

Calvin slapped an 8-track tape into the player. 'My Favorite Things' came out. The hymn coiled around the jazz solo, reminded me of matins at St. Matthias Anglican Church in Barbados; and especially evensong and service. I could picture myself walking in that peaceful sacred light, one hour after the sun had gone down behind the tall casaurinas, when there was slice of a moon, like this one here in Birmingham, and walking between thick green sugar canes in my black John Whites that kicked up almost as much dust as the tires of this old VW. And each time Coltrane repeated the main statement of the tune, I could hear and recall the monotony of the tolling bells. There, my mother walked beside me, in contented sloth of age, of sickness and of Christianity. Here, I bent my neck to the charmed pull of the music.

Calvin is silent beside me. This music is his. I have heard this music before, probably, all the places and things and colors that the music is showing me I have faced in Toronto. The tape is scratched badly.

In the distance, pointed out to us by the weak left headlamp, is a bam, or a factory; perhaps something that was once used as a portable camp for soldiers. Soldiers are always on my mind in Birmingham, this summer. The Civil War, which a magazine swears in its cover story, is about to be fought again: white people versus black people. Soldiers with muskets, vertical straps of leather aslant their shoulders, fighting for the *other* cause. And the flag of their confederation with its own two vertical blue slashes across its broad bloodied shoulder, signifying something different. This building in the shortening distance sits in a square stubbornness in the middle of the single headlamp, with no grace of architecture like the white-painted gazebo. From this distance it is black. It soon looks brown. Light from inside the building is being forced through small windows that are covered by blinds made of sacks of sugar not for Bohemian style, but from economy. And as we get nearer still, the truth of its dimension, size and color, are exposed to us.

The tenor saxophone reminds me of the singing of old women, repeating the verse of the hymn as if their age has crippled their recollection of succeeding verses. So, I begin to think again of my mother, leading the song at the Mother's Union service, going over it again. 'Rock of Ages.' This saxophone is not speaking of such desperation, though.

We are approaching Gwen's wooden house.

Calvin stops the VW, for no reason; and I realize he's always doing this, but this time he parks it, and it rocks forward and backward, just before the engine dies. We are now bathed in the light from the naked fluorescent bulb on Gwen's porch. I did not see this light the night of the party. The rain was too heavy that night.

"You're really into Trane playing 'Love Supreme!'" he said.

"Not 'My Favorite Things?'"

"'Love Supreme,' brother."

How many other things in this city of Birmingham, this South, in this culture, in this short time here had I got wrong? I had heard a train, but was there a train rolling through the green fields like a lawn mower? I had seen a moon, but now that we were stopped, there was no moon.

"A love supreme, a love supreme, a love supreme," Calvin said. "Nineteen times Trane chants it." I can see movement in Gwen's house, at the side; for the bedrooms are at the side.

Calvin got out, leaving me in the car; slammed the door shut, and stood beside the car. A splattering of water hits the gravel. I imagine steam rising. I can smell the sting of the water. And then I too get out, and shake my legs, each one to straighten the seams of my tight-fitting jeans. Calvin is still peeing and shaking. Some men can pee as long as horses. But it looks more as if he is being shaken by the peeing, in short spasms of delight and relief. Each time I think that Calvin is finished, he shakes again. I was wrong about the name of the tune on the 8-track. I am wrong about my mother. It was not 'Rock of Ages.' It was not even the walk through the country lane going to St Matthias Anglican Church for evensong and service that had pulled those memories from me. It was I myself. As a chorister in the St. Michael's Cathedral singing a song of praise. Was it Easter I was thinking about? Easter? Or Christmas? Rogations Day? Quinquagesima Sunday? Could it have been Lent? *O, all ye beasts of the sea praise ye, the Lord. O, all you fish of the sea, praise ye the Lord.* Could it have been that? Yes. That was the comparison of the repetition which the beauty of the saxophone ought to have brought back.

"Every time I hear Trane playing 'Love Supreme,' I gotta have me at least *one* smoke, and . . . " He seemed short of breath, all of a sudden. His words were cut short. Nevertheless, there was a lingering, a drawing-out of the enunciation of his words. His words would be cut off. In mid-sentence. As if he were struggling. For breath. And trying. To talk at the same time. The middle door on the porch opened and light flowed weakly out, and I could see Calvin's eyes, now red and fierce and at the same time, peaceful and filled with water. But he was not in tears. He was happy. "Want a joint? Can you handle this shit, brother?"

"I'm cool man."

"Shit'll kill you. It's a motherfucker. It kills the black artist, and the black musician."

"I'm cool, man."

"Know something? Let's not waste time with these chicks. Forget Gwen." I was wondering what kind of a man Calvin was. "Let's talk, brother. You're going back up to Toronto, next week, and when you're gone, ain't nobody I can talk to, nobody on this campus, in this city, in this fucking country. Let's talk And I gonna cut-out all these "motherfuckers" and "shits" in my speech, and just talk." I was sure he was reading my mind. But I was getting accustomed to his speech, peppered with this Southern or American violence. "I've been checking you out back there, while you were talking to yourself, as Trane was grooving. Bet you didn't realize you were talking to yourself? 'Love Supreme' is a motherfuc . . . is a fantastic piece, freaks me out, too, every time I listen to it. At least five. Times a day. And if I have a joint, shee- . . . well, it's fantastic." He took the last, deep, noisy pull on the cigarette, now no longer than his fingernail. "'Love Supreme' brings back memories of something my grandmother used to hum, just after she lit the kerosene lamps every evening. Some white folks calls this shit a canticle. Took me years to stop confusing canticle with cuticle. Heh-Heh! But, anyhow. This canticle thing has a Latin name. Man! I kicked more ass, I was superior to everybody in my class in Latin in high school. Hate the thing now, though. But I know it all, by heart. Had to learn it by heart. Been learning it by heart from hearing my grandmother, singing it for years. Listen. *O, all ye works of the Lord, bless ye the Lord; praise Him, and magnify Him forever.* Want to hear more?"

"Didn't know you were Anglican."

"Baptist! To the bone. But I read that shit in a book that had words like Works, Nights, Days, Whales, Water, etcetera etcetera, and all were spelled with a capital letter. Isn't that something? The English be strange motherfuckers. Strange people. In the South, right here in this city of Birmingham, we worship the English, culturally I mean. The English use colons like Coltrane uses the E-flat! Baptist to the bone! Baptist to the bone. And anti-English, except culturally." He threw the marijuana cigarette, now smaller than his fingernail through the window. The VW's engine started as if the whole car was about to explode. It stuttered, and finally, it turned over. "Life is better without chicks around. Sometimes. We're going to the Stallion's Club where there's the best rib-sandwiches and fried chicken in the whole city of Birmingham! If not in the whole South!"

Pandemoneum, sweet as pecan pie and ice cream, struck me full in the face, the moment the door of the Stallion Club was opened, when Calvin pushed me inside, first. The room was dark. Bodies were moving. The laughter was loud and sweet and black and jocular and exaggerated. Smoke was rising and swirling. And above the lighter darkness of the bodies in the room, the smoke remained there like halos. The music was climbing the walls. Music such as this I had never heard. It was like a baptism, a final submergence into the hidden, secret beauty of the South. Loud and full, enunciating each vowel, each nuance possible of behavior, each instrument, each riff. I heard a voice pleading, *Didn't I do it, baby? Didn't I? Didn't I do it, baby?;* and I looked towards the stage, in the deeper darkness there, through the large, slow-moving dancers, expecting to see Aretha Franklin in the flesh. What a victory it would be, to know her, in this thick-fleshed Southern, warm night! I was overcome by the music. I could feel my entire body relax. I could smell the odors around me. I could feel my blood. I could feel the difference, and the meaning of my presence in the South. The fried chicken. The barbecued ribs. The tingling, sweet nausea of burnt hair. The cosmetics and lotions in the glassy, bushy "pompadoos," as Calvin called it, on the fat, healthy jowls of the men and women dancing. I could feel my own body give off a stifled exhaust of smell. I could feel the sweat and the excitement under my armpits. A house fly was in the room. It came and rested on my top lip, and I did not brush it away. I was, for the first time, at home in the noise, the smells, the fragrance, the sounds and the voice of this city of Birmingham. And they all made me nervous, as they made me good. *Didn't I do it, baby? Didn't I . . .* I was like a man drowning in this foam of a wave that one moment ago had been wafting me in its freshness; I was moving towards the front of the swaying crowd that was coupled in its own sweetness. I looked into their faces. And those faces that were not buried into the necks and shoulders of men and women, wore flat expressions. Masks. No one was smiling. No one was grinning. No one was laughing as he danced. No teeth showed in this relaxed, coagulating, heavy and soft coupling of the music with the voice. It was as if the voice was giving them a message they all knew and desired. I could feel and taste the powerfulness in the large room. It was like a country. A country of men and women, all of the same color, the same breathing. And this became my baptism: I had never imagined it was possible to be in a room so large with only black people. Never in Toronto. Never even in Barbados. I looked around to see, just in case. And there was none, not one white person. It was a beautiful sensation, and it frightened me. This is why I thought of powerfulness. And now I knew what it meant. I could feel it in my blood.

Two large women, heavy in their thighs, heavy in their bosoms, heavy in their arms, heavy in their waists, each one about fifty-five years old, were tied together in the slow almost unmoving dance; their breasts pressed against each other, thighs glued together beneath their mini-skirts, looking like logs of mahogany polished to a high magnificent sheen, arms lassoed to arms like tentacles, or in a Boston crab, and with the weight of their waists pressed together, begrudging space and denying any man's hand from forcing itself between their impenetrable love, close as if they were Siamese; love for the music and for the voice that pumped this love from one into the other, blood through veins, these two women moved in their heaviness like oil on shining glass, oblivious to the fact that there were hundreds dancing along with them. They moved as if they were on ice. They moved only because I had seen them leave one spot small as a dime, and occupy another dime's area, not that they themselves could ever know that they had moved. They were close to me now, and I stood for a moment and watched them. I watched them grinding out their satisfaction and their ageless joy in this heavy, segregated world, in this black section of this city, safe amongst numbers, and amongst blackness created through the dance: *Didn't I do it, baby?;* a black world and a black poem which the dance itself had formed and had drawn a circle around. "This is a black world," Calvin said, having to shout to be heard.

I was now only three paces from the stage. I stood. I had to stand, for the bodies were not moving now. They were grinding. I was the only one who moved. I was the only one out of the rhythm. Inching to the stage, I was the only one out of place.

Didn't I do it, baby?

The face of the singer was bathed in black perspiration. It was like the water of baptism and of revival. And it was growing out of the body, like strength. Not dripping like an exertion. The thin, tight body looked as if it was being tormented. I could see this through the slits of space in the crowd as the dancers moved. I could see it as a slice of a fish; a slice of a human being slithering in the shimmering sequins on the long dress that was like an extra skin. She was bathed in the white material of the dress, like a dolphin. *Didn't I do it, baby?*

"This sister can whup Aretha's ass any . . . " And Calvin's voice was blocked out, for a moment, by the passing of the two women between us, "any mother . . . any day!" Here in this room, I needed space even to hear. The song came to a perspiring end. It was a soft end. And it was followed by an explosion of applause. Handkerchiefs, fingers and kleenexes came out to repair the cheeks, and wipe away the beads that had damaged the neckline and the collar, and the forehead for the duration of that love-making rendition. And before the women and men had completed the renovation of their cosmetics, the mermaid of a woman on the stage began another song. *A midnight train to Georgia . . .* Without warning, without even a desire to join in this dance and in this circle, for I was out of place, inarticulate, foreign without speech and gesticulation, one of the fat ladies took me into her arms. It was like a mother knowing before the expression of pain is made, taking her child in the safety of her breast and bosom. I sank deep and comfortable in the billows of her love; as her arms wrapped my smaller body in embrace so much like my mother's, that I felt I could fall off into a sweet slumber and surrender myself to her; except that the song was raging through the magnolia and pine and poplar woods of a land that held such frightening memories. And Calvin was there to witness my surrender, and perhaps, in a seminar on black behavior, live to tell the story. But she held me close. She held me tight. She held her left arm round my waist, and her right hand on the softness of my bottom. I began to travel all those miles between the never-ending rails of steel going from one place I did not know, to a place which was even farther removed from my present; but to a place which was identifiable, as I was able to *know* where I am now. And so, I buried myself in her flesh, her perfume acting as a mild chloroform, and I found that Gwen and the woman in Toronto climbed into the sweet delirium along with the woman holding me, and I paid no regard to those two encumbrances, and allowed myself to be moved so very slowly by her, by her body that was guiding me, and by her blood which I thought I could taste. But that would have been, in addition to the unseemly unnatural acts, incest. I was dancing with my mother. The smell of her body, and the strength in her legs which were tightened round my left leg was like the tightness of a thick towel after a bath deep in winter. I could hardly breathe. But I could just as easily have died in her arms.

The house fly I had seen earlier, returned and lighted on the woman's mouth. She pursed her lips, unwilling to release one hand and let go of my body; and the fly fled. It probably had learned, through its ugly leaden antennae, what thunderous violence her anger would give rise to, in the slap the woman would have used.

Her lips were rouged in a deep red. Like the blood inside her body which I felt I could feel and taste. But I was not entirely passive in my enjoyment. My eight fingers were pressed deeply into her soft flesh. With difficulty I tried to move to the music, in my own slow, sweet time. It was like poetry; and I thought of poetry. And green and golden I was huntsman and herdsman . . .

"Are you screwing me, nigger?" she asked. And then laughed. A breath of Jack Daniels came to my nostrils when she spoke. I could feel her weight. I had made a wrong step, and her weight fell upon me. And I wondered what it would be like, if by accident, I were to make another wrong step, and she were to fall on top of me. "You want me?" She whispered this into my ear. I smelled her lipstick. I smelled her Jack Daniels again. "You're screwing me, ain't you?" Her mouth was at my ear. I smelled her perfume, and the cosmetics and the treatment in her processed hair. She tightened her grip on me. She tightened her grip more. My breathing became more difficult. And then she groaned, in a short spasm. My wishes raced through the house high hay, and nothing I cared . . . that time allows. "You like me, don't you, small-island man?"

Whatever Georgia was, whatever was the ruggedness of its landscape, whether of rocks or of stones, green fields of sugar cane or of cotton and corn, the concluding journey was before me. The singer was washed in perspiration, pouring out of her body with a sensual righteousness; the sequins in her dress moved as she breathed, from her ankles to her covered arms, like pistons on the very train that was pulling into Georgia, long after midnight. *Oh, as I was young and easy in the mercy of her means, time held me green and dying though I sang in my chains like the sea.*

"I want you, nigger. I have to have you."

I could feel it. I could feel the soft inside of her thighs. I was hard. The singer was coming home. Two sequined arms dropped at her side, in victory like that which concludes exhaustion of the flesh. And sudden so, the strong feeling thundered down. The rain had arrived.

"You want me, don't ya? I want you."

"No, I don't want you," I said.

"Well, fuck it! Nigger, you's *mine!*"

"Clovis!" It was Calvin, like a referee forcing himself between two locked boxers. "Clovis! Take your motherfucking hands off the brother! The brother's with me, motherfucker!" And Calvin ripped at Clovis's head, as if he was delivering a jab to the face. And when Calvin's hand returned from the face, in it was the wig which had contained such allure and fragrance of Duke Greaseless Hair Dressing for Women. His head was shaven bald, and was shining, and he was shaking with anger; and he said in a huskier voice, "Shit, Cal! I thought the nigger was mine!"

"Motherfucker!" Calvin pushed him off.

A few men and women danced close to us, looked at me and danced away. I stood looking at Clovis's shining head.

"Motherfucker, this is a Yale professor!"

"I could've *swear,* Cal honey, the nigger was mine. I am very sorry, sir, I am very sorry," Clovis said, offering me his hands. I remembered his hands were very soft. But by this time, I was feeling the eruption in my bowels; and Calvin, sensing this, and intent upon freeing me from this assault, this offense, and knowing that I had lusted after the wrong person, was easing me with some force, through the thick of the crowd, to the entrance.

On the way out, I barely recognized Clovis's voice, as he stood where he was, saying, "I knew the nigger looked strange, as if he didn't belong here, weren't one of us, weren't from the South, so what the fuck was I supposed to think?"

I could not wait until I was on the gravel patch in front of the entrance of the Stallion's Club, before the vomit spewed down on my white dashiki, onto my white cotton Levis, into my shoes, with the noise and the slime and the bad taste, and Calvin talking and talking.

"Shit, brother, couldn't you *tell?"*

"How?"

"Didn't you see the motherfucker didn't have no breasts? Couldn't you see?"

"How? I was mesmerized by the woman singing 'Midnight Train to Georgia.'"

"That motherfucker was a man, too, brother!" The vomit punctuated whatever else he was about to say. It was coming out with pain and with violence, as if I was trying to rip something awful something vile, some sin, some hurt clean from my insides.

"I was in love with the woman singing 'Midnight Train.'"

"The woman singing is also a man," Calvin said. Pity and disappointment in me, registered in his explanation. "The woman is a motherfucking man, brother! This be the South. Birmingham. In the South, it be so fucked up, you can't tell one motherfucker from the next."

"I thought the man was a woman."

"It's a motherfucking *man,* Jack! A man!"

He lit a Salem. "Sure's hell ain't Toronto, Jack!"

1992

Doing Right

I see him and watch him, I see him and watch him and I start to pray for him, 'cause I see him heading for trouble. Making money. "In five or six years, I want to have a lotta money. Only when I have a lotta dollars will people respect me."

I had to laugh. Every time he say so, I does-have to laugh, 'cause I couldn't do nothing more better than laugh.

"Look at the Rockefellers. Look at the Rothschilds. Look at the Kennedys."

I was going-ask him if he know how they mek their money, but before I could-ask, he would be off dreaming and looking up at the ceiling where there was only cobwebs and dust; and only God knows what was circulating through his head every time he put himself in these deep reveries concerning making lots o' money and talking 'bout the Rockefellers, the Rothschilds and the Kennedys.

I was still laughing. 'cause the present job he had, was a green-hornet job. He was a man who went to work in a green suit from head to foot, except the shoes, which was black and which he never polish. His profession was to go-round the St Clair-Oakwood area putting parking tickets 'pon people cars. Before he start all this foolishness with Wessindian cars, he uses to be on the Queen's Park beat for green hornets.

A big man like him, over two hundred pounds, healthy and strong, and black, and all he could do after eight years, is to walk-'bout with a little book in his hand, putting little yellow pieces o' paper on people windshields. He like the job so much and thought he did-doing the right thing that in the middle o' the night, during a poker game or just dipsy-doodling and talking 'bout women, he would put-back-on the green uniform jacket, grabble-up the peak cap, jump in the little green car that the Police give him, and gone straight up by St Clair-Oakwood, up and down Northcliffe Boulevard, swing right 'pon Eglinton, gone down Eglinton, and swing left 'pon Park Hill Road, left again on Whitmore, and all he doing is putting these yellow pieces o' paper on decent, hard-working people cars. When he return, he does-be-laughing. I tell him he going-soon stop laughing, when a Wessindian lick-he-down with a big rock.

"I have fix them! I have ticketed one hundred and ten motto-cars today alone! And the night I leff the poker game, I tick-et fifty more bastards, mainly Wessindians."

I start to get real frighten. 'cause I know a lotta these Wessindians living in them very streets where he does-be ticketing and laughing. And all them Wessindians know who the green hor-net is. And being as how they is Wessindians, I know they don't like green hornets nor nobody who does-be touching their cars. So I feel that any morning, when one o' these Wessindians come home from a party or offa a night-shift and see him doing foolishness and putting yellow tickets 'pon their motto-cars, I know um is at least *one* hand brek. Wessindians accustom to parking in the middle o' the road, or on the wrong side, back home. And nobody don't trouble them nor touch their cars. And since they come here, many o' these Wessindians haven't tek-on a change in attitude in regards to who own the public road and who own the motto-cars.

So whilst the boy still ticketing and laughing, and putting his hands on people cars which they just wash in the car wash on Bathurst, I continue worrying and watching him.

One night just as we sit down to cut the cards, and before the cards deal, he come-in grinning, and saying, "I ticket two hun-dred motto-cars today alone!"

"One o' these days, boy!" I tell him.

"When I pass in the green car and I see him, I know I had him!"

"Who?"

"I see the car park by the fire hydrand. The chauffeur was leaning back in the seat. One hand outside the car window. With a cigarette in tha' hand. The next hand over the back o' the seat. I look in the car, and when I look in, I nearly had a fit. I recognize the pipe. I recognize the dark blue pin-stripe suit. I recognize the hair. With the streak o' gray in um. And I mek a U-turn in the middle o' the road . . . "

"But a U-turn illegal!"

"I is a green hornet, man!"

"I see."

"I size-up the car. And I see the licents-plate. ONT-001! I start getting nervous now. 'cause I know it is the big man. Or the second most biggest man in Toronto. I draw up. The chauffeur nod to me and tell me, "Fine day, eh?" I tell he, "A very fine day, sir!" And I get out. I bend-over the bonnet o' this big, shiny, black car . . . "

"Limousine, man. A big car is call a limmo."

"Well, um could have been a limmo, a hearse be-Christ, or a' automobile, I still bend-over the bonnet and stick-on one o' the prettiest parking tickets in my whole career!"

"The Premier's car?"

"He mek the law. Not me!"

"And you think you do the right thing?"

"My legal bounden duty. Afterwards I did-feel so good, like a real police officer and not a mere green hornet. And I walk-through Queen's Park on my two feet, looking for more official cars to ticket. And when I was finish, I had stick-on *five* parking tickets in their arse . . . One belongst to the Attorney General, too."

"The same man who does-defend Wessindians?"

"I put one 'pon Larry Grossman car, too."

Well, that whole night, all the boy talking 'bout and laughing 'bout is how he stick-on tickets on these big-shots cars, or limousines. And to make matters worse for the rest o' we, he win all the money in the poker game, too. I feel now that the boy really going-become important, maybe even become a real police, and make pure money. Or else going-lose a hand, or a foot.

But we was feeling good, though. 'cause the big boys in Toronto don't particular' notice we unless um is Caribana week-end or when election-time coming and they looking for votes or when the *Star* doing a feature on racism and Wessindians and they want a quotation. So we feel this green hornet is our ambassador, even if he is only a' ambassador o' parking tickets. So we laugh like hell at the boy's prowess and progress.

And we does-wait till a certain time, on a Friday night, nervous as hell whilst cutting and dealing the cards, to see if the boy going-turn-up still dress-off in the green uniform, meaning that he hasn't get fired for ticketing big-shots cars. And when he does turn-up, dress from head to trousers in green, we know he still have the job, and we does-laugh some more. But all the time I does-be still nervous, as I seeing him and watching him.

Then he start losing weight. He start biting his fingers. He start wearing the green uniform not press, and half-dirty. He start calling we "You people!"

I getting frighten now, 'cause he tell me that they tek-him-off the Queen's Park beat.

So um is now that he up in St. Clair-Oakwood, and I feel he going-put a ticket on the *wrong* motto-car, meaning a Wessindian car. And at least one hand brek. Or one foot. And if the particular motto-car belongst to a Jamaican, not even the ones that have locks and does-wear the wool-tams mek outta black, green and red, I know um could be *both* foots and *both* hands!

I see him and I watch him.

"I have live in Trinidad, as a police. But I born in Barbados. I leff Trinidad because they won't let me ticket one hundred more cars and break the all-time record. I went to Guyana after Trinidad. I was a police in Guyana before Guyana was even Guyana and was still Demerara, or B.G. They make me leff Guyana when I get close to the record. Ten more tickets is all I had to ticket. From Guyana, I end up in Dominica. Same thing. From Dominica, I went to Antigua, and um was in Antigua that a fellow came close to licking-me-down for doing my legal duty, namely ticketing cars. In all them countries, I ticket cars that belongst to prime ministers, ministers of guvvament, priests, civil servants and school teachers."

I see him and I watch him. I see him getting more older than the forty-five years he say he was born; and I see him drinking straight rums, first thing every morning lately, because he say, "The nerves bad. Not that I becoming a' alcoholic. I only taking the bad taste o' waking up so early outta my mouth. I am not a' alcoholic, though. It is the pressure and the lack o' sleep."

But he was drunk. Cleveland was drunk drunk drunk early early early every day. He had to be really drunk after he outline his plan to make money, to me.

"Remember the Rockefellers, man!" he tell me. "This is my plan. I been a green hornet for nine years now. They promise me that if I ticket the most cars outta the whole group o' hornets, they would send me to training school to be a police. First they tell me I too short. I is five-four. But most criminals is five-three. Then they tell me that my arches fallen. Jesus Christ! What you expect? After all the beats I have walk in Trinidad, Guyana, Antigua, Dominica and Grenada, my arches bound to fall! And eight-nine years in this damn country pounding the beat ticketing cars! But they can't beat me. Not me. This is the plan I got for their arse. Tickets begin at five dollars. Right? There is five dollars, ten dollars and fifteen dollars. Right? Twenty dollars for parking beside a fire hydrand or on the wrong side. Right? Now, I write-up a ten-dollar ticket. And I change the ten to a forty. The stub in my book still saying ten. But the ticket on the car that saying ten also, I going-change from ten to a forty. Then I rush down to the vehicle registration place on Wellesley Street where they have all them computers. And I tell the fellow I know from Guyana something, *anything* to get him to look up the registration for me. And then I get in touch with the owner o' the said vehicle and subtract ten from forty and . . . "

"You mean subtract ten years from forty!"

"You don't like my plan?"

"I think your plan worth ten years."

"Okay. What about this other one? People don't lock their cars when they park. Right? Wessindians is the biggest criminals in regards to this. Right? A fellow don't lock his car. And um is night. And I got-on my green-hornet uniform. Right? Meaning I am still operating in a' official capacity . . . "

I see the boy start to smile, and his face spread and light-up like a new moon. The face was shining, too, 'cause the heat and the sureness that the plan going-work this time make him sweat real bad. But I watching him. I know that Wessindians don't have much money, because they does-get the worst and lowest jobs in Toronto. Only a certain kind o' Wessindian does-have money in their pocket. The kind that does-work night-shift, especially after midnight, when everybody else sleeping; the brand o' Wessindian who I not going-mention by name in case they accuse me of categorizing the race. And being a reverse racist. But *certain* Wessindians, like hairdressers, real estate salesmen and fellows who know race horses backwards and forwards, good good good *plus* the unmentionable brand, namely the illegal immigrants, the illegal parkers and them who hiding from the Police, them-so would have money to burn, inside their cars that not locked.

The boy eyes smiling. I see dollar bills instead o' pupils. I even hear the money clinking like when a car pass-over the piece o' black rubber-thing in a gas station. *Cling-cling.* "Gimme just three months," he say. "Gimme just three bare months, and I going-show you something."

Just as I left him and walking 'cross Northcliffe Boulevard going to Eglinton, I see a green-hornet fellow standing-up in front a fellow car. The fellow already inside the car. The fellow want to drive off. But the green hornet standing up in front the man car. The fellow inside the car honk the horn. And the green-hornet fellow take out his black book. Slow slow. And he flip back a page. And hold down a little. And start to write down the car-licents. The fellow honk the car again. The hornet walk more closer. He tear off the little yellow piece o' paper. And getting ready to put it on the man brand-new gray Thunderbird. Just as the hornet was about to ticket the man for parking next to a yellow fire hydrand, the fellow jump out. A Japanee Samurai wrestler wouldda look like a twig beside o' him. Pure muscle. Pure *avoirdupois.* Pure *latissimus dorsae.* Shoes shining bright. White shirt. Stripe tie. A three-piece gray suit. Hair slick back. And long. Gold 'pon two fingers on each hand. Gold on left wrist. More gold on right wrist. The hornet par'lysed now. A rigor mortis o' fear turn the whole uniform and the man inside it to pure starch or like how a pair o' pyjamas does-look when you left um out on the line in the dead o' winter.

"Goddamn!" the man say.

"You park wrong," the hornet say.

"Who say I park wrong?"

"You park illegal."

"Who goddamn say I park illegal?"

"Look at the sign."

"Which goddamn sign?"

"The sign that say No Parking between four and six. And No Stopping Anytime. You not only park, but you stop. You stationary, too." The Indian green-hornet man's voice get high and shaky. "You have therefore park'."

"Ahmma gonna give you two seconds, nigger, to take that goddamn ticket off my car, motherfucker!"

"What you call me? I am no damn nigger. I am Indian. Legal immigrant. I just doing my job for the City of Toronto in Metropolitan Toronto. *You* are a blasted American negro!"

Well, multiculturalism gone-out the window now! All the pamphlets and the television commercials that show people of all colors laughing together and saying, "We is Canadians," all them advertisements in *Saturday Night* and *Maclean's,* all them speeches that ministers up in Ottawa make concerning the "different cultures that make up this great unified country of ours," all that lick-up now, and gone through the eddoes. One time. *Bram!*

The Goliath of a man grabble-hold of the hornet by the scruff o' the green uniform, the peak cap fall-off all like now-so, the little black book slide under the car, the hornet himself lifted up offa the ground by at least three inches, and shaking-'bout in the gulliver's hands, pelting 'bout his two legs like if he is a muppet or a puppet; and when I anticipate that the fellow going-pelt him in the broad-road, the fellow just hefted him up a little more higher offa the ground, and lay him 'cross the bonnet of the shining Thunderbird, holding-he-down like how you does-hold-down a cat to tickle-he under his chin; and the fellow say, "Now, motherfucker! Is you gonna take the goddamn ticket off mah Bird?"

I pass 'long quick, bo', 'cause I know the Police does-be up in this St. Clair-Oakwood district like flies round a crocus-bag o' sugar at the drop of a cloth-hat; and that they does-tek-in anybody who near the scene o' crime, no matter how small the scene or how small the crime; and if um is Wessindians involve, pure hand-cuffs and pelting 'bout inside the back o' cruisers till they get you inside the station. And then the real sport does-start! So I looking and I looking-off, knowing that a green hornet, even if he look like a Pakistani or a' Indian, but is really a Trinidadian, or a Guyanese and only look a little Indian, going-get help from the Police. Not one police. But five car-loads o' police. All like now-so, the road full up with Wessindians and other people, and these Wessindians looking on and laughing, 'cause none o' them don't like green hornets, not even green hornets that come from the Wessindies.

I pass 'long quick, bo'. I got to face the Immigration people in a week and I don't want nothing concerning my past or present to be a stain through witnessing violence, to prevent them from stamping *landed immigrant* or *immigrant reçu* in my Barbados passport! I may be a' accessory before the fact. But I was still thinking of my friend, the other green hornet, so I look back to see what kind o' judgment the Thunderbird-man was going-make with the Indian gentleman from Guyana, who now have no peak cap, no black notebook, one shoe fall-off and the green tunic tear-up. And as my two eyes rested on the scene *after the fact* I hear the Charles Atlas of a man say, "And *don't* call the motherfucking cops! I got you covered, nigger. I knows where you goddamn live!"

I hope that this Goliath of a man don't also know where my Bajan green-hornet friend does-live! I hope the Thunderbird don't be park all the time up here! And I start to think 'bout getting a little message to my friend to tell him to-don't put no tickets on no grey Thunderbirds, or no Wessindian cars, like Tornados, whiching is Wessindians favorite cars. And I start to wonder if he know that a Wessindian does-treat a Tornado more better than he does-treat a woman or a wife; and with a Wessindian, yuh can't ask his woman for a dance at a dance unless you expecting some blows. Even if he give you permission to dance with his woman, don't dance a' Isaac Hayes or a Barry White slow-piece too slow and too close, yuh . . .

I waiting anxious now, 'cause I don't see the boy for days, these days. I feel the boy already start making money from the scheme. I walk all over St. Clair-Oakwood, all along Northcliffe, swing right 'pon Eglinton, mek a left on Park Hill Road, a further left up by Whitmore and find myself back 'pon Northcliffe going now in the opposite direction, and still I can't rest my two eyes on the green hornet. Fellows start telling me that the boy does-be going to the races every day, on his lunch break from ticketing people cars, and betting *one hundred dollars on the nose* and *five hundred to show* on one horse, and leffing the races with bundles o' money. And laughing like shite.

I walking 'bout day and night, all over St. Clair-Oakwood, and still no sight o' the boy.

Then, *bram*! I start hearing horror stories.

"I come out my apartment last Wednesday night to get in my car, and my blasted car not there! It gone. Towway!" one fellow say.

A next fellow say, "Be-Christ, if I ever catch a police towing-way my car!"

"I don't like this place. It too fascist. Tummuch regulations and laws. A man can't *breathe.* I can't tek up my self and lodge a complaint with the police 'cause I here illegal. No work permit, yuh know? No job. Now, no car! You park your car, and when you come out in the cold morning to go-work, at a lil illegal job, no fucking car?"

"I was up by a little skins one night. I tell my wife I going by Spree. I tack-up by Northcliffe at the skins apartment. I really and truly did-intend to spend only a hour. Well, with a few white-rums in my arse, one thing lead to the next. And when I do-so, and open my two eyes, morning be-Christ brek, and um is daylight. My arse in trouble now, two times. Wife and wuk. I bound-down the fire escape, not to be seen, and when I reach ground, no blasted car!"

Stories o' motto-cars that get tow-way start spreading through the St. Clair-Oakwood neighborhood, just like how the yellow leaves does-fall 'pon the grass a certain time o' year. Stories o' fellows getting lay-off, no work permit, getting beat-up, can't go to the police, in case, and getting lock-out, all this gloom start spreading like influenza. The fellows scared. The fellows vex. The fellows angry. And they can't go and complain to the police to find out where their cars is, 'cause , yuh know, the papers not in order. As man! And the lil matter o' *landed* and *recu* and so on and so forth . . .

They can't even start calling the police "pigs" and "racists" and "criminals." And all this time, nobody can't find the green-hornet boy at all.

Well, a plague o' tow-way cars rest so heavy on my mind, even though I don't own no wheels, seeing as how I is a real TTC-man, that I get real concern. 'cause drunk or sober, blood more thicker than water . . .

"As man!"

I hear the voice and I bound-round. And look. I see cars. I see Wessindians. I don't see no police, but I frighten. I see a tow-way truck. And I still don't see nobody I know. But I think I recognize the voice.

"As man!"

I bound-round again, and I see the same things.

"Over here, man!"

God bless my eyesight! Um is the green-hornet man. My friend! Sitting down behind the wheel of "DO RIGHT TOWING 24 HOURS." I do-so look! I blink my two eyes. I seeing, but I not seeing right. I watching, but I having eyes that see and that watch but they not watching right.

"Um is *me,* man!"

The tow-way truck real pretty. It have-in short-wave radio. Two-way radio. C.B.C. F.M. Stereos. *And* C.B. It paint-up in black, yellow and white. The green-hornet boy, dress-off now in overalls and construction hat, cock at a' angle on his head, cigar in mouth and shades on his face, like if he is a dictator from Latin Amurca.

"Remember the plan? The plan I tell you 'bout for making money? Well, I went to my bank and talk to my bank manager and squeeze a loan for this outta the bitch." He tap the door of the tow-truck like if he tapping a woman. "And I had a word with a fellow who was a green hornet like me. I is still a green hornet myself, but I works the afternoon shift. This fellow I know, the ex-green hornet, couldn't take the abuse and the threats to his person of being a hornet, so he open up a little place up in Scarborough where he *enpounds* the cars I does tow-way. And me and he splits the money. I brings in a car, and quick-so, um lock-up and enpounded. If a fellow want-back his car, fifty dollars! You want piece o' this action?"

I get real frighten.

"You want to get cut-in 'pon this action?"

"But-but-but-but . . . "

"You see that pretty silver-gray Thunderbird park beside that fire hydrand? I watching that car now, fifteen minutes. I see the fellow park it, and go in the apartment building there. I figure if he coming back out soon, he going-come-out within twenty minutes. I got five more minutes . . . "

I start getting real frighten now. 'cause I see the car. And the car is the same car that belongst to Goliath, the black Amurcan fellow. I so frighten that I can't talk and warn my green-hornet friend. But even if I couldda find words, my tow-truck friend too busy talking and telling me 'bout a piece o' the action and how easy it is to tow-way cars that belongst to illegal immigrants and get money split fifty-fifty, and that to remember the Rockefellers . . .

" . . . and I had to laugh one day when I bring-in a Cadillac," he tell me, still laughing, as if he was still bringing-in the Cadillac. "Appears that my pound-friend had a little altercation or difference of opinion with a Murcan-man over a car once, so when I appear with the silver-gray Caddy, he get frighten and start telling me that nobody not going-maim him or brutalize him or cuss his mother, that before anything like that happen, he would go-back home to Guyana first and pick welts offa reefs or put-out oyster-pots down by the Sea-Wall . . . Look! I got to go. Time up!"

I see him, and I watch him pull off from 'side o' me like if he didn't know me, like if I was a fire hydrand. I watch him drive up to the shiny gray Thunderbird car, not mekking no noise, like if he is a real police raiding a Wessindian joint after midnight. I see him get-out the tow-truck, like if he walking on ashes. I see him let-down the big iron-thing at the back o' the tow-truck. First time in my eleven years living here as a semi-legal immigrant that I have see a tow-truck that didn't make no noise. I see him bend-down and look under the front o' the Thunderbird. I see him wipe his hands. I see him wipe his two hands like a laborer who do a good job does-wipe his hands. I see him go-round to the back o' the Bird and bend-down. He wipe his two hands again. I see him size-up the car. I watch him put-on the two big canvas gloves on his two hands. I watch him cock the cigar at a more cockier angle, adjust the construction hat, tek-off the shades and put them inside his pocket, and I see him take the rope that mek out of iron and look like chain and hook-um-on 'pon the gentleman nice, clean-and-polish gray 1983 Thunderbird. I seeing him and I watching him. The boy real professional. I wondering all the time where the boy learn this work. He dance round to the tow-truck and press a thing, and the Bird raising-up offa the road like if um ready to tek-off and fly. I see him press a next thing in the tow-truck and the bird stationary, but up in the air, at a' angle, like a Concorde tekking-off. I see him bend-down again, to make-sure that the chain o' iron hook-on good. I see him wipe his two hands in the big canvas gloves a next time, and I see him slap his two hands, telling me from the distance where I is, watching, that it is a professional job, well done. I think I see the dollar bills registering in his two eyes, too! And I see him tug the chain tight, so the Bird would move-off nice and slow, and not jerk nor make no noise, when he ready to tek she to the pound to enpound she.

And then I see the mountain of the man, tipping-toe down the metal fire escape o' the apartment building where he was, black shoes shining in the afternoon light, hair slick back and shining more brighter from a "process," dress in the same three-piece suit with the pin-stripe visible now that the sun was touching the rich material at the right angle o' sheen and shine, and I see, or I think I see the gentleman take off a diamond-and-gold ring two times, offa his right hand, and put them in his pocket, I think I see that, and I see how the hand become big big big like a boxing glove, and I watching, but I can't open my mouth nor find voice and words to tell my former green-hornet friend to look over his left shoulder. I seeing but I can't talk o' what I seeing. I find I can't talk. I can only move. A tenseness sei*f*ze the moment. I do so, and point my index finger like a spy telling another spy to-don't talk, but look behind. But at that very moment, the black Amurcan gentleman's hand was already falling on my friend's shoulder . . .

1985

In An Elevator

It was mid-November and after five o'clock, and most of the staff had left. It was snowing. And the evening, early as it was, looked like midnight. Hundreds of men and women had already streamed out from the building heading for the trains to the suburbs, and, except for one woman who was in the ladies' room, almost the only people in the twenty-nine storey building of glass and steel were the heavily-built Portuguese and Greek women who cleaned the offices and the washrooms.

The occupant in the ladies' room was Susan Cole. Tainted seafood eaten at a place by the lake, the Fish, Tackle & Bone Cafe, had given her a touch of diarrhea all day. It had magnified itself into a constant run to the bathroom. She waited in slight pain and with great embarrassment in the locked cubicle, while other ladies entered, chatted and gossiped while doing their business, and left.

Susan was a careful woman. She was tidy. She dressed well. Perhaps, above her means and salary. But the job was temporary: she was heading for Osgoode Hall Law School. She lived at home with her parents. Her father had been in hospital from June until two weeks ago, lying in silent writhing misery from his back which he had "put out" from playing old timers' hockey, after his wife had told him not to skate at his age, and he went and did and "put it out." She loved her father.

Susan was sensitive. Not only to the dirty language some of the women used in the ladies' washroom, and to the corny, horny jokes of the supervisory male staff, but also to the changing face of the city, and to the fabric of her own office: faces and accents. She was above all, sensitive to smells. On the subway, at a quarter to eight each morning, she travelled from home to office and had to stand for the thirty-one minutes of the journey because the train was jammed. She would be very close to men and women from lands she had not even come across in geography books at school. And she would smell and become aware of their lotions, their after-shave and the hair-sprays.

Earlier this afternoon, the chief executive officer had called her into his office, and had dictated a letter of such length and questionable syntax, that she cringed in her seat, sucked on her breath, gritted her teeth, and spent most of the dictating time looking through the window into the foreboding gray sky that hung over the Lake. Her stomach was grumbling. The curtain of bad weather was hanging round her like a mood, and she could barely make out her club, The Royal Canadian Yacht Club. But the sky began to clear. And the name of the restaurant she had eaten at came through the clouds, and the sight brought her lunch close to her mouth and lips. Half an hour before, she had vomited in the ladies' room. Now, she placed a man-sized white Kleenex to her red lips and missed a very technical phrase in the CEO's dictation. She closed her eyes. When she opened them, the nausea had passed. Clouds hid the name of the restaurant. And the dictation was at its conclusion. For a moment she could not move. But she had to think of the missing phrase. She was capable. Very intelligent. And inventive. And very uncomfortable.

She had rushed to the ladies' the moment her boss got up from his deep-seated leather chair, and she sat on the cold porcelain bowl and was about to surrender to the turmoil in her stomach, when Grace entered with Joyce, carrying on a conversation. Susan raised her shoes, for she wore shoes that were distinctive in style, in color and in quality, and she was known throughout the office as Shoes.

This afternoon, the two of them did not talk in whispers as they were sure they were alone.

"From ten this morning, she started. I counted three times before lunch."

"Didn't you tell me last Christmas, that she's engaged?"

"Me?"

"You said she's engaged."

"Not me."

"Must've been Anne, then."

"Couldn't've been!"

"Anne and her were reading about the man who molested the woman in the elevator last Friday."

"You think she's pregnant?"

"Could be."

"It happened at seven o'clock. It wasn't even midnight. At *seven*, imagine!"

"And in an insurance company building."

"Look! See my whistle? I don't leave home without it. But I wish I didn't have to catch the five-thirty so I could go with you to those classes."

"Last night, they taught us how to overpower a man with pepper spray."

"The papers said she was in the elevator with the man for four floors. Did you say pepper spray?"

In all this time, with her shoes raised, out of sight, adding a tightness to her stomach muscles, and trying to control the rage within her bowels, Susan remained quiet and in great discomfort, barely hearing and unable to pay attention. But then she lost control. The toilet bowl erupted, and she hoped that the smell was not equal to the echo.

"Somebody!" Joyce exclaimed.

"I have to catch the five-thirty!"

"Have a good weekend."

"What're you doing this weekend? God, I have eight minutes!"

"This pepper spray thing. You have seven and a half minutes . . . "

Susan was grateful when they'd gone. And she settled on the toilet seat, and tried to think of the cause. "It's the oysters!" She spoke it loud enough for the person who had entered after Grace and Joyce had left, to hear, and know that the bathroom was occupied at this late hour.

"Some person?" the cleaning lady asked.

There was silence, and then the noise from the locked cubicle.

"Some person?"

The cleaning lady retreated and closed the door; and parked her trolley and walked to the end of the corridor, where another cleaning woman inside the men's room was mopping the floor, with its door held ajar. They stood talking, waiting like watchmen for Susan to come out.

When Susan got up from the bowl, she could hardly stand, she was so weak. And when she walked to the wash basin, her high-heeled shoes clipped over the tiles, with less noise. Susan Cole was twenty-eight. And she had learned to walk this way, making noise with her heels, even when, at Bishop Strachan School for Girls, her shoes were Oxfords with half-inch rubber heels. At Bishop Strachan she'd been captain of the field hockey team, captain of the wrestling team, captain of the junior track and field team and ended up as Head Girl.

Grace and Joyce were convinced she looked down on them. They had attended a collegiate institute for boys and girls of working class background from Leaside. Once, Susan left a copy of the Bishop Strachan Alumni magazine on their desks. The two of them felt it was done to remind them of their place. In fact, Susan had left the magazine mostly to show them what she looked like at age ten.

Susan was not married; and they wanted to be able to say that in spite of her clothes from Holt Renfrew, and her Bishop Strachan schooling, her red shoes of leather and of suede, she would find herself in precisely the predicament both of them had known. Grace was a single parent. And Joyce barely escaped that state through an abortion, suggested by her mother. So it was a digestible piece of gossip when they hoped that Miss Susan Cole would find herself in a state of want, rejection and dislocation they themselves had known.

Susan went back to her desk. It was now ten minutes past six. A woman in a blue uniform came along the corridor with a trolley that was silent as an expensive European car. The woman held a dusting mop in her left hand, and humming under her breath, absentmindedly, she passed it over the tubular pencil and ball-point holders, over the man-sized boxes of Kleenex, over the framed photograph of Susan's sweet-hearting man. This cleaning woman was once in a school of dress designers in Athens. She liked clothes and designs. Her first three years in this city, were spent bending over a power sewing machine, putting buttons on women's blouses in the garment district on Spadina Avenue; and sometimes falling asleep. She watched and waited and cursed her husband a little for being too slow in pulling himself up by the laces of his construction boots. She knew that if she got the chance, in two years she could make a woman of herself; and a man of her husband. And be successful like this woman, sitting at her desk, whom she would watch closely and love from a distance. Susan hated her.

Each morning, standing in the subway train, one of hundreds of jostled women, thrown against people from places like the one the cleaning woman came from, with her breasts and waist pressed against those men and those women who stared at her with lust and love and envy, all she could smell during those short minutes of the long ride was the aroma of garlic. And once, in an honest confession of her allergic reaction to it, she mentioned it to Joyce, not remembering that Joyce was Joyce Maviglia before she became Joyce McCarthy, before she became divorced.

Now, after all this time, she got it. It was the garlic she had eaten at Fish, Tackle & Bone Cafe. But the garlic had been buried in the fresh shrimps large as little lobsters. She sniffed the air now. The woman with the silent trolley went about her cleaning humming under her breath. Susan knew she smelled garlic.

Returning from lunch on Wednesday, in the brilliant life-giving afternoon, and taking a last puff on her Players Light, Susan moved without paying attention to the elevator whose arrow was green and pointing upwards. She wanted the twentieth floor. The elevator she got into went only to the fourteenth. In she went, and did not press a number. Before the door closed, a black man stepped forward, barely missing the aimed palm of the door, intent it seemed, on cutting his body into half. He smiled at her. Susan did not smile. He smiled again, and said, "Jesus Christ!" The door missed him. He smiled again.

It was warm inside the elevator. A voice in the mechanism said, "Going up." Music started to play in the middle of a song. She did not recognize the song. The elevator was moving. The black man had not yet pressed a number. She noticed this, and wondered. The elevator became very uncomfortable. Susan passed her left hand, with the ring on her little finger, across her neck. On the ring was the crest of Bishop Strachan. Her hand remained on her neck for a longer time than she would take to remove a thread from her collar. Danger came into her stomach, like the first signs of diarrhea.

This man was thinking of the interview he was going to; that he was late. He tightened his tie, slackened the knot, and tightened it again. He looked at the piece of paper in his right hand, realized something was wrong, and when the elevator stopped and the door opened, he knew he had taken the wrong lift.

Back at her desk, that afternoon, she'd accused herself for having *those* feelings; and she searched in her past and went back over her days at Bishop Strachan: Amantha was from Barbados, wasn't she? Yes, I remember her accent. And she was good in class, especially in Latin and she was in my House and played field hockey better than me, better than anybody else, and the time I knocked her down, did I knock her down because she was challenging me, because she was smaller, because she was Amantha? Or? And that other one from the Bahamas who thought she was the cat's meow better than any of us, the best of us with her father the prime minister; and getting her parcels special delivery and couriered to her; and that time when I told Miss Sweeney that it was *her,* she was the culprit who had written the dirty word on the blackboard about Miss Sweeney: *lesbian;* and she travelled over every remembered detail of those years of childhood and of pleasure as they were meant to be, without bias but with the perspiring competitiveness of bright, privileged young girls. "Could I have offended any of them?"

She was tugged from these reveries and confessions by the ringing of the telephone on her desk.

"I'm seeing that bastard again." It was her father. "The bones-doctor." His voice revived her. "Drinks after work?" That put an end to her acrimonious sadness.

So, on this evening, two days later, she began to fix her face in the silver compact she had bought at Chanel on Bloor Street, pursing her lips, drawing them up into a thin line, making them into the shape she used to kiss the man who used lubricated condoms with her; drawing them to one side, the right, as if she had undergone surgery for a disfigured face; and then she did the same thing, drawing her lips to the left.

She removed a speck from the corner of her left lid, checked that her eyes were clean, and then applied mascara. The lipstick was red, full-bodied and strong. She tilted her bottle of Chanel Number 17, and placed the finger with the invisible drop on her left wrist, and with that wrist rubbed her right wrist. And then she passed the bottle under her nostrils, and rested it lightly against her neck.

In the oval looking glass in the compact, she caught the cleaning woman's eyes. The were in full focus watching her, studying her. She became agitated. She went back over that time when the word was written on the blackboard. *Lesbian.*

The woman was standing in front of the trolley, and she seemed to be imitating Susan's motions, her left hand raised as if it was holding some small object; and her right hand reproducing the touching of nostrils, neck and wrists. Susan kept her full in the center of the looking glass. She could see her eyes, the color of her cheeks, and the mole at the corner of her mouth, on the right side. The cleaning woman's eyes were green.

Nervously, Susan examined her own eyes, going over the makeup, and snapped the compact shut, intending by that action to shut the prying green eyes out and obliterate that dirty word written years ago on the blackboard.

She breathed on her fingernails, at the red nail polish on her manicured hands; passed her hand, while still sitting on the leather chair with the protecting cushion for back pains, over her well-shaped and endowed hips. She glanced at her legs and promised, that in spite of the pain, she would have to do something about her veins. The veins that were beginning to crawl in irregular blue rivulets beneath her light-gray pantihose: have to take time off, have to check my health benefits, have to tell them about the hospital and co-ordinate with the surgeon, have to tell Mother and Father, have to put my desk in order and have to give my tickets to Joyce or Grace . . . Anne? . . . someone who'd appreciate ballet and, "Oh my God! Look at the time!"

And she rose from her chair, put her purse into her bag strapped over her right shoulder, and walked out with her heels reverberating against the tiles, noisier now that the entire floor was empty.

Smoking was not allowed on her floor, but she took the box of Players Light from her purse, placed a cigarette into her mouth and then removed it. The red smear from her lips stained the tip; and then she put the cigarette back into her mouth, and fished for the box of wooden matches in her large black shoulder bag made of imitation crocodile skin. The gray-green small box with two capital P's written back-to-back on it, she held in her hand, until the elevator came to her floor. She got inside.

She was about to press G, when she noticed that every single floor button, from 20 to G, had been pressed and illuminated, even that for the basement. She lit the cigarette, filling her lungs with the first deep pull, and kept the smoke there for a long moment, and exhaled and relaxed and felt the weight of the day and the annoyance with the diarrhea dissipate, and thank God it was over; and the cleaning woman looking at her in that way, as if she was about to ask her a question; but "What the hell did she want?"

And then the door closed and she endured the slight nausea of her stomach falling as the elevator started to descend; and then the smoother sailing down the shaft in the enclosed, paneled cage. Alone to enjoy her cigarette, alone to travel down the twenty floors, alone to smoke her prohibited cigarette, alone and with some sense of regaining strength after love. She thought of the man. And only after enjoying the expectation of this privacy that she knew was going to last only until someone else got into the elevator, "The building is empty," did it really sink in and become anxiety, that each of the twenty illuminated circles representing the twenty floors would first have to be obliterated, that the cage would stop at each circle before they all could be wiped out, before she could reach ground.

The first stop was sudden. She looked out at plants on a receptionist's desk, and compared the office displayed before her with her own, and decided that hers was a more prestigious place to work. When the door was about to close, a man in a blue uniform, with his name written on it, came into view hauling a long fat rubber connection; and just as the door closed, she heard the hum of a vacuum cleaner. She was becoming irritable. "Why would that bitch do this to me?"

She looked at her watch. It was seven. She had no dinner appointment, no places to go, but she still continued looking at her watch.

She was on the nineteenth floor. The elevator was descending to the eighteenth and she was now between floors. They say that during the power failure in New York City, men and women were caught in elevators between floors for hours together, and when they came out, some of them were pregnant. And she looked at the button marked *emergency,* and she glanced at the telephone behind its glass protection; and she wondered how long it takes for someone, police, superintendent, repairman, ambulance attendant to arrive? And how would they arrive? Do they come through the top of the elevator?

The eighteenth floor. A man steps into the elevator. He is wearing sneakers. The laces are not tied. They are the kind that basketball stars use for making shots slam-bang, and defying gravity. They are white with red and blue slashes; and she cannot make out the name of their manufacturer. The trousers are black jeans, down over the tip of the sneakers which look like boots, they are high above the ankle; and the bagginess of the trousers causes her to wonder how tall this man is. She moves her eyes from his sneakers up his legs, his waist, and down again. She cannot bring herself to look into his face. Not yet. "He's taller than me!" And her eyes reach the bottom of his coat or windbreaker, and she can imagine how large the shoulders are, and can see the colors of red and green and yellow against the black background of the windbreaker. And then she sees the expanse of his chest and the thin yellow line of electrical cord joining the yellow Walkman's noise to his ears, going deaf. For she can hear the noise, even though she cannot follow the rhythm. "Rap!" she says to herself. And in the slow descent, for she is now travelling with someone she does not want to be travelling with, the cigarette is still in her mouth, and she allows the ash to grow. And she stands in the middle of the small space shared with the intruder in this cage, realizing that the man is facing her, and has not moved an inch since he violated her right to be safe and silent and alone in this elevator. For after all, she works here. And was here first.

And the elevator moves slower now, taking as much time to reach one floor below, as all the nineteen to travel and in the deathlike quiet, with nothing else to do, for she has already painted a picture of his attire, and could pick him out of any police lineup with her eyes closed, she goes over in her mind, with the tough cigarette in her mouth, with smoke and ash getting longer, word for word, her accusations of rape and assault. A kick in the crotch. A scream. Where is my goddamn whistle? Did I leave it on the desk when the goddamn cleaning woman was staring at me? My whistle is attached to my subway tokens holder. Press the button marked *emergency,* and scare the bastard? Do not give him the impression I am scared. Be aggressively defensive. Remember the lessons in karate. Wish I'd attended those classes Joyce goes to, with that pepper spray thing! And look the son-of-a-bitch in his eye.

She raises her eyes. He is staring at her from behind tinted glasses. Disguise! And sees the earphones. And the baseball cap. With a white large X. And turned backwards, so that she can see he has one of those haircuts popular with rappers. And thinking of music, she realizes with some shock that she has not heard music since he entered the cage. It was music already piping through the speakers above their heads. And it was not even Rap.

And the man, in panic, standing before her, placed in this closeness against his will watched her as she lit another cigarette, as she coughed, as something in her throat went up and down, as he saw her hand that held the cigarette, shaking.

Holy shit what am I gonna do stuck with this bitch in this elevator? If it wasn't for my Mom, I wouldn't be in this. Forcing me to take a part-time job. Dad said no; study hard and you will get to college. I'm studying hard, for college, and now this. What with me and her in here, how the fuck now am I gonna explain I didn't do nothing that I am only delivering a parcel?

He's waiting for the seventh floor. Perhaps, the fifth, the fourth? He will stop the elevator between the eighth and the seventh. That's why he's wearing dark glasses. Why else would he be wearing dark glasses in an elevator, seven o'clock at night? I see them on television wearing dark glasses. I see them all the time in the news, in dark glasses.

Boy, am I gonna be glad when this reaches the ground floor. Holy shit am I glad I have this Walkman in my ears! And I was gonna put it in my pocket before I entered this building. I wonder if she could know that I ain't listening to nothing, since this stopped working. Batteries dead. So, it's only style and to prevent people from staring at me like it keeps me invisible. I wonder what this chick is thinking? She sure smokes like all those white girls in my grade thirteen class. Like Jane. Now, if Jane and me were still dating . . . Twenty a day? Shit!

And the elevator, passing through all this time in its slow journey, reached its destination sooner than either the man or the woman expected. In a strange way neither of them desired the end. And he could see her body relax as if she had just finished exercising and could now breathe easier. He saw her hand, no longer shaking, drop the cigarette on the floor of the elevator, and how she crushed it with the tip of her high-heeled shoe. She grounded it into the carpet until it turned to brown flour. They were red suede shoes. And he said to himself, "The last time. Never again."

The area of the lobby was bright. He could see the winter light reflecting on the tall sheets of glass and metal in the building across the street. Outside, there were people walking. They looked happy and secure. Would they know, or care that he had just come through a baptism of fear and of violence which could have been done to him, because of that fear? And what might he have done to her?

She pushed past him. He stood at the front of the cage, allowing her to pass. She looked to see if the night security guard was behind the counter. This counter with its lights and buttons and controls and monitors looked like the controls in an airplane. It made the guard and the job he did more important than it really was. She too could see women walking in the street. Some of them were alone. Two women were standing up, chatting and laughing; and all of them oblivious to her experience with this ass-hole, from twenty floors above their heads right down to this saving, thank God, protected lobby, because I was *here* first, and I work here, and no goddamn immigrant or cleaning-woman or black son-of-a-bitch, nobody's gonna make me feel threatened and live like a victim in my own fucking country, province . . . in my city.

Now, did Cecil lock the doors before he went on his coffee break?

The man was beside her. And he too wondered if they were about to face another hindrance. But holy shit, at least people outside on the street can see me and her, and I can tell my side of the story, and they gotta believe my innocence.

She knew she could pick him out *like that* from any lineup in a police station, even if he left his dark glasses at home to hide the fact. And she knew that never again, not ever, would she be found *dead* in an elevator with a black man. She'd get off first! And wait until a white man came in! Or remain standing in front of the elevator, even if it took till time for work the next day! I can pick him out *like that,* in any lineup. But why didn't I get off at the very next floor after he entered? Why? Why?

The door onto Yonge Street was unlocked. He had used too much force, anticipating the hindrance, and so when he pushed the door outwards, he almost lost his balance. But he smiled. And turned and looked her in the face, and smiled once more. And he said, "Lady?" She was surprised to hear his voice. His hand was on the polished horizontal bar, holding his half of the glass door open, allowing her to precede him. He had forgotten his ordeal in the cage locked up with her. She did not say thanks for opening the door. She walked out as he held the door.

Before she reached the edge of the sidewalk, she had the white cigarette pack of Players Light in her left hand, and the matches with the two P's on the box, in her right: "I'm *safe* here!" Her purse and handbag were on the cold cement of the sidewalk between her feet. He turned to her and said, "Lady, so much smoking not good for you. Says so on the box."

She looked at him with no change of expression. Her expression before he had spoken was of relief, of victory mixed with a tinge of anger at having been helpless and without inventiveness to control the terror of his company. She placed the cigarette back into the box. She dropped the matches into the large black imitation crocodile shoulder bag. She took the bag and the purse from the cold pavement. She wanted to see in which direction he was going to turn. And then she stood and watched his jumping strides, as if he was a basketball star or a ballet dancer, moving as if he was walking on air. The unbuttoned multi-colored broad-shouldered jacket blowing in the wind, made him look like a bird, free and dancing in his stride to the inner music pouring through his ears.

Her face felt warm and flushed. Her hands began to feel the weight of the purse and handbag. But she was accustomed to this every day on the packed subway train. This new weight, however, made her feel her body and the blood in her cheeks and the slight pain in the veins in her legs. But more than that, she could feel something like excitement, like new life in her body, a kind of transfusion changing her blood to desire.

And he was disappearing fast from her, going in the direction of the lake, and the Fish, Tackle & Bone Cafe, towards Harbourfront. Were they having a concert, or a poetry reading tonight at Harbourfront? And even when tears began to wash her face and cloud her eyes and vision and made it impossible for her to identify him in the distance, she blamed the cold air that now brought the tears. She knew she would still remember the white sneakers with their slashes of blue and red; and the baggy trousers that fell over the top of the sneakers that looked like boots, above the ankle. And he was tall and his head was shaven in the new style; and she could see the large white X, and the yellow cord to his ears.

1993

If The Bough Breaks

Where they were, on the second floor of a building that squatted at the corner of Bay and Davenport, whose ground floor was taken up by a store that sold milk for five cents more than you could buy it in any supermarket, and beside which was a store that sold everything, these five women were chatting while two others sat in the hairdresser's chairs. The hairdresser was a man. Christophe. A big strong man with a black complexion, from Barbados. He had never learned French at school; had never visited the islands in the West Indies where French is spoken; but he understood what French meant in his business in this city, so he changed his name from Granville Da Costa the moment he graduated near the bottom of the class from the Marvel School of Hairdressing; went by bus to Montreal and stayed there for a long weekend, Labor Day weekend; and when he returned, by train, he had the name Christophe and a new accent. He called every customer, cherie, which came out as "cherry." He had two women working for him. They themselves had graduated from the Marvel School of Hairdressing three months ago, near the top of their class.

On the front of the building, on the second floor where these five women were now sitting, emblazoned in lights, was CHRISTOPHE'S SALO . The lights that formed the letter N in "salon" never worked. But Christophe was known throughout the city as the best hairdresser, the only man, or woman, who knew how to "fix" black women's hair.

One woman had curlers and grease in her hair; another woman's hair was lathered in shampoo, so thick and rich, you could not tell her age, although she was the youngest in the salon. And the five waiting together were all over forty and well-dressed; and two of them had foreign cars parked below; after one hour, they had given up running down the stairs to put loonies into the meters.

The girl in the chair cried out as the shampoo ran into her eyes, stinging her, "Are you trying to blind me Christophe? I'm too old to learn Braille, hear." She was a fourth year student at the University. She was studying psychology. She was very good-looking. She came from a rich Barbadian family who owned a very small sugar cane plantation that grew sugar cane no longer. "I have theories to read."

"Cuddear, cherry!"

It was three o'clock, Thursday afternoon. They could hear the traffic below and the voices of people passing, for the windows facing the street were open for the breeze.

Christophe had forgotten to call the repairman to come and fix the two noisy air-conditioners, taped round their perimeter with electrical tape which his friend Cox, a plumber, had left. So, the room was warm. And the five ladies were using the boxes of Kleenex, passing them from hand to hand, mopping their brows, their embroidered hankies already saturated. And the prospect of the ironing comb, not really a comb made of iron by a blacksmith as many used back in the West Indies, but its modern version, which performed the same function, making their hair "white," making their temples hot, threatening burns on their scalps, certainly singeing hair in the wrong places, all this made their waiting more uncomfortable than the patience they knew they must have each time they visited this salon, always too crowded, too slow, and too understaffed. They had been Christophe's customers for years.

In with a whiff of wind which cooled the salon came voices of a quarrel below on the street. The room was quiet for a moment. Then, a siren screamed through the buzz of voices, and the humidity seemed to clutch the women's bodies, and cause them to breathe more heavily. The noise increased and it seemed as if the ambulance or the police cruiser was going to climb right up the flight of stairs and join them. And in fact, it did stop in front of the entrance. The five women ran to the windows.

There was a hiss. The sirens stopped. And the hissing sound lasted a few more moments. The two assistants dropped their instruments into some kind of liquid. They joined the others at the windows. Christophe continued fixing the young woman's hair.

There were three large windows. The lower half of each was pulled up. So the women could lean their bodies out, and see. And they could look at one another leaning out the three windows. It was not an ambulance. There were three police cars. Stopped in the middle of the road, blocking all traffic. The owner of the store who sold high-priced milk came out to meet the policemen. They had left their car doors open. The women could hear the three radios crackling. The six policemen had their guns drawn. In the distance, coming towards them, was another cruiser, flashing in red speed and urgency.

"I bet you," one woman said, "it's some black man in there."

"And not eighteen yet," another said.

The policemen and the store owner were now inside the store.

"These *people*!" one of the assistants said. "I was walking through the Eaton Centre one night, and just as I take up my parcel with the things I bought in it, and paid for, all of a sudden I feel this hand on my shoulder, and when I turn round . . . "

"Blasted people, eh?"

Two of the policemen came back out. Between them was a young white girl. No more than sixteen. They took her to a car, and put her to sit in the back seat, while the other four officers exchanged words which the women could not hear; and then they too got into their cruisers, and drove off. The few men and women who had stopped to look walked on. One man took a red box from his pocket, extracted a cigarette and lit it. He walked at a faster pace. A bus was coming. The wind was blowing again. The store owner came back outside with a broom, sweeping the sidewalk; and they could see because of the stains from chopping meat and pork and roasts on his white apron that covered his body from his neck to his thighs, that he sold other things than milk.

"What you think they got her for?"

"Shoplifting."

"They begin young."

"Well, it was a good thing," the assistant continued, "that I had keep my receipt that Friday night. It was the Friday before the Caribana parade, and I was thinking of stopping at the kiosk-thing to buy a Lotto, 'cause I had had a dream the night before. But before I could walk more than two feet from the counter where I had bought the pantihose, this blasted man's hand on my shoulder. I look round. And staring me in my face is this blasted man. Security guard. Accusing me. Of something. Say I shoplifting. Well, I not ashamed to tell you, I let-go some bad words in his arse, that caused all the people in the Eaton Centre to stare at me. These blasted people, eh?"

"How old you think that girl is?"

"I could only see her head."

"I wonder if she have a mother?"

"From the back, which is all I could see, I would put her at sixteen."

"So young? And to have a record?"

"She's sixteen, as you say. She can breed."

"Christ, waiting here on Chris, my mind all the way up in Pickering, wondering if *my* child went home straight from school. We moved up in Pickering to get away from crime and violence down here, but child, I tell you, up there isn't any better than down in Jane-Finch corridor, if you ask me."

"In the weekend *Star*, did you read the thing about teenage pregnancies?"

"Wonder what time Chris intends to get to my hair? Four o'clock, and school must be out a long time."

"What happened?"

"You mean the article?"

"No. The security guard and the pantihose."

"I looked him straight in his face. The whole store watching me now. I faced him and I said, in my best manner, 'Let me tell you something, nigger-man.'"

"You called him that?"

"Was he black?"

"What was his complexion?"

"If you want to," I tell him, "you could put your hand in my bag. But let me tell you something. When you put your hand in my bag, I am going to take off my shoe, and *drive* it right into your two blasted testicles."

"No!"

"His complexion was what?"

"Not black."

"And you called him a nigger-man?"

"He was a white man."

"No!"

"And what happened?"

"He didn't say another word to me."

"*No!* But the teenage pregnancies is what I want to know about."

"I didn't read the newspapers that weekend."

"Anybody have that article? Joyce, you think you still have it? You clips things from the *Star*."

"Was in the *Globe*."

"I don't take the *Globe*. The *Star* is my speed."

"Mr. Chris, how much longer before you getting-round to fixing my hair? I have a child at home waiting on me."

"And a husband."

"Had!"

"You divorced, cherry? I didn't know you and the old-man had break-up, cherry?"

"In name only, Mr. Chris, a husband in name only."

"That girl that we just see being arrested by the police, I am sure that they're going to take her down in that station and make that girl's life miserable, and they may even do . . . "

"Do what to her? Do what to her? What you mean by miserable?"

"Child, every other day in the newspapers there's stories about the police and women they have in their cruisers."

"But that child, though."

"She's sixteen. She can breed."

"You mean rape."

"Who said anything about rape?"

"Sexual assault. Sexual assault is the name for it nowadays. Everything nowadays is sexual assault."

"Growing up in the West Indies . . . "

"You're a damn liar!"

"How can you accuse me before you hear what . . . "

"What you're about to say? I already know it, before you even say it. You were about to say that growing up in the West Indies, we didn't have anything such as what we witnessing nowadays in this place."

"Well, how the hell could you know what I . . . ?"

"Because I know you. And I know the West Indies. And I . . . "

"You know too blasted much. You must be working *obeah,* that you can read my mind."

The five women were sitting again. The wind came through the windows in a slight gust, and for a moment, it was as if Christophe had fixed the air-conditioners.

"Every year. Child, when you see Christmas come and the 28th is here, I longing for home. But I won't go home *before* Christmas. Christmas isn't Christmas unless you have a tree and snow."

"Child, all over the West Indies nowadays is trees, and *real* Christmas trees too! Not the artificial ones we had in our days!"

"Snow, too!"

"Snow, too? What the hell I hearing?"

"You didn't know? Didn't hear? For *years* now, the tourist board people in Barbados been importing snow from Canada. For years now."

"You don't mean the Tourisses from Canada? You not referring to white people?"

"I am no prejudice. I talking about the snow. I understand it comes from Toronto, whiching . . . "

"*And* Montreal!"

" . . . whiching is the best snow in North America."

"Who's next, my cherries?"

Christophe removed the plastic bib from the neck of the woman who was now almost two hours in his chair. The smoke from his cigarette rose gently. He put the cigarette to his lips; pursed his lips as if he was about to kiss the woman dismounting clumsily from the high chair; put the cigarette in the glass ashtray, and said, "Who's next, my cherries?"

The five women looked at one another. They had had lunch together at the Four Seasons Hotel nearby. They had had two martinis each. And when they arrived, giggling, after discussing their children and their families and their husbands, as they did each time they had lunch, once in two weeks, they were fortified, through food and drink, to wait the long wait in the old, hard plastic-bottomed chairs. The plastic made their dresses stick to their bottoms and they could feel the lumps where the upholstery had collapsed against their soft well-cared-for skin.

"You have a child coming from school soon. You go."

"Charmaine can look after herself, man."

"You're not concern about that little girl walking the street and going home to an empty house with all this *worthlessness* you read about in Toronto?"

"Well, child, I would never allow my Suzianne to enter an empty house. Nor go to the mall with her friends. Some o' these friends, I tell you."

"Charmaine's the same age as that child the police had downstairs a few minutes ago."

"Talking about bringing up children. Do you believe we bring up our children better than them?"

"Well you getting me mad as hell now! The evidence speaks for itself." One amongst them, who had been quiet, now spoke up. "How you could compare *them* with we, with us? The facts speak for themselves! If it is only once, in my twenty-something years living in Toronto, I have lived to see the day when a police go in a store and don't bring out a black boy or a black girl but a damn white girl. And all o' you spending your time taking up for that girl? I haven't heard nobody amongst you, in the two or three hours we been sitting down waiting for Mr. Chris to fix our hair, nobody, not *one* of you haven't uttered a word in support of the police! Not one of you!"

"Wait! She fooping a police?"

"She's a married woman, child."

"Her husband would break her arse if he only heard!"

"Are you sleeping with one o' Metro's finest, on the sly, girl?"

"The girl is a little whore!"

"She was unfaired by the police."

"Not the police. The man who own the store is who called the police. Blame *him*. He could be the son-of-a-bitch."

"Who's next? Cherries? Who's next?"

"We're talking business, man."

"Just a minute, Chris, man."

"The fact that it was a white girl and not one of ours, well, that answers the question. We raise ours better than *them*."

"We had just moved to Pickering, in the house we're living in now, and it was a day like this, in late July; no, it must have been in August, 'cause we had just come back from watching the Caribana parade on University Avenue, and . . . "

"You see? You see? Christ, they couldn't let us parade on University, 'cause University Avenue is too good for black people, so they moved us down beside the Lake, where nobody can't see us, whilst they leave right-wingers like the Shriners to ride all over this city on tricycles as if they are blasted kids! You see? You see?"

"Nevermindthat!"

"Why never mind that?"

"Nevermindthat! We had just moved into Pickering and my daughter was nine, my son was six and my other daughter was eight, and we had just got home from sweating-up ourselves in the Caribana parade, and it was so hot and we had nothing cool in the house to drink, so me and my husband . . . "

"The cop you was seeing on the sly?"

"And fooping with? I did-hear that."

"Fuck you."

"Me, child? I can't do it by myself!"

"Was nothing in the house cool to drink, as I was saying, so we send the eight-year-old to the convenience store, just across the street, in the mall to buy a large bottle o' pop, 'cause we had just got a bottle o' Mount Gay from a girl friend who had gone home on holiday and me and Percy opening this forty-ounce and waiting for the child to come back from the plaza, and when we hear the shout, these blasted sireens going like hell in front our house, and four police in three cars jump out and my child in the back seat of one o' them police cars, handcuff. Well, BeJesus Christ, you shouldda seen how my husband *react*!"

"No!"

"Good dear!"

"Oh God! This happened to you?"

"And you never mentioned a word of this before?"

"Some of the things you have to keep to yourself, eh?"

"No! Not a' eight-year-old child, handcuff, in the back of a police cruiser! *No!*"

Christophe struck three matches before he could light his mentholated cigarette. The smoke shot through his nostrils without sound, in two long piercing white streams. The cars outside the windows were moving fast. Horns were blown in exasperation. And the women could hear a few complaining voices. When the cars passed they could hear the footsteps of people on the street, and the scratching of the broom as the store owner swept the sidewalk; and then they heard the scratching of a match on a box, and the inhaling of the first lung-full of cigarette. It was one of the two assistant women hairdressers, smoking a Salem.

"Go on. Pass her a fresh Kleenex to dry her eyes."

"*My* eight-year-old. We send her to Sunday school every Sunday. From the time she was two, every Sunday as the Lord send, she was in that Sunday school class. We send her to piano lessons from the time she was five and last year, taking the advice of a friend of ours, she's been taking ballet lessons, and . . . "

"*That's* the way we bring up our children!"

"And her ballet teachers at the Ballet School just down there on a side-street near Church, her ballet teachers tell us that the child have a future in pirouettes. And, don't laugh, that August afternoon at five, four police have *my* child handcuff, in the back of a police cruiser and all the neighbors looking out and pointing. When we moved up there, four months pass before the one on our left said a word in regards to good morning or good evening; and the afternoon my husband brought home the new car, you should have seen them staring from behind their curtains. We shouldn't have those things. We shouldn't live the way *they* live. We shouldn't."

"What your husband did?"

"Pass her another Kleenex."

"It's too sad. It was too sad that August afternoon. It was too sad. And too shameful. I can't talk about it, no more."

"Don't then. We know everything you were going to say. It happens to all of us. We know. You don't have to say any more, 'cause it is the history and the experience of each and every one of us in this room."

"Well, who's next?"

"My mind is still on that white girl."

"Are you her god-mother?"

"She's a child."

"A child? She's a white girl. And she is the daughter of the four police in those three cruisers who molested this woman's eight-year-old daughter and handcuff her. She is the daughter of that landlord who didn't rent me that musty, stinking basement apartment years ago, in 1961 on Walmer Road. She is the daughter of the woman at the Eaton Centre who had the security guard come up in my face accusing me of shoplifting, a decent person like me. She is the future mother of all the racists we come across in this city. She is just herself."

"Is a hard sentence, though."

"At least, she's a thief."

"I won't put that judgment on her, though, 'cause as I said, when my husband saw those four police having my daughter in the back of that cruiser, handcuff, well . . . "

"Sins of the fathers, my dear. Sins of the fathers. I didn't say it, and like bloody hell I didn't cause it! You can find it in your Bible, if you ever read the Bible."

"And what sins have we committed in this place, since all of us were living here, coming from various parts of the West Indies? Name me one. Go right ahead and name me one. Name me *one*. The only sins we committed in this place is obeying the blasted law. And from what I see, there is one law for us, and one for *them*."

"We raise our kids better than them."

"There isn't no argument 'gainst that, as far's I concerned."

"We're sitting down here in this hair-dressing place, in at Christophe, five middle-class bitches with not one worry in the world, except if our husbands going-crawl home before three in the morning, cattawauling."

"And with some o' these same white bitches!"

"Look at the five of us! I dress well. She dresses well. You dress well. Look at the dress that one is wearing. Five well-off bitches like us, with two-car garage, educated, decent and have more education than most women, than the average Canadian white woman. And with *all* this, we have to walk-'bout Toronto with our head down, and . . . "

"Shit! Not *my* head!"

"Christ, I looks them right in their blasted eye!"

"I know, I know. Individually. But I'm speaking as a rule, as a general rule. You know what I mean. Back home, we'd be ruling the roost. We'd be women with men and husbands that make decisions and run things. But here, if it isn't some bloody parking-lot attendant who hasn't been here for six months, and can't even talk English, if it is not some woman in the Eaton Centre, and don't mention Holt Renfrew or some o' them places in Yorkville Village, if it is not some damn racist cop, if it isn't some woman in a beat-up Toyota, while you or she are driving a BMW, or I behind the wheel of my husband's Benz, *anything*, any-blasted-body, we always have to explain *some* thing to them. Explain ourselves. Explain."

"My husband been driving a '68 Chev for ten years and would come home and curse *me*, and say how the cops in Toronto are the best. Last year, the son-of-a-bitch got his hand on some insurance money from a policy we had take out fifteen years ago, and he bought this second-hand Mercedes Benz I just referred to. It spends more time in the garage round the corner than parked in front our house. He bought a note book from Grand & Toy. A black little note book. Guess what he puts down in that little black book?"

"'Course, he puts down the mileage!"

"Or the miles!"

"What's the difference? Miles is mileage!"

"Not in my book, cherry," Christophe said.

"Every week. After ten o'clock. When he gets off the Don Valley Parkway. A cop. A cop in his arse! Three times a week, a cop pulls him over. As an average."

"They want him."

"Sending him a message."

"To go back to the '68 Chev."

"And here we are worrying about a little white girl that got picked up for shoplifting from a Mac's Milk. Ain't that something? We five black bitches, in a black hairdressing place, sitting down this lovely summer afternoon, worrying over a little white thief!"

"Harsh, though! Too harsh, cherry," Christophe said.

"How would *you* know? You ever given birth?"

"You don't have to be a woman to know that."

"A woman is a woman."

"I suppose you gonna say next that we have the same *thing* between our legs!"

"I wasn't getting personal, I was barely stating that a woman is a woman, and a mother is a mother, and . . . "

"A child is a child. Is that what you saying? That the one out there a few hours ago, arrested by the police, is the *same* as my eight-year-old? I bet you. I bet you *anything* that they took her a little way down the street from the Mac's Milk, and let her go, and that poor man who owns the store will never get satisfaction for whatever it is she took."

"What she took?"

"What she could've taken to justify the way the police came, with sireens blaring?"

"That's a strange comment coming from a black woman like you! With your eight-year-old?"

"What was her crime? We sitting down here all this time, and nobody knows what is her crime?"

"Stealing!"

"Who's next? This is my last time, cherries!"

"And being white."

"Suppose, just suppose, they took her away for her own good. Suppose it's the owner of the store down those stairs who did that to her?"

They could hear the footsteps coming up the stairs. Another customer, probably. The breeze was cooler now. No one snatched a white tissue from the jumbo-sized Kleenex box. The thin smoke from Christophe's cigarette moved in their faces. One woman sneezed.

"Bless you!"

"Sinus?"

"Allergies."

"Is these blasted cigarettes Christophe smoking!"

The footsteps stopped. All of them turned to look. It was a young white girl. No more than sixteen. They continued looking, not speaking, not believing their eyes. In the short silence that was heavy as the earlier humidity in the room, they went back over the scene down below on the street, the police cruisers and the policemen with their hands on their guns, and the short store owner in his stained white apron sweeping the dust from the entrance of his store. And when they saw her, a gasp came from their mouths, and they were paralyzed for a moment. And then they all rushed to the little child. A newspaper was in her hand. She was sixteen perhaps, as in their recollection; but her appearance rendered her helpless, unprotected and much smaller, a child in their eyes; and she seemed unable to move another step up the stairs. She had stopped at the round, hand-polished newel ball at the head of the banister. Christophe had tied a red ribbon round the newel last Christmas Eve, as decoration, and it had remained there ever since.

Her face was red. Red from the color of the blows that had struck her face. Her lips were thicker than the lips of any of the five women. Her face had no expression. At first, the women could not tell whether it was fright or shame.

They were sure that what they would hear from her mouth would be tales of pain, of assault. The thought went through each of their minds at the same piercing moment and, with five slight variations, their minds sped to their homes where they could see their own children. She looked as if she could be drugged. As if someone had given her something to drink that contained a drug. They did not believe she had taken it herself, by herself. They believed she was too innocent, too nice a little girl. She was a child. A newspaper was in her hand.

"Lisa!"

She held the afternoon *Star*.

Christophe said the name; and said it two more times. The third time he called her name, it was astonishment turning to unbelief. "Lisa?"

"You know this girl?"

"She's his niece. She delivers my paper."

"The corner store man?"

"Mr. Macdonald's niece, Lisa. She lives with him."

"This girl's in trouble, Chris, you can't see that? We have to do something for this poor child, man."

"Come, come," one of the women said. "Come."

"Ask her what happened?"

"Not now, man, not now. This is an emergency."

They half-carried her, surprised at her solid weight, to the chair where the last customer had sat; and they turned the tray with the shampoos and the pins and the curlers and the straightening agents aside, and they placed two soft cushions on the black leatherette bottom, to give growth and height to her body; and someone in the meantime was filling a sink with hot water; and the steam was rising higher than Christophe's cigarette smoke; he was holding a cigarette at the corner of his mouth, with one eye closed against the sting of the mentholated smoke; and one woman stood behind Lisa and held her gently against the hard black leatherette back of the chair; and one woman stood on each side, rubbing a hand over Lisa's chest which was rising and falling as if she were running from something, while the remaining two women took turns testing the heat of the water pouring out of the hot water tap, soaking white towels and testing the heat against their faces and gauging Lisa's ability to withstand the steam.

The hot towel made her start. And close her eyes. And it was then that they saw the tears on her beautiful skin. The towel moved over her cheeks, and she winced. She closed her eyes each time the towel touched her, but they could see the blueness of her ears. They could see the holes pierced in her ears, for earrings. They could see her teeth, pink against the strong fluorescent light pouring down from above; and when they shifted their position, running the warm towel round her neck, her teeth became sparkling white. They could see a scratch at the bottom of her neck. "Take off her dress." She still had the newspaper in her left hand.

"Not the whole dress, she's a child, after all. Just lower the blouse."

But someone raised the hem of her dress, and they saw it. For a moment, they stopped passing the lukewarm towel round her neck. They took the newspaper out of her hand and handed it to Christophe, and he dropped it on the floor. And the women who stood at the back of the tall leatherette chair, kept their hands on her wrists and on her left shoulder. Christophe stubbed his cigarette into a jar of hair pomade. The grease embedded the cigarette into itself. It was blood on her leg. On one leg.

"Blood?"

"Jesus Christ!"

"It's blood, all right."

The five women thought of their children, daughters and sons. The five women thought of their husbands. And one by one, but together in their fear and in their horror at the spectacle and what they knew the spectacle could mean, they went back over all those times, when their own children had been left with uncles and brothers-in-law, with close friends of their families, with their own husbands, fathers of their children, and they dared not travel back with too much memory and clarity and honesty. It was blood on her leg.

No one wanted to ask the question.

They knew the answer without having to pose it, even to themselves. They knew it could be one thing only. One cause. One kind of violence. It was the violence they knew. That they had lived with from birth. Pain and blood. Blood and pain, in a combination of joy, of sorrow, of natural function, and for those blessed with fertility, the pain and blood of giving birth.

"Why does it always have to be so?" said the woman whose daughter had been handcuffed. "Why does it have to be so, all the time?"

Her eyes were filled with tears. And she made no effort to hide her disconsolation. She was now holding the child's body, in her arms, and was rocking back and forth, her tears falling into the blonde hair of the child, who was now sobbing, and who had in all this time not spoken a word. "Why is it always this way with women? And for women?"

"Call the police."

"Who have the number for the police? I never had to call the police before."

"Call any number. Call *all* the numbers. One must be the police. Call 7-6-7!"

"That is S-O-S on the telephone dial."

"So call the police.

1993

An Invitation to Join

It was a bright day in the small Southern town. The rains had fallen all week, and the forgiveness in the weekend sky meant assurance for the dwellers in the low-income housing project. This day would be a blessing, and it would last gloriously until the sun went down behind the tops of the pine trees which towered over the metal clotheslines in the yard of the project. The clotheslines were bright with washing. There were pieces of clothing and bedding which had seen better days, but had been rendered almost new by the careful hands of the women. And they certainly were clean. A few patches were in them, here and there, where eagerness for cleanliness had tampered with the lifespan of the fabrics.

The women who washed these clothes were sitting among the spiral clotheslines after a long week of hard work as maids and as factory workers, at homes or in the small businesses in the town; and as they sat, they seemed relaxed. They watched with pride the evidence of the end of their week on the swinging clotheslines.

It was early Saturday afternoon. The yard on to which all the kitchen doors faced was crowded with these women and their children. The large hips and big breasts of most of the women told you something about their eating habits: not many thin women were among them. Occasionally a man, recovering from the previous night's party in the project, or just come from his job, come perhaps to visit his child and to deliver the support-money, would draw closer to the crowd and sit beside a woman. But there would be no conversation. The large women seemed to be all queens in the middle age of their heavy bodies and wisdom. The man would then stand, not talking still, not even to his child, and when another man recognized him, he would gladly move away. And you knew that a heavy burden of having to say something to the mother of his child, or to his estranged wife, or to the child, would be taken off his mind. Just his presence would be there. And the children, his children, would acknowledge and respect his presence by an occasional glance, and then they would crowd around the four strapping muscular black musicians who were untangling the electric wires from their speakers and setting up the drums. The project yard was having a bazaar and dance.

The men, all of them, held cans in their hands. They would raise these to their lips, and when they took them away, the feeling in their faces would change, the color in their eyes would become heavier, and they would laugh from their bowels. Some women drank from these cans, and the same thing happened to their faces, and also to their already slow movements which were beginning to be as sluggish as the dying wind which had now left the clotheslines almost alone.

The young woman in the house with the man visiting her felt she was above the project and never hung her clothes outside. She felt more secure hanging them on the shower curtain and on chair backs just outside the bathroom door. She was smaller and younger than the other women, and was living in the project because of a mistake in her marriage, as she put it. Religiously she kept her distance from the communal yard, deciding instead to spend the afternoon arranging her few new pieces of furniture bought on time to make her living room appear as no reflection of her marital fortunes. The furniture was as cheap as the meat she bought to feed her daughter with: for she had no alimony and no child-support, because her husband had caught her with a man. But her living looked grand. She always made a point about appearances. There was a lamp table which looked like polished mahogany, substantial as the pines beyond the horizon of clothes poles; until you leaned your weight against it, by mistake or by design, and then you found out that it was made of firm cardboard.

She had just wiped the dust from this table with the back of her arm when the front door was temporarily covered by a shadow. The man visiting her thought that perhaps the sun was not keeping its word. But soon there was a gentle knocking, a touch, intended neither to scare nor to interrupt unduly. The light returned, and there, before the front door which nobody used, was a tall straight young man dressed in a black suit which could have just come from the cleaners; and beside him, equally respectable in bearing and in clothes, was a woman. The woman was old enough to have been the young man's mother and the young woman's mother, too. She was thin and her white pleated dress was well below her knees. She and the young man both wore hats. And the sun was sweating them.

They were not project dwellers because the young woman would have recognized them, even at a glance. But she was face to face with them now; and she felt they tried by their presence to make her think more deeply and with more regret of her own presence in the low-rental project. They had come to talk to her about her soul, they said. She became nervous, and excused herself; and came back to the man in the kitchen. She made one last gesture of tidiness over the fake table, carried the gesture over the hips of her cut-down jeans, and having found enough courage, she went back to the door.

She wore a smile on her face. The older woman outside the screen door smiled back. The younger woman was glad she had kept the screen door locked. The old woman's smile was a genuine one, practiced after many mornings of disturbing housewives. She had learned how to smile. The younger woman's smile was false: she smiled because she knew she was expected to smile at people who called; and this version of her smile had something to do with the way the man was dressed, so differently from those in the yard.

They told her that they belonged to some religion, and she smiled also because she felt the Christian woman was a lady. She called anybody a lady if they were tidily dressed; and she thought she saw her mother's face in the old woman's smile. She smiled as she had been taught to smile by her mother when as a child she had accompanied her to church — a habit she had continued until the church had instructed her about the future of what a Christian-minded black woman should achieve: a good stable marriage, and the sure hope of a long lasting respectability. She had in fact seen respectability for two years, with her husband who married her one year after he got her pregnant, and who lived with her one more year, to balance off his conscience. Church to this young woman was now a risky business.

"May we come in, please, miss, to talk to you about Christ?" The woman said it just before the man did. She seemed to know it would be easier for her to impose her age upon the younger woman; and perhaps, with her Christian knowledge of the world, she felt that the man's attention had already begun to stray to the frayed edges of the younger woman's improvised tight-pants.

"I'm busy," the woman said. She was thinking of her housework. And she was thinking of getting away from the project before the bazaar and the noise started. She always talked of getting away from the project for good. She felt she had to move to save her daughter's ears from the obscene language of the project children around her, and she had to protect the child from the pounding of the electric guitar and the drums which had now started up in the yard. "I'm busy." She was a woman of few words, just as she was of small means.

"But, it won't take a minute to talk about Christ." The older woman seemed by now to know she had imposed her age and the memory of mother upon the younger woman; but what she did not know was that the younger woman was very determined, and that she prided herself on being independent. "I don't need a man," she often said. And yet it was, in spite of her boast, not really independence, rather more like stubbornness and hard-headedness that guided her life. The man in the house with her had pointed this out to her, and it was then that she had first used her chorus, "I don't need a man."

The older woman was saved from knowing this. However, the invitation about Christ was not taken up; it was rather pleasantly despised. The young woman went into the kitchen where the man was sitting, listening, and said, "Gimme a quarter. Or a dime. A dime would do. Lemme deal with these two motherfuckers at my door." She went back to them. The old lady was preparing her words in her mind, and her eyes focused on the young woman's face. She opened her mouth to talk, just as the young woman opened the screen door a crack, and, caught between her first and second words, the old lady felt the dime dropped into her palm. She did not realize that her palm was open. For when the young woman slammed the door shut and started to move away, the old woman was still about to speak.

When the young woman returned to the man, she looked relieved. The man watched her, and before he could make up his mind whether or not she had turned them away from her door because she was busy washing dirty dishes, she let him know through an expression of her body and her attitude that indeed it was more than a small victory which she had won, through the help of the dime. It was a victory of her independence.

"I know how to deal with them Christians. A dime stopped them from bugging me. They ain' too much for me to deal with!" And she laughed, as she would laugh to celebrate a petty theft, when she passed through the check-out line in a grocery store, or in a department store, with a seventy-nine cent item which she always claimed, with the proper ideology, she had "liberated." The man was watching her now, and trying to understand her logic about those things. He found himself studying her body more than her mind. But he could see that it was very important to her that she had *dealt* with the two Christians, with a dime. She brightened and the slump, which would sometimes rest on her spirit and be reflected on her shoulders like a downcast brooding mood, disappeared.

The music was lively and loud in the yard. Her daughter was upstairs moaning about having to go to the bathroom to wash, and to brush her teeth. She wanted to go outside to see the people and to play with a little boy next door. Yesterday, this little boy had struck her on the crown of her head with a toy wooden baseball bat.

Suddenly, there was a scream in the yard. The music did not stop. The woman's eyes grew larger, her hands moved away from the greasy dishwater, the slump came back to her posture; she cursed herself for being in the housing project, and ran to the screen door. She beckoned the man to look. "Look! Come and see!" She was as furious as when she had heard her own daughter scream. "That little goddamn bastard. When're you going to take me outta this damn project?" Her daughter's four-year-old friend was striking an older girl on the head with the same baseball bat. "He should be in the goddamn major leagues!" she said. And when the boy had beaten the little girl down to the cement in the unswept yard, he opened his mouth and yelled for help. A woman emerged from among the clotheslines and the garbage pails; and when she saw her little boy crying, she parted the screen of the two hanging bedsheets with her head; bent down, and took up the girl from the cement. Then she raised her hand, and when it fell, it landed flat on the girl's face. It fell a second time. This time, on the girl's ear. The woman looked satisfied now. She had aimed for the girl's ear in the first place. She then disappeared into one of the opened back doors, with her son on her hip.

The sun came out again. The two Christians emerged from among the clotheslines, and entered the yard where the musicians and the men and the women and the children were dancing. All of a sudden, it looked as if the yard with the people in it was taken up in the noise of the music, and that the music was voices and laughter and screaming and men greeting each other with palms outstretched and then slapped, and screaming children. A few dogs sniffed at people's ankles and then wandered off.

The little girl in the house with the man and the young woman pressed her face flat, her nose broadened against the curtains in the kitchen window, looking through them, longing to go out.

"Get away from there!" the woman shouted. The little girl was transfixed to the view in the yard. The young woman kept her hands in the dishwater, and she seemed to forget, for a while, that the child had not obeyed. "Out there is not for you! Get upstairs!"

The sun had left the yard, and was now in the kitchen, like a finger compelling the child outside; and the child, feeling the warmth of the sun on her face and the music in the yard, shuffled a little and then ran upstairs. When she reached her bedroom, she threw herself noisily on the hardwood floor. The mother kept her hands in the dishwater. The child had thrown herself on the floor, in her own way, many times before. The man imagined that the woman was clapping her hands in the detergent suds in a kind of victory over the child. For the child was farther away now from the noise and the music and the yard and the people out there; and the man was made to feel that the young woman wanted to shield this part of the project's obscenity and noise from her daughter. The child was quiet now. The slight slump in the mother's shoulders disappeared.

The two Christians were walking like strangers through a dancing clump of women, as they went up to another door. The music continued. The two Christians were too far away for the man to hear what they were saying; but the housewife who answered the door must have told them the same thing as the young woman; must have shown her displeasure at their coming to talk to her about Christ, on a day like this, when all her neighbors were around taking part in the bazaar and the dance. She must have been embarrassed by the Christians' choice of visiting her on this Saturday afternoon, when there was all this noise and gaiety and drinking out of cans and short glasses with designs on them, right outside her door; and with the Christians witnessing all this sodom of riotous living, and neither of them being from the project, or from any neighboring project, she must have felt that her women-friends were disappointed in her, were calling her a traitor, suspecting her, for they had now begun to look at her with questions in their eyes, wondering whether she was really "together" or had been slipping out of the project and going to church on Sunday mornings, after she left them at the long parties in their kitchens, while they slept all day to recover from the cheap wine and the beer and the grass.

The sun was making the old woman's dress more chastizingly severe; and the primness of its style and cut took her face out of its natural mold and fashioned it into a stronger, more vengeful face. The white dress made her look blacker than she was; and her clothes seemed to be the voice of her disgust at these people with the bare backs and short skirts and bright colors and jeans cut-down so short and fitting so tight that you could see the creases of their private parts. The Christian man held his peace and his place, and he watched the women's bodies. He stood just a pace behind the old woman.

The music burst out in a loud rhythm and blues number, and the drummer went wild, and more than once the man visiting the young woman thought that the drummer had seen Africa on the faces of the dancing people. The two Christians were like statues in the midst of this bazaar yard. Through this music, these two Christians passed like deaf-mutes, like two missionaries moving through the thickness of an infested and infected jungle; two strangers in a small town upon which they had happened, by mistake. The children were interpreting the music through their improvisation of the movements of the men and the women. They were moving from side to side, correct in their following of the drummer's hands and head; and they looked like small black penguins. But they were penguins with the difference of precise movement to the beating of the drums. The man on the guitar did something wondrous with his blocked chords, and the bodies moved with his fingers, and became more abandoned; the children improvised their steps out of the proportion of the older dancers' movements, and the two Christians just walked to another door, to save a soul, to get a donation for their church, to call the person inside outside to witness the presence of the Lord, to make him realize that He was out here in the midst of all this Babylonian noise. The little girl upstairs in the house with the young woman and the man was moaning, and out of tune with the music. From the distance, something like oily water appeared on the drummer's back; and the muscles in his torso snapped and shook like the sticks on the snare drum, plucked in that rhythm of the song.

The two Christians moved to another door, because no one answered the door they had just left. And their pride or their self-assurance told them not to ask any of the dancers in the yard if the person who lived there was now here, was one among the dancing people crowding round the musicians, among the bizarre outfits in the yard. The people did not talk to them. The two of them walked against the beat of the music which seemed to touch neither their ears nor their bodies. All of a sudden, they seemed to be invisible persons. The man in the house with the woman, and the little girl upstairs, were the only two persons who were seeing the Christians. The young woman merely looked at them, and tried always to stop her daughter from watching them.

They were now marching from door to door, and the yard was full of people who continued dancing and drinking; and they were talking to each other as they were walking; and in all this, they seemed very far away from the people and the yard, upon some Galilean dream, ignoring the people, far from the joyfulness in the stormy music. The man playing the bass guitar began jumping up with the music in his fingertips, and he paused once in his plucking to take off his shirt, to give himself more freedom. The two Christians stopped at another door. Nobody was inside. They were all outside. But nobody was watching the Christians now: they were all watching the musicians. The Christians knocked at the door. And the music became louder and wilder. The children grew braver in their steps and in their imitation of their elders, and then recklessly, they jumped like the bass player was jumping.

Nobody came to the door at which the Christians were knocking. The man in the house with the woman could not tell whether the music had taken the Christians' knocking up in its hands, or whether they were knocking against the rhythm of the blues song. He could not tell whether there was anyone inside the house, or whether the music had killed the sound of the Christians' knocking. But suddenly, a woman appeared at the same door, looked at them, and walked past, and joined the dancing in the yard. She was the same woman who had earlier parted the hanging bedspreads on the line to slap the little girl whose head was in the way of her little boy's baseball bat. She carried the bat in her hand. It looked as if it was an overgrown finger. This woman was the only one who stole a glance at the Christians. Everybody else was drinking and dancing. The little girl in the house with the young woman washing her dishes was dancing too. And the man felt the music come right up into the bright kitchen like the rays of the sun, and he could not prevent his feet from tapping on the soiled linoleum floor. The young woman took her hands out of the greasy dishwater, and, as she wiped them on her jeans, she moved just a little bit with the music. The music was brighter, stronger now, and more fierce than the sun. It was a glorious Saturday Southern afternoon. The children were being baptized in the music, in the meaning of their lives in the project and in the beautiful noise. They roamed about, like the dogs, in a trance.

The Christians held their Bibles firmly in their hands, together with the religious magazines. And when they realized that nobody was coming out to welcome them, the man bent down to the mat at the door, deposited a magazine on the doorstep and then left. Door by door, he and the Christian lady moved around the bazaar and the dancing, trying their luck, depositing magazines, until they were back at the house nearest the bandstand, which was almost hidden by the people.

"Look! Look out there, and see something," the young woman said to the man. "Even the way they dress. Even the clothes they wearing. They don't even look like black people!" The man had never before heard her give so much attention to any matter except her own appearance at work and on the street; her comments now made him look outside. And indeed, the old woman's long, sedately cut white dress took on a strange meaning in the midst of all the colors in the clothes and the skins of people in the yard. The old woman held her head high, and apparently she knew how to keep her ears closed to everything but that which she intended to tell these happy people. She carried her head with great pride. The man walked behind her, in attitude and in posture. "You know, I look at that bitch, and I see my mother. Pardon me for saying so. I don't mean my mother was a bitch. She was a Christian, too. But something about that one out there, how she's interfering with the bazaar . . . "

It was at this point that they had reached the door of the last house they thought of visiting. The music was now too much for their knocking. The sticks and the drums and the guitar were in rhythm with the expectations of the people in the yard, and with those few who were still indoors, not with any knocking by the two Christians. Nobody saw them: nobody saw their knocking. They stood with their backs to the musicians and to the people. The people were dancing. A few men were dancing with children in one hand, and liquor in the other; holding the children close, very close to the music in their own veins, so that the children might feel the pulsation of older blood, and in time learn through that surging blood the message which future drums and sticks and guitars might suggest to them. A few men were dancing with beer cans in their hands. The women were dancing by themselves. Even those few, too heavy and too fat from beer to move easily, who had decided to remain on their chairs leaned against their doors, these women rocked the chairs, or moved their heavy bottoms in the seats of the chairs. The yard was one: the people and the yard and the music: threaded on a string of black beads, joined to the noise and the laughter and the music in a circle of mind. The two Christians stood like their judges at the door, demanding whoever was inside to come out, to face the music of their dancing lives, to listen to the music of chastisement which they had come to preach on this bright afternoon. Nobody among the dancers, some of whom were within touching distance of the two Christians, offered a word to them. They ignored the Christians: and the Christians ignored them.

"And look at that blasted man. A young man like he! He should be somewhere else, with a woman." And she laughed, and conveyed the real meaning of her words to the man by the winding of her small tight, cut-down jeans, as she went upstairs to tell her child to shut up and stop moaning. The man's eyes climbed the stairs on her hips, and he thought he should follow her, but the child was upstairs, and the music had stopped in the meantime.

The man went to the door to see whether the two Christians had finally silenced the people, had killed their joy, or had succeeded in being heard and were now preaching to the bazaar. The man pictured all this in his mind before he looked outside: had the Christians used their power over the power of the music?

But the two Christians were not visible. Only the people. All of them were standing up, in a circle. But it was most unlike the circle of dance, or ritual or of emotion. It was a tense, enquiring leaning of bodies towards some center. It was a center of activity. Their bodies were leaning over to the magnet of a hidden attraction within the circle. The bare strong body of the drummer was shining through the other bodies; and the guitar player was standing on his toes, straining his body as he had previously been straining his fingers and his face muscles, to reach the pitch and tone of the note he wanted. Then the man saw the baseball bat. It was over the heads of the people, as if a batter was loosening up before taking his turn at the plate. And then it was gone.

The sun was behind the horizon of trees and clotheslines and bed sheets; and there was no sound in the yard. Only the rushing of expectation in the blood and in the breathing; something like the presumed noise of anticipated explosion. The children were either held back on the fringe of the circle deliberately; or their small bodies prevented them from pushing closer to witness what was happening inside the circle. It seemed to have been a circle of wisdom and of knowledge that was understood to contain too much for their tender apprehension. Or it could have been that in their wisdom, they understood that they could only be on the fringe, and like the other customs that ruled their lives in the yard, they held back, instinctively.

And then the circle broke. People walked casually back to where they had been standing, near to the musicians, to where they had been sitting before. The sun broke through the trees, and it was bright again, and it was lively again, it was a yard full of noise, and the drummer was caught in the act of sitting on his seat. The drummer was regal in this sitting posture. And his hands began to express a more complicated understanding of his past; his past in music, and his present in life; and his face became wilder and at the same time, more beautiful. The other musicians were like men transported on some journey of mysterious but acknowledged beautiful essence.

When the last of the women reached her seat, she placed the baseball bat beside her, as a musician would rest his instrument, and the people were all dancing again; only the children were standing near what had been the circle. But they soon moved away, no longer drawn to the circle; and they took up their places just as their parents had done. Custom had already run its heavy-handed finger throughout their young limbs.

And on the ground, in what had been the center of the circle, were the two Christians. Their Bibles and religious tracts were scattered on the ground. The wind was ruffling them like discarded public notices. As the man watched from the door, he saw the old woman rise from a sitting position and bend closer to the young man. When she challenged her position, the man saw that blood was splattered on her white dress. The blood was coming from the young man on the ground. He could not tell whether the man on the ground had moved, or was able to move. For a long time, the old woman did not move. Both their bodies were motionless in the same way as their bodies had been dead to the music. Their bodies were motionless, the man could see that now, and very still, and very ugly on the hot cement yard, with the Bibles and pamphlets scattered around them in a rough crude circle of silent witness.

And then, running down the stairs in the apartment where he was visiting, was the young woman, with her child in her arms. She had gone upstairs, and must have seen the circle when it first formed, from her upstairs window. Now, she was rushing back down, cuddling her child, with her right hand on the child's forehead. Her hand partially covered the child's eyes.

Outside the house, the people continued dancing. There was the wildness of the music in her eyes, and the meaning of the circle in her tense body. She was wild in a different way from the fierceness in the music. And she was not in the rhythm of the yard as she came down the stairs.

She looked in the man's eyes to find the meaning of the yard; and when she could not find it, or thought that the man had no answer to please her, since he did not speak, she held her child closer to her, and pressed her against her small bosom. Her tears fell on the crown of the child's head. "You know why they did that? Why the people didn't raise a finger or stop their bazaar . . . "

The man became very frightened to hear the answer. For he knew the answer. He felt the meaning of the music was the answer: the answer and the music and the yard and the woman with the baseball bat were the answer, he felt. And then she said, "When're you gonna get me outta this damn project?" She moved back upstairs, pressing her daughter close to her bosom. "You ain' no man. That's why I always say I don't need no man." The man opened the door and walked out on to the yard. The yard was full of noise and sun and people dancing. But the two Christians were still on the ground. He looked for the woman who held the baseball bat and wondered if she was the answer; but he was more intent on getting away from the project.

1971

When He Was Free and Young and He Used to Wear Silks

In the lavishness of the soft lights, indications of detouring life that took out of his mind the concentration of things left to do still, as a man, before he could be an artist, lights that put into his mind instead a certain crawling intention which the fingers of his brain stretched towards one always single table embraced by a man and a wife who looked like his woman, her loyalty bending over the number of beers he poured against the side of her bottle he had forgotten to count, in those struggling days when the atmosphere was soft and silk and just as treacherous, in those days in the *Pilot Tavern* the spring and the summer and the fall were mixed into one chattering ambition of wanting to have meaning, a better object of meaning and of craving, better meaning than a beer bought on the credit of friendships and love by the tense young oppressed men and women who said they were oppressed and tense because they were artists and not because they were incapable, or burdened by the harsh sociology of no talent, segregated around smooth black square tables from the rest of the walking men and walking women outside the light of our *Pilot* of the Snow and had not opened nor shut their minds to the meaning of their other lives; legs of artless girls touching this man's in a hide-and-seek under the colorblind tables burdened by conversation and aspirations and promises of cheques and hopes and bedding and beer and bottles; in those days when he first saw her, and the only conversation she could invent was "haii!" because she was put on a pedestal by husbandry, and would beg his pardon without disclosing her eyes of red and shots and blots and bloodshot liquor; the success of his mind and the woman's mind in his legs burnt like the parts of the chicken he ate, he was free and young and he was wearing the silks of indecision and near-failure. But he mustn't forget the curry for the curry was invented by people and Blessings, Indians; or perhaps they were the intractable Chinese, the curry was the saviour of his mind and indigestion just as the woman guarded for no reason in the safe soft velvet of her unbelieving husband's love, guarding her in her turns as they sat opposite each other in the different callings of paint and metals and skin and negatives and thirst during all those dark days in the *Pilot*, the curry was the saviour of a madness which erupted in his mouth with the after-taste of the bought beer and the swirling bowel after the beer and after the curry; she was like the lavishness in the light except that the color surrounding her in the darkened room hid everything, every thought in his mind just as the wholesome curry in the parts of chicken hid the unwholesome social class which it could not always distinguish from the bones any suitable dog in shaggy-haired and shaggy-sexed Rosedale would eat, and if the dog in Rosedale and the dog in him did eat them the dog might make them, like this woman sitting with her drinking man, into an exotic meal packaged through some sense of beer and the sense of time and place, and looking at it in one imaginative sense, turn it into something called *soul food*: now, there are many commercial and irrelevant soul food kitchens these days in night-time Toronto, and any man could, if he had no soul and silks on the body of his thoughts, if his soul were occupied and imprisoned only with thoughts of *her* sitting there badly in the wrong light of skin, he could make a fortune of thoughts and sell them like dog meat and badly licensed food to all the becauseful people who wore jeans and heavy-weave expensive sweaters walking time into eternity in dirty clothes and rags because they were the "beautiful people" as someone called their ugliness, like her of soon-time piloted to a tavern, married to a man who did not deserve the understanding of her; these the becauseful people, people who didn't have to do this because they didn't want to think about that, because they were people living in the brighter light of the soft darkness which they all liked because they were artists and people; the becauseful people like her, liked her and likened her to a white horse not because of the length of her legs nor the gray in her mind, but because in the lavishness of the wholesome light of the *Pilot* she looked as secure and was silent as the fingers of the tumbling avoirdupoids of the man who made mud-pies in the piles of quarters and dollars mixmasterminding them in the cash register. It is so dark sometimes in the *Pilot* that if you wear dark glasses, which all the artists wore on their minds, you may stumble up the single step beside the fat man sitting on a humptydumpling stool and where she always sat on her pedestal of distance and protection chastised in pickled beer, and you may not know whether it is afternoon on Yonge Street outside, for time now has no boundaries, only the dimensions of her breasts which her husband keeps in the palm of his flickering eyeballs; it is so dark in the early afternoon that with your dark glasses on, you might be in Boston walking the climb in the street climbing like a hill to where the black and colored people live; or you might be here in Toronto walking where the colored people and the kneegrows say they "live" but where they squat, here where E. P. Taylor says he does not live but where his influence strangles some resident life and breeds racehorses of the people, where Garfield Weston lives in a mad biscuit box crumbling into broken crackers; in the lavishness of the night thrown from your dark glasses, you might stumble upon a pair of legs and not know the color of time, or what shape it is, or where you are, or who you are: he thinks he should haul his arse out of this bar of madness and mad dreams, drinking himself into an erection stiff to the touch of ghosts in her legs and the legs of the tables. He had seen her, "this young tall thing," walking to the bar through winter in boots and rain in blue jeans and sandals, insisting without words in the fierce determination of her poverty and dedication to nothing she could prove or do that this was her personal calvary to the cross of being Canada's best poetic-photographer, unknown in the meaning of her life beyond the tavern, unknown like the word she would use, "budgerigar," having years ago thrown out Layton, Cohen, Birney and Purdy in the dishwater of her weatherbeaten browbeaten body and heavy sweaters; he could see her mostly among women stuck to their chairs by the chewing-gum beer, free women freed by their men for an afternoon while art imprisoned the men with beer, wallpaper along the talking walls like flowers, their own flower long faded into the dust of the artificial potato chips they all ate in the nitty of their gloom because it was like grit for their reality, their "dinner" an unknown reality like her word, "budgerigar," in the despised bourgeois vocabulary and apartment-lairs of their lives; and in this garden of grass growing in their beds he had handpicked her out five years ago, this one wallflowering woman who wore large hats in the summer-street, and cream sweaters in winter. She always sat beside the man who sat as if he was her husband; tall in her thighs with the walk of a man, this white horse woman with the body of a bull; and the eye of her disposition through the bottom of the beer bottle warned him that "the gentlest touch of his desire might be fatal to the harmony" of the two ordered beers which they drank like Siamese twins in the double-bed of their marriage. He, the watchman-man, was harnessed by island upbringing and fear in the lavishness of the dim light, ravishing her ravishing beauty with his eyes they could not see, eyes they saw only once and spoke to once when they saw him entering or leaving; for five years. For five years of not knowing whether the sun would sink in the space between her breasts, or whether butter ever dried in the warmth of that melting space, he watched her like a timekeeper. Once he saw her leaving her husband's side and he followed her spinster's canter all the way in his mind down the railing guard of parallel eyes honoring her backside sitting on the spinning stools where the working class reigned and into the bathroom, past two wash basins and the machine that saved pregnancies and populations with a quarter, on to the toilet bowl, under the dress she had plucked her hand and had pulled up her dress and did not soil her seat or sit on it because it was in the *Pilot,* and he smiled when she reappeared with fresh garlic on her lipstick mouth; and he looked at the edges of her powder, and he looked into the lascivious dimness and saw her and smiled and she smiled but the smile belonged to the mudpiling man at the cash register or to another table where they were talking about the Isaacs Gallery and the Artists Jazz Bann where Dennis Burton's garter belts were exhibited in stiff canvas and wore houndstooth suits and the thick heavy honey of colors and materials thicker than words. He had walked around her life in circles and bottle rings of desire and of lust and she was always there, the center of dreams frizzled on a pillow soaked with the tears of drinking; he followed her like a detective in the wishes of his dreams, and from his inspection of a future together got a headache over them and over her, and over the meanings of these dreams. *Mickey* and *Cosmospilitane* and other dream books did not ease the riders of the head in his pain, and nothing could unhinge his desperation from the wishful slumber of those unconscious nights of double broker vision. And then, like a cherry falling under the tree because the sun had failed it, after long thoughts and wishes of waiting she fell into his path, and he almost crushed her. He remembered the long afternoons waiting for the indelible rings of the melting bottles to ripen, waiting for the departure of shoppers who lived above the Rosedale subway station to stop shopping in the Pickering Farms market so he could shop and not have to listen to the loud-talking friendly butcher in the fluorescent meat department, and whisper loud under the sun-tanned arms of the meaty housewives and commonlawwives, "One pound of pigs feet, chicken necks and bones — for soup," and hear the unfeeling bitch, "Er-er! Who's next?" behind the counter dressed like a surgeon with blood on his chest, saying, "You're really taking care of that dog, ain't you, sir?" Godblindyou, dog! godblindyou, butcher! This meat is for the dog in front of you; and he remembered her now, single, on this summer-street under the large hat as she was five years ago under the drinking mural under the picture of hotdogs and fried eggs that some heartless hungry painter drew on the wall where she sat beneath when she was in the *Pilot*. He fell into the arms of her greeting like an apple to the core and he looked down into her dress and saw nothing not even one small justification for the long unbitten imprisonment selling his nuts next door. She was away now from the *Pilot*. And he did not even know her name: not for five years, he never was introduced to her name: "Hurley or Weeks . . . Weeks or Hurley . . . " either one would do? "they are both mine, and I use either one any time," but Weeks is her maiden time; although she was no longer a maiden, though single and with no husband for weeks and months now. There was no large gold ring on the finger of her personal self-regard, which she said ended mutual on a visit of her once-accompanying husband warming radically, like forgotten beer, into her haphazard lover; there was no bitterness in the eyes of her separation because she missed only the cooking which he would do every evening, when she said she was too tired, or couldn't be bothered to cook, which was every evening, when he would do the cooking in her kitchen and leave her afterwards like the dishes, panting from thirst and a thorough cleaning, so her eyes said on this summer afternoon, hungry in the frying pan of their double-bed bedroom, where he kept the materials of his stockings, feet and trade, his love of meddling with medals and metals and sculpture, and where she kept a large overgrown blow-up of her brother's success in the cowboys and movies in the West, shooting the horses over the head of the never-setting bedpost, her brother with a gun in his hand, a gun loaded at the ready to be fired at the nearest rivalry of badmen and badwomen, a gun which he gave her, a gun which remained nevertheless loaded, hung-up, cocked and frustrated and constipated from no practice or trigger-happiness; and this she talked about; she did not stay in one place, she said she was rambling, not along the streets because she did not like to walk, but that she was rambling and that she had to be alone in the constitutional of her thoughts, from one bar to the next bar; she admitted she might have a problem, but it was not this problem which changed her husband's heart into a dying lover drifting apart at the semen in the widening sea of her jammed ambition: "I do not know what I want to do, I know what I don't want to do, and that is stay married, but I don't really know what I really want to do"; she bore her wandering in her hair, loose and landing on her broad shoulders like the rumps of two cowboy horses; and her dress was short, short enough for the eyes to roam about in and follow her over all her landscape at a canter — that's how she was put away; she was put away as if she could be put to pasture for work and for love and for bearing responsibility: "I know I don't want to have a child. What am I going to *do* with a child? I know I can have children and I know I can have a child. I want a child, but not now, because a child *needs* love . . . and and and I I I haven't any left right now for . . . " He looked at her and wandered and wondered why she couldn't give a child a chance, a chance of love, with all the pasture in her body, all her body, with all her breasts, with all her milk bottled in brassieres that had no bones stitched in them, with all her thighs that spilled over her dress-hem, "A-hem!" But perhaps she was really talking about another kind of love and another need for love, which was not the same as the need for love her lover-husband needed from her when she was a child in his arms late at night, and was crying with him in the double-minded cradle of his sculptures. *Haii! Austin!* He looked into her eyes and made a wish that her body under his eye would not be completely bloodless as her hands sometimes seemed five years ago when she was fresh from the basement washroom, and the snow on the women walking out of the cold corner of Yonge and Bloor in the arctic months; that her body would not reveal the theft he had in mind to put it through, the theft her husband had put it through; that she would not be like Desdemona and wax, but that she would be a queen from the entrails of Africa and Nefrititi, plucked out in olive blackness luscious to the core of her imagined seed, like the Marian from the alligator troughs of Georgia. He dreamed a long dream standing there on the street with summer before her, and he killed the color of her body because it needed too much Eno's before it could go down; and he wrapped her in a coffin stained in wood in blood, and made her again to look like Marian from way across the bad lands of enroped and ruptured Georgia. *Haii, Austin!*: he was back in those good old days, good because they had no responsibility for paying the good deeds artists incurred in debts and made them bad, bad debts and artists on the segregation of walls and memories; he was here and he was there in Georgia in the double ghost of a second, for artists were bad for debts and for business in those young days when he was free and the only silk was his ambition; he remembered her in those days, and on this summer afternoon already obliterated in the history of the past, nights in the crowded *Pilot Tavern*, searching the faces of the girls and women for one face that would have had a meaning like Marian's, and he could not find one head with truth written in its clenched curled black-peppers of hair, one mask with the intelligent face of Nefrititi the history of Africa from Africa, not from the store on Yonge Street, "Africa Modern" selling blackness cheap to whites, written brazenly upon its ivory; a mask, a mask from that land not unlike Georgia, he had watched for one face like a timekeeper keeping a watch that had no end of time in it, and he had to paint the faces black, blacken them as he had blackened the red clay sculpture a woman did of him once, like an Indian in his blood, and had made it something approaching the man he wanted to be, something like the man Amiri Baraka talked about becoming in the later years of his new muslim wisdom; he remembered the sweet-smelling Georgia woman in those soft nights when the bulbs were silk as moths among the books overheard like a heavy chastisement to be intelligent, like a too-self-conscious intention; with the sherry which she drank in proper southern quantities, like bourbon warm to the blood, and her fingers were long and pointed and expressive, impressing upon his back, once, her once beautiful intent, as they writhed in pain with glory and some victory, after she lay like a submarine in a watery pyre of soft soapy suds, white flowers of *Calgon* upon her black vegetation, going and coming, he remembered her in the shiny cheap stockings proclaiming her true color of mind and pocket and spirit and background and intention: a *black student*; a black woman, black and shining in that velvet of time and black skin, a black woman, black and powerful down to her black marrow; there was something in the ring of her laughter, perhaps in the gurgle of her bourbon, in the *ding-ing* of her voice when she laughed in two accents, northern and southern, something that said she was true-and-through beautiful, and because she was black, and because she was beautiful, she was beautiful; she could withstand any ravages of history, of storms, of stories that wailed in the rope-knotted night of Georgia; she could stand on a pedestal under any tree which no village smithy in white Georgia would dare to stand up to: a man who had no burning conviction could not put his arms as high as her waist, for she had seen certain sheets of a whiteness which were wrapped around a black man's testicles in a bestial passion-play, and she had seen, in her mother's memories, this play as it showed the germ of someone's bed linen made into sheets that were worn as masks of superiority testing a presumption that some men would always walk on all-fours like a southern lizard; *haii, austin!* This woman standing on the summer-street in the silk of time stopped without desire; and that woman lying in the rich water with her smell whom he remembered best holding down her head in love, in some shame, looking into a book of tears because his words were spoken harder than the text of any African philosophy. He remembered that woman and not this woman, well: Marian, his; ploughing the fields of poverty and a commitment in her barefoot days, dress tangled amongst the tango of weeds, sticking in the crease of her strength silken from perspiration, and her dreams cloggy as the soil, and in her after-days in the northern rich-poor city, her long-fingered hands again dipping into the soil of soiled sociology Jewished out of some context, maintained backyards, maintained yardbird poverty, backward in instruction the smell of soil the soiled smell of the land in which she was born, the smell of poverty, a new kind of perfume to freshen her northern ideas, a new kind of perfume truer than the fragrance of an underarm of ploughing, more telling than the tale in the perspiration of her body, in the fields, in the sociology, in the kitchen, in the bed, in the summer subway sweaty and safe with policemen and black slum dwellers from Dorchester, in the heat, in the bus stations, in the bathtub in Boston; a perfume of sweet sweat that clothed her body with a blessing of pearls, like a birthwrap of wet velvet skin: "Honnnneee!" The word she always used; honey was the only taste to use; honey was the only word she used always; for it was a turbulence of love and time from the lowered eyelids from the vomiting guts up to the tip of the touch of her skin. She was a woman; she was a woman without woe; she was to be his woman, she should be here in the summer-street; now in the summer-street, he watches this alter-native of that woman, he understands that the transparency of this dress, tucked above her knees by the hand of fashion, is really nothing but the vagueness of this doll; he sees now that this transparency is the woman, like the negatives she meddled in, for five years' time, like the film on a pond's surface, like white powder, like a glass of water with Eno's in it, like a glass of water in the sun, the water clear and unpolluted, the water the top soil of the sediments at the sentimental bottom; he wanted to mix this water with that water in the bathtub in Boston, the water and the mud into some heart, into that thick between-the-toes soul of the Georgia woman; he wanted to break the glass that contained that water for the *Calgon* bath and the sherry and the bathwater; break the vessel, spill and despoil, spill and expel this wateringdown of the drink of his long thirst; stir it up and mix the sentiments in the foundation with the upper crust of the water, shake it to the foundation of its scream and yell and turn it to the thickness of chocolate rich in the cup, thick and rich and hot and swimming with pools of fat, so he could drink, so he would have to put his hand into the black avalanche of feeling and emotion and sediment, deep and gurgling as the tenor in her laughter, down the tuningfork of her throat resounding with love and make her say a word, speak a thought, be some witness to the blood in her love. This was his Marian in the vision in the summer-street. This was Marian. And the five-year stranger, estranged from her husband's love in a transparency, in the costume of a lover, this woman who used to sit upon the pin of his desires, now on this summer-street where he thought he saw her, she is nothing more vivacious than a feather worn in her broad-grinned hat: not like the scarf she wore with conch-shells and libertyscars and paisley marked into it with water; this negative of Marian passed like the cloud above the roof of the *Park Plaza* where one afternoon she sat drinking water, when he was playing golf in the new democratic diminutive green of the eighteenth-floor bar; and a cloud passed overhead like the loss of lust of a now dead moment, with the woman; and when the sun was bright again, when the sun was like the sun in Georgia, fierce and full, when the sun was a purpose and passion, when the sun was as bright as the sweat it wrung from the barrels of a black woman's breasts, the laughing beautiful Marian was there, not in his mind only but larger, dispossessing the summer-street in the buxom jeans of her hips, red accusing blouse belafonted down the ladylike tip of the gorge of sustenance between her breasts, and around her neck around her throat, a yellow handkerchief and a chain of a star and a moon in some quarter of her sensual religion. He saw her with passion and with greed, he saw her clearer than the truth-serum syrup of a dream, than the germ of love, true as the guinness in the egg and the Marian was his stout, this woman. He remembered all this standing in the summer-street: when before she climbed the steps to her hospital, she held his hands like a wife going in to die upon a cot, and drew him just a suggestion of new life closer to the relationship and her breasts, and with the sweet saliva of her lips she said in the touch of that kiss, "Take care of yourself." He was young and free again, to live or to travel imprisoned in a memory of freed love, chained to her body and her laughter by the spinal cord of anxious longdistance, reminders said before and after, by the long engineering of a drive from Yale to Brandeis to Seaver Street to Brandeis dull in the winter Zion of brains, dull in the autumn three hours in miles hoping that the travel won't end like an underground railroad at the door of this negative woman, but continue even through letters and quarrels and long miles down the short street up the long stairs in the marble of her memory, clenched in her absent embrace but rejoicing with his fingers in the velvet feeling of her silken black natural hair . . .

1973

Sometimes a Motherless Child

She went back on her knees beside the bed, but the words did not come. "I can't commune with you this morning, Lord." She got up, rubbed the circulation back into her knees, pulled the pyjamas leg from sticking to her body, passed her hands over her hips, promised to eat less food so late at night, touched her breasts for cancer, said, "Lord, another day, another dollar!" She walked out of the bedroom and into the cold hallway, four paces long, passed through the living room which served also as a dining room and kitchen, and into the tiny bathroom, colder than the short hallway. She looked up at the color print of a man with a red beard grown into two points, strong piercing eyes, thin face and sallow complexion. The man's heart was not only bare, but exposed. Something like a diadem, or a crown made of two strands of branches, thick and plaited with thorns sticking into the man's head, was causing drops of blood to fall from his skull. The color print was above the sink. "Father God," she said. She closed her eyes and continued to pee. The man's hand was raised, the right hand, in a salute like that made by a boy scout, or like a gesture giving benediction. It was this gesture which made her say, "Thank you." And with that, she felt better. But the words they were saying, and the words written about the Jamaican; and the sad memories that the snap shot of her husband brought back; and the drying up of her own words so necessary to begin the morning with; and the snoring behind the wall, all these worries passed from her mind, and made her step light and carefree as she stepped into the shower. She hated showers. But they were quick. And this morning, in her hurry to be happy, she pulled out the new-fashioned circular knob, and the water, cold as winter, pounded against her body, as if it contained small pellets of ice. She shrieked.

And before the scream died down, she was on the telephone to her landlord, who lived above her head. She hated that more than she hated showers.

"*Mister* Petrochuck!"

"Yes, my dear?"

"Am I paying you rent for this place? And I can't take a proper bath in peace, without the water turning cold, cold, cold as Niagara Falls, and freezing my blasted body?"

Through the receiver she heard his hearty laugh, and words in some foreign language which she hated next to having to take showers, which after five years she still did not know the origin of; and when his laughter abated, and her anger lowered, she heard Mr. Petrochuck explaining the difficulty.

"I tell you two times now, Mrs. Jones," he was saying, no longer with laughter in his voice, for in a way he both feared and respected her. "Two times I explain it now. You turn knob to left for the cold. And you turn knob to the right for the hot. And you turn before you pull out knob."

She felt ashamed to have to be told these explanations again. "So, how the hell am I to know that? Where I come from, you turn to the left for the hot. To the left!" She tried to imitate his accent, to diffuse both her frustration and her anger. "And you turn the knob to the right for the cold."

"That's right!"

It was her time now to laugh, and to laugh and talk as she teased him.

"Thanks, Mr. P."

"Thank you, Mrs. J."

"Sometimes, I feel like a mother-less child!" She was already in the shower, and the water was warm, and her voice was beautiful and clear above the sound of the water which came out in jets, as if it was mixed with marbles that had been taken from a furnace, and mixed in cold water. *"Sometimes, I feel like a mother-less child . . . "*

When she was dressed, she started to prepare a sandwich, using Wonder Bread and canned salmon. She put a slice of tomato and a leaf of lettuce between the soft white slices. She wrapped it in a large white napkin, then into grease-proof paper, then into plastic. She dropped it into a brown paperbag. She placed a five dollar note on the paperbag and secured it with a paper clip.

She pushed the door of the small room behind the wall where she was standing in the kitchen, and looked at the large body curled in the shape of an embryo, on his left side, breathing heavily through his mouth. She looked down at the sheet and the blanket torn away from his body. And she admired his smooth black body, muscular in the places where men his age are muscular; and with his hair cut in that odd style which she never liked, with two things that looked like lightning marks shaved deep into his short hair; and after she had taken in all this, as she does every morning during the week, she turned the light on.

"You!" she shouted.

This is the way she greeted him every morning;the way she chose to rouse him from his sleep. There was a smile in her shout, as she stood by the door, blocking it, sturdy as if she was a prison guard. "You!"

Her voice penetrated the sleep he had been embracing, and it might have penetrated also the nightmare that his sleep had wrapped him into, for with the second call, he sprung upright, and started to tremble in terror. She noticed that he had a hard-on. But she was his mother.

"Don't shoot, don't shoot!" There was terror in his pleading.

"Who shooting you? Boy, who are shooting you?"

"Sorry, Mom."

"Is somebody shooting you? Look, fix yourself in front of me, do!"

He pulled the sheet up, and covered his nakedness.

"School isn't this morning?"

"Yes, Mom."

"Well, get up, you!"

"Thanks, Mom."

And she laughed, and hugged him tight, as if it was a farewell of love. He wrapped his strong black arms round her body, and she could feel his heart and she was sure she could feel his blood. Then, she released him. She turned the light off. She closed the door. She shook her head from side to side in profound satisfaction at the way he was getting along, making plans for him and for herself, but more than anything else, making plans for his future. She was so proud of him. So proud. And he was growing so well. She gathered up her purse. She selected a large bag. She folded it and put it into the leather bag in which she carried her purse and other things. She turned the lights off in the rest of the apartment. But she was worried about something. Why would he say, "Don't shoot, don't shoot?" But just as soon, she put it out of her mind. He was such an obedient boy. She began to hum, and before she closed the front door, and before the clock on the mantelpiece chimed seven times, she heard him say, "Bye, Mom. Have a good day."

Her shower this morning was warm and embracing and the water soaked her body as if she was still bathing in the waves of the sea. She was feeling better. She would manage her work today, and not complain. She would even change her mind about taking showers.

"Life is so good!" she said, turning the key in the lock. When she walked down the short path, covered with snow with ice beneath, her steps were gingerly, and she didn't mind the winter. *"Some-times, I feel, like a, mother-less child . . . "*

"BJ! BJ! Hey, man! It's Marco, man! BJ!" He waited as usual, until he was sure, until the caller had identified himself by name, before he even moved from the chair where he was reading a book, *The Autobiography of Malcolm X.* He wanted to be sure. He had to be sure that he was opening his mother's door to the right person.

"Hey, BJ! It's Marco, man!"

Years ago, when he skipped school on the smallest pretext, and felt he was clever in doing so, his mother got the landlord, Mr. Petrochuck, to check on him; and Mr. Petrochuck asked her how he would check on her son, and she told him how. "He can't fool me, Mr. P., so don't let him fool you. Just look along the alleyway between my place and the house next door, and see if you see if my son left. Make a note of the footprints in the snow, and I sure, Mr. P., that a man with your experience in the Second World War, as you always telling me you was in the Alpine Batallion with skis and a gun on your shoulder, that you would know what time my son passed through the alleyway on his way to school." The landlord's laughter, and hers, and his remark that she was a better spy than any he had faced in the Russian Army, lasted throughout the rest of the conversation that ended with her giving him her number at work, with the instruction to call her back. She spent that morning, with her hands in the rich foamy water in the double sink, washing crystal glasses from the party the night before. But her laughter turned to anger and violence when she heard Mr. P.'s report; and when she got home at seven o'clock that night, she was tired and blue with fuming, but her energy came back to her, just as she was revived from the morning shower, and she stood over him, ten years old on that cold Monday night, and she counted twenty-one times that the leather slipper was raised and landed on his back, and she stopped counting, and did not hear her words, as she drove the slipper across his back, ripping away one of the thongs, and shouting and muttering and screaming, as she flogged him, "Let me tell you something, you hear me? Let me tell you something, young man. If you don't want to go to school I will take you myself to the nearest police station, and let them lock you up, you hear me?" And it went on that way, the sharp blows from the slipper rising in their unsatisfied anger, and her voice piercing the peace of her place which she kept clean and in which she made no noise, careful to be decent and respectable, " . . . and, and-and, living in this place with all the things happened to black people, to men and boys like you, and you wanting to turn out like them?" And it stopped only when there was a pause in her energy, and in her anger, and she heard the pounding at the door. At first she thought it was the police. And she got scared. And then she felt grateful that they had come to take her son away. "Serve you damn right!" And then she was terrified. She saw herself in handcuffs, taken out to the police cruiser, and placed in the back seat, with the road of neighbors watching, and led into the station, the same police station she was going to take him to, and have her fingers placed on the ink pad, and in ten small spaces, printed as a criminal, and the charge of assault, or bodily harm, or violent assault whichever charge they wanted to lay on her. And then, she recognized Mr. Petrochuck's voice. "Are you going to kill this boy?" And the relief, and the protection his presence brought, as if he was still in the Alpine Batallion and had rescued a detachment of his men ambushed and encircled by their own loss of control and of nerves, she did not lower the broken leather slipper again, but held it in her right hand, as her eyes filled up with tears. And she embraced Mr. Petrochuck, and she asked him to sit with her for a while, and she remained silent and heavy with her grief which shook her body in spasms from time to time. That morning when they had spied on him, as he explained it to Marco on the telephone, hours later, the snow had betrayed him. It had remained firm and pure, clean and like innocence itself, without a blemish, because he had remained in his room all day, listening to music. Marco had supplied the school principal with a note of excuse, with his mother's signature forged on it. But he learned his lesson and deceived the landlord who continued to report his activities to his mother; and he excelled in class through his brilliance, and because he was bright he had more time to do the things he wanted to do. So, this morning when he heard her leave, as he has been doing for years, he put his coat, a fur-lined jeans jacket over his pyjamas, put on his sneakers, and walked from the back door, his private entrance, through the deep snow, right to the alleyway, and through the alleyway to the front of the house.

Then carefully, he walked backwards, placing the sneakers exactly into the footprints going away from the back door, retracing his steps, right back into the house. He had been doing this so often that he no longer regarded it as a skill. Or as deceit. It was like brushing his teeth as the first activity after getting out of bed. He took off his sneakers, brushed them off on the mat covered with a copy of yesterday's *Star*; he dusted the snow off his jacket, as he had brushed the low hanging branches of the tree in the alleyway, and put it back into the cupboard where he kept his stereo and CD player, and his clothes, and which he had covered with a piece of cloth he had bought from the Third World Books & Crafts store on Bathurst Street. The cloth was Kente cloth. He had read somewhere in his voracious appetite for books that Malcolm X was married in Kente cloth.

"It's Marco, man."

He closed the book, after putting a book mark between the pages; the book mark was a sliver of Kente cloth; and replacing it into the shelves which took up two complete walls in his small room. The shelves were crammed with books. All the books were paperbacks. All the books dealt with black people, and were written on black subjects, in fiction, philosophy, religion, art, culture and his favorite, biography. He kept his school texts under the bed, on the floor.

"BJ! Man, it's Marco!"

He was not impressed by the impatience in the voice, and before he went to the door, he rested the Gaulois cigarette into an ashtray, lit some incense, and he turned down the volume of John Coltrane playing 'A Love Supreme.' He put his housecoat on and went to the door. The ashtray was a square crystal one, which his father had bought eight Christmases ago, and had never used. His father did not smoke.

"Fuck, man!" Marco said, stomping one foot after the other, on the worn coconut husk mat. "It's fucking cold out here, man!"

BJ looked at Marco sternly.

"Sorry, man."

A trace of a smile came over his thin lips as Marco remembered his aversion to foul language. His father had drilled that into him, with a few beatings. So, he opened the door wider, and Marco squeezed between the post and him, and went in, and stomped one foot after the other, although his sneakers were already wiped clean on the mat. He hunched his shoulders,and pushed his hands into his jeans side pockets, and said, "It's fucking cold, man!" Under his arm were newspapers.

"You should control your emotions better than that."

Marco looked cowed, and said, "Sorry, man. But it's all right for you, man."

They embraced, touching bodies, and slapping each other on the back three times, as if they belonged to an old fraternity of rituals and mystery. They let go of each other, and did it a second time, with their heads touching the other's shoulders. It was Italian, and it was African, and it was this that joined them in their close friendship for the past nine years. They saw each other every day, either at school or here in BJ's room. Their parents never met. And did not know of their sons' deep friendship. And it never occurred to either of them that they should bring their parents into their strong bond of friendship. BJ's mother went to every school event that required a parent's presence. And Marco's mother and father attended them too. But they never met.

BJ went to the small square table in a corner and with an African print covering it, and on which he had put a large leather-bound copy of the Holy Qur'an. Two glasses and a bottle of vodka were on the table. Ice was already in the glasses. He had been expecting Marco. The ice was already melting.

"Punctuality," he told Marco, "is also not an Italian characteristic, although we are blamed for inventing CPT."

"Fuck, man! Gimme the drink!"

And BJ poured two strong vodkas. He had not forgotten the orange juice, but he could not risk taking it earlier out of his mother's fridge, just in case. He did this now, and when he returned, Marco was sitting in a straight-back chair, with his drink already at his lips. He poured each of them some orange juice.

Coltrane was at the stage in his song, chanting "a love supreme," over and over. Marco joined in the chanting. His voice was deep for his age, eighteen, similar to a bass.

"A love su-preme, a love sup-preme," he chanted. "Nineteen times, fuck, you say he does that. Sometimes, you don't know, BJ, but I feel he's gonna sing it maybe twenty times, or eighteen times! Fuck."

"Unless your concentration diminishes, Coltrane won't."

"Fuck!"

BJ went back to the table, brushed a piece of ice from it, and ran his hands over the cover of the Qur'an. It was covered in brown paper, cut from a bag from the Liquor Control Board of Ontario, weeks ago when he went to pick up his weekly supply of vodka. He was seventeen then. But he looked older. He always looked older. This did not fool the manager at the LCBO store around the corner from his home, and he knew it; so to save the embarrassment, he used forged identification, including a school mate's birth certificate. He felt guilty about doing this, on the first three occasions; but it was the style of the times. Only last week he read in the *Star* that the police had caught five immigrants working illegally under false names and with forged social insurance numbers. It was the way of the times. And he was a born Canadian, so, "Fuck!" Marco consoled him, and himself. On the brown paper cover he had printed HOLY BIBLE. On the bedside table, beside his single bed that had an iron bedstead, he had placed the Bible, just in case. He read the Bible, too. His mother had given him the Bible. But he devoted his devotions to the Holy Qur'an. Coltrane was now into the second part of his song. The music came out at them with equal balance, and power, even though he had turned down the volume out of the four speakers. The speakers were four feet tall and more than one foot in width. He had built them himself. The other components in the stereo, he and Marco had reconditioned from spare parts and odds and ends thrown out by neighbors in his district in the Bathurst Street area, and in Marco's neighborhood up in North York. Every piece but the CD player, they had reconditioned themselves.

"Did you check out the things for me?"

"Yeah, man," Marco said. He was almost perfect in the speech of black people. It came out easy and almost natural. "I got me the Form, man."

"Well, let's spend a few moments scrutinizing the entries, and adding to our fortune."

"All these books. Fuck. Man, you's something else! All these books!" Marco would busy himself by taking out a book, flipping its pages, replacing and repeating this until he had touched almost every book in the shelves. And he did this to allow BJ to concentrate on the Racing Form. "You're like, like a walking 'cyclopedia, man. And also a genius at the track. Fuck!"

"All it takes is concentration, Marco. I've been telling you this for years. Concentration. And dedication."

"I gonna give you something Italian to read. You know anything about Italian classics? Man, I gonna lay some Italian literature on you, one o' these days. Like Dante, man."

"Third shelf, sixth book from the right. Second bookcase."

The book Marco picked out was *Seven Systems of Dante's Hell.*

"Fuck! I didn't know he wrote this, too!"

"Imamu Baraka wrote that, Marco. That's a different inferno," BJ said. "My mother is fine. She didn't ask for you this morning."

"Fuck!"

"This morning, she pushed my door and greeted me in her usual way, *"You!"* I pretended I was sleeping, but all the time I could see her face, and the worry in it, and the worry in her body about her work, and I was pretending I was sleeping. I was up all night, reading."

"This black power shit?"

" As a matter of fact, Marco, I was reading Shakespeare." Marco got up from his chair and went to the bookcase. He knew this one. This one was, in a way, his favorite bookcase, for it contained books he too liked. The bookcase was made from unpainted dealboard, sawed and cut by him and BJ; and it occupied the space in the wall between a window and a cupboard. It ran from the floor to the ceiling. BJ liked everything in his room to run from the floor to the ceiling. It had something to do with perspective, he said. Marco did not understand, and said, "Fuck!" to show his sentiments. If his room were larger, BJ knew that they would have built the speakers from the floor to the ceiling. In this shelf in the bookcase were books by Shakespeare which Marco liked, and did well in, in school preferring *Romeo and Juliet,* "Fuck! Not because I'm Italian, man!;" and *As you Like It,* and *The Merchant of Venice,* which they stopped studying in his school the term before he reached that grade. BJ preferred *Henry IV* and *Othello,* "because you're black, right? Fuck!" But BJ told him, "because it contains the best and perhaps, the most noble of Shakespeare's noble poetry. I don't even like the character Othello. Iago is a more realistic character. I see Iago's every day in class." And to all this, all Marco said, years ago when they had this conversation the first time, was "Fuck!" They have had this same conversation many times since. And Marco uses the same single word to express his sentiments.

"Today is the last day. I suggest we go out with a bang. But how many classes would you miss if we got there for the first?"

"Lemme see. Biology? Physics? English? And basketball practice."

"I will do your Biology and Physics assignments for you. Or we can do them together at the track."

"Fuck!" Marco said. He rubbed his hands as if he was cold. He poured himself another vodka and orange juice.

For young men, for eighteen-year-old boys, really, they had an enormous prodigity for alcohol which is the term BJ used laughingly, when they would sit in his small room, and consume half of a twenty-six once bottle of imported Absolut Vodka; and if his mother had returned home and had seen them, she would shake her head in pleasure at their hearty liking for orange juice, "You two boys don't know how good I feel to see you drinking orange juice, instead of all this damn Coke and Pepsi!" And after these long bouts, their speech was not even slurred, afterwards.

"Did you remember the *Globe*?" BJ read the *Globe* everyday. He read the racing tips first. He read the sports section second, the editorial third, and the foreign news section fourth. He read nothing else in this newspaper.

"Woodbine, here we come!" Marco said. *"They're at the post!* Fuck!"

"Should we invest a hundred each? What is your opinion, Marco?"

"A hundred bucks? Fuck! Why not, man? I deposited yesterday's winnings in my account. Those tellers're *weird,* man. She look at me with all that bread as if I was a drug dealer! Fuck, man."

"Today's the last day," BJ said. Marco noticed the tone of his voice.

"You all right, man?"

"You have to do something with the money in your bank account. Something. *Some* thing. And we have to think about the car, too."

"Today is the last day, man. So, if we lose . . . "

"Don't say it!"

"Sorry, man."

BJ went to his dresser, a narrow, tall piece of furniture which his mother had bought at the Goodwill Store on Jarvis Street, to save money, and which he had stained to make it look like mahogany. It looked like a mahogany antique piece of Georgian furniture, although he did not know that. It had five drawers. In the top drawer, under his handkerchiefs which his mother starched and ironed and folded into four, he kept his cash, arranged in denominations in ascending order, inside a box that contained cheques from the bank. He opened this drawer now, and took from it a metal box that had a key. He brought the box to the bed, and unlocked it. There were four boxes that used to contain cheques in the metal box. They were full of bank notes. No note was smaller than a ten. He did not count his money every night, but his memory was good, and he knew that with the withdrawals and the deposits into his private "safe," that he had five thousand, three hundred and five dollars in it. He could not tell his mother about this. He could not offer to lend her money, not even when he saw her moaning and crying and cursing his father for having abandoned them; not even when her rent of four hundred dollars a month was in arrears. And sadly, not even when she had to postpone her registration for one month, and never caught up, in the Practical Nursing course at George Brown College. She would kill him to learn that he had so much money, in her house, in all the time she was seeing misery, in all these days when she had to cut and contrive. But he had prepared for her. At such a young age, it seemed ominous, too adult, too final a thing this preparation by someone so young. He had opened a savings account in her name, at a different bank from the one she used. Marco put his winnings in a chequing account. But he kept his in cash.

"Here's twenty tens, Marco. I'll take twenty, too. This is the last day, so I'm staking you. What we win we keep. What we lose, well."

"Fifty per cent of our winnings should still go in the kitty, man. Fuck!" It was their business arrangement. And they stuck to this code, like members of a gang. "And look for a longshot, man!"

"There's no such thing, Marco! No such thing. My father went to the races every day. Faking illness from work. And family crises and emergencies. He had to be there. In summer and winter. He even walked there, once. Not to mention the times he had to walk home. And he bet on longshots, because he was a gambler. He was a gambler. And was greedy. He was a fool. A damn fool. He thought he could get rich from the track. We are different. We are investors. Don't ever let me see you betting on a longshot! Longshots are for racetrack touts."

"Why can't we use the car?"

"How many times do I have to tell you it's not safe to be driving that kind of car in Toronto? It's safer to drive it in Montreal."

"Oh man! What's the point of having the wheels, and not using it? Fuck!"

"Have you told your parents you own a white BMW? Or more correctly, a fifty per cent share in a 1992 white BMW?"

"Well, fuck no, man! For them to execute me?"

"Exactly! My mother doesn't even know I can drive. As long as our friend respects our confidence, the car will remain parked in her underground garage in Scarborough. Now, I have to make my *salats*."

"Make your salads, man. Make your salads. Fuck."

"Are you going to respect my religious principles? Or are you leaving?"

"I'll respect your salads, man. I'll respect your praying, man."

The Timex watch on BJ's wrist began to buzz. It was the hour for prayer. Marco poured himself a vodka quickly, wanting to stop the racket of the ice cubes in his glass, and the sound of the vodka pouring out of the bottle, now almost empty, before BJ began his prayers.

BJ pulled a cheap Persian rug from under his bed, unrolled it, and placed it in front of the table on which were the Absolut Vodka imported, and the Holy Qur'an. He placed the Qur'an on the floor, in front of him, and he placed his hands before his heart in the demeanor of prayer and concentration.

All this time, Marco was looking into the pages of Plutarch's Lives, which he had taken from the bottom shelf of the narrow, unpainted bookcase that contained only classical literature. And he sucked on the vodka straining it through his teeth and the melting pieces of ice cubes, as his friend *ommmmmmmed* and *ommmmmmmd,* and intoned *"alla hack-bar"* which is how Marco understood the pronunciation of the Muslim prayers. Fuck, he said to himself, this mother-fucker is real serious. If I didn't know he was serious, fuck! It was nine o'clock. The morning was crisp and cold and clean.

The boy flung the newspaper, aiming for a different spot, and it banged against the window where she was with her hands in the thick, white dish water, foaming like the waves that banged against the rocks near the Esplanade, and then retreated back into the calm, blue sea. She was thinking of home. She had seen him. "You little bastard!" And the boy jumped back on his bicycle, and sped out of the circular driveway over the crunching snow. It was ten o'clock. The morning was cold. When she had got off the subway and was walking to this mansion, the wind ripped into her body, and made her think of going back home the moment she made herself into a woman, meaning when she had money; and it made her feel as if she was naked. The wind had the same brutal touch as his fingers on her backside that day when she was bending over the vacuum cleaner. He had not touched her. She imagined it was his intention. And imagining it, it made it real. The wind swept up her legs, right between her thighs, clawing at her pantihose with such force that she thought she had left home without putting on her underwear. She felt the shame in the touch of the wind. "I should have been born a man," she said, to the boy disappearing over the smashed snow, but really not for his ears. Men don't know how lucky they are, she said, continuing her thoughts; they don't know how damn lucky they are to be wearing pants to get more greater protection from this damn cold. "And in other things, too!" Her thoughts went back to her son. For she had seen the photograph of the Jamaican family on the front pages of the *Star* newspaper many weeks ago, and now this morning, when that damn boy pelted the paper that almost broke the window where she was, here was another one. She wiped her hands in her apron, and studied the newspaper. It said that the young man was seventeen, and it said that he was living with his mother in a big house in the suburbs, and it said he was in the car with another young man about his same age, and it said that he was not going very fast and that the traffic policeman didn't have to follow him with the sirens on, and it said he was shot in the back of his head. She felt sad. And wanted to cry. She was leaving her own son at home, so often, by himself, before the dawn broke, in bed, and she wondered if he was safe. "But praise God, he doesn't have any car. A car is the surest thing to make a police shoot a black man dead. Praise God for that!" And she wanted to take up a cause, and hold a piece of stick with cardboard stapled on to it, and a message written on the cardboard, in thick black letters: THIS COUNTRY RACIST. THE POLICE TOO! "Yes! And put an exclamation mark after it, too!" She wanted to cry. She wanted to scream. But who would listen to her? A simple woman like her? That's why, she said to herself, a man has it better; for "I am the least amongst the apostles."

The young man's face, and the face of his mother, wringing her body in tears, filled the space of the double sinks, as she returned to her work. Her employers were having a party at five. And when the image of the mother and the son evaporated like the foam of soap from the two sinks, in their place were the faces of her own son, and his no-good father. She pulled the plug in the second sink out, with force, and the face of that bastard disappeared. She began to hum, *"Sometimes, I feel like a mother-less . . . "*

BJ got out casually, and with self-assurance, from the taxi, at the front of the tall apartment building somewhere in Scarborough; and as he walked across the lawn, he passed a blue car in which two men were sitting. The men were watching the same entrance BJ took. They had been there for the past three hours; and they had started watching the door since last Sunday. BJ paid no attention to the blue car. He walked straight to the panel of names, and pressed one of the buzzers. It was a buzzer beside the name, G. Harewood. He did not know G. Harewood. He could have pressed any buzzer. It was only two o'clock, and his school friend who allowed him to use the underground parking, without her mother's approval and knowledge, was still in school. This was the only way to retrieve the car.

"Who's it?" a woman's voice, mangled by the malfunction in the speaker system, cried out. The voice came through louder then he expected, and he made a start. It stirred him more than usual. "Who's it?" The voice was now irritable. "Is it George?"

"Yeah!" BJ said, trying to change his voice to George's voice, without knowing George's voice.

"Come on up!" the woman's voice screamed. It was less irritable. "Come on up!"

And when BJ entered the lobby, he could still hear the voice saying, "Come on up!" and the buzzer on the door to let him in was still being pressed.

He pressed the button in the elevator to P2, and went down into the bowels of the building. Three women were in the elevator with him. The three women stared at him. When the three women were tired of staring at him, they stared at the floor. Pools of water from melted ice were on the floor. When the three women were tired of staring at the floor, they stared at the illuminated numbers on the panel in the elevator. When it came to P2, the three women stood where they were. It seemed to BJ that they were standing in such a way to suggest that they had taken the wrong elevator. BJ got out. BJ walked straight to a corner of the large dimly lit underground parking area. Glimmering in the bad light of the dull fluorescent bulbs was the white BMW. He stood beside it. He looked at the front tires. He looked at the hood. He looked at the windshield. The elevator door was still open. The three women were watching him. He went round to the front of the BMW and he looked at the bumper. He looked at the cap which covered the hole to the gas tank. He screwed it tight. It was already tight. It was locked. One of the three women got off the elevator when it reached the main floor, and walked straight to a door marked superintendent. The superintendent answered at the first ring. He was eating a salmon sandwich that had bits of green things it in. The woman started talking to the superintendent.

BJ looked at the licence plate. He passed his hand over it. He was about to brush the dust from the plate onto his trousers, but he remembered in time. He was wearing expensive clothes. His trousers were black. They were full in the leg, and narrow at the ankle. His socks were white. And the shirt and jacket fitted him as if they were three or four sizes larger than his weight and size. He took a handkerchief from his pocket. The handkerchief was white, and folded into quarters. He wiped his hand, and then he passed the handkerchief slowly over each letter of the car licence. When he was done, the licence plate was glimmering almost as much as the BMW itself. The licence plate was BLUE. His beeper was beeping. So, he got into the car, with the doors locked, and the engine still turned off, and he checked the beeper. It was Marco.

He turned the engine on. Gradually, the interior of the black leather got warmer and warmer until he felt he was as comfortable sitting in it as he was in his room surrounded by all his solid state stereo and CD equipment and books. In this car, he had installed an equally expensive system. John Coltrane was playing. He had left the cassette in the tape. 'A Love Supreme.'

The car was warm. BJ's two large eyes filled up the rear-view mirror, and he could barely see, in periphery, the elevator door open, and a man and three women; and the women were pointing in his direction as they talked to the man; but the BMW was warmed up, and it moved without noise over the caked ice in some parts of the underground parking; and he manoeuvred it through spaces left by bad and careless drivers, past large concrete pillars, and mounted the incline to the exit door, in no hurry, and all the time speaking to Marco on the telephone, and he had to repeat himself two times, for the aerial struck the top of the last exit door, and finally he emerged into the brilliance of the winter afternoon, bright in the sun but still cold. The women had just told the superintendent, "I'm sure he looks like one of those drug dealers, and I feel he is, not because he's . . . "

The two men in the blue car saw the white BMW. And the two men made a note of it. And they registered BLUE in a notebook. And they made a check on their computer. And they began to talk on the telephone. BJ was heading for Victoria Park and Kingston Road to pick up Marco at the subway station. He was in a good mood. The last racing day was something else, fuck! as Marco put it. They had won and won and won . . .

Facing her now was the most magnificent slender white sculptures of branches on the trees in the backyard. She had seen these trees change their form for three years now, and she still did not know the name of one of them. But this afternoon, around three, with the clear light and the brilliance of the sun which gave no heat, she marvelled at the beauty and thought of men travelling in olden times over this kind of landscape, walking in shoes made from skins; and following in the tracks of wild animals they had to kill to stay alive. It was as if an artist had applied pearls and other kinds of jewels, with precision, on the branches of the trees. But she was not happy inside herself. Something was bothering her. And she picked up the telephone and called her landlord.

"Did you really see him?"

"Yes, I tell you, Mrs. J."

"Go out, dressed? In his school clothes? In time for school?

"Everything."

"You sure it was my son? You didn't mistake somebody else for him?"

"Sure!"

"Well, thank you, then." And to herself, she said, "I don't know why I am in this mood."

She had selected the crystals and the silvers and the plates, and all she had now to do was choose the serving dishes, and put the place mats on the shining mahogany table. She checked the roast beef in the oven, and shook her head at the amount of food she cooked, with most of it being thrown away the next morning, since neither husband nor wife liked to eat left-over food; and with all this damn food wasting day in and day out, and so many people on the streets of this city starving with nothing to warm their stomachs, and that blasted boy I gave birth to, refusing this good rich food, saying he is a Muslim. What a Muslim is? Is a Muslim a person who doesn't have commonsense inside his head, that he would refuse all this richness. And she laughed to herself. It was a joyous laugh. A hearty laugh. A laugh from the bottom of her belly. She looked round to see if anyone was close by, to mistake her for a fool that she was going out of her head, laughing and talking to herself, like this. "And come telling me that he is fasting. *Fasting?"* And all this food, all this food going to waste. I wish I knew somebody on my street, without foolish pride that I could leave a plastic container full of this food! And she began to hum. *Some-times, I feel . . .*

As BJ pulled off from the curb in front of the subway station in the East End, with Marco strapped in beside him, and laughing and turning up the volume of the saxophone solo, the BMW was so loud with the music contained within it that Marco himself felt his head was about to explode; and BJ himself was becoming nervous that perhaps the BMW would become conspicuous with the two of them in it with so much noise. The windows were rolled up. The BMW took the first entrance on to the 401 West doing 80. BJ settled behind the wheel, with a Gaulois unfiltered cigarette at the corner of his mouth, one eye closed against the smoke, and he put the car into fourth gear, and the car still had some more power, and moved like a jungle animal measuring its prey, and receiving additional power because of the certainty of devouring its prey. The prey in this case was their destination. But they did not have any anxiety of time and distance to reach that destination. It was simply that BJ liked to drive fast. That was why he convinced Marco to buy the BMW instead of the Thunderbird. And that was why he got it with standard transmission. They had won the money at the race track, one afternoon when Marco made the mistake of buying the three horses in a triactor race for ten dollars, instead of five which was their custom. The name of the horse that won, that went off at 50 to 1 odds, was Blue. BJ knew he could not keep all that money in his room; and he knew that he could not open an account without questions asked. He knew he could not give it to his mother, even with the explanation that he had won it at the track. What would he be doing at the track? Why was he at the track on a school day? So, he bought a white BMW. He paid a friend of his, a real estate salesman three hundred dollars to cover for him. Real estate was at rock bottom at that time, and the salesman was more than happy to keep his mouth shut and to pocket this unearned commission. But BJ knew all the time that he had to be careful and that a time might come when the real estate salesman, still at the bottom of the unsold rocks of houses on the market, would need more help in keeping his mouth closed. He had to be careful.

He turned the music down a little more, and he reduced his speed to 80. As these thoughts entered his head, he had been doing 150. He had just spotted a marked police cruiser, with 52 painted on its white side, parked alongside the 401. But he did not know that as soon as he had pulled off from the subway station in the East End, that at that precise moment, a blue sedan with two men in it had pulled off too, and had followed him until he entered the 401 going West. The marked police cruiser was expecting him. And as he had swooshed by, the traffic policeman was on the radio to another one, somewhere farther west along the 401. Conversation passed between the policemen in the cars. "Drug dealers for sure!" And through another system came, "Question of being armed and dangerous." And the two policemen in the parked blue car up in the suburbs of Scarborough added their contribution. "We were hoping for a red Camaro but you never know with these drug dealers, they have the money to change cars . . . " And Coltrane was playing his ass off, as Marco would say, still fond of the way he thought BJ talked, and should talk. "Trane's playing his ass off!" he said, eventually. He said it three more times. BJ grunted something. In his rear view mirror he saw the police cruiser pull into the same lane as his, tailing him. He knew this stretch of the 401 like the palm of his hand. He was west of the Allen Road, approaching on the highway a little north, the area in the city known as the habitat of drugs and guns and gangs, and called by two names — one, the name of a woman, a whore: the other name of a bird, which may also be a woman and a whore. Jane-Finch. He knew this stretch of road well. He knew he could get into the express lane within twenty kilometers. The cruiser was gaining on him. Marco was oblivious to this, as he listened to Coltrane. The cruiser's red light was still not on. But BJ surmised that any time now, it would be. And the siren would start. The lanes ahead of him were crowded with slow drivers who had themselves seen the cruiser. All four lanes heading west were crowded. But that was what he wanted. He put the BMW into third. He was gearing down to stop; and the car was not so noisy with the music, and that was when Marco had commented about Coltrane's mastery of 'Love Supreme,' when BJ changed his mind about stopping, to face the consequences. For how would he know the cruiser was following *him*? Of the hundreds of cars on the highway, why should a police cruiser pick him out because he was driving an expensive car, and was a young black man? He told himself he must not be fooled by the logic of a man, or of a woman, or of a time, a better time than was taking place in this city; he remembered that logic had absolutely nothing to do with it. He was intelligent in the ways of the hunter and, in this case, the hunted. He was relying upon his instincts. Somewhere in his vast reading, he had come across something about this. He was not quite sure, nor could he remember the exact quotation; but it had something to do with instinct and emotion and gut feeling. His mother lived by her emotion. So, he geared up to third, and the BMW lurched forward. Marco said, "Fuck!" and tightened his seat belt. "Let her ride, let her ride!" It was already in fourth. And in and out of traffic, from the slow lane to the middle, to the fast lane, and when the fast lane was not fast enough and the entire width of the four-lane highway seemed to be creeping, the white BMW swerved like a top spinning near the end of its revolutions. "Fuck!" Marco said, when they were safe, for the time being, in a secondary road, somewhere near Dufferin. "What the fuck was that all about?"

BJ smiled. He turned Coltrane up. The car was filled once more with the beauty of music, with the pulse of emotion and with the feeling of the time; and they remained quiet in the waves of this melodious tune they both liked so much, and argued about. BJ insisted, because of his new religion, that it was a religious chant. Marco, equally insistent, said it was a love song.

"A love supreme," he began chanting. *"A love supreme.* Nineteen times the brother says *a love supreme!* Nineteen times, BJ!" He never lacked enthusiasm about this aspect of the song. "Fuck!"

"Nineteen times," BJ said. And he turned the music up even louder. They were cruising along Eglinton Avenue, passing record stores from which reggae and dancehall blared out upon them, past barber shops and restaurants and shops which sold curry goat and fish and oxtail and peas and rice, and they felt they could smell and taste the food even in this breathless afternoon so cold, and so uncertain. Young men, some younger than either of them, walked with a patience that came closer to loitering along the lively street, stopping now and then to place their hands on the parking meters, as if reassuring themselves and the ugly pieces of metal that life was still going on, even in this cold afternoon when it was difficult to breathe; in this heart of West Indian life, when there was no attention paid to the depth of the fall in the coldness and where life remained constant: the laughter and the lightness of dress and manner. "What about lunch?"

"Yeah!"

"Curry goat? Or oxtail?"

"Fuck! Goat *and* oxtail!"

BJ and Marco were driving around. Listening to Coltrane and taking in the sights. It was about four in the afternoon. The white BMW had just been washed at the car wash on the corner of Bathurst and St. Clair. And the music was sounding better it seemed, now that the car was spotless. As they handed in their chit, the four car washers who were polishing another car paused in their work to admire the white BMW. And they looked long at the car and then longer at the two teenagers, and said something with their eyes and said something to themselves, and went back polishing an old black Pontiac. BJ was accustomed to people looking at him and then at the BMW. And when Marco was with him, they looked at Marco, at him, and at the car. And sometimes, if it was in the parking lot of a supermarket, or in a mall, they would go through the order of looking and staring a second time in reverse.

They were cruising along Bathurst now. It was Friday afternoon about five. And the trafflc was heavy. And BJ was driving within the speed limit. And as he turned left into the street before Dupont, to tack back on to Dupont because there was no left turn there, from under a low-hanging tree came a police cruiser. BJ and Marco were alone on this stretch of road. And the cruiser came close to them, and BJ understood fast enough, and pulled over and stopped.

"Get out! Get out!"

"Yes, officer."

"You too! Get the fuck out!"

"Yeah, officer."

The policeman was out of the cruiser, and he had his hand on the T-shaped night stick. His other hand moved to his gun to make sure, it seemed, that it was still there.

"Out!"

They were already out.

"Okay, okay!"

"Who're you talking to like that? Eh? Eh? Who're you fucking talking to, like that? Eh? Eh?"

And with each "eh," he poked his T-shaped stick into Marco's ribs.

"Up against the car! Up against the fucking car! Both o' youse! Both o' youse!"

It seemed that in his training his lecturer had had a hearing problem and he had to repeat each answer two times; for he was now saying the same thing two times, as if it was his normal way of speech. Or as if he was also accustomed to talking to fools, or immigrants who didn't understand English, and he had to speak in these short, truncated, double sentences.

"Spread your legs! Spread your legs! Come! Open up! Come! Open up!"

And they obeyed him. BJ could feel the dust from the side of the cruiser which needed a wash, going into his nostrils. He could feel the policeman's stick moving around his legs, round his crotch, up and down, up and down. He could feel the policeman's hands, tough and personal, strong as ten pieces of bone, feel his thighs, his chest, under his arms, between his legs, and feel his penis and his testicles; and then the ten pieces of bone spun him round, so that he now faced the policeman. BJ stood silent and calm as the policeman did the same thing to Marco. He thought the policeman was treating Marco more severely.

"Where you get this goddamn car?"

Before BJ could answer, the policeman was talking again.

"Where you get this goddamn car?"

BJ was about to say something when the policeman cut him off.

"You steal this car! You steal this car?"

Marco opened his mouth to speak, and thought better of it.

"Who owns this fucking car? Who owns this fucking car?"

BJ put his hand into the breast pocket of his suede windbreaker, and was about to pull out his driver's licence, when the policeman came at him. His hand was on his gun. His gun was in his hand. The policeman seemed to see red. The policeman seemed to feel his life was being threatened. The policeman was behaving as if BJ had taken out, or was about to take out, a dangerous weapon. The policeman turned red. He came at BJ with great force, as if he was tackling a running full back, and when he hit him, he had him flat onto the side of the cruiser. Dust rose from the side of the cruiser. The cruiser leaned for a short time off its tires. Marco was about to intervene, when BJ raised his hand to stop him.

"Come on, nigger! Come on, nigger!"

And he slammed BJ into the side of the cruiser a second time.

He put his hand behind his back, and when he brought it from behind his back, he was holding handcuffs. He snapped them on BJ's wrists. He poked the T-shaped stick into Marco's side, and ordered him into the cruiser. And he pushed BJ towards the cruiser, and threw him into the back seat, beside Marco.

"You could put away those! You could put away those!" BJ's licence and ownership papers were still in his hand.

The policeman went to the white BMW, stroked the tires with his T-shaped stick, and was about to smash the front side window, but something made him change his mind. He turned the engine off, put the key into his pocket, and came back to the cruiser.

He drove off. Voices of other policemen and of a dispatcher babbled on the radio. He seemed impervious to the racket of the voices. He drove south on Spadina and turned right at Bloor; and left on Brunswick, and into a few short one-way streets, and then he was back on Spadina going south of College; and then he turned east onto Dundas. BJ recognized the Ontario College of Art and the Royal Ontario Museum. He visited the ROM twice a month on Saturdays, to study African cultures and art. And Marco went along with him on many occasions. They have been doing this for three years now. BJ recognized Division 52 police station. And his heart sank. He had heard about Division 52. Wasn't it a police officer from 52 who shot a Jamaican, many years, ago? The policeman moved on to University Avenue, and turned left, and took them northwards on University Avenue. Apart from the crackling of voices from the other invisible policemen and dispatchers, the cruiser was quiet. It was six o'clock and the winter light was fading fast and made the afternoon seem like night. And if night should catch them in this cruiser, alone with this policeman, oh my God! The policeman had not spoken in all this time. He had smoked two cigarettes. They came to Queen's Park, and took the roundabout and were beside Trinity College, and back onto Spadina. Marco had a cousin who was attending Trinity College; and he took BJ there, one Friday night at dinner, and they ate fish that had no peppersauce. BJ loved the huge oil paintings and the black gowns the students wore. In all this time, BJ said nothing. And Marco said nothing. Marco was slapping his trousers' legs. BJ sat with his eyes closed, his teeth pressed down tight, and if you were sitting in Marco's place, you would have seen the slight movement in BJ's jaws.

"Get the fuck out! Get the fuck out!"

It took them a while to realize who had spoken to them. It took them a while to recognize where they were. The policeman came round and unlocked the cuffs from BJ's wrists.

"Get-outta-here! Get-outta-here!"

He had let them off beside the white BMW.

His mother remembered it was a big day on Saturday, a wedding she had to go to, and she rushed from work to get to the hairdresser before he closed. They were many women there, some of them had been there since early afternoon. It seemed that every woman in the place had an important church service on Sunday. Or an important dance date. Or a wedding to go to. She was tired, too tired from a long day, and she dozed off as she sat in the chair. She could barely hear pieces of conversation around her.

"I know a Jamaican man that the cops kill."

"But that was five years ago, child!"

"And in Montreal too. Not here. As a matter o' fact, this particular Jamaican had a daughter who went to school with me, in . . ."

"I mean the Jamaican man. The Jamaican who get killed and brutalized by the police. Those ladies you was having the discussion with, do they know the Jamaican man?"

When she opened her eyes, she realized that the hairdresser, Mr. Azan who was rubbing the grease into her hair, had been talking too. He turned now towards the ladies who were still with their heads over the square sinks, and to the others under dryers. But he did not say anything to them.

"How long is this going to take? I have to get home and see that boy."

"How the boy?"

"Bright as anything. Doing well in school. Someday he going-crown my head with pride and glory. Praise God. But apart from that, sir, he's a boy. And that means he has his ways. How long?"

"Well, let's see. It's going on seven now. Comb. Folding. Gimme a few minutes. You'll be done in no time! No problem. Not to worry. Yeah, man. You'll be out in no time."

And when his mother left, a new woman, years taken from her appearance, years taken from her gait, years taken from her attitude to herself; and with her hair a bright mauve, and shining and smelling of the lotions and the smell of the hairdressing salon, it was eight o'clock the night. But she was beautiful and looking young and feeling sprightly and full of life. And that was what she wanted for the wedding on Saturday afternoon.

The yellow police cruiser was stopped a few yards ahead of her. It was a dark night. She had looked up into the heavens a few moments, a few yards farther back, and smiled as she wondered and remembered that in this city you don't see stars as you see stars back home, when you can become dizzy counting more than three hundred in one raised head and spinning eyes. But when she saw the police cruiser, she became tense and the feeling of paranoia which came to her every time she saw a police cruiser came to her now. The black-clad police officers always brought a tense, angry tightness into her chest. And the tightness moved swiftly into her guts. And without knowing she always felt that it was a black man, or a black woman, but more frequently a black man, who was stopped by the policeman. In all the time she has been living in this city, she never saw a white man stopped by a policeman. But then, of course, they had to be some white men stopped by the police. All couldn't be so much more better than black people, she said. And she always felt the black man was innocent. She assumed that. He had to be innocent, she figured, because he was black. And she always thought that the policeman stopped him for no reason at all; that he was not breaking the law; but that the police was merely testing him, and anticipating that he would break the law, showing the black man who had power and pull. And the way she always saw the police hold his truncheon, as if it was a long penis, in an everlasting erection, as if he was telling the black man, "Mine is more bigger and more harder than yours!" This is the way she always felt whenever she saw a police cruiser stop a black man in a car.

The night was darker now. She was walking on Davenport Road going towards Bloor Street, and the cruiser was still too far from her for her to see clearly. But she was sure that the man inside the cruiser was black. She hurried her steps. And when she drew almost abreast of the cruiser, it was still too dark for her to see the man's face. The roof light inside the cruiser was not on. But she would bet her bottom dollar that it was a black man, a black youth, a black child. Her stomach became tight. There were two policemen. She remembered the argument in the hairdressing salon. Two? Or three? There were two. And they were standing beside a car. It was a lovely car. She had seen cars like this one all over the Ravine where she worked in a mansion. It was a beautiful car. Many times, standing at the cold, large, picture window, looking out into the blank, white afternoons, with the rhythm and blues music from the Buffalo radio station behind her, she had admired these beautiful cars coming and going along the street in front of the large house. This was a beautiful car like those. It was gleaming. It was white. And it blended well with the snow that was not falling. And she wondered why the licence number plate did not contain numbers like other licence number plates. All it said was BLUE. What a strange licence to have BLUE? And she was feeling so good just a few moments ago. She understood blues. But what was this blue? He must be in a blue mood. What a strange licence to have! BLUE? But she laughed to herself: she herself liked the blues. Rhythm and blues. She stood up to investigate. She was sure there was someone in the back of the cruiser. She had just passed the show window of Mercedes-Benz, when the bright color of mauve in her hair was reflected back to her and showed her bathed and professionally coiffured, and hennaed. It startled her. The color did. For the instant of the reflection, she could not move. She stood up. She looked at herself in the reflection. She leaned her head slightly to the right, and then to the left; stood erect before the show window and could see not only her reflection but also a salesman in the window looking at her, with his right thumb raised in approval. He had smiled and she had smiled. And then she had moved on, after having stolen a last glance at herself. This was before she saw the police cruiser. And when she saw it, all that gaiety in the reflection in the show window evaporated. She was beside the cruiser now.

The two policemen were walking away from the cruiser, going to the white BMW; and she caught up with them. She stopped three feet from the policemen.

"Keep moving ma'am."

She wondered who was in the dark back seat of the cruiser. And she thought of the Jamaican man, the poor man and his two fatherless girl-children. They said that when the policemen burst into the house that Sunday afternoon, just before the peas and rice were dished and served, and the shot was fired, his head burst open just like when you drop a ripe watermelon from a certain height. They said his head burst open, clean clean clean.

"Why you-all always bothering black people? Why you-all don't go and try to catch real criminals, them who molesting children? And women?"

"None o' your business, ma'am."

"Who say it isn't none of my business? I pays taxes. I obey the law. I have a right to ask you this question, young man."

"Move on, lady! Or I arrest you for obstruction."

"Obstruction? Who I obstructing?"

"What did you say?"

She stood her ground. But she was not so stupid to repeat what she had said.

"Lord, look at this," she said under her breath. She felt she dared not pray, appeal nor talk to her God, aloud with the policemen to hear. And the policeman who spoke to her was about to forget about her, when she started up again. "I hope you're not taking advantage of that poor boy you got locked up in that cruiser and I hope you read him his rights and I hope he has a good lawyer to defend him, oh God, for if it was me I would surely lodge a complaint against the two o' you with the Human Rights Commission and complain and tell this policeman to please kiss my . . . "

"Lady!"

The policeman knew there was something said, although he did not quite know what was said. He knew there was this bond and agreement which he could not break. And he became uncomfortable, and nervous, and felt threatened, as if somebody, this woman standing in front of him, with nothing in her hands, save her handbag and a plastic bag full of left-over roast beef, was going to take his life from him. And he rested his hand on the side of his waist where he had his gun.

She took a last glance at the beautiful car, and shook her head with some disappointment that she could not see through the heavy tint of the glass to make out the person inside, and satisfy her prejudice that it had to be a young black man. But she was not going to give up so easily. So, she leaned over the bonnet of the car, being careful not to smear its sheen, almost feeling the cold of the glass, as she peered through the obstructing glass. Inside, on the passenger's side, was a young man. She could see that much easily enough. But she wanted to be sure, to be certain that this tinted glass was not playing tricks to the young man's color. Perhaps he was black, and this tint was changing his color. She could touch the glass now, and feel the coldness of it, and at the same time, the comforting heat from the engine, even though it was turned off. She stared, and saw him. It was a young man. A young white man. And the man inside the car, feeling his own shame for his predicament, held his head aside, as if he thought his profile would hide the identity of his face from this malicious woman whom he had seen five minutes before. He did not know her, could not remember ever seeing a woman with her hair dyed mauve, and sticking up in the air as this woman's hair was doing in the tricky changing light caused by the passing cars. He held his face in a profile against her staring eyes. And felt the curiosity in her eyes, and thought he could feel the love and the sadness in her manner. If he was not handcuffed behind his back, he would push the door open, and invite her in. But what would he say to her? Perhaps he would call out for help. She moved away, walking backwards for the first few steps, and the smallness of his space, and the fit of the manacles made the car seat large, and it became larger and embraced him in the growing space of his temporary imprisonment. She was walking backwards to get a last glimpse of the licence plate, BLUE, which still made her smile at its eccentricity. And when she walked past the police cruiser, her body flinched, and the tightness that she sometimes deliberately put her body into, to prevent the cold from climbing all over her bones, came to her, as she moved beside the cruiser. She could smell no similar smell of polish as she had done standing beside the beautiful car. She could sense no powerful fragrance of leather in the interior, as she had surmised with the white car, named BLUE. And she could feel no warmth from the engine of the police cruiser, as she relished in that short moment when her curiosity challenged her wisdom. The police cruiser was cruel and ugly and tense and made her feel guilty. And in this shame, in this surrender of self-control she walked away not being able to tell, should she be asked, what was the color of the cruiser. But she made a note of the writing on its side. Division 52. She would never forget that number. And she amused herself, heading to the next bus stop, and if no bus came to rescue her from the gnawing cold, the subway station at Bay, that if she was a gambling woman, she would play combinations of 52 in tomorrow's Lotto 6/49.

Time, and not the consequences nor the cause of his presence here, this evening where he was, was heavy upon BJ'S nerves. He paced up and down, with various thoughts entering his head, and his panic and isolation made the space much much larger, so that he was buried in its vastness, and the time and the consequences, what they could be, and the cause became real and he could see his life, his entire life in three short hours that had passed. All these things passed through his mind, and for each of them, he had no solution. He paced up and down, not having enough length in the square space to make his pacing more dramatic, and less of pathos. And when he again realized the restriction of the square space, his mind bounded backwards to a time, which he had almost wiped from his memory, recalling a time when he had spent four hours in this same police station, in another cell, alone and not knowing really why he had been locked up, not having had a charge laid against him, not having had a policeman enter the warm cell and interrogate him about the alleged theft of a kid's bicycle that afternoon in August when he and three other kids were horsing around and pretending to be bagmen — they did not play with girls near the corner grocery store, trying to beg enough quarters to buy ice cream, when his mother was at work down in the Ravine, this other kid came wobbly on his bicycle, his first, a present *his* mother had given him for Christmas past; and one of the other three kids took the bike playfully from the little kid and the little kid started to cry and ran home with tears in his eyes and told his mother, and his father returned with sunburnt arms bristling with black hairs and chest like a barrel covered with the skin of an animal with the black hairs punching from under a nylon undershirt and with his underpants showing just above the waist of his green trousers, when the kid pointed at the colored fella, dad; the colored fella is who took my bike; and all hell broke loose with *mama mia's* spewn all over the road in white vomit, and as if it was still Christmas and hail was falling, and the cops came screaming down the avenue going against the pointing of the white arrow, two carloads of them, to solve this ghetto delinquency, that began as a small neighborhood kid's prank, "I didn' mean nothing" and slam! into the cruiser, nigger; into the goddamn cruiser, you goddamn nigger, *mama mia* Hail Mary's and BJ not understanding the various languages and accents being vomited against him, no explanation in the eyes of the man who owned the peddling grocery store, no explanation from his three friends who did not know Italian and Greek and were no longer within ear-shot and speaking distance to translate this crime, no understanding from the father with his chest buried in black hairs ripping the air with gestures which BJ thought at first were karate chops, but later knew their meaning even though he knew no Italian and no Greek, and no understanding from the four cops who descended armed and sunburnt like the father, to solve this serious crime, git, goddamnit, git! into the goddamn cruiser! no, not in the goddamn front seat, in the fucking back, where youse belong; and they took him down, and did not book him, and put him in a nice large warm cell large for his age, bigger, goddamnit nigger warmer than the piss-small room you and your goddamn mother lives in! you fucking West Indians! and they left him there to stew and to mend his thieving ways, and then, hours later when the time for his supper of plain rice and boiled king fish and boiled green bananas had come and gone, the truth was known and the kind sergeant came with a styrofoam cup of steaming coffee, Have a cup, come now, have a cup; and then said, A little mistake, if you can understand what I mean, you being such a little fella to know these serious, big things, a little goddamn mistake and you happened to be the goddamn unlucky one. So, beat it, kid, and don't let me lay my goddamn eyes on you again! Git!

Too young to know what he had done; not knowing what he had done; not knowing what the policeman in the cruiser had done; not knowing the exact shape of his fate this time, but wise enough to know that he was going to have some fate, BJ paced and paced. And then, perhaps because of his Black Muslim sense of destiny, he stopped walking up and down. He decided not to worry. "Let the motherfuckers come!" he said, but within his heart, he was calmed by the small square space, and by his history. And then he worked it out, in detail, and with a logic he was capable of, but which in the circumstances of the steel surrounding him in the four smells of impatience and of no restraint, the smell of vomit and old urine, in the circumstances of an unclear head, he had permitted to elude and overwhelm him. But when he had worked out his plan, he lit a cigarette, all that they had left him, and in his mind, for his mind was clean and not touched by his circumstances, he took out the long-playing record, could see his fingers ease it out of the jacket, and put it on his stereo, and remained standing, listening to the words of Malcolm X's speech, *The Ballot or the Bullet.* He was asleep, standing, before the introduction of Malcolm X had finished. And he was stirred from his reverie by the opening of the door, and walked out into the dark cold parking lot, to his car now buried and made invisible by the falling snow. Marco was somewhere else: in another cell, held until his parents could come down from North York, to sign him out. Two men walked beside him. They were not in uniform. He recognized his car, for the snow had not touched the letters, BLUE, on the licence plate. And he made the gesture to go to it, even though he did not have the keys. And he was corrected. "We're going for a little drive . . . " And he was put into the back of the cruiser. Left alone, to himself, behind the plastic protector thick as brick, strong as steel, and with his two hands free. The blue unmarked cruiser drove off in white pouring quiet.

From the top of the street, near Bathurst, she could see the red lights. They were whirring. They scared her each time so much just to see them, that they gave her the impression they were making great noise, and that the red lights were silencers of that noise. She could see the four police cruisers parked in the middle of the road, and one at the side. She could see the large red, ugly vehicle of the fire department. She could see a smaller, but equally ugly white-painted ambulance. And from the distance she was, turning into the smaller street where she lived, she could see the road filled with people. People were leaving doors open and running and passing her as she walked, heading in the direction of the spinning red lights on top of the police cruisers and the fire department truck and the ambulance. She had never witnessed a fire of this bigness in this city before, and so she walked as fast as she could, in the deep sliding snow, to reach the sight.

The road became more crowded when another police vehicle, a small panel-type truck marked Tactical Squad, forced itself into the road, from the other end of the street. She was sure now that someone was holding someone hostage. She had watched many of these scenes every day on the soap opera shows in the mansion down in the Ravine where she worked. And tickled by the transformation of a movie into a slice of her real life, she tried to hasten her stride, but without success, for the snow was too deep. She felt the excitement the spinning red lights gave off, the curiosity of staring at these kinds of lights on a highway ahead of you, and she passed each house from one end to the next now as long as a block, her blood quickening, and not once through her mind passed the thought of "Who's sick?" and she did not once consider her neighbors nor the landlord in this absent thought of compassion. It was the excitement she was heading to. People, she could see them now, people were being kept back behind a ribbon of yellow plastic, and one policeman stood guarding the yellow plastic ribbon, which measured the area round one house, and disappeared out of sight, perhaps down a lane, or the thin unwalkable space between two houses, and this ribbon reminded her of birthday parties back home, and of Christmas morning, and once when she was no longer a child, taken by her mother to an opening of something where they had a long ribbon like this before the entrance. On that occasion, the vicar of her church cut the ribbon with scissors. Her excitement was now in her blood, and with her blood hot, she was no longer recognizing things, and landmarks and the shape of the uneven concrete steps the landlord had incorrectly built to save money, and that caused her to slip even in the summer. She was forcing herself against these strangers to reach the entrance. And she could see the splotches and the drying small pools, the spots, taking some time to be registered in her excitement as blood. She could see the blood on the steps and blood along the narrow lane, and the lane became difficult to see, as it went beside the house on the left. A dog walked out as if it was drunk. And when it vomited, what came out was like grape juice.

She could see policemen inside the room, collecting things, some of which they were already bringing out. And she could see the attendants from the ambulance arranging something heavy on to a stretcher. She could see the clothes being brought out. She could see the stereo equipment, speakers, CD player, amplifier. And the books. And the small Bible. She wondered who lived here. She could see the books. Books always interested him. And then she realized she was thinking of her son. He always had his head inside a book. And one book she saw was the Holy Qur'an. She wondered if this was the wrong address.

She could see the policemen inside the room, at the back near the door to her kitchen, walking round the small space, nervous and silent. The street outside was silent too. No one was talking. But she could hear their anger and their resentment and their hatred. She was beginning to learn how to listen to this kind of silence.

And then, there was a sound. A sound very similar to surprise, or to shock, or even to the satisfaction that what you are about to see, is the shock, but that you are not prepared for it.

They were bringing a body out. Two ambulance attendants carried the stretcher which had wheels like a bier of a coffin, but which had to be lifted part of the journey, the short journey from the back of the house down the two short cement steps which the landlord had not got around to fixing properly, a little way to the right of the rear door, and to the ambulance after going through the thin lane, down two more steps and up the three steps of the basement apartment front door. As they lifted it up the steps, the wind which was cold and strong blew the cloth off the body of the corpse. A cry went through the people. It was a young man. A boy, still with his mother's features. No more than sixteen or seventeen or eighteen. A black youth, with a close-trimmed haircut, with Zeds for patterns and an X for style, dressed in a black woolen jersey, black slacks, white socks and black shoes that could, if he was alive, help him to jump against gravity, like a basketball star. Or Michael Jordan. And when the wind had taken the blanket on its short wild curtsy to the wind and to the night, the people made that sound again, like a gigantic taking in of wind.

She could see it too. And she saw the head, and it was out of shape from something that had hit it. Disfigured. And the blood was covering the face. And the stretcher was covered in thick blood. And the black clothes the youth was dressed in were red now, more than black. The blood seemed to have its own unkind and disfiguring disposition, and it seemed to drip and mark the journey from the room at the back of the basement apartment through the room itself, through the small backyard, through the lane and out into the cold wind. It looked as if a cannon had struck the head, and the head had exploded and had been cut into pieces, like a watermelon that had slipped out of the hand. To her, it seemed as if the brains of the young man were coming through his mouth, as if his eyes were lost against the impact of the bullet. To her, it looked like a watermelon that was smashed by the wheels of a car.

It was too much. It was too cold. It was too brutal. It was too cruel. And there was too much blood. Worse than the American soap opera she had watched earlier the afternoon of this Friday night, down in the Ravine.

"BJ! BJ! Fuck!"

It was somebody screaming. She did not know the voice. She looked around, in this crowd of people only one of whom she knew, her landlord, and then she saw the owner of the voice. It was a young man. There were tears in the young man's eyes. He was dressed in a black jogging suit, black Adidas, and white athletic socks, and he seemed to have something wrong with his right hand or his right side, for he was doing something with his body which made it shake, as if he had a nervous habit, like a tick, hitting his right hand against his right thigh. He looked Portuguese to her. She did not know him. "BJ! BJ! Fuck!"

1992

Ship, Sail! Sail Fast!

She did not take the taxi through the unknown streets to see him off. It had been his first visit to the small town, where she lived in a place popular among students with a dog which she'd found and kissed and slept in bed with; and before he had finished dinner, she removed her plate with half the food eaten, and placed it on the floor for the dog to lap up, and relish. He had stopped eating after that. He had not spoken another word. Now, he had fifteen minutes, through this meandering slow town, in the taxi driven by a man who did not seem to know the town, to catch the train. It was not the last train, but his anger made it seem like that, and helped to justify his fury and his nervousness, and his dislike bordering on hatred for the innocent, slow taxi driver. They passed through the streets he had walked two days ago, hand in hand with her, comfortable in his new love, anxious for the bed that would follow the cool, long, uninteresting stroll beside the river, along desolate streets with solid buildings on them where men and women who looked like students moved just as slowly as this taxi; he refused to be impressed by the beauty which people say you can find in small towns. He did not like small towns.

He felt like a man escaping custody. But during his incarceration in the small, dog infested room, he had grown accustomed to the plastic cover on the toilet bowl which he had to sit sideways on; to the shower which beat against the sides of its tin enclosure; to the dining table which his knees knocked against, causing the legs to buckle and almost fold and toss the food untouched to the dog, as it was a folding table made for playing cards; and the bed made of three found mattresses of three different sizes, which slid each time he mounted them, and her. He had got accustomed, like a man who has acknowledged that he has to spend time against his wishes, in a confined space, getting to know the restriction and abiding with it, because there is no other way.

"How much farther?"

"We there soon."

He looked at the cluttered dashboard that had more instruments on it than he had ever seen in a taxi in the city; and was searching for the one that told the time and speed.

"Why are you doing twenty-five?"

"In this town, the limit is thirty, sir."

"So, why are you..?"

"Can't go faster, in this town."

They were on a street where the buildings were large and empty, and he thought of olden times when sugar or flour or sawdust must have been made in that building, and the streets were crowded and the traffic moved like this creeping taxi, as the townsfolk travelled in polished, scrubbed carriages, with rubbed-down horses.

On his left was the vast body of water the color of lead; they called it The Lake, but he had never seen a lake this size; and close by, to the side of the street, was a ship that stretched for two blocks, looming, and he thought of disaster. What was she doing now, left alone in the angry farewell of silent words? Was she kissing the dog to make up for his anger? Or kicking the dog to transfer her disappointment with the man who had entered her life, just as two ships pass each other in fog or falling snow? He thought of the ship which was large enough to enter oceans, faltering in its arrival at this port, and hitting a large rock, with its invisible dimensions below the surface, and crumpling; and voices raised in terror and frustration.

When he had seen her body, and the softness of her limbs; her breasts which his anxious hands covered; and he felt her body shudder and then collapse, as his touch became lighter, moving over her not quite brown, not quite white, cool skin, she had held her eyes closed against his passion; but her body kept shaking. In her eyes was something like terror, something that said she was fearful of the ecstasy she had started to enjoy.

And he'd told himself then, that he knew.

A horn sounded. He did not know about trains. It could be the train signal getting ready to leave. He could not see any building which looked like a train station. But in these small towns, the station could be a shed. Buried behind the two-storied brown-painted buildings which flanked the street. The street was crowded. And the slow-moving cars reminded him that it was Sunday; and he guessed that no one here took a train on a summer afternoon on a Sunday, preferring to be in Sunday school, or walking beside the unmoving Lake with dog and kid and girlfriend and lover, watching the ship that has not moved in years.

"Here we are!"

And the ride he was taking with his eyes and imagination has come to this sparse end, with men and women loitering outside the station, and the train huffing and chugging. The ticket seller pauses to ask a woman how was her trip to the big city, and whether her son is still in the hospital, when the horn goes again and he wants to pull the ticket seller from behind her cage and spread her on the floor. The town is slow. And the talk in this town is slow.

"Have a nice trip sir, there is no hurry as the train ain' going nowhere, it just got in and I'll tell you when you are to board, if you want a coffee just around the corner or potato chips or a pop you can sit here then, and I'll see you and tell you."

She is lying on the three-tiered bed and her eyes are soaked in water and they seem like soft slits of passion and they are looking into the eyes of the white-haired dog who looks like an African albino through a meeting of two bloods, and she asks the dog why her man does not like him, that he is only a dog.

He sits by a window. The train cuts through a village on the outskirts of the town. And he can see the barbecues belching smoke; and a man with thick pieces of dead animal in his hand in a bowl with forceps. The train is going through the backyard of village after village. The roses are still red. The green is the grass on which the children fooled the rules of football, touching the football and touching the grass. And then there is only corn. In the city the corn is already dead. But in this rumbling, inhospitable cutting through the privvies of these homes, the corn raises its head and can reach a tall man to his shoulder, hiding secret and compelling crimes, unseen by the eyes of the woman, old as an aunt, who sits on a collapsible chair and breathes in the perfume of the red dead animal. Beef.

Years ago, he would walk through the ears of corn, and rip the blonde hair from the stalk when no one was looking and turn himself into a European with a silk moustache. Or if he was reading a book about buccaneers, make a beard like Sinbad the Sailor, and mow through the waves of the green and the corn and come out at the end, miscalculated like a pilot who had not learned his lessons, on the compass. A wrecked frigate.

"Ship, sail!"
"Sail fast!"
"Hommany men 'pon deck?"

"Twenty!"

"Give me twenty grains o' corn, you idiot! I only have three in my hand. How-haw-haw!"

Five years after that evening when the sky was golden, as if there could be autumn in the island, and the sea, not a lake, was blue and white with the waves like the moustache of old Englishmen, she held his hand, and led him into the ocean of corn, where there was no current and no neighbors, where the trade winds could not reach, with the girl his only rudder, leading him into the valley of information and learning; and it must have been three minutes at the most, but three minutes filled with a lifetime of the mystery of this young girl's experience; his hand was trembling; and he thought she was taking him into this deepness to continue, she and he, the children's game. "Ship, sail! Sail fast!" It was he who had told her five nights before, when their school books had been put under the table for the weekend, "Twenty! Twenty men 'pon deck!"

"You little idiot!"

Now, the train has moved from the crowded yards with the small swimming pools, many of them raised above the lawns, with a ladder for a midget taking the shaking steps from the grass to the brink of disaster. It was the woman who had told him, just as he came out of the small shower walled-in by tin, where each drop sounded like a cataract, it was the woman who had told him, "Last summer, you know? Ten children drowned in swimming pools, the round ones, you know? This summer, and it's early in summer, August only, you know? Already thirteen fallen off step-ladders into the water, and drowned." The yards are larger. And the pools are dug into the green ground. It is very peaceful. It is Sunday afternoon, and no children are splashing in them. The corn comes right up to the kitchen garden bed in a corner of the paled backyard, far from the pool, and he can see green tomatoes and some red lettuce and other green things too far in the distance to name; he can see moustaches and beards on the corn. He wonders who were the first boys and girls, men and women, who ran through these green tunnels, hiding from danger; and who rode these green rails hiding from the inhabitants of the other country across the vast body of water? He had forgotten to ask the man the name of the lake. And in the book about the town, he had not reached that paragraph of its history.

The fields are running beside the train. They have the same speed. But he does not know the miles per hour. Two passenger cars and a truck come into his view on the right side, the farther side of the window. He pushes the shade up. They are beside him now, abreast, well within range. If he had a gun with power with a scope glass for accuracy, the cars and the truck would be brought into his sight, and *pow!*, with just one shot he could explode them. In his mind he aims, using the cigarette in his mouth as the rifle; but the smoke clouds his aim, so he exchanges this for the pencil he was using to write the entry under Sunday the 6th in his diary; and all of a sudden, the two cars and the truck are left behind in the rumbling of the train as it goes into a bend. The fields of corn are running beside this monster of iron.

And in them he sees the figure of a woman. Jane. He knows her name, because her name is the name of her plight. Her clothes were originally white, long and flowing over her legs which have caused so much pain and brutality and loving longing, and which have become the legs of any man assuming he was white. Jane is running beside the train. Her eyes are balls of horror, for in them he can see himself, without having seen her in that large yard on the other side of the body of water; can feel the cow-skin rip into her soft black back, the skin was no longer beautiful and black. A painting of barbed wire with thick powerful brush-strokes of red became her back. And she was the one who carried the largest bale of cotton, the largest collection of twigs, the largest of her seven children on her back. Her strong legs keep her abreast of the train, and her arms reach to the side of the train, where the short steps are, the same size as the step-ladder from which the thirteen children, not her children, not her cousins, fell into the raised, plastic swimming pools in the first short part of this summer. But with all her strength and desperation to jump on board, the train is still too fast for her agility.

Jane walked the hundred miles from the place across the water, without knowing how to swim, without knowing how to read the geography of the map, and all she knew was that the map had a meaning less intractable than geography and theodolites and compasses. The sun this Sunday afternoon is crisp and warm. Jane walked during the night, and slept like a big city bagwoman wherever her bodily strength exhausted her mind that held this promise of walking through the endless corn fields, beside the iron rails of this monster taking him away from the woman with the dog to the big city where no corn grows.

No cotton grows on the streets of the big city. Only a sign on a store on Yonge Street, and racks outside in the whirling wind, that say *Au Coton*. It is not the same cotton that Jane knew and lived through, and nearly died of. And just before Jane grows small and smaller in the disappointed distance, he sees the large black body of a man, naked down to his shorts, covered in perspiration. Jane's husband, Jim. And even though Jim cannot stand beside the road and raise his finger, and cajole the driver of a car to slow down and stop, he understands the protocol of catching rides. He sent Jane, a woman, to do his dirty finger-raising business. It was like that back in that yard in the other place across the body of water, when chickens and ducks, pigs and cows, and some snakes, roamed in a greater freedom of space than even he and Jane; and in that time, it was he who understood that a little mistake, a word said under the breath but loud enough for Mas'r to hear; the misappropriation of one of those freed hens in the yards; the miscalculation in the pouring of molasses for the horse and jackass, leaving too deep a bottom in the bottom of the pail; and his ignorance of mathematics and addition, but his proficiency with subtraction: twenty hams was put in the smoke-filled shed with the hickory leaves and the smoke broke out as if the whole goddamn place was on fire, Mas'r; and he said, under his breath, but too loud, Amma wish this goddamn place were going up in flame with these hams; but when he checked their smoking and their curing, one was gone. One gone! These two words became like a bell in the night, like a boot at the door, like a tap on the shoulder in a crowd, like the leather in the boot of the Gestapo, all over that land across the body of water. "One gone!" And dogs barked. Lights came on. Lanterns were carried. Dogs yelped, tasting the sweetness of blood. Whips were cracked for suppleness. And for length. And for deadliness. And men jumped on the backs of horses. Rifles and pistols were taken from their shelves, already oiled and ready for use. Bullets and shots were fired for practice in the air. And the small children, who knew those two words, laughed in their sleep, and wished, and wished. So that small miscalculation of arithmetic; and how was he to know, since no one had sat him down under the tree in the large yard, after his endless chores, to say, "One and one is two. Two and two is four. One from four is t'ree!" And for the love of his body; and for the love of his woman, and the love she bore him, he sent her forward, he pushed her forward, to take her rightful place of leadership, and she took and endured the sting of justice. It was a chastisement he could no longer bear. It was a punishment his black body held no unmarked area the size of a postage stamp to endure. That is why Jane came closer from the deep green patch of corn to hail the train.

He can see the man's disappointment. And the man's shame. For the man knew he was a man, even in the circumscribed circumstance of his life and of his woman's life. But he had no power to behave as a man. As the way he knew, if he were living in a different land, he was to behave. It was surprising that the man naked down to his shorts, torn and tattered from catching them against branches and barbed wire and the teeth of howling dogs, perhaps the almost deadly flight of a bullet; his clothes in the same condition as his woman's, it was surprising that he did not take his failure out on his woman and beat her in the full sight of the disappearing train.

"Never get tired of that scenery," the conductor said, punching a hole in the ticket. "Ya know. Years and years I been making this trip. In summer, winter, the fall and spring. And ya know. Always grabs my attention just to look out and see the things and the fields. Interesting, ain't it?" He gives back the ticket, takes another from his pocket and places it above the seat. He does the same thing two seats beyond. Those two tickets are of a different color. So, the color must mean destination. Did Jane have a color scheme for her hoped destination? Could Jim have told her what to choose? "Tell ya something, " the conductor says, sitting in the opposite seat. "You seem to be a sensible gentleman, educated I would say. And I hope you take this the right way, but I would swear that in them fields o' corn, there's people living. I don't mean living as against dead, you understand. What I mean is this. There could be people in them fields carrying on a life like you and me. With differences of course. If you see what I mean! You ever seen it that way?"

"Could be."

They sit in silence, and the passing of time coincides with and runs besides the scenery they are watching.

"Well, have a good trip for the rest o' the way. Been good talking to ya."

He moves away, down the shaking corridor. The tune he is humming is barely recognizable, *Georgia on my mind . . .*

Why were there no mile posts beside railroad tracks so a man can tell how far he has travelled? Or how fast? It was so strange that you had to be in the carriage, the cage, the hub, or was it the *caboose,* to see where you were going. He is getting tired, and the monotony of the speed measured against the lasting green fields is beginning to dull his mind and his attention, just like the sensation in a plane, looking through the window shaped like a toilet seat, at clouds that bury the bulk of the plane and come harmless and dangerously close. He is not the kind of a man who could slump into a seat, take out a paperback book and read, and then fall asleep. Or talk to the stranger beside him. What would he say to this unknown man? Normally, he closes his eyes and pretends to be invisible. Or asleep. But during this trip, an escape from the woman who loved kissing the dog, and kissing him afterwards with the same lips, escaping from the dog as much as from the woman, he has pressed his head against the plate-glass window and the images of his conscience strike against the cool glass; and he sees the half-dressed Jane and her naked husband, Jim.

Now, the train is beside water. And he thinks of that childhood, years ago in the sun, when there was only water at the end of his reaching eyes, wherever he looked. *Ship, sail; sail fast!* There were ships, many ships; ships with sails bringing cod fish from Newfoundland; and the crows of the sea, those carrion-eating birds were numberless on the decks like albatrosses; and when the crows regain their dignity and sail away from the rotting, rotten fish, all that is left are the bodies of men and women. He cannot see the faces of these men. He cannot see the faces of these women. Only their skin and bones, no more covered with the salty delicious flesh of the cod fish but with its bones and white scabs and greyish skin, like the sin of age and disease and withering sickness. Every Saturday morning, his mother soaked a saucepan full of that cod from the Banks of Newfoundland, and after hours of softening the flesh, removed the bones, scrubbing away the white and the grey from the slab of cod no thicker than the cover of his green-backed exercise book, in which he wrote exercises in English composition: *the boy stood on the burning deck!;* and then the fresh small tomatoes grown in plots that were miniatures of the fields he passes on this train; and the lard oil, the sickened thin cod came alive in taste and deliciousness, as she poured it thick and richer after her operation, all over the thick, *cloiding* dish made from corn, dried and shelled and husked and ground by hand in Mr. Thorpe's Corn Grinding machine; and called it cou-cou. They told him when he left the island where this feast was manufactured, that cou-cou was from Africa; and now, in this body of water through which the train passes, over it , on a bridge, that past is bridged by the memory, and he can see those dying bodies left by the carrion-eating birds. Amongst them, there is no Jane. That was not a name she was christened with in Africa. There is no one called Jim. But he knows no African names. Once, in a fit of anger, he erased the name his mother told him he was given, while she stirred the okras into the slippery pot with the ground corn, and put in its place a large *X*. But *X* means nonentity. *X* means illiteracy. *X* marks the spot. Once, in the cod fish sauce thickened with tomatoes and fresh eschalots, he found a bone the shape of an *X*. It did not hide any mystery. So, he spent the afternoon, roaming through the village sucking it, as the boys played cricket; as the girls played rounders and as the men drank rum. His mother was at home reading *Revelations,* chapter 13. She loved *Revelations*. She loved chapter 13. And she loved the first verse most of all. A crumbling, dried cross, or an *X*, depending upon his haste or impatience to read the verse five times each night, marked the spot. *And I stood upon the sand of the sea, and saw a beast rise up out of the sea, having seven heads and ten horns, and upon his horns ten crowns, and upon his heads the name of blasphemy.* They were surrounded by water, the Caribbean Sea or the Atlantic Ocean depending upon which hill he sat on and watched the sea. And later in the fading day, at dusk, the boys and the girls gathered in a circle, and played the game, *Ship, sail; sail fast!* Later still, the same night, the mothers and his mother sat in the backdoor looking out into the yard filled with sleeping chickens and ducks and centipedes, and his mother held them in thrall, "Once upon a time, there was horse that had seven heads, and ten foots, any my God, one dark night as I walking home from the Marine Hotel where the Englishmens stay . . . " His mother never worked at the Marine Hotel. But the vision of seven heads and ten feet crippled him and he drew closer to the same girl who had taken him into the corn, to feel her comfort, to be protected from these beasts of the land, and to feel her breasts. "Wait!" she said, in an embarrassingly high voice, a stranger now to his advances, "who you think I is, boy? Who you think you feeling-up, boy?" She pushed him aside, and he was spared greater embarrassment in that cool darkness where he could not see even his own feet in its thickness, and no one could see his furtive trembling hand, similar to the hand of Jane, disappearing from the side of the rails going back into the dense green corn. It was fifteen years after that rebuke before he had the strength to raise his hand from his side to touch a woman on her waist. And he saw the horse his mother was talking about, and which had ten heads and forty feets; and he was in a road by himself, and the horse was coming in his direction and the eighty crescents of iron in its cantering madness were like the fright in a dream of standing in the middle of a tunnel with lights at the side, overhead, and curving in the short noisy distance round an invisible bend and hearing the loud clatter of an approaching train but not being able to decide which end of the tunnel is the entry or the exit, and then in his confusion all goes black, and only the noise now closer to a roar, brings him to resignation and the making of the sign of the Cross, two times on his shaking breast. Just before Jane had disappeared out of the rectangular train window, the man had seen her make a sign, and now that he had vomited that part of his past, he realizes that it was a Cross she was tracing in her broker ambition to hitch a ride to a big city where she thought her rags would be replaced by silk and stockings and pumps.

And he is in a dream, rumbled to sleep by the level of the sliding rails, by the lulling movement of the speed. He can hear his dream and he can hear the train. His head hits against the cold plate glass window, not hard enough to wake him, but strong enough to pierce the dream with the reality of knowing he is not dead, that he is disappearing from the small town, and without watching or counting the miles in the darkness outside, he sits like a man drugged from gin waiting for this journey to end. Jane passes through his dream one more time. She is wearing silk and black pantyhose that is ribbed with an almost invisible design. And she has pumps on her feet. Her legs are strong from all the running she has done. Her breasts are prominent in a style and fashion of dignity and determination. His mother would have told her, "You walking like a woman now. With your chest push-out. If you have it, show it off, girl. Show it off." She is walking beside Jim. Not that the two of them are a couple. There is not that kind of love between them. She is walking beside Jim, because she could not get rid of him, her encumbrance, her disappointment, her hindrance, from catching that train that would have brought her sooner to glory and to the freedom she was seeking. Jane is in a dress that tells him she is a working woman, a woman who rises at five to make food for her children, two from Jim in the five years of her new life in the big city, and in that time, two years more than the contended legal space of decentness and trial and error to make her into spouse, woman, wife; and to make up his mind; Jim walks beside her as if he is not tied to her; as if he was plunked there by masculine ego; and not as her partner. He is dressed in a very expensive suit of shiny silk material. The bottoms of his trousers are narrow, and the "play" in the legs gives them a zoot-suit look. He has a long chain from his fob pocket hanging in a sweep by his knees and up again into his left trousers pocket. It looks like gold. The waist of the jacket is small and it shows the rippling muscles of his back that had chopped wood in the plantation yard. The shoulders are flat and broad. And the jacket hangs like the flair in the skirt of the dress Jane is wearing. "Why're you always walking beside me dressed like a pimp? Am I picking fares for you? You'se my pimp? Or my *man?* The man I want walking beside me is a man dressed in overalls, and open-necked shirt in summer, a heavy sweater in winter, and boots reinforce with steel. A laboring man. A working man. A man who works. A man who knows sweat and who carries a lunch pail to the site." Jim has not worked since he arrived in the big city. "What do I want with a man walking beside me carrying a purse in his hand like if he is some *faggot!* And with a beeper like if he is some, some, some *pimp!* Or crack dealer! Or time-keeper. Who're you keeping time for?"

"Bitch!"

It was as if he was fighting to catch his breath, so bitter and short and fierce was the way he uttered the word. It was a new word. It was a word he had heard her called by, years ago in the large plantation yard, swept so clean by him when he was a boy, and drenched in the life-giving sun, when his knowledge of the new language he was growing up with, English, was sufficient for him to ape the word *bitch,* spewed out of the mouth of the Master of the Slaves.

The towns and hamlets are fireflies in the darkness that surround the train as he moves in the snoring silence, coming into view, and before he can surmise where he is passing, and even after the trainman announces the place, it is gone. Like the dream of Jane and Jim. He wonders if they caught another train. But it could not be: this was the last train. The last train from the small town the short distance of a bridge spanning water that no longer moved. He can sense the smell of destination: the air is heavier; the cigarette smoke in the coach is thicker. The fireflies change into the eyes of cats in the darkness that is not so thick. Around him now, are lights as numerous as Christmas, but in the moving distance, all the same color, against the black trunks of roads and intersections.

The woman in the small town becomes lovable the farther he is from her. Her dog is no longer a pest, but a pet that he could, with some understanding, cuddle and kiss, if he had three rums in his system to give him the strength and stomach. The small economizing room was as spacious as the coach, and the toilet with its sides made of tin, did not reverberate to the noise of his peeing as the shaking latrine on the train did, spewing his urine on the seat and making it difficult for him to aim in the unsteady bullseye of the soiled oval. The lights in the coach go out, just as the trainman announces the last town before his destination. And in that temporary darkness he forgets dog and woman, room and enclosed bathroom. He is standing, pushing papers into his leather bag, putting on his shoes, taking a last drag on the cigarette, checking that his Walkman is not left for a dishonest passenger to find and keep, getting into shape to manage the rush from the train and into the subway, and bounce women with large bags out of his way, and ignore the begging man, hungry at this time of night, as he can spare the time it takes to dig into his pocket less than he can spare the change.

All he is thinking of now is how short is the time to get from this train and the hissing steam down the stairs into the subway off the platform four stops north, and into his house to pour himself a stiff gin and tonic and listen to the midnight program of contemporary jazz. Before he leaves the train, stepping on the rickety iron step; "Watch your step, now," the same entreaty as "Spare any change?" and he has already wiped woman and dog, Jane and Jim out of his mind. He is back again in the big city. And it was only a train ride.

1993

From *The* Tom Clarke Columns

GRENADA SECRET DOCUMENT 1: SCROON'S TELEPHONE CALL

"Who I got there? Who I talking to? Hello? Hello?"

"Señoras, señores! Con la frente contrita de los americanos que no han . . . "

"I keep-telling these revolution-boys to fix the blasted telephone lines, and you think they would listen to me? You think they would listen to a humble man like me? All they want is Cuba and Castro . . . All I hearing 'bout-here is Spanish, and nothing but Spanish . . . Hello? Barbados? Who I got there?

"This is Scroon! Scroon. A' 's' at the front o' the name! My name have-on a' 's' at the top. Yes! Scroon! The Governor-General! I trying to reach Barbados. Tha' is Barbados? Good. Lemme talk to the Brugguh-dear. Yes, The Brugguh-dear formerly the Feel-marshall."

" . . . Han podido entrar aun en America . . . "

"Tha' is New York? I got Amurca? I just hear the word. 'Amurca', call . . . "

"This is the Brugguh-dear! Brugguh-dear! Scroon, there?"

"Brugguh-dear? Man, I so glad to reach you! All I hearing 'bout here is Spanish and more Spanish, and I never get the chance to learn none, so I really don't know what they saying. But Brugguh-dear, I glad you on the line."

"Is the Brugguh-dear talking to you."

"Brugguh-dear, things bad, man. We need help down in here, yuh. They killing people. They shooting-up people. People falling-off walls all round the place where they have me in custody."

"Give me your logistics, then. I have to know your logistics, before I move in . . . "

"But Brugguh-dear, I thought we talk last night 'bout the logic o' moving-in with your Eight Army, and the Armies o' Dominica, Sin-Lucia, Jamaica and Sin-Vincent? You haven't change your mind concerning this rescue, have you, Brugguh-dear? 'cause they got me surround. All round-here in the background is pure bullets firing and heavy equipment. I thought you say um was logical to get a Carbean arm-force with a Carbean capability, to liberate we and all o' we who don't know Spanish . . . "

"I don't mean logics. Scroon, I mean logistics. How we going-move in? How we going-tek-over? How we going-say we had to move-in when we move in. Them is logistics."

"Oh! 'cause you had me nervous for a minute there."

"Wha' is that I hearing in the background? Them is cannons? Artilleries? They sound real pretty. Mortars? I hearing land-to-air missives that the Cubans plant there?"

"Oh! You mean the noise? I playing classical music. Um is the *1812 Overture . . .* "

"Scroon, turn-down the blasted radio or stereo or whatever um is you playing, man! And listen to wha' I tell you. First, we got to get permission to move-in. *Some* kind o' permission. You know 'bout any old treaties sign between wunnuh and we?"

"Permission? Treaties?"

"You think you could duss-off the Instrument the Queen give you when you was sworn-in, in 1974, as Governor-General?"

"My instrument clean. My instrument with me. It here, look! Look! 'Course yuh can't see my instrument 'cause we talking 'pon the phone. But if you couldda been here, in Grenada, in the flesh, I would tek-out my instrument and show you, and show you the power I have."

"Any lawful person in Grenada, somebody *within* the law o' the land we need. We got to get *that* person to invite we in, before we could move-in. You understand what I saying?"

"Um I is me! Is that person then! I is the legal and lawful head o' down here. But concerning the old treaties, I think I hear somebody say that Maurice tear-them-up before he dead, yuh."

"Well, look at um, this way, then, Scroon. You think you could sneak-out something write-down 'pon a piece o' paper, in your own-own writing-hand, telling we in Barbados, to wit, that you, in your capacity as head o' state, inviting-we-in, to clean up the place? Yuh could write-um with lead-pencil, if yuh can't find official letter-head stationery. And sign-um Governor-General?"

"*Wait!* Look! Brugguh-dear! Why wunnuh don't just come-in. Come-in, man, and if the whirl-press, particularly Rickey-Singh and then-so, say anything, we could-always say that wunnuh come-in to save the precious lives of the Amurcans going to the Medical School."

"You know, as a Brugguh-dear, that invading forces don't have to have no legal nor moral right to invade nobody. Invade, and *then* find some reason or the other, man. We can't tek all this Spanish I hearing 'pon the radio, and in the telephone, every time a man try to make a overseas call. We can't tek-um. We prefer to speak with a Yankee-accent. Well, even with a Bajan-accent then. Listen to wha' I tell yuh. "Scroon! Find you Instrument. Write the thing. Even 'pon a piece o' paper, with a lead-pencil, as I tell you. Do wha' I tell you . . . "

"But Brugguh-dear! If, for arument sake, I is the Governor-General. Using the logistics that you just tell me 'bout, can' people like Rickey-Singh and George Lamming argue that Sir Eric Gairey is still the Prime Minister?"

"Look, Scroon! I is only a Brugguh-dear, hear. I know 'bout mortar and pistle. AK-47's, missiles, and missives, logistics and capabilities. I don't know one damn ting 'bout the state o' heads o' states, or nothing so. I don't even care. All I is to do, according to the commission that Manningheim just hand me, is to get you out, outta there, and if I can't get you out, then you got to get-out that piece o' paper, sign in *your* name, giving we the word to come-in.

"So, are you going turn-down the stereo so I can't hear no more classical music with them cannons in the *1812 Overtures,* and sign your name? Or are you going-let Castro and the Cubans turn your head with all that Spanish . . . Scroon! Are you still there?"

"Who I got there? Brugguh-dear? You still there? We like we get cut-off, yuh. Brugguh-dear? . . . When I write um, and give you and Manningheim and Eugeneus and Shagguh and them-so, the go-ahead, wunnuh had-better come straight to where I staying and relieve me from these blasted revolution-boys . . . "

" . . . *Con el serono conocimien-to del puesto y valer reales del gan . . .* "

"Brugguh-dear, tha' is you? Brugguh-dear, you still there? Cuddear! Brugguh-dear?

"Oh loss! I keep telling Maurice to fix these blasted telephones that always cutting-in with Spanish."

1984

Grenada Secret Document 2: General's Call

"Manningheim? Manningheim, I just hear from Scroon! No, Scroon safe so far. But when I thought I was hearing real warfare and artilleries in the background, all um was, was Scroon playing a lot o' blasted classical music.

"Tchaikowsky's *1812 Overture* . . . But listen to this. This operation more bigger than I want to handle all by myself . . . Scroon safe, as I say, but we still got to find something to base our actions 'pon.

"I mention a treaty to Scroon. But Scroon say that Maurice tear-them-up. Maurice really-and-truly tear-up all the old treaties, or Gairey tek-them-up in Virginia with him when he was last here, in August?"

"Lemme handle the diplomatical dipsy-doodling, and you handle the guns-part. Hear? I don't know nothing 'bout Gairey. What I want to hear from you is hummuch men we need? And don't forget, we not tekking no soldier-girls 'pon the invasion. I already hear 'bout them Cuban-mens they got down in Grenada.

"Leff them nice soldier-girls 'bout-here. We got people like Lammy-C, and them-so, and I won't hear my ears if I allow you to tek soldier-girls down in Sin-Georges."

"And, Manningheim? This may or may not be the time to raise this lil-matter, but I got to ask you, wha' I going to do if this mission fail?"

"Fail? (expletives deleted.) You (expletive deleted), say that (expletive deleted) going (expletive deleted) fail? Fail? Man, don't lemme quote *Macbeth* 'pon you, yuh! Fail? With the Amurcans backing we? With Eugeneous backing we? We fail?

"Listen to this. You think I spend tha' term in the Modern-Six at Harsun College, before I went up to Oxford, for nothing? Fail! *Screw your courage to the sticking place, and we not ging-fail,* Feel-marshall!"

"I thought you just-mek-me a Brugguh-dear?"

"Well, if you go-on talking 'bout fail, I like I going get to tek-'way some pips offa your shoulder-blade, yuh, and turn-yuh-back into a simple Feel-marshall. No, man. Brugguh-dear! Fail? *Who dare receive it other,* Dipper-barrr or Rickey-Singh, *as we shall make our griefs and clamour roar upon his death?* Fail? You mekking (expletive deleted) sport?"

"But, Manningheim, you know that they have a general down-in-there?"

"He went to San-hearse with you?"

"Nobody up in San-hearse don't know nothing 'bout a General Austin!"

"Well, wha' you frighten-for?"

"I been thinking that um would look more better if a general from here, was facing a general from there, in combat and warfares."

"Oh! You seeing stars, now! You seeing some more stars 'pon your uniform? Well, let me wait and see if the Cubans and the Russians going-mek yuh see stars somewhere else, before I consent to mekking you a general."

"Not that I aping Odo down in Guyana, or even General Austin down in Grenada, but I just want to know what in this for me? I got a wife and thrildren, as you know, and if anything should happen to me whilst I liberating the Grenadian people, I would like to know that my wife could live offa my pension, and a general's pension, and I already look-um-up in the Orders-book, would just do she good . . . "

"Who tell you we liberating Grenadian people? Where you get that clap-trap from? From Scroon? Scroon tell you so, in your telephone conversation with him at six o'clock this evening? I didn't hear nothing so. All I hear was a lotta Spanish brekking-in 'pon your conversation . . . "

"Wait! But Manningheim, you mean you was listening-in 'pon we?"

"I is a Spanish-radio station! I does-have to know everything that going-on 'bout here! Who you think is Prime Minister o' here? Dipper-barrr?"

"Well, if we not liberating the Grenadian people that Scroon want we to come-in and tek-out, why we going-in sovereign territory, then?"

"Because I say so! Yuh like you don't live 'bout here, yuh! You like you don't see that my popularity poll going-down. You like you don't see the blasted people, including the electorates grumbling.

"Costs costing more. I weas spraining my brain all last month, trying to come-up with something to tek the people mind offa the economy and offa the Govament. You don't like power?

Who mek you Brugguh-dear? And going-mek you a general when this over?

"Well, Brugguh-dear, um is the calculus o' politics. George Lamming. Rickey-Singh, and Cammie could call um wha' they like. Um is the mattimattics and calculus o' political power. Um isn't nothing 'bout liberating no Grenadians!

"You know anybody from here who went-in there to help them elect Maurice? So, what clap-trap you talking? And to-besides, you have something 'gainst the big wall-house you living in, free? The big motto-car that I give you don't drive good? Well, tell me, nuh!

"I could get a 450 Benz send-down for you. You don't like power no more? You don't like to tek the salute with me, 'pon a Independence morning, no more? You like you don't know that Dipper-barrr *praying* for you! Dipper just waiting till he get-back-in, to demobolise and demote people 'bout here!

"So, you had better do wha' I tell yuh! We going-in Grenada to mek-sure that for the next five or six or seven years, you going-still sleep free in that big wall-house and drive-'bout Barbados in a 450SEL Mercedes Benz. Tek yuh pick! You call the Amurcan ambassador, as I axe you?"

"I call he. He say that they going-be more war-planes 'bout-here than wha' land in Pearl Harbour during the Second Whirl War."

"You didn't call the Canadian high commission-man, though, as I tell you to-don't call . . . "

"And that is another thing. The Canadians real vex. They say that they going-have to advise Trudeau to-don't give we no more aid, and that we only dong so because we already get a big new airport offa them . . . "

"Next time he tell you any (expletive deleted) foolishness, quote a piece o' *Macbeth* his (expletive deleted). Tell him quote, *'that I with wine and wassail so will convince, that memory, the warder of the memory, the warder of the brain shall be a fume, and the receipt of reason a limbeck only'*. We can't fail.

"To-besides, Trudeau believe tummuch in peace and mekking peace. But this is the Carbean. We does-live here. Um is *we* basin on initiatives, and *we* po of influences . . . "

"And as you tell me once, a Canadian dollar-bill only worth one-forty or one-fifty. If yuh lucky! Whilst one *in-God-we-*

trust worth two something! I learning fast fast, from you, Manningheim.

"And if you don't mind repeating yourself, tell me a next time, the namne of that piece o' Shakespeare you want me to quote to the Canadian high-commission man! Um sound real sweet."

1984

GRENADA SECRET DOCUMENT 5: SCROON'S CALL TO EUGENIOUS

SCROON: Miss Prime Minister, this is Scroon.

EUGENIOUS: Who you say? Coon? Boy, I don't know no Coons in Grenada. Who you say your name is?

SCROON: A' "S" 'pon the beginning o' the name! Scroon. I is the Governor-General o' Grenada, and I calling in my capacity as Governor-General.

EUGENIOUS: Bishop forget you? I thought you had-leff Grenada with Gairey. I know there was one or two Coon families in Grenada. I know a lot o' Grenada Coons. But I never thought that Bishop had leff-back a Governor-General all the years he been in power!

SCROON: Bishop didn't app'int me. Gairey didn't app'int me. I get my Instrument during Gairey days, but not from Gairey. Um is the people o' Grenada that have me still as their Governor-General.

EUGENIOUS: You could prove that by law? 'cause I got President Reagan 'pon the other line, and me and he trying to put this invasion 'pon a legal footing, and the more we try, the thinner the evidence o' law is. And we now trying to see if there is any old treaties that we could bank this action 'pon.

SCROON: Miss Prime Minister, I know you . . .

EUGENIOUS: And another thing. Stop calling me Miss Prime Minister. Because I is a woman you can't call me Mr. Prime Minister? The prime-minister-job is a manjob. I doing a manjob like a man. More better than nay man before my time!

So, because I not married, and don't have no damn man hum-bugging me when the nights come, and because you is this play-play Governor-General, you think you can't have the comma-decency to address me by my rightful entitlements? I is a prime minister. And saving Margaret Thatcher and Indira, all the rest o' the prime ministers in this God's whirl, is man. So, call me Mister Prime Minister.

SCROON: Well, Mister Prime Minister Eugenious. I got to talk to you.

EUGENIOUS: I like how um sound. You like how um sound? Um sound as if I is a man, no? Anyhow, lemme hear wha' you want. I got Reagan on the next line. He telling me he bringing-in the Marines, the FBI, the CIA and the IMF in Grenada. So, if you have something new to tell me, tell me now, so I could pass-um-on to Reagan. I can't trust nobody nowadays. I here bargaining with Reagan that Dominica contribution worth 30 million Yankee dollars.

Manningheim already got to Reagan first, telling him that Barbados have a airport big-enough to on-load war-plane and transport plane, and his share have to be 50 million. Talk fast, Scroon. Reagan got to get to his ranch to ride horse and pony before the weekend done. I don't understand wha' happening to the CARICOM we got.

SCROON: Mister Prime Minister Eugenious, you know 'bout any treaties, sign or unsign that I could quote to get the Brugguh-dear from Barbados to come in Grenada and tek-me-out from amongst these Spanish-speaking revolution-boys?

EUGENIOUS: That is exactly wha' Reagan and me spraining our heads over. I do know 'bout one that we sign in CARICOM, but that CARICOM treaty demand unanimous support. I know 'bout a next one that Dominica sign with South Africa, in the days when Corporal John was running this place.

But I can't mention South Africa to Reagan, seeing as how I got the man on the point o' signing something to give we in Dominica a few million. Wait! Scroon? You still there? What is that I hearing in the background? General Austin tekking-over before the CIA come in to help him. That man so damn impatient.

SCROON: You know 'bout General Austin? That is the big-gest most guarded secret in Grenada. General Austin and the CIA. Mister Prime Minister Eugenious, I got to tell you something. All 'bout-here, we was saying that you have spies plant in every Carbean country that getting more 'Murcan aid than you. In Grenada I even hear the revolution boys say you wukking for Uncle Sam. And now, you telling me something concerning General Austin and the CIA . . .

EUGENIOUS: Not now, Scroon, Reagan 'pon the other line . And I got to get Reagan ears before Seaga get to Reagan. I could handle Manningheim. But Seaga is different fish, of a different ideology altogether. He might be the shagguh in the moss' of Carbean political affairs. Incidentally, they got any shagguhs in Grenada? Or have Bishop export all to Cuba?

SCROON: I serious, Eugenious, man. Axe Reagan if he can't come in? We could find reasons afterwards. We could mention the Medical School, and . . .

EUGENIOUS: Before I pass-on that message, I want you and everybody in Grenada to understand one thing. I not in this invasion-business for my health hear. I not backing invasion because I have no lot o' love for Grenadians. As a matter o'fact, Maurice tek-away some land that belong to a Amerindian fourth-cousin o' mine. I vex with Bishop for that.

And another thing. As I tell you. Manningheim getting 50 million Yankee dollars for letting Reagan land the planes 'pon Barbados soil. I know that Barbados more richer than the lil pooh pooh islands 'bout-here.

Incidentally. Scroon. Um is Scroon, isn't it? Not Coon? Scroon, you happen to have a Canadian telephone directory handy? One for Ottawa? I trying like hell to remember Trudeau telephone number . . . Trudeau give me his number once when I was up in Ottawar, but I write-um-down 'pon a match-box. To-besides, um was in French . . . summuch foreigners talking foreign language 'bout here! . . .

1984

Grenada Secret Document 6: Manningheim's Call to the Trinidadians

"Tell Sparrow to-don't come back in Barbados. Tell Sparrow he ban. If wunnuh down in Trinidad does-listen to what calypsonians does say, and think that calypsonians could run guvvaments, well, not me! I is a Bajan. And the only thing Bajans like and does sing is *The Lord Thou Gavest*, outta Hymns Ancient and Modern."

"Eh-eh! And what 'bout Gabby? The Mighty Gabby? All you don't know that Sparrow and Gabby hooking up? And that they going paint the whole Carbean with political rhetoric and political criticism, during the 1984 carnival? All-you just playing that the arse . . . "

"Gabby getting ban, too, then! Um don't mean that because Gabby born here, that I can't slap a ban 'pon Gabby. I not tolerating no clap-trap and no infelicities and no calypsonians 'bout-here, who think that they could embarrass me in son. Boots was enough. I had enough o' Boots. Gabby get-bout-here and sing' bout Boots? Well, I going show wunnuh something 'bout real boots. Wait till me and Reagan put some more boots in Grenada!"

"That is only a bluff, Manningheim. I know you from up in London, in the Students Centre. That is pure bluff. You may pull a gun 'pon somebody at a press conference, but down here we not frighten for you."

"I tell you that Trinidad not joining all-you in Grenada. Half o' Trinidad is Grenadians. We Trinidadians have a more closer and peaceful relationship with Grenada. And we say Grenada ain't do nobody nothing."

"You think you is the muhguffy of the Carbean? Well, wait and see wha' we going-do to all-you with all-you shirt-jacks that all-you does-export down here!"

"Wait, and see wha' we going-do to all-you with all-you small industries, like mannifracturing. All-you got oil? A lil hole in the ground up in Sin-Phillips that won't even full-up half o' the Mercedes Benz that driving-'bout Port-o-Spain, is wha' wunnuh call oil?"

"Sparrow still not coming-'bout here."

"Eh-eh. Sparrow got Gabby. And we intend to mek Gabby a Order o' the Humming Bird. We tekking-out Trinidadian citizenship for Gabby. You don't own the air-waves o' the Carbean."

"Wait till the calypsoes that Gabby and Sparrow write 'pon you and them soldier-boys, and the Brugguh-dear! You going-ban them, too?"

"I did-know I couldn't trust wunnuh. I trust wunnuh with the secret mission that me and Reagan carrying out, and the whole whirl know. So, tell Chambers he can't frighten me."

"Tell Chambers from me, that in future, I not telling he nothing 'bout the invasion nor 'bout CARICOM. As a matter o' fact, I shouldn't even be telling you nothing. 'cause the kind o'person wunnuh Trinidadians is, wunnuh, or you, or Chambers, would swear blind that I didn't consult wunnuh."

"I bet that when the Amurcans and the Brugguh-dear overrun Grenada, wunnuh going-start telling people that I didn't call you in, and tell you nothing. I bet that history will bear out this, this stinking infelicity in all o' wunnuh."

"But Manningheim, you forget that I know you from up in the Students Centre? I know everything you uses to do up in London. You forget the calling-cards that you print-up, and write a certain African princess name 'pon? And how Grantley had to fly-up in London to ease you up?"

"Well, let me tell all-you something! Trinidad chase-out the Amurcans from Chagauramas. Trinidad chase-out the Amurcans that come-in here with the Peace Corps. Trinidad got oil. And as a certain person say, 'Oil don't spoil.'"

"Wunnuh might got Shell, but we got Mobil."

"And you can't start stopping me, nor no other Trinidad diplomat at Seawell airport, and tek-off we pants nor search we like how you search the diplomats from Grenada during Maurice days."

"Trinidad diplomats don't carry guns. So, you don't have the excuse to search and lock-up, without habeas-corpuscles. Wait till we put Sparrow in your arse! Wait till we put your own Gabby in your a . . . ! Wait till Carnival 1984! Wait till Kitchener come back down here with a soca 'pon the Brugguh-dear! Wait till Crazy start singing 'bout the Girl From Brandons!"

"Let me tell you something right now. From now, from this-very-now. I want you to leff 'bout-here. Diplomatic immunity or no diplomatic immunity."

"You leffing. Well, don't even bother to go home and pack. I got a car senning for you. I want you out outta here. All o'wunnuh commanisses, all o'wunnuh radicals down in Trinidad who advise Maurice, I want all o' wunnuh-kind offa Barbados shores."

"So, tell Chambers to recall you. He don't even have to re-call you, then. I throwing you out, right now."

"Eh-eh! But all-you brave! And when all-you throw me out, wha' going-happen to all-you in '86? Or '85? Or whenever all you get the nerve to call elections?"

"I know all-you don't like doctors, 'cause one, all-you ban, one, all you deport; and the third one got all-you spending sleep-less nights 'pon a night. But um won't be long."

"Remember that I remember you from up in the Students Centre! Remember the grave-yard? Remember the hose with the water through the louvres down Brandon Hill?"

"Remember the English-man who get he work-permit tek 'way, because of a certain brown-skin girl? But let me tell all-you something else. When all-you call me 'pon the 21st o' October, all-you didn't tell me that all-you was going-invade Grenada. All-you tell me that a contemplation was contemplated. I study English at Oxford. And I know English."

"And 'contemplate' isn't to do. Or even, to want to do. And 'contemplate' don't mean going-do. 'Contemplate' is when you feel peckish and you see a gash, and your eyes do the work that your tom-pigeon contemplate to do."

"You didn't tell me you was talking officially, neither. You talk to me like if you was contemplating a back-raise, or like if you was wishing you had a Ace in the hold, when you playing Kings-and-lil-ones down by Maxie."

"So, don't come now telling me that all-you advise Chambers. Chambers was not advise, 'cause a contemplation is not a intention. I-myself have had contemplations concerning Trinidad not buying no more CARICOM goods offa Barbados. I myself, as a humble diplomat, have had contemplations 'bout becoming Minister o' Foreign Affairs, or even Prime Minister. Everybody does-have con-templations."

"Even Gabby tell me once, in the Trinidad Hilton, by the pool, that he had a contemplation concerning getting you to spend money 'pon butter and less 'pon boots. A contemplation is a dream. I dream once that you, was leader o' the oppositioners. And as far as I can see, I don't know wha' Richie waiting for? Tha' is a contemplation. Eh-eh' but all-you brave!"

1984

NOT MY CHILD!

MOTHER: Not my child! I say, not my girl-child! She can't come telling decent people that to don't allow their thildren, that they give birth to, to not wear short uniforms that tight. Now that she in the Cabinets, corning money leff and right from the big-salaries I hear Mr. Arthur, who we is to call Prime Minister, does-share-out; and for her to now come telling decent people that their girl-thrilren dress too short and too tight, and that to make it longer and less tighter . . . not my child! My girl-child wearing her dress six inch over her two knees, and not a' inch more longer. Material too dear, soul.

FATHER: It is the prerogative of the Minister of Education to imbibe and im-bue the very highest moral standards into the minds of our youths.

MOTHER: Wha' you saying? What you just say to me? Looka man? Talk English, do! So that a person could understann what the hell you saying! Who is her to come telling me, a mother that birth this child, anything 'bout imbribe and imbued? Is them the two words you just-now? Imbribe? And imbued? I talking 'bout dress material, and how it suh dear, even when it 'pon sale! And you come talking a lotta shhhh —

FATHER: And that's another thing, too! This vulgarity that permeates the speech of our society. I embarked a ZR-van Monday, because I was rushed. My car had some mechanical problems, I got into that ZR, and immediately disembarked. The language I heard!

MOTHER: Wait, wait, wait! Wait just a kiss-me . . . cotton picking minute! You talking to me? Man, you talking to somebody you know? Me and you is miles apart through the language you using to me this blessed Sunday evening!

I tell you that no minister, be she the Prime Minister, or just a plain minister in the Cabinets, she can't come telling me, a woman who give birth to this girl-child, that to don't allow my child to cross Sin-Michael's door, wearing a uniform unless un covering her shins?

My child is to wear uniform making her look as if she is some old maid, or something drop outta . . . outta. Man, you mekking me damn mad, you don't know! I tell you once, and I telling you two times, um is the cost o' dress materials.

She going-pay for this? She going-open her cheque book and write-off a cheque in my name, legal-tender, so I could go-in Abeds and buy a' extra half-yard to satisfy her Dress Code? Um ain' my dress-code! Is her own.

The next thing she going come telling decent people is to dressup the thrildren in more longer socks and stockings, so they won't show their legs off to the public. Wha' wrong with a girl showing-off her two legs if her two legs nice and isn't like two match-sticks?

FATHER: I am appalled. I as this child's father, am fundamentally appalled by the disgusting attitude you're taking in this matter of such national significance. It distresses me, profoundly. I have to say it.

MOTHER: I tell you, that iffing me and you talking, and talking-over something as serious as this, that you is to talk in plain English, that I could understann! You like you been in the Civil Service too long, yuh! You had-better come out, find a private enterprises job, and see how the outside-whirl does-behave. And don't talk to me as if I is some some damn musty file. Hear?

FATHER: I'm merely pointing out . . .

MOTHER: You wha'? Say that again! You pointing-out something to somebody? Well, lemme tell you something, man! Is the dress-materials. For me, a person who give birth to that girl-child in there, to have to fork myself down in Town, and go in Abeds and add-on a next half-yard o' material to mek a uniform to satisfy her, when things suh dear; you ain't get the increment Mr. Arthur promise you; she isn't to tek no more ZR's; and your motto-car not wukkin! Looka, man, don't mek me vex as shhh . . . vex as anything, now, yuh! Girleen? Girleen! Fork yourself in here, right this-very-now!

CHILD: Yes, Mummy?

MOTHER: Bring yourself in here, and settle this dry-row me and your father having. Girleen, lissen carefully to me. Lissen to your mother.

FATHER: Do not influence or persuade the child . . .

MOTHER: Who talking to you? Somebody axe you something? I addressing my child. You suffer any birth-pains with her?

Girleen, lissen to me, dear. Wha' you think 'bout this damn business that schoolgirls shouldn' wear school uniforms that short nor tight? Tell me your honest opinion, as a Sin-Michael's high-school girl.

Don't be 'fraid to talk in front of your father. He can't eat yuh! You could tell Mummy how wunnuh girls see this think 'bout wearing more longer uniform dresses that not tight, and this other thing 'bout having your undies under-neat; and not showing.

CHILD: Last Friday afternoon, Mommy, as a matter of fact, we sixth-form girls had a significant debate on this matter, examining the nuances of it, from the moral and religio-cultural aspects, and we took in all the parameters of the question of nationality as it impinges upon the real essence of Dress Code, and whether the concept of Dress Code is inversely proportionate to discipline, and . . .

MOTHER: Wait wait wait! Wait one kiss-me-arse, cotton-picking minute, before I lose my temper with you! You talking in English? You just like your blasted father! Wha' I senning-you-school for?

1995

I Can't Tell She Nothing

I can't tell this woman nothing at all. She come home from wukking. First thing she does-do is run in the bathroom. And tek a shower. When I think the woman going-put on she "home-clothes," and start mekking dinner, she emerge from inside the shower, telling me, "Come!"

I tell she, "Come for what?" She stannup in the middle o' the bathroom door, telling me, "Come."

I get so frighten, seeing she there, in her birthday suit, with lipstick, rouge and Evening-in-Paris smelling-down the place. And when she move-off, my heart start to flutter, and I can't think at all, at all. Nor axe she nothing.

"Why you don't put on something," I tell she. "Why you don't cover yourself? All the lights burning, and the n'igbours going-see!"

She leff me sitting down at the dining table, that ain't set for no food. And she gone in the bedroom. I start to feel more better now, 'cause she gone in to put on clothes, and start mekking the food 'cause I hungry-hungry.

"What you hungry for?" And when she say so, I start trembling again, 'cause she dress-off now in a negligée, stanning-up in the light. "What you hungry for? You is a man or what? You mean to tell me that it tek a white woman from Amurca who doeswrite in the NATION to tell we Bajan women what we been missing all these years?

"And wunnuh wirthless men walking-'bout the place, bragging 'bout how wunnuh does-do this, and does-do that to a woman? And in all these years I married to you, I can't testify to having *no satisfaction* outta you?

"And now you want me to turn-off the lights? And be in the dark? But I got something for you, though! I buy two. I purchase two down in town 'pon my lunch hour today. So, if yuh slip a next time, yuh slide . . . "

I can't tell this woman nothing at all. I frighten to axe she what she buy or purchase down in town. But a mind tell me to-don't axe she, yuh.

"Wunnuh is only *talk*! Pam Groton, the Murcan lady, tell we wunnuh is *only* talk?

"But lemme tell you something, see? I not putting up with no more talk from outta you? I not putting up with no more slackness from you? I not turning off these lights, no more. We going-do wha' we have to do with the lights on. You hear me?

"And in case you is one o' them mens that fall in the category o' men who is *pure talk only*, and can't perform nothing, I will tell you, you the man I married all these frustrating years, that I learn — thanks to Mistress Pam Groton the Murcan lady — how to fix you. And fix you good-good-good as anything? Hear me?"

I can't tell she nothing, nor axe she nothing' bout the two parcels that she buy down in town 'pon her lunch-hour. I trembling. A biological thing happen to me. I feel that cold water pouring over me. All feeling gone outta my body, all like now-so.

I not hungry no more. Food gone outta my mind. I want to run. And hide from she — never mind she is my wife. I scared o'she . . .

"And something else? I giving you your *last* chance. In future, I want you to tek my hand, and lead me inside that bedroom there, and put me' cross that bed that I mek up and put clean sheets 'pon.

"And I want you to light them four red candles that I buy from the Indian store, with the incense; and I want you to talk to me, and tell me wha' you want; and wha' you going-do; and how you want what you want; and I want you to pass your two hands over my body that I put Evening-in-Paris on; and I want the lights on, you hear?

"And I want you to touch my ear, and whisper in my ear, 'Doo-doo, love-bird, darling, roses is red, roses is blue, the love inside my heart is only for you, and it blue blue-blue?' You think you could please me with that?

"Cause if yuh don't? If yuh slip this last time, yuh *slide.* You hear me?

"And a next thing. You see the commercial 'pon CNN that we does-watch? The one with the bunny-rabbit and the batteries that don't run-out? You see the morals in that commercial? You had-better wake-up, yuh! 'cause, with the two parcels I purchase 'pon my lunch-hour this afternoon, I had the presence o'mind to buy *two* boxes o'Duracell batteries, that does last and last and last.

"And I going-see if you going-talk to me, and don't be in a rush as if the house 'pon fire. I going-see if a Duracell battery going-outlast you?

"Mistress Pam Groton, child, you don't know how I thank you! And if *you* was a real man, you would thank that Murcan woman, too!"

I still can't talk to this woman. And I too frighten to axe she, what in the two parcels from down in town? You think um is chocolates?

1995

Baby Want Shoes

Life is a gamble. To gamble is life. Wha' wrong with mekking the whole o' Barbados a gambling-den? It would make people live more longer. And baby want shoes!

The present Guvvament can't share-out shoes to every last Bajan. So whilst the grass docs-be-growing, and the cow yuh-know-what, why we can't tek up we-selves 'pon a Sunday instead o' going-church, and fire a few dices, brek-off the handle offa a one-hand bandit, and mek some sport, and mek some money, whiching the Guvvament not sharing-out, yet.

Life is a big-able gamble. Yuh drink yuh tea with a slice o' sweet bread to cloid yuh, and yuh step outside, and bram!, a ZR-van lick-yuh-down!

Or, you driving your lil motto-car that yuh paying off the bank for, and when you turn-out outta Highgates Gardens, brug-gah-down! yuh fender lick-off, the steering wheel mash-up, and you in the Casualty with your head bandage-up, from the wemms that you get. Who going pay for that? Guvvament?

To gamble is to live. When they release you, tek the first ZR — never mind the dance-hall music they does-play, and the speed they does-tek! — jump in one. And find the nearest casino, mek the sign o' the cross for luck, and pelt-'bout some dice, and see if yuh can't throw a seven or eleven.

Baby want shoes! And a man need lil sport. And the Guv-vament need money in the Treasuries. And a woman, even a "deputy" or a "kip-miss" need a new dress when the Christmas come. And seeing as how none o' them 30,000 jobs I hear 'bout, all during July, August, September up till the 6th o' October, haven't materialise yet wha' you going-do? Lock-up Mr. Arthur for saying "job number one is jobs?" Or lick-he-down?

Baby want Christmas shoes! You want one o' them 30,000 jobs? I looking for one, too, yuh! If you win a jackpot, you would be doing the Guvvament a favour. They won't have to sprain in their brain, looking for no job for you, or for me. And if you mek a thing in one of the six casinos I hear they building, wha' job you want? Baby got shoes! The "deputy" please! "Kip-miss" loving you more bad, and the wife satisfy. You is a millionaire. You ever hear anybody get to be a millionaire from wukking so hard and so long in the Post Office down Cheapside?

Mek-sure that wunnuh build one o' them casino-things near tha' Post Office, yuh! Be-sure to ereck one 'pon Roebuck Street, near a certain place that is the headquarters of a certain political party in Barbados. Richie want one near where he living, too. Share-them-out fair and square. Give every stripe o'political derivation a picking. Baby want shoes! And it don't matter if the child belongst to a father who is a Bee, or who in the Cabinets. Um still want shoes to wear 'pon he two feet. Cuddear, wunnuh going-make the child of such a powerful man in the land, walk-'bout barefoot?

Baby want shoes, don't mind if um born up in the country! Um still want shoes! So, don't leff-out my friend. David-Tee, yuh! Wunnuh spiting the man, and talking 'bout dumping a dump in Sin-John, the site of one o' the most oldest institutions o' higher learning, namely Codrington College, whiching is where a lotta fellows who didn't have the wherewithal, namely no access nor availabilities to a casino nor money 'pon the bank, had to went-school to learn Classics and get a thing behind their name! Jeff, and Sam and Greenie — and I think Sleepy, went there, too!

So, leff-out putting any dump in Sin-John. Hear? Give the man a nice, big casino, instead. One big and pretty like Caesar' Palace in Vegas. Paint-um-up in the colours of yellow and blue. I myself won't mind being the Head Cruppier. I got some fellows who say they willing to wuk under me. One is my friend from up by Naz, who does-be running out o' beer and barbecue chicken when you see nine o'clock come.

Think of all the shoes that the babies in Sin-John could walk-'bout in. Christmas morning in the Park, or next year for Crop-Over. Neither the Guvvament nor the Treasuries; the Authorities to the Tourisses or the BDS-forget BIMAP and the TDC and the CBC! — wunnuh can't mek no change offa them. 'Cause, baby want shoes!

I is no great, or small, educator. But I happen to bring-'long most o'the men and women that running Barbados and the Guvvament, in the ways they should go. In other words, I teach them.

I know I teach them good-good. Look where all o' them is, today! — or was, day before? One Prime Minister; two bishops; a mob-o'-ton o' school teachers; civil servants too numerous to count or mention; reverends and vicars, enough to full-up two cathedrals; a couple o' lawyers (let the two o' them draw-up the legal papers); three doctors; forty-'leven ZR van drivers; one Postmaster-General; five Inspectors o' Police; a handful o' corporals; three hundred privates, and a murderer.

I is a man that teach the spine and backbone o' Bajan society. And if I say we need a casino — (not one! What we going-do with one casino in a big place like Barbados?) — If Tom Clarke say Barbados need six casinos, all o' them pupils o' mine who now running Barbados, got to, have to, bound and 'blige to lissen to wisdom.

Baby want shoes! Some o' them former pupils didn't wear none to school. I not teaching them nothing so different from how I teach them, "je suis, tu suis, il suit"; "one and one is two"; or "Life is a gamble?"

Don't gamble no more 'pon one o'them 30,000 jobs. Grabble-on 'pon the handle belonging to a slot machine. And build the slot-machine inside a nice, pretty casino. 'Cause, baby want shoes!

1995

Don't Mind Them. Nod Off Justice

The Honourable Mr. Justice Eric Bishop, Esq., Queen's High Bench Judge, Retire (formerly) The Supreme Court of Barbados, Coleridge Street, (or forward to Sherbourne Centre, near where Mr. Arthur, whiching we is to call Prime Minister, does live, seeing as how I do not stand in possession of the right address — Barbados, Wessindies).

MY DEAR honoured Sir, Mr. Commissioner, I writing you as a alternative to appearing before you, in persona and furthermore, in altero, to submitting my submission before your honourable Commission regarding gamblers and consequentially, disregarding all them who stand against gambling in casinos.

Don't mind them. Nod-off when they open their mouth.

I is a Barbadian. I want you to know that first. I stand in direct consequence to reaping a lil something offa casinos in case, you Sir, in your jurisprudential judgement say the right word, utter the right legalistical Tort and give Mr. Arthur, whiching we is to call Prime Minister, the lil push that he need, to alter his hue-and-cry concerning Crusades of Power, and make him say-even in the House of Sembly! — that "job No. 1 is casino-jobs and casinos".

Iffing, on the other hand, in altero dextero, you can't have your way with Mr. Arthur, he whom by nomenclature, we is to address as Prime Minister, my advice to you, Sir, is to just nod-off.

You is a gentleman who travel the lengths and breadths of lands whiching and in which you dispense jurisprudences of law and justice.

You is a hard-working man, who sit on the highest Benches in far-off lands of the Carbean, and who now, after toiling and labouring in the vinyards of untractabilities in law and Torts, to say nothing concerning contracks, have come home to take a sea-bath.

Ipso-facially speaking therefore; and as a consequence to the afore-mention, you is a gentleman in who should take it easy.

Primer-facially, then, you ought to nod-off. And don't mind them, if they don't like casinos. Nod-off, the minute they talk.

The primer-faces of the matter say, in explications that you is not to sprain your brain, taxed and exhausted hitherto in distant

Carbean lands whiching was where you dispense some o'the sweetest justice documented in learned journals of law and jurisprudence and Torts, Nod-off.

Don't lissen to no foolishness, particular the kinds and the res and talk emanating from the mouths of neither preachers nor prieses; neither vicar nor dean; cannon nor bishop; neither lord-bishop nor archbishop; nor none-so. Lissen to the gamblers, first. And then, nod-off.

A gentleman of your high esteem, steep in the tractabilities of jurisprudence should remind all of them-so, of the Theological and Ecclesiastical Law, namely and towit;

"Render under Caesar the rewards and gains that Caesar wins, even in a casino."

Have you ever went to Caesar Palace in Las Vegas? You don't have to answer.

The stenuating evidence of my catastrophe whiching is the consequential cause of my not being able to be before you, in persona is two things.

One is the motto-car; the second is the job that Mr. Arthur whiching we is to call . . . you know the rest. I loss all-two-both.

Notwithstanding my incapacitations, there was trepidations that I harbour concerning appearing before you, in persona.

However, as I am now a in absentia supplicant before you, I hope that the sanguinity of my legal argument, couch in legalese and supporting Torts, will convince you of the legal presidents, therein.

Namely, don't mind nobody who tell you, in written form or even in viva-voce that a lil casino plant in Sin-Peter, going hurt Mr. Arthur, whiching we for the time currently being, is to call Prime Minister. Take a nod, if anybody tell you so. Nod-off.

Furthermore, and notwithstanding, one in Sin-Michael's South East, can't subtract from the fees that patients paying nobody. Don't mind Richie. Nod-off upon that point.

I retiring just like you. But I retiring up in Sin-Philip North.

See what you can do for me up in there. And drop three in Sin-Philip North. I need action in my retirement years. The Sin-Philip nights too dark and too long.

I sleeps alone, and I need to make a lil sport, in altero, by vapping and nicking.

My brain is not sprain from measuring law and jurisprudence, and I find I can't sleep nor nod-off before three o'clock in the morning. To-besides, up on Sin-Philip North, does-be dead after six in the evenings.

This may or may not be relevant. But somebody show me a document that haveon, Eyes Only. You know what Section 1, sub-1 of that document say?

This information privilege. Don't utter a word or a iota even to Mr. Arthur, cause he would get vex with me, and next time he sharing-out motto-cars and jobs, I know I won't be getting none.

Between me and you, Sir, it say, and I quoting now:

"1.i: Whereas hithertofore, the Oppositioners sought to advise the people regarding our clandestine intercourses with a unnamed money-lending international agency; and whereas that infelicitous, dirty-minded accusation did not stick-on, the geopolitical infrastructuralities of the macrocosmic realities of public policy, have now cause this Guvvament to take a next look in the direction of that unnamed agency, with the intention of . . . "

I sorry I could not read the last part. The person snatch-it-way, and tear it up.

But a gentleman with your perspicacity, know what it mean.

If therefore, they don't come clean with you in that regards, nod-off.

So, consequentially and in conclusion, Sir, and without prejudice nor discrimination, I lay my submission before you in your lap.

To-wit: one, share-out as much casinos as you like. Two, don't forget me.

I going-be residing in Sin-Philip North.

Yours respectively, Tom Clarke, LLB (inter) (London) (External) — (Failed).

PS: I hear Lowe Downes want one. He too shame to axe. But he axe me to please axe you to drop one in Morgan Lewis.

1995

Breadfruit Cou-Cou

After wunnuh went-church this morning; and come back home, and look in the larder, and didn't see nothing; no leff-over Kentucky-Fry; no tin-salmon; no piece o' pork; not a pullet at the door, and wunnuh can't borrow one, nor thief one offa the n'ighbour, wunnuh think, "Wha' I goin-give this man to eat, now, nuh?" Don't grieve. Mek he breadfruit cou-cou, with beef-stew, prickle and pear.

Get a fair-size breadfruit, with the stem still in; and wash-she-off; and cut-she-up in eight pieces; peel-off the skin. The skin gotta be turning almost yellow. Put she in a skillet o' cold water, enough to cover-over the breadfruit; and before you cover-she down, sprinkle a lil salt over she.

A n'ighbour may have a few extra pieces o' salt-pork, or pig-tails; but pig-tails more better. Wash-off the pig-tails under cold water. But remember something: Bajan pig-tails don't got in summuch salt and brine in them, so yuh don't have to bile them once, throw-off the water, bile them a next time, and throw off the water, till they loss the salt and the brine. Yuh could bile the pig-tails one time, only.

But this is wha' wunnuh going-do with the pig-tails. After they wash-off in cold water, sprinkle some oregano 'pon them, after yuh dry-them-off, though, and in a real heavy buck-pot, throw-in some lard-oil, and some onions slice in cart-wheels; and when the oil hot, throw-in the pig-tails; and let them stann, till the skin sear, without the pigtails cook. When they sear, and they looking nice, throw them in the skillet with the breadfruit; and turn-down the fire a lil more higher than to simmer. Yuh still got-back yuh fry-onions in the buck-pot. So, throw-in with the onions, a few clove o' garlicks, two more big big onions, slice in cart-wheels, and let them fry, till they almost burn. They got to almost burn. When they almost burn, tek-off the buck-pot offa the fire.

Now, if yuh could put yuh hands 'pon four to six Irish potatoes, peel them whole, and rest them 'pon the counter. In the meantime, check the pot to see if the slices o' breadfruit cooking; and since yuh checking the breadfruit, yuh may as well check 'pon the pig-tails, too. Pig-tail does tek more longer to cook, or bile, than breadfruit. But yuh drop-in the pig-tails with the slices o' breadfruit, to give taste and flavour to the breadfruit. Um won't hurt yuh to bile the pig-tails separate, in case. Like the potatoes.

Now, so said, so done; the breadfruit bile, the Irish potatoes bile; the pig-tails soft, and sweet, and juicy, and nice. This is the time to fire one. Yuh can't cook, not even a bake, if you don't fire one. And since um is Sunday forenoon, what more better to whet the palate with, than a rum-and-soda. Fire one. Yuh going-need um.

Wunnuh don't have things in the supermarkets or in the shops, or nowhere, called "braizing beef?" How you mean? What, braizing-beef ain't nothing more than beef-bones! Or a spare-rib mek outta beef, instead o' outa somebody old pig or boar-hog! Well, get some then, nuh! Yuh going-need four to six piece o' braizing-beef, or two pungs. Cut-she-up by the bones, mekking each cut have-in a bone. Wash-she-off in cold water. Dry-she-off 'pon a towel. Sprinkle she with lil salt; a lotta black pepper; some fresh thyme; a handful o'garlick cloves; and slice-over-she a bunch o' eschalots, fine fine fine. Put yuh hand in the bowl with the brown sugar, and sprinkle-over-she, enough to mek a thing; but don't bury-she in brown sugar, though, 'cause you ain't mekking sugar cakes, nor rolly-poley.

Let we go over the ingreasments for the braizing-beef. The braizing-beef in a pyrex baking pan, or some kind o' baking pan, that could go in the oven. Yuh got yuh salt, yuh pepper, yuh onions, yuh eschalots, yuh fresh thyme, yuh fresh garlick cloves, whiching, needless to say, yuh going cut-up, or squeeze in a garlick press that does press.

With the pieces o'braizing beef in the baking pan, and using the two hands that God give yuh, mash-in the ingreasements in the braizing beef. And um is when yuh finish mashing-it-in, that yuh adds the brown sugar over she. Throw a few drops o' Worchestershire Sauce 'pon she, but don't drown she.

And since you just fire one, toss-in a snap o' rum, or a snap o' sherry, brandy, wine, or falernum — but not tummuch: falernum does-be sweet. Yuh oven 'pon broil; and throw she under the broiler, *not* to cook she, nor bake she, but to sear-she-up. When it sear, tek it out. Now the sport going-start.

Yuh need a more bigger skillet for the braizing-beef. Remember the fry-onions? Well turn all the juice that in the baking pan, in the buck-pot that have in the fry-onions. Put the braizing beef in the more bigger skillet. Put some fire under the fry-onions, and add all the curry powder you could handle. I does-use a tablespoonful full-up to the brim. Stir she. Drop a fresh pepper that hot, in she. Stann-back. And smell she. And fire a next rum. When she *saw-tay*, turn-she out in the more bigger skillet that got in the braizing beef, stir she, bring she to a bile, and cover-she-down, and let she simmer . . . Oh, Lord, she now smelling!

Back to the breadfruit. Mash-she-up with a potato masher. Mash-up the Irish potatoes, in a separate bowl. Get yuh pig-tails. Add a quarter cup o' cream, or less. In a next clean big big skillet, yuh now got yuh potatoes, yuh pig-tails and yuh breadfruit; and yuh going mash-them-up, and when they mash-up, add yuh cream, and yuh pigtails, and turn she like yuh does-turn meal-corn cou-cou; and when she done, she mellow. Turn-she-down under a low fire, to keep she simmering.

Yuh prickle. Cumcumber slice thin like pages outta the *Good Book*; yuh salt, yuh fresh parsley, a lot; and yuh lime and lemon, a teaspoon each — without the seeds. Slice yuh pear — if pear in season — and lay-out yuh prickle 'side o' yuh pear. By now, yuh-going-be blind-drunk! But the food done. Serve um when you sober-up, nuh!

1995

Essays, Poems, Memoirs and Interviews

Harrison College and Me

There were always cockroaches — large and lazy, crawling up the closet pit, and looking into my eyes, as I looked down on them, and then tried to shoot them dead or cripple them, with the pellets of my shit. And there were flies. There were always flies in the island, particularly in the hot season in the island. If I were to look back over the snapshots of my youth in Barbados, I would have to remember the wind, and the music in the wind, as it ran its fingers through the rustling hairs of the sugar canes in the mornings of cold baths and warm green tea: bright and early; and hungry sometimes. But my life in Barbados was not all cockroaches and flies; not all wind and sugar cane. It was also carefree: but with a freedom restricted by the history of that parallelogram of life drawn for us many years ago by the English (who historically "owned" us, and who represented the top line and the two parallel sides of the figure); and by our own ignorance of ourselves (which represented the bottom line).

It was this restrictiveness which followed me out of the backyard of cane stumps not entirely hidden by time and barefoot-trampling; through the laneways which, yesterday, were fields of canes and sweat and labor and villagers and buckets of swank and foul explosive language — villagers who lived and died upon the hard bottom line of the parallelogram of my past. And it followed me right through the iron gates of that strange building on Crumpton Street, which boasted a curious religious fatalism (which not even the best scholars in the Classical Sixth could translate with final authority): "In Deo Fides." Harrison College!

I had arrived. I had come to stand and confront Harrison College, that old, time-honored and timeless bastion of higher learning, higher snobbery. But in a truer sense, I did not "confront" Harrison College. I had stepped across the Canal (some called it a gutter) from the old Combermere School on Roebuck Street, which was the Maginot Line segregating Harrison College from the stench of Combermere and the Canal itself, in which floated the jetsamed lives of the flotsamed flying fish heads and tails and guts, and some of the bones of the fish sold at the corner of Constitution; and also the deaths of many ambitions and reputations of civil servants and fathers.

I was unfortunate. But some said they were not as fortunate as I. I was fortunate because, some said, "Because I ain't have no father." What they meant was that he was neither school teacher, nor civil servant in white dealboard drill, nor inspector looking for "larvees and shit in my people's closets." This apparent neglect, or oversight, on the part of my mother to legalize her sex-life, apparently was very important at Harrison College (and Combermere, too), because I can remember that three times a year I would be reminded of it, by the deliberate half-inaudible sniggers behind me, whenever the master asked, "To who, Clarke, this report card going? Miss Luke?" (although she was, legally, Mrs. Luke!) . . . the impossibility of saying *Mrs. Clarke* was a tragic shortcoming.

But the sniggers in my past, both at Combermere School and Harrison College, did not end there. The most traumatic experience I met with, in the world of higher education at Harrison College, was when I attempted to join their cadet corps. I had been Sargeant-Major at Combermere. And since I remembered that at one time both cadet corps shot with "board guns," I expected that even although Combermere cadets had not graduated from drilling with mock guns hewn out of pine and dealboard by Wiltshire the Carpenter (and some few relics from the Boer War), and whereas the Pansa troops of Harrison College used real 303's (which, however, could no longer shoot!) I would at least be appointed a sargeant. But after some kind of military examination which had to do with real warfare (in Barbados?), and which I passed, I was given my new rank, posted among diverse important orders, on the notice board. *Acting* Lance Corporal!

Amidst the shock and the humiliation, and the first taste of the sociological repercussions of what it is like to crawl under the wire and cross the Canal from a second grade school to a first grade school, I could not find out, and have never found out, whether the position *Acting*, in my new appointment, was more important and significant than the rank itself — Lance Corporal. It was the first blow. It was the deadly blow. Perhaps I might have been the first black general, or commander deployed by the British Army to put down the racial disorders in what was formerly British Guiana!

And now, fifteen years after that sad, blearing, sun-scorching afternoon, near the Tower in Harrison College, I have looked back, and by-George! cannot hunt out anything about that experience which singles me out as the most unfortunate school boy at the College . . . a Trinidadian scholar of Modern History, with a PhD degree is offered a job as a porter, on the Canadian National Railways; a Barbadian civil servant with ten years' experience and boredom in Treasury is given a job as a watchman in a Toronto factory . . . we are all cockroaches in the same closet pit. But the pits in Barbados are so different from those in Canada.

All my ambitions of generals and machine guns and surrenders and armistices had evaporated in that hot inhumane afternoon . . . for I could remember, as a small boy at elementary school, marching to time, martial in time, oh God, man! and the shouts of our headmaster-general, Wardie, who always wore khaki, "hip-pip," and *Onward, Christian Soldiers,* we the little black ants of soldiers, Christian and English, screeling the song, and saluting the flag ("Wait, that flag we does salute so, that is we own-own flag?"), the Union Jack; and having to learn its origin and history (" . . . and, and the one with the red thing crossing it like a cross on the white background, that one is the flag o' Sin George or Sin Andrew?") . . . and, the innocuousness of the sheckling coins of the 1937 Coronation in my sweating hands, shackled by colonialism and ignorance and hunger; and the thumping of my bare feet in the unpaved stretches of marl and dust and school yards (many of my classmates developed a disease called "chigger-foot," and only God knows how I escaped it!), pounding out in martial strains, *Rule Britannia! Britannia rules the waves* . . . never say we were slaves, what with those bags of buns, stale and bilgy as the ginger beer, given gratis when I was a boy, because there was a new Majesty on the wall; and when I was old enough to hold a musket in my hand, and do something to the situation or to myself, or about Majesty and buns and bilgy beer, they, the commanders and the officers, by-George! made my musket out of board — dealboard!

Nothing was shot through its muzzle, but pride.

And we would stand beneath a relentless sun, at the zenith of its hate for black skins, at the zenith of fainting from the sun and from hunger.

("Jesus Christ, boy, look, I ain't have even a half-loaf o' sweet bread to put in your guts before you go down there 'pon the Gar'son Pasture parading for the Queen! But come, drink this little miraculous bush tea, 'cause it going bring up some o' the gas, still . . . ")

While the Union Jacks were banging the wind with their own jubilation, beneath them stood so many mock-soldiers, tied in allegiance and at attention, because there was a Queen or a King, somewhere up in London: *Royal salute, preee-sent arms! Orrr-der arms! Slope arms!* and the Queen's or King's representative, the Governor, with a fowl cock on his head, fluttering like authority and royalty, unknown to most of us, except that handful who went to church at Government House tea parties, to have tea and cucumber sandwiches in 90-degree three-piece suits made in the same cold climate where the Queen or the King was probably drinking sherry (while they should have been in Marcus rum shop drinking rum and eating bread-and-fish and talking something sensible) to show some visiting dignitary or a captain from a man-of-war, that in our splendid island of Barbados, *Little* England, master and slave could meet in other circumstances than those constitutionally arranged by colonialism . . . these are the memories of growing up with a dealboard musket on my shoulder, my memories of a proud, little, black, English childhood.

Let me not give the impression that I did not, in those barefoot-after-school days, swagger with equal or even greater contempt and conceit with the Harrison College students at the lesser mortals: the Combermerians. Do not let it be said that I had no pride, and found none, in the white shirt and the khaki shorts, the college tie of red and gold, with matching flashes, and a book bag slung over the handle of my black bicycle (black — a choice color for bicycles only!), crammed with knowledge which I garnered then, and never could use since: Virgil, Cicero, Tacitus, Caesar, Livy and other trinkets of useless battles and bridges crossed, and something about a man named Hannibal who crossed the Alps, without its being pointed out whether that crossing was tantamount to crossing his racial Rubicon, without being told that this Hannibal was not an Englishman, but was rather black like me; and many books of Shakespeare without being taught the one tragedy significant to me as a black man in a white society — Othello — which above all the other snippets of learning could have anchored me down, steadfastly, to my birth, my culture, my origin.

In the Hall, where a diminutive voice conducted Prayers, the language used was English, identical to that in the prose of Burke, or Goldsmith, or Macaulay. A voice not out of my past, because of that past I knew nothing; and was taught less than nothing — there was never a West Indian history book in my bag, which for six years

I pulled through Combermere School and through Harrison College for three years, like a wharf rat pulling a lighter.

That voice had once told me to leave the class, because the mauby and buns had settled too soon, too heavily and too finally in my stomach, and had sent me on the afternoon wings of negritistic drowsiness: that foreign voice which said on my school-leaving recommendation (without which no school boy leaving school can exist in the "outside world"), merely sketching the skeleton of potentiality: *Austin C. Clarke entered Harrison College in 1950, as a transfer from Combermere School. He has recently taken the Oxford and Cambridge Higher School Certificate in June, in English, Latin and Roman History. He was an outstanding athlete, and has a flair for writing. Signed: J.C. Hammond.*

Hendrik Verwoerd could not have said less on a kaffir's pass book! And had I this ability to summarize a piece of English prose, I might have been a Barbados Scholar — or I might have got a distinction in English! Equipped with this testimonial arsenal, I was left to forge my advance into a society built on recommendations. The gentleman who wrote it had made certain (could he have forgotten?) that there was no mention of my "demeanor", my "behavior" and my "manners." And since Barbadians believe that "manners maketh man," I could not be considered a man.

It was a recommendation based on the fact that I had dared to fall asleep in his class that had something to do with English Social History, in which a lot was droned about England and not very much about society or sociology or history. And remembering now, I wonder what that same gentleman would have done (what did he in fact do?) had he the opportunity to recommend to the "outside world" another gentleman who came to Harrison College with three academic degrees: BSc, MSc and DSc, which, it turned out, he had none of? There is a way of dealing with cockroaches in the closets of Bank Hall and the cockroaches of Hastings Village.

I was left then, with nothing but aggression and ambition, which I could use as antidotes to my poverty. I sometimes wonder, from my new mental safety of Canada, whether fate alone divided those who writhed a shitty living out of their poverty, and those who were buried in the shit and the poverty. I cannot yet understand how I escaped its death knell. Perhaps it was my aggressiveness. I remember the energy I used in order to combat the ingrained prejudices and other disadvantages in my life at Harrison College; and my determination to be outstanding in something.

During my days at the College, to be outstanding with the books (the ability to write a good distinctive Latin prose was the exception) was not accorded any unnecessary honor or seriousness. I understand that the island regards scholarship more seriously nowadays: because the island is becoming "free." Everybody who had ambition could not be named Griffith, or Smith, or Williams. But I had to shine. And I chose to shine at athletics. For me, athletics was a more acceptably aggressive way of fighting back, than coming first in Latin Unseen — because apart from the questionable virtues of this acquired foreign knowledge, I thought at the time, that scholarship was a more passive way of presenting myself to a society in which social acceptability was not only superior to book learning, but was also based on hereditary considerations.

Athletics implied a fight: a competitiveness, a visible defeat and a visible victory. It was something that could be seen; and read about; and applauded — (and I needed applause); and since I could not lay claim to the applause of a plausible legitimacy of birth, nor to the plausibility of a knife-and-fork-eating middle class background, the plausibility of my existence had to be won *by me*, alone.

I understand now (I was not, nor could I be expected to understand it, then) why I did compete in individual sports. I could not share my honors with anyone. I must be in front, alone, in victory, as I had been alone in the defeats caused by virtue of being, firstly, black; secondly, poor; thirdly, illegitimate.

It was easier to come first in the 100 yards sprint than to bowl all day, and depend upon the slip fielder to take my catches, in order to see my name in the score book.

My promotion from Sargeant-Major in the Combermere cadet corps to the rank of Acting Lance Corporal in the Harrison College cadet corps, further convinces me that Barbados, Harrison College, and other institutions in my island, are not so very different from South Africa, southern Rhodesia, the United States and even Canada.

It is one thing to want to be a soldier (and be permitted to be soldier), and to be given a musket of dealboard with which to hunt for the enemy: a hunt which, by-George! takes you into the pits of Hastings and Bank Hall, among the cockroaches and the flies. I had to leave.

1966

Two Poems from Barbados

Fishermen Looking Out to Sea

Why do you sit beneath the burning August sun,
And stare so madly at the sea?
Why do you stare so madly at the sea,
As you sit so half-despondently on the burning sand?

That is your sea, your life and your grave:
The sea that draws you magnet-like
On the dark, dead nights
That frighten the bait from the dead fishes' mouth.

Why do you sit beneath the burning August sun
And stare and watch,
And hope? What hope
Could you hope, with that August stare of yours?

The sun is burning hot,
And so are the waves and sands
And the resentment of the fishermen,
Looking out to sea, beneath the burning August sun.

Do not go to sea tonight, old fishermen.
Something says this is a fishless night,
A night of tears,
        With a tear-stained tomorrow
        Full of old maids' sad-wrung hands.

Yet, you will go.
But tomorrow they would come,
With ripe expectant eyes
Looking at a dead, sun burnt sea
For the dead; the dead of the fishless night.

Their hearts would tell their searching tearful eyes:
"You are not drowned. Perhaps, only drifting round."
And they would come again;
        beneath the burning August sun,
And look, and listen for the sounds of the dead . . .
The last death-note of the old fishermen,
That sat beneath the burning August sun.

From My Lover's Home

From my lover's home to me there is the sea,
There is the sea from my lover's home and me,
The sea, the sea, the sea;
There is the sea from my lover's home and me.
Right down my side, right down my left side
There is the sea, the dark sea,
The midnight sea, the dark, dark midnight sea.
The black sea separates my lover's home from me,
It is the sea, the sea, the midnight sea
That separates my lover from me.

These are the poems of a young man, a student, at Trinity College, University of Toronto. They appeared in the College literary magazine, The Review, in 1957.

Fishermen Looking Out to Sea received the prize for poetry that year.

Ed.

In The Semi-colon of the North

Going straight north as an arrow I looked at a map to shoot my direction and progress, the Ontario Northland Railway was taking me to Timmins where I would work on the *Timmins Daily News* as a reporter for thirty-five dollars a week. It was December, nineteen fifty-nine. One week before Christmas.

One week before Christmas, six years ago, I was sitting in the warm friendships built from birth in Barbados, inhaling the fumes of new polish and varnish and paint that was green and dark blue on the furniture that surrounded me like the knowledge of those friendships. And six years later, now, I am sitting in a crowded coach of this CNR train, surrounded by women and by men who look like trappers out of the adventure books of the West I had read in Barbados, and out of the conversations I had heard from university students who came from the West, and who said they hated the East. My closest friends at the university were Westerners. But where are these Westerners now that I am taking this long journey into the semi-colon of the unpunctuated North?

The men sitting around me on the slow-moving train, making up my mind on a divorce from Toronto where I had lived for five years, all looked like miners and prospectors. Their skin was rough-hewn and burned and tightened as if by a different kind of climate or sun-lamp from those I had seen in the tanning bedrooms of Rosedale and Forest Hill in Toronto; and they all looked half-asleep just as those women in the sun and under the lamp seemed to be. They resembled the Indians I had passed on Spadina Avenue, men and women of tanned skin, inheritors of abuse and scorn I had listened to in the streets of Toronto.

"Would you sell a *Molson's* to a goddam Indian?"

I was myself like a prospector, travelling light and lightened by the uncertainty of expectation, no bags and baggage to suggest permanency, enough clothes to ensure personal hygiene, no notebooks and no typewriter for I was not yet a writer of fiction, no writer at all, but a dreamer of ambition larger than the land over which the train was taking me. I was equipped with the music, the memory of the music I had listened to in the jazz clubs and bars of Toronto, and in other places; and the three pieces I had selected to memorize and bring along on this journey, were

Milestones by Miles Davis, Beethoven's *Third Symphony,* and the *Russian Easter Overture* by a Russian composer whose name I could hardly pronounce.

Milestones was the metaphor and the definition of this horse of a train, this horse of iron, with its slow pace, its excitement and strange smell of coffee weakened by the touch of cold hands, hardly any steam as it touched the lips, and no recognizable strength of caffeine to deaden the disorientation of the journey; Canadian apples that reminded me of cider when they were crushed by the strong teeth of these men, only because I had heard that you could make cider from apples; the smell of clothing, heavy shirts that were famous for their plaids in another country, and for some reason, the smell of fish, although the only sea was the waves of snow through which we were travelling. The music in my mind showed me a horse trotting slowly and surely, aware of its pace and destination. The snow outside the train was like a large white pasture over which the hooves were travelling; a "comforter" of pure white which looked blue in the distance. The wheels of iron, and my speculation of the time they took to make one revolution, were the hooves of the horse in the music, and the tempo of the drummer as he beat his measurement on skins and brass.

But the music that was in my mind belonged to a different drummer, to a faster means of travelling, to a land in which I was at one with the color of sweat and the creed of labor and exploitation: Miles Davis was not a "comforter" on the brittle, rasping and sometimes piercingly clear trumpet; he was defining a journey of changing destination, of changing intention, of changing purpose. And it was making me nostalgic for Toronto. The journey on which my body was now being carried could not tolerate that excitement. For I was surrounded by nothing but whiteness. Snow.

Not even the wind outside, and I imagined that there would have to be a wind no matter how slight; not even the wind had succeeded in altering the patterns of mild undulations, careful hills of snow, without any purpose of rhythm and beat; and the wind gave the snow no threat of ever being conquered. Valleys and dales looked smooth, not treacherous, and exciting enough for the cover of a galvanized pail with a child in it, to slide down the disappearing sides from the train. It was all snow, and the windless caress of white rectitude and order and a puritanness of the snow itself.

I began to think of different music. *The Russian Easter Overture* composed by that man of Russian origin with the unpronounceable name, which I recognized on sight but could not put vowels to; this music which reminded me of Barbados and its own colonial puritanism, where the only snow, at Easter and at Christmas, is the make-believe whiteness of the "marl" from the rock quarries; and which we spread around our homes in devout obedience to the purity of those two Christian holidays, or eating days. We ate more than we worshiped the sacred metaphors of those days. And in Toronto, where I had first heard the *Overture*, one Christmas Eve night among friends and drinks who were "artistic," I gained a more focused understanding of the Russian countryside. It comes to me now, and with it comes that Group of men, Seven in number, who gave their art the same name as the number of their membership; and I wondered if they too had listened to this Russian music and had seen the fierce snow in its chords; if they had captured this part of the northern country with its desolate weather, or whether they had drawn the reality of this North, purely from the warm comfort of picture postcards and Toronto beer parlors.

The sun must have been still high in the Russianed sky, and fierce as the music, even at four; or was it already seven o'clock? for I could feel light and life and wonder within the wilderness outside the murmuring train. The life outside was stronger than the life of the snoozing well-travelled passengers. Inside the train, these men and women had already arranged their bodies in a resignation of comfortable position to the well-known long journey. Although the journey was beginning to be broken up by constant interruptions of stops and stations. Miles Davis changed the pace of his journey on the trumpet from a gallop to a canter. And my understanding of the riffs of his climb was altered and heightened. But these men and women seemed to know when the train would stop, when their portion of the journey would end. They had become no longer so impatient as the colonial from the South about the clattering of miles. Their sense of destiny and music and long living was stronger.

They also ignored, through custom and perhaps with love, the coming and going of the "colored" porter. He was a fact of the train, and a fact of their lives; a metaphor of this kind of railroad travel. They looked up, smiled, bought a cheese sandwich from him, or a red Canadian apple, and steaming styrofoam cups of dark liquid which made their faces redder, and then, as quick as it takes to forget a stranger, they closed their eyes, and re-settled themselves among heavy coats and blankets. The few children in the coach with me, were chewing gum to help them fight their restlessness. Two strong, handsome, unwarlike Indians stomached their steaming black coffees just as gamblers try to stay awake, to cut the journey into gulps.

And the trees; for I was looking and watching and hearing the *Overture,* and not eating nor drinking as the others were; the trees, green even at this death of time, unaware of the inhuman coldness that was sharp enough to kill a man, manly as a trapper and as noble as the two Indians, including those in storybooks, the trees were just a little similar to the genius in the paint boxes of two of the members of the Group of Seven, I had seen in exhibitions.

I could have been crossing the Steppes, or the Himalayas, or the Canadian Shield, for the music was so international in its wideness, just as the land around me was wide; and the music could have been invented by a Barbarian to be played in any small Christian-Missioned church on a green hill, so constricting was it to my far smaller context of origin.

A man can imagine any color to give to the whiteness of the snow outside, or to the gold of a sunset. And if he is fused to the electricity of genius, or if he is infused with enough of the natural means of keeping the body warm, as it was becoming almost impossible to do inside this train, then in his drunkenness of originality and craftiness, brought about by his heavy drinking and by the inordinateness of the alcoholic and surrounding beauty, then what he does do with the colors in the eyes of his art, is not so commonplace a trick as bending the normalness of color and perception, but is merely the adding of his conviction to it.

I was now travelling on the brass and reeds of Russian movement, no blanket to match the white and green-bordered regal robes of the two Indians who sat facing me to make myself comfortable. They did not talk, nor blink, nor smile. They were mysterious masks.

The heat in the train was turned off after we pulled out of North Bay. This may not be a fact, but it is an artistic liberty of the fiction writer whose craftiness and words can see the land and the passengers becoming more wedded to their freezing surroundings; since he has seen with his artist's eye that there are no longer any politicians, nor reeves, nor managers of banks, nor cold-blooded southerners after we have passed North Bay, and that the only residents of this slowmoving cold-storage train are Indians and "colored" porters, and people who are stupid enough to live in the North.

I had heard of North Bay before. Once. But I imagined it to be closer to Toronto. When it came, and when the train changed its tempo after it disappeared on the narrowing lines, I sensed that I had come to the end of the line, the end of all reasonable expectations and of survival without extreme violence. I had reached a state of awareness of a time before men became avaricious and greedy and adventurous, and sought to pan for gold and kill for skins, and kill everything that was not gold or bears, everything that lay in the sights of their transits. I could imagine men in the coach with me, as *those* men who had first prospected on the land which they thought was covered in gold, just as the streets of New York and Toronto were glittering with golden success for the immigrant. A colonial's dream, and a fool's fantasy. North Bay must have been crawling with men like these, my companions on a train, before the time when those two Indians and their families were pushed back even farther, back into the reservation and into extinction, as the buffalo and the trees that impeded progress and development were shot and axed.

Were there Italians among these first "Canadians"? Were there Jews then, too? Some bears are like this "colored" porter, and like me, only in color.

It is too cold now, and too late, back in Toronto, for the Italians, the worker ants of the Fifties, to meddle in trenches and on scaffolds from which they fall like flies, and die like martyrs in their new hyphenated Canadian experience. "On the street cars, when you get too close to them, all you can smell is garlic . . . "

I can see a time before the Indian was skull-capped by versions of his resistance to national development, and how from scalping and raping he was turned from flesh and blood into symbols on coins, and into names of insurance companies and exclusive resort areas and lakes; and I turn to the Indians sitting before me and try to compare their silhouetted forward look to their images on American coins. My body is cold. And the coldness becomes the disposition of their fortunes and their prospects.

This train bound for my personal glory, stops nowhere. It has stopped, it is true, in a certain ordinary meaning of time, because I can see the trees are no longer evading the thrust of the train through the vagina of this Indian territory. But in the bigger meaning of time, this train stops nowhere. Little insects of specks of snow scurry just above the surface of the sheet of milk. A man gets off. There is a gust of steam like the overdue passing of gas from a tired human body.

I am scared. I am terrified that this man has pressed the wrong stop. And then I wonder how do you stop a train, except to lie in front of it? But this man gets off like a man would get out of a taxi. He must be an Indian. Or a fool. He seemed too much in a hurry to reach his destination, unwilling to remain in the belly of the train, and had decided to get out, and end the rhythm of movement. And now, I see him through the mist of the window, wandering through a path in the uncut wilderness. He seems more knowledgeable than the rest of us, who are too frightened, too unwilling to take up the heavy ploughs of chord in Beethoven's *Third Symphony*, of which I am thinking now, and become a part of that tragic retreat through a different country, but in the same thickness of snow. So, we sit and wait for another destination to come, one that is more habitable, for some unpure station that offers a habitable ordinariness.

The man injures the snow as he moves in a straight line in the lineless landscape, and he constructs his own highway, just as the Italians do on virgin land in a Toronto suburb, or as the tentativeness of retreat had done in the Symphony. And then, before the train abandons him altogether, before he can change his mind, as I would have done, and run back to the ordinary safety of the train, he walks and walks in the shrouds of interminable bandaging snow, and approaches a hill on which there is a tall noble tree, the sentry for many more, and then, from the distance he is from me, all of a sudden he finds his bearing in the rudderlessness of the field. I envision drums and horses and soldiers tired as construction workers, and silent defeated cannon and artillery that look like gigantic cement mixers.

The train is now at another angle of his departure. There are houses now in my view. And I become disappointed that he is not lost, that he is not going into a field of defeated battle and more snow, and possible suicide.

If I were a painter I would paint this snow black. Last month, or last year, in the previous season, this whiteness was a field of wild growing grass, with flowers which we from the city could have picked or cut and put into a vase, or into a wine bottle of cheap Italian wine that we had had for dinner, to decorate our crowded space.

The man who has left the train, is perhaps, now home.

But before that, before he enters the door, I see him as a black dot. I had ignored his progress before this diminution, to think of the rails and miles before me. The train takes me headlong into more towns in this disregarded North. I count the hours and I count the sheep in those hours, and I wonder what has driven me from the comfortable house on Grace Street near Bloor, to enter this landscape which I could have been satisfied to have *seen* in the music of Beethoven's *Third?*

I think of the thirty-five dollars I am to be paid each week, perhaps at two in the afternoon on each Friday, so that I might sled through the streets of Timmins to the bank on time. I think of the size of an immigrants' wages, which is merely his means of buying necessities, which is the dignified alternative to begging and unemployment insurance, and which is not the important impetus for the immigrant's contribution to this country's wealth. It is my dignity that I can spend, and pay for things. Not my wage.

So, the wage may be a small wage. I cannot ask questions about its size simply because I have the immigrant's surrealistic optimism that says that larger wages will come with larger experience, even if, for the moment, that experience is called "Canadian experience."

I wonder if I can get the larger knowledge without the larger insults and the larger unhappiness?

I will therefore accept this pittanced wage, and leave the North when the time is golden. And afterwards, with this "Canadian" experience, conspire to climb faster than the newest immigrant, rapidly, and suffer the castigation for being "uppity," in the silence of my integration.

I count the trees that run along the wires, with my eyes, until I must have travelled around the sea that surrounds Barbados, one thousand times. And if the line does not end where I am heading, if the line could not end, and the train becomes a ghost train after the ghost towns we have passed, and could go on and on, I can conceivably end up right where I have started out, in the small village of Flagstaff, since too far North must be South. I begin to put my mind into that deceiving discipline of informing it that this is the best, most enjoyable journey I have ever taken. I tell myself that the journey is really not simply the two parallel lines which refuse to end within my sight, but that they are joined to each other in the unseeable distance. The drums in the retreat of the music are heavy, and I can see mothers along the way, including my own; discarded lovers hot from the shortened exhilaration of a climax of victory and orgasm.

I pretend that I have fallen out of the train. The train does not stop. I am merely a dot left to blacken the snow in one spot.

The "colored" porter has just helped an old grey-bearded man down the slab of iron of the stopped train, to the ground.

"Been South?" the porter asks.

"Yeah, Joe."

He put his hand into his pocket and puts that same hand into the porter's hand.

"Been visiting the kids. Last girl got married. Temagami, ya know. She been living south these two years."

The music of retreat rushes over the snow, like an avalanche of thick spoiled milk. And before this conversation is off my mind, before I can fill in its spaces with faces and bodies of snow-bitten, beaten soldiers, we are at Haileybury. A little north of the South.

The train is warmer now. I had travelled through many towns with the heat off and my body was now acclimatized to the fresh northern Canadian experience. The distance between these towns was now speeded up like a magic-lantern slide show, played at the wrong, faster speed.

New Liskeard, Englehart and Swastika . . .

Swastika?

Could this train have passed through compass-points while I had been dozing between stations? Perhaps, this part of the wild bush had been an iceberg and had been drifting backwards through a slower snow that did not melt; perhaps this part of the bush was ignorant while other trains criss-crossed Europe bearing this same Swastika, and filled with different passengers whose namesakes in Toronto could not rent a cottage in the weekended lakes. Perhaps other men than I were dozing while other passengers were being gassed and then buried. Perhaps, it was this cold that drove us to this drowsiness.

Through the breathing glass window that showed the hissing steam: rub the palm of the hand on the ice that has formed there, and clear the two-temperatured air, and see if there is a swastika painted on the station door, if there are people goose-stepping on the platform. See, too, after you have seen that, if there are any persons who "look like Jews," who have not got summer cottages to rent down South, and who are now come, or forced to come, to this destination.

I try to imagine how a namesake of those European times, would feel entering this northern Ontario town with its brazen name, for the War is still raging in our painful memories.

Look and see if you can recognize anyone in the small crowd of thick coats and furs, and women in mink's clothing, if there is a journalist like Pierre Berton investigating here, as he has been investigating everywhere, including the pages of the Toronto *Star.*

Kirkland Lake was bellowed out, but it was too dark, and I was too sleepy and too numbed to see.

Ramore I could see. I saw the second "colored" man in the North at Ramore. And an American army base was there, and many American "colored" boys, so the porter said, were living there.

"Don't bother nobody none," he said, "and nobody don't bother them. You won't think they were such nice boys. When you think of it . . . "

I decided I would spend my weekends in Ramore. It is closer than Toronto. Ramore was also close to Rama, and although it had some similar sound to that Biblical city, I still was not discouraged to invest in its brotherhood.

But what were the Americans doing in the Canadian North? Had they come to gain "Canadian" experience, too?

After Ramore, with the "American colored boys" changing the town no doubt, and making polka-dots of the beer parlors, dancing to the rhythm of the Ska and rock-n-roll, Fats Domino and Billy Eckstein and Jimmy Brown and James Brown, wriggling their black asses on the football fields of these northern white corsetted climes and times, like Friday nights along Spadina Avenue in Toronto, after Ramore, came Matheson and then North Porcupine, South Porcupine, and then, as God would have it! . . . Timmins. I had reached the end of my line.

1982

AUSTIN CLARKE/MALCOLM X

AUSTIN CLARK: Within recent years, there have been many forces responsible for bringing attention to the problems of the black man in America and other parts of the world. One of these forces is the Muslim movement, black Muslims, which is a very active movement in New York and other parts of America. With me is Mr. Malcolm X, minister of Mosque Number Seven in New York, and who is regarded as one of the better known spokesmen for this movement.

Mr. Malcolm, could you tell me what is the history of the movement in America?

MALCOLM X: Well, number one, when we are referred to as the black Muslims, actually this is incorrect. It is true that we are black people who are Muslims because our religion is the religion of Islam, but in the west, the word, black Muslims has been used in the wrong way. When I say I am a black man who is a — and I am a Muslim, I mean I am black in the sense that black is an adjective, and when it is used by the Press, usually they say Black Muslims; they capitalize the letter B and attach it to the word, Muslim, and make it Black Muslim, the name of an organization.

AUSTIN CLARK: You say they are trying to differentiate between a white Muslim and a black Muslim?

MALCOLM X: Yes, and they do this purposely, for propaganda purposes, to try and make it appear that we are — that we are using the name, Black Muslim, as the name of an organization that has nothing to do with a religious connotation, but we are Muslim; we are black people who are Muslim, because our religion is Islam, and also in America here they oftimes try and say that we are not Moslem but Muslim, and they are successful in doing this simply because most Americans aren't aware that Moslem is only the anglicized or westernized way of saying Muslim. A Moslem is a Muslim and Moslem. Most Americans don't know this so most Americans end up in referring to the followers of the honorable Elijah Mohamed, they will say, well, we aren't Moslems, we are Muslims, and this actually displays or reflects the ignorance of the average American concerning other religions and here in America we are followers of Mr. Elijah Mohamed, the honorable Elijah Mohamed. He is the religious head or spiritual leader of the ever-increasing number of black people who are coming out of the Christian church and accepting the religion of Islam, the religion of our forefathers, and accepting the one God, Allah, rejecting the trinity of the Church and accepting the unity of God.

AUSTIN CLARK: Could you put your hands on the forces or the motivation for this exodus from the old traditional religion and the new one?

MALCOLM X: Well, you mean by the old traditional . . .

AUSTIN CLARK: The old Christian religion.

MALCOLM X: Well, most of the black people in America are well aware that the Christian church as we have known it has definitely failed us. It has failed to solve our problems. It has failed to produce brotherhood between black and white Christians. It has failed to eliminate the conditions of poverty and discrimination and segregation that our people experience in this country. It has failed us, period, and it has failed to make us a godly people. It has made us more ungodly, so especially among young black people today, we are able to see that Christianity has failed. It has failed to do all of the things that it professes to lead one toward and this has produced an atmosphere or climate or season in which the religion of Islam, as taught by the Honorable Elijah Mohamed, has found fertile soil and has been very productive, with productive results.

AUSTIN CLARK: What element of the Negro population seems to be most interested in being Muslims?

MALCOLM X: All elements, only the interest is usually reflected according to the element that one happens to be in. You take the bourgeois Negro, the so-called — the Negro who refers to himself as the bourgeois, middle class or professional Negro, he is interested, but usually his crumbs, the crumbs, the economic crumbs he receives come from the white man, so he has to hide his interest. He has to camouflage his interest. He has to camouflage his sympathy. He has to camouflage his support but still he is intellectually honest enough to admit that what Mr. Mohamed is teaching actually will solve the problem of the masses of black people, but at the same time being a realist and knowing that his crumbs come from the white man, he has to hide his agreement with Mr.

Mohamed and then you have the masses of black people in this country who suffer the brunt of the white man's discrimination, segregation, who live in the slums and the ghettos. They also are interested, but since they have nothing to lose, they have nothing to hide, so they reflect open interest. They reflect open sympathy and they actually also reflect open support and what I am saying to you in essence is that all black people in America are interested but the differences in their interest is in the form that it manifests itself.

AUSTIN CLARK: What are the aims of the movement, the practical aims?

MALCOLM X: Yes, the aims of the honorable Elijah Mohamed, his reason for teaching us the religion of Islam, is that this is the only thing that will solve our problems. It will clean us up morally. It will awaken us intellectually, mentally. It will show us how to stand on our own feet economically and it shows us also — it instills within us an independent desire to govern our own affairs, plot our own destiny, control our own future, and one of the reasons that it is so important for the black people in America to develop this kind of thinking, this kind of concept, you have to understand the religion of Islam. The religion of Islam teaches us to believe in one God whose proper name is Allah and by believing in one God we believe in all of the prophets, because we believe that there being one God, he only had one religion, and therefore every prophet who walked on this earth had to teach the same religion so once we accept Allah as God, the oneness of God, that means we also accept the oneness of God's religious message and we also accept the oneness and the mission and the objectives of all of the prophets, the oneness of their source, the common origin that all of them had, and in accepting this, we also accept the scriptures that were taught by all of their prophets, all of these prophets, and all of the prophets always mentioned, that there would come a time when God Himself would manifest Himself in the flesh on this earth and bring about an end of all wicked kingdoms and then establish a kingdom of His own that would be based upon freedom, justice, equality, righteousness, peace, love and brotherhood. This would be heaven on earth.

AUSTIN CLARK: How close is the white man's kingdom — I mean, how close in association between the wicked kingdom and the situation of white prejudice?

MALCOLM X: It's impossible to separate wickedness, corruption, slavery, colonialism, exploitation and oppression from what we would call Europeanism, or westernism, or whiteism, or, as they say, white supremacy — only — when the white man practices it, he doesn't call it white supremacy, nor does he call it slavery. He calls it colonialism. Colonialism was slavery. Colonialism was white supremacy. This was wickedness. This was oppression. This was corruption. This is what it is predicted God Himself would bring an end to at the end of time when He manifests Himself in the flesh, and when the prophets in the scriptures refer to the end of time, they didn't mean by the end of time, the end of earth, but they only meant the end of a system on this earth that was wicked or the end of a world on this earth that was wicked and most Negroes in America, by having a limited, narrow, religious concept, when they hear the religious leaders say 'the end of the world,' they think that this is meant to be the end of everything, but the honorable Elijah Mohamed, our religious teacher, teaches us that God does not intend to bring an end to the earth, but an end to the world, and on this one earth there are many worlds, the world of socialism, the world of capitalism, the world of communism, the world of colonialism, the world of Buddhism, the world of Judaism, the world of Islam, the world of Christianity; there are many worlds and when the religious reference is made concerning the end of time, Mr. Mohamed teaches us that this only means the end of time for a certain world or a certain race or a certain system, and as a religious people who have accepted the religious teachings of the honorable Elijah Mohamed, we feel that we are living now in the last days of the white man's world, or at the end of time for the white man's world, and because we feel religiously that his time is up or that his world is approaching its end, its doom, its disaster or its judgment, we have no desire to accept his belated offers of integration into a corrupt, outdated society that has been sentenced to doom and destruction by the God or Lord of all the worlds, whom we refer to as Allah.

AUSTIN CLARK: If you are not willing to — let me put it this way: if you do not want to accept any of his crumbs or be in a partnership with him now, because you think he is on the way out anyhow, are you in effect suggesting some form of apartheid? This has been one of the criticisms I have read of your movement.

MALCOLM X: Apartheid is misunderstood, unless you translate it into English with the proper counterpart. When you translate the word — I think it is a Germanic word apartheid, into English, under the word segregation, does *apartheid* mean segregation or does —

AUSTIN CLARK: The existence of the two races independently of one another.

MALCOLM X: Does apartheid then mean segregation?

AUSTIN CLARK: Well, the apartheid we know of in South Africa seems to suggest some sort of segregation because the black man is not given all the facilities, but in your case if you are going to establish yourself independently of the white man, I am wondering if this cannot be termed some form of apartheid.

MALCOLM X: You see, apartheid has been used or translated or come to be known in the west now as something very derogatory, because it is associated with South Africa. America practices apartheid too, but she preaches democracy, but she practices the opposite. Now, the reason I ask you for a definite distinct definition, we are against segregation but we are for separation and Mr. Mohamed teaches us that the difference between segregation and separation is segregation is that which is forced upon inferiors by superiors. As you hinted, separation is done voluntarily by two equals. The people of South Africa practice segregation, apartheid in a segregated sense. We are against that but we are for separation which means the voluntary separation by two equals. I have everything that I need to control my destiny, my future. You have everything that you need to control your destiny, your future. An example here in America: an all-white neighborhood is never referred to as a segregated neighborhood. It is only a Negro neighborhood that is called segregated, because the white neighborhood is controlled — it is lived in by whites. The economy is controlled by whites. The politics are controlled by whites. The society is controlled by whites, whereas the Negro community here in America is also controlled by whites. The housing is controlled by whites, the educational system is controlled by whites, the politics of the Negro community is controlled by whites, the economy is controlled by whites. All of the businesses in the Negro neighborhood are controlled by whites. The banks are controlled by whites, and this means that the Negroes, even though they live in their own neighborhood, are controlled by whites. This is segregation and this is why a segregated neighborhood is usually deteriorated economically, politically, intellectually and otherwise but the white neighborhood is separate for they control their separateness. They are in command of their — of what they have now. We believe, as followers of the honorable Elijah Mohamed, that the white man should have his own and that the black man should have his own. The black man should control his own and the white man should control his own, but we don't believe that the white man should control us politically, economically, religiously, intellectually, educationally or otherwise. We believe that we should be in complete command of our own.

AUSTIN CLARK: You have been reported to desire certain states set apart. I think this goes back to what you were talking about, being separate but equal. Could you tell me how you would go about arranging your business interests, your educational facilities, even what system of education would you have to institute in order to set up your separate state?

MALCOLM X: First, you have to know the background, as to why Mr. Mohamed suggests separate states. He says that the government has shown its inability to give justice to black people in this country. The government has shown its inability to give freedom or equality to black people in this country and since the United States government has shown its inability to treat us as human beings in this country, Mr. Mohamed says that the United States government should let twenty million black people in this country leave here and go back into our own homeland, but the government doesn't want the world to know that it is incapable of giving democracy or freedom and justice to black people so that the government puts forth every effort imaginable to keep a mass number of black people developing an idea or desire to go back home among our own kind, and so Mr. Mohamed says since the government doesn't want us to leave here and go back home among our own people and the government can't treat us right here, mixed up with them, then this government should separate this country and give us a section where we can live to ourselves. Give us separate territory where we can go and solve the problems that the government has proven its inability to solve. We are trying to secede from something that is bad and from something that has proved its inability to treat us good and to treat us in accord with the principles of freedom, justice and equality.

AUSTIN CLARK: If you did get these states, do you think that there would be a clash, let's say, in foreign policy or even in economic policy between your states and the rest of America, which I presume would be white by this time?

MALCOLM X: I don't think that any clash could ever develop worse than the clashes that are developing right now between black and white, in our so-called integrated society. Whenever you live in a country that refers to itself as a democracy and refers to itself as the leader of the free world and in that country you see pictures on the front pages of cops sicking dogs on black people, simply because they want to vote, simply because they want to exercise what the government has professed to be the constitutional rights of black people? Why, sir, the relationship between the two races couldn't get any worse, and the attitude toward each other couldn't get any worse, so we feel that since the government is hypocritical, the white man is hypocritical, the American is hypocritical, Uncle Sam is hypocritical whenever he speaks in terms of freedom and justice and equality where black people are concerned, the best thing that Uncle Sam can do is let the honorable Elijah Mohamed take our people, who are unwanted here in this society, into a separate territory and there we will establish our own farms, our own agricultural system by which we will feed our people. We will stop begging the white man. We will set up our own factories, our own industry, by which we will clothe our people and employ our people. We will stop begging the white man. We will be able to take the surplus that we produced and put it on the world market and do trade with our darker brothers from the east, from Africa, from Asia, from Latin America. This way we will be able to somewhat control our own destiny. We will cease to be a burden on the back of the American white man. We will be solving our own problem, instead of sitting around here waiting for a hypocritical American white man to solve our problem for us which he knows he can't solve.

AUSTIN CLARK: Would you — let's say, would you trade with white America if this came about?

MALCOLM X: Well, I think that even your black countries in Africa who were colonized and oppressed and exploited by whites trade with the white man today. All the black man in Africa wanted was his freedom, which meant control over his own land and once he controls his own land, then that which he grows, that which he raises in his own soil he is able to trade on the world market with white, with black, with brown, with red, with yellow, with anyone who will do business with him, and then he is recognized as a man. He has something to offer. He has something to exchange in the society of human beings but as long as whites were in control of the African continent, this meant that the black man didn't even have control over what he produced. The whites controlled it. It put whites in the position where they were able to exploit the wealth of the black man's land, take it into their own country, take raw materials from the black man's land to their own country, back to Europe, feed their factories with it, produce manufactured goods and then turn around and sell it to the black man at a higher price, sell his own goods to him in a manufactured form or finished goods form at a higher price and this made the economy of the white man at a high level and it has only been since the black man in Africa has gained possession of his own land that Europe now doesn't have access to free raw materials, so this has affected the European economy to the point where it has driven the European countries, in desperation, together into what they call the European Common Market, something that they can use to offset their loss of free materials. Whenever the black man in this country begins to get some kind of access or freedom of operation over his own economy, this affects the economy of the white man in America to the point where he doesn't have the economic power that he once had and you will find, sir, that the white man in America is not going to give up that economic position freely any more so than Britain wanted to give it up or France wanted to give it up or Portugal or Belgium wanted to give it up, and I only say that to point out that just as those countries over there were colonial powers, because they colonized dark people and exploited them and oppressed them, America has colonized twenty million black people in this country who are just as thoroughly colonized as the Africans in Angola or the Africans in the Congo or the Africans in southern and northern Rhodesia. The black man in America is just as thoroughly colonized, only America is shrewd enough to camouflage her colonial practices by classifying her colonial subjects as second class citizens instead of calling them outright colonial subjects.

AUSTIN CLARK: Going back, Mr. Malcolm, to the subject of integration and efforts to integrate certain institutions, talking specifically about Dr. Martin Luther King, how do you regard his achievements, if you regard any of his actions as achievements?

MALCOLM X: There are people in America who have made no progress, economically, politically, intellectually or in any way, shape or form when you take into consideration the progress that America itself has made. This is a country that is supposed to be for freedom; then why should black people — if this is a country in which the Supreme Court says American policy is for integration, the Congress says that policy is for integration, the Senate says that American policy is for integration, the President of the United States is supposed to be for integration. His brother, the Attorney General, is supposed to be for integration. Now, you have got these Negro leaders like Martin Luther King who have to get down and allow themselves to be beaten and jailed and spit upon, but they can't get integration. No, we haven't made any more progress in 1963 than our people were making in 1863. The whole thing is a farce. Integration is just another political trick that the American white man uses to make black people think that we are making progress when we haven't made any progress.

AUSTIN CLARK: Your movement has been subjected to certain criticisms, you have been called a hate group, you have been referred to as violent, seditious Americans and instigating or advocating a black supremacy. Could you answer these charges for us?

MALCOLM X: Number one, I don't see how anyone can accuse the honorable Elijah Mohamed of teaching hate. He teaches black people to love each other. He teaches black people to respect each other. He teaches black people to work together in harmony, in unity with each other. Now, because he doesn't waste his time telling our people to run around here and drool at the mouth over white people, the white man jumps up today and accuses him of teaching hate. How can you teach black people in America to hate after we have spent four hundred years in a country that made us slaves? We have spent four hundred years in a country at the hands of whites who kidnapped us and brought us here and sold us from plantation to plantation, like you sell cows and horses and chickens and bags of wheat. We have spent four hundred years in the hands of a white man who has lynched our fathers on trees, which is murder. We have spent four hundred years in the hands of a white man who has actually treated us like a beast, more cruelly than a beast would treat another animal, and then the past hundred years this same white man has used every form of deceit to keep us from being recognized as human beings. Now, behind that kind of treatment, if black people in America don't hate the white man, we would look like we would be fools trying to teach our people to hate someone who had done these things if they didn't hate them already. So what Mr. Mohamed does is he teaches us love, but he teaches us to love our own kind and he says we would be fools to be running around here trying to love white people before we learn how to love each other or before we learn how to love our own kind. The white man in America has a guilt complex. He knows that he is so guilty, he has blood dripping from his fingers, the blood of black people dripping from his fingers. He has the blood of black people dripping from his lips, from his mouth, and he knows that if the black man had done to him what he has done to the black man, he would hate the black man, so it is his own guilt complex that makes him think that someone is teaching hate. He — not only does the white man in America think Negroes hate him, he thinks the whole world hates him, because when a man is guilty, he knows that everybody should hate him, so this is Uncle Sam's complex that makes him put out the propaganda and project a religious man, like the honorable Elijah Mohamed, as a hate teacher instead of a teacher of love, unity and harmony among black people and he accuses us of — Mr. Mohamed of advocating violence because the honorable Elijah Mohamed says that the black man in this country should defend himself against the brutalities practiced against us by whites and because the white man is used to exercising brutality against black people without black people defending themselves. Whenever someone comes along and says that we should have the right to defend ourselves, instead of the white man admitting that he is the one that is violent, he accuses the one who was defending himself of advocating violence. It is like if someone was putting a rope around my innocent neck and I struggle vigorously to keep that man from lynching me, that man has the audacity to accuse me of violence and I am his victim. So this is again the trickery of the American white man. Every time a black man stands up and tries to defend himself against a brutality practiced against black people in this country by white people, the white man puts out the propaganda that we are violent. He never says that these people in Mississippi who are sicking dogs on our people are violent. He doesn't say that the man who coils the lyncher's rope around our neck is violent. He doesn't say that the people who are bombing the Negro churches are violent, but when a Muslim says that it is time now for black people to defend themselves, since the government has proven itself incapable of defending us, it is time for us to defend ourselves, then the government puts out the propaganda that we are advocating violence. We are not a hate group. We are not a violent group. We believe in loving our own kind. We believe in defending ourselves. What was this other thing you asked me about, black supremacy, was it?

AUSTIN CLARK: Black supremacy.

MALCOLM X: Supremacy means to be over someone. To be supreme, to be over someone. Now, our whole philosophy is separation. We don't even want to be with the white man, much less over him. We believe the white man should be with himself, over himself. We believe we should be with ourselves, over ourselves. We believe that white people should be supreme over white people. We believe black people should be supreme over black people. We believe white people should rule white people.

AUSTIN CLARK: Where would the children of mixed marriages fit into this?

MALCOLM X: They are in trouble. The mixed — if you notice, the white man always rejects children of mixed marriages. When you become of mixed blood you're never white but you are always considered non-white.

AUSTIN CLARK: What is the degree of black blood you must have in order to be black?

MALCOLM X: Well, as far as we are concerned, as long as we can tell that you have black blood, you are one of our brothers and when you get in that borderline where you can't tell what you are, or it's questionable, then it's best for you to get some papers, especially nowadays, because you are going into an era today where the color of your skin might. Save your life.

AUSTIN CLARK: Mr. Malcolm, what do you mean exactly when you say a black man?

MALCOLM X: Well, when Mr. Mohamed teaches us, when we use the term, black, we include within that black everyone who is non-white. That is, black, brown, red and yellow. He teaches us all of the non-white world in Africa or Asia are the same: they are brothers, and even the white man himself uses that terminology. He speaks of white and non-white. Well, we take the non-white, all of them, to be the same, black, and we include them all, and whenever a person of mixed blood reaches the point where you can't tell what he is, then this is why it is referred to as the judgment day. This is where God comes in and those people who are at that borderline, it will be left up to God Himself to determine which way their heart beats, which way their heart is turned.

AUSTIN CLARK: Suppose they wanted to be identified with the Muslims; would you accept them?

MALCOLM X: Mr. Mohamed teaches us that anyone who accepts Allah as God and practices the principles of the religion of Islam is a Muslim. His skin coloration has nothing to do with it, and Islam is the only religion in which this type of brotherhood prevails. When you are a Muslim, the color of your skin is not what is looked upon. It is when you are a Christian that the color of your skin makes a difference. In Christianity you have what is known as a white Christian and a Negro Christian or a black Christian, but in Islam you are just a Muslim. The color of the skin makes no difference. Now, when we refer to the white man, when you read the history of the world, you will find that the religion of Islam spread rapidly and easily and voluntarily in Africa and Asia, but when it reached Europe it ran into a white stone wall. The white man has a tendency to go for Christianity but he also has a tendency to rebel or reject Islam. Islam is a religion based on brotherhood, whereas Christianity is a religion where they can preach brotherhood but they don't have to practice it.

AUSTIN CLARK: But one of the tenets of the Christian religion seems to my mind to suggest brotherhood.

MALCOLM X: As I say, it's a principle. It's a preachment but it's not practiced. It is what the white man has always used. He has used a doctrine that he would get others to practice but he himself doesn't practice it. When he came here to this country he sent his priests to talk to the Indians, to pave the way for his soldiers. In the history of Africa, they sent their priests, their missionaries, to talk to the Chiefs, to the Africans, and the missionaries were followed up by the soldiers. This is the history of the slavery of Africa. The white man has always used this tactic. He will send a religion to you to get you to believe in it and he himself will pretend to believe in that religion, but if you observe closely the difference between what a white man practices and what he preaches, then you will see how he has been able, as a minority, to rule the vast majority of dark people on this earth.

1963

THE CONFESSED BEWILDERMENT OF MARTIN LUTHER KING AND THE IDEA OF NON-VIOLENCE AS A POLITICAL TACTIC

During the hallucinatory climax of something called Integration, Martin Luther King wrote a book called, perhaps mistakenly, perhaps over-optimistically, *Why We Can't Wait.* More significant than the content of this book, which dealt with Dr. King's misgivings and hopes for integration of the black man into American society, is the advertiser's blurb on the front cover of the book jacket. It refers to Dr. King as "the moral leader of America." (Note, not white America; nor black America: but America!) It also says that Dr. King was stating the case for freedom now. That was in 1964.

Then as now, it is as much a presumption, if not a hallucination, on the part of a black man, to allow himself to be referred to as "the moral leader" of a country, which in its daily dealing with him, and others like him, is immoral in certain important functions of its genitals and its arteries. But his presumptuousness does not raise as many eyebrows of cynicism, as it raises the question now very relevant, particularly when we consider the history of "morality" in America since 1964. This question arises out of the results and practices of that "morality" which is concerned with the presence or absence of freedom that Dr. King has been talking about. Bluntly speaking, that question is, *What* freedom, Dr. King? Was it a freedom to eat at lunch counters with whites, the food at which counters was, in cases, worse than the grits and the cornbread and the collard greens that have been known, mythically, as the characteristic fare of some of those Americans of whom he is supposed to be the "moral" leader? Or was it a freedom to demonstrate against evil wrongs; and demonstrate non-violently; and suffer violence from the white population of America, (of which he is the moral leader), peacefully? Dr. King made no gains of freedom, even with his nation-wide liberal support, and his emotional appeal to white liberals, and black bourgeois liberals. The only significance of the NAACP, through which organization Dr. King came to prominence as a "Negro" leader, was that the violent suffering of black people, whom he insisted should suffer non-violently, was witnessed on television by the whole American nation, both black and white. All the world saw the degree to which sections of American society is "immoral." In this respect only, was he ever a leader, a "moral" leader: he led a march of civil demonstration which brought out in the open, certain hidden and subconscious realities of American morality. But he was merely the present, coincidental agent. Those realities had to be faced, someday.

Dr. King's basic inadequacy as a leader of national civil rights, was that he attempted to appeal to white conscience and white morality. It was this same conscience and morality which brought about the presence of black people, Negroes, slaves, *niggers, negars,* on the American landscape. But that historical conscience spent more than one hundred years before it could see the natural inhumanity of slavery. And up till now, 1968, it has not faced the inherent immorality of refusing to admit that blackness of skin has nothing to do with the presence or the absence of dignity in that blackness. Historically, Dr. King is wrong: wrong in a moral sense; and in a very real social sense. A national leader must know the full implications and nuances of the history of the people he is leading. Dr. King should have known in 1964, and he should know by now, that one cannot present a social problem clothed in moral terms against a people whose lack of morality in the first place, brought about the existence of that problem. This is the basic mad unreality of Dr. King. It is Dr. King's idealism. And though this idealism is couched in Western Christianity, it does not make it any more acceptable to the very people he is trying to "free"; nor does it make it relevant to those white people, Christians like himself, to whom he has addressed his brand of morality. In the context of the harsh reality of white America, historically speaking, and morally speaking, his entire moralistic approach renders the entire tactic of a conscience-oriented socialist philosophy, highly anachronistic.

If Dr. King had known about a Spanish law, passed even before Spain imported slaves from Africa, *Las Siete Partidas,* which ironically, was framed within the same Christian doctrine he adheres to; and which stipulated that the "slave had a body of law protective of him as a *human being"* (italics mine); and which was not honored in America until after 1789, in a modified form, then he would realize that it is more important to comprehend the psyche of white America through its historical behavior, than through its Christian and moral considerations. The law, *Las Siete Partidas,* states in part, a very interesting set of rights for the slave. The significance is that these rights were on the statue books of one of the countries involved in the slave trade; and that they were unacceptable to America, during the height of her material profitability from that slave trade. It says: "A slave became free against his master's will, *by denouncing a forced rape against a virgin, by denouncing a maker of false money . . . He who killed his slave intentionally must suffer the penalty for homicide, and if the slave died as a result of punishment, without intention to kill, then the master suffers five years exile*" (italics mine). Think then, of the hundreds of white Americans, from 1789 until 1968, who would either be hanged for murder, or would be serving prison terms for their maltreatment of the slaves of that era, who are now the Negroes, *niggers,* of this era.

The dream that surrounded, or that was conceived at the March On Washington, has long been deferred, and has now become a nightmare. It is a nightmare without direction, without commitment. Dr. King's most recent book is called ironically and instructively, *Where Do We Go From Here?* The answer is more harshly realistic than his former dream of integration. It is: *Nowhere!* At least, not under the leadership of Dr. King. It is obvious that in his development as a "Negro" leader, Dr. King has not found freedom *now;* nor will he *ever;* and it is obvious that he does not know which tactic will lead where. This is a kind of confusion that a leader of a socialist movement (provided Dr. King considers his leadership to be socialistic, and based upon the realities of life for those at the bottom of the social ladder; and provided also, that he does not conceive of it as a Christian-oriented, intellectual leadership), the kind of rhetorical question he cannot afford to ask, cannot afford to make known to his followers and his adversaries. The mere mention of it, and the suspicion of it, disqualifies him from that kind of leadership. At the very least, it renders his leadership ineffectual. And this is really the crux of the matter. Is Dr. King's leadership ineffectual? Is Dr. King morally responsible for the "freedom now" hopes he deluded thousands of black Americans (and some whites too), into believing would result, particularly after his March On Washington speech, from his appeal to emotion and conscience and white guilt, which have been uncomprehended by white America for more than four hundred years? And even if his tactics were more appropriate to the problem, could he promise "freedom now" to a people (legal citizens), who are not (legally), regarded and treated as citizens, but rather as property in the twentieth century attitude of that slave trade version? And is he aware that these very people had been unloaded upon the American landscape because of a previous annulment of whatever freedom they once had in Africa; and which annulment has now come to be synonymous with their presence in America? The word, *Negro,* conjures up more implicit lack of freedom than the term, *DP.* Could it be argued that in the event of "freedom" and power accruing to black Americans, when the society is reorganized, that Martin Luther King Jr., within the strict context of revolution, should not be found to be a traitor for the national disillusionment he has nourished, directly and indirectly, in the minds of black people?

Dr. King's effectiveness as a leader of a national socialistic movement breaks down on the historical reality against which the movement itself is based. The NAACP and the southern Christian Leadership Conference, which are the two great exponents of non-violence, have based their philosophy on the Indian example, practiced (it must be admitted, successfully) by Mahatma Ghandi. But the analogy was wrong from the very beginning: wrong because there was no consideration given to the differences that exist in the two models. In the Indian model, the Indians constituted the vast majority of the population demonstrating against British injustices. In America, the black man is twelve percent of the population. In India, religion bound the Indian in two strong cohesive groups; in America, the black man is multi-religioned; multi-denominational. In the Indian context, the Indian had his land; land to the Indian was indivisible from freedom; if he succeeded, he could *own* the land. (Canadians own Canada; Germans own Germany. Negroes do not own anything called Negroland!) In America, if the black man did win, he could not inherit the land; and even if he won in such a way as to partition the land in some sort of geographical and cultural separation, then, because of the system of capitalism in the rest of America (homogeneously white by now), this partition would still be subjected to the worst functioning of that greater, more powerful capitalistic system. The most important factor, was that the Indian version of non-violence demonstration was carried out, homogeneously, by Indians. Also, the sheiks were killing British soldiers in the rural areas, while Ghandi was praying and fasting in the urban areas. There were no British citizens in India, no British liberals taking part, against the British, in the non-violent demonstrations. In America, the great ineffectiveness, among other weaknesses, of the non-violent movement, is that it is not only integrated along racial lines, but also political lines (some are moderates, some conservatives), and moreover, its orientation and its direction is non-black. For more than fifty years of the existence of the NAACP (the leading force behind Dr. King's moral non-violent tactics), the president has been a Jew. It is conceivable therefore, that such a movement would contain conflict: both with the real and other white liberals who sing, "We shall overcome someday." Would these Jews and white liberals *overcome* themselves, or their relations, to give Dr. King and other black people, their freedom? It is obvious that Dr. King has been used.

Dr. King's moral responsibility (and this is a serious, strong accusation) for the useless suffering of black people: the killings, the beatings, the murders, the burnings, the time spent in jail, the bail money, the traumas of those who suffered the jeers, the insults to their humanity, their manhood, their virginity, is a very great one, indeed. It is a responsibility that a leader must be aware of, before he embarks upon any campaign in which this kind of suffering must take place, in the process of carrying out the objectives of that campaign; it is a suffering that he must instruct his followers is inevitably necessary as a means of achieving what the campaign is motivated to achieve; but this suffering is not to be projected as the end product of the campaign itself. Suffering in a social movement, in a social context is essential to the achievement of a state of mind, a state of being that is going to bring about, no suffering at all, or less suffering than in the previous social condition. After ten years, this cannot be said about the kind of leadership that Dr. King has been guilty of, has been advocating. The responsibility of a leader, is to try, through means that lie outside the basic structure of the society he is trying to change, to bring about a new condition based upon his idealism. Dr. King's idealism is a kind of integration in which the black man has freedom: in terms of better housing, fair job practices and opportunities; in which, in other words, the black man in America can *operate in the society with the same freedoms as the white American.* But this conviction of integration is wrong. Its thesis is wrong: for the black man to be integrated into the American society of the mainstream, to Dr. King's way of thinking even within the terms of white liberalism, is really and fundamentally, an impossibility. Such an integration would mean the integration of an alien revolutionary body into a conservative body, within the existing structure of society. Such an integration, if it were possible, would mean that the entire mores of American life would have to change; it would change the moment this kind of integration became a fact, *ipso facto:* morally, culturally, educationally, ethically, and otherwise. And this change need not be for the better. But it would be a change. And one cannot bring about this kind of change by working within the existing to-be-changed structure; not by using the techniques and logic common to that structure. A leader's responsibility lies also in the need to forecast change. A great responsibility lies in his *acknowledgement of the impossibility of that change;* and in the final responsibility of resigning from that leadership, the moment he sees that his promised change, his "freedom-now" dream, is unattainable. In blunt terms, this is called sincerity, or honest leadership. In parliamentary terms, it is called confidence. Dr. King, at some time, did see his responsibility in this sense; but either through white liberal pressure to stay on, and be a catalyst to the Black Power movement (and before that, to act as a "sane balance" against the realism of the late Malcolm X), he has not resigned. And the fact that he has, brilliantly (one must admit), correlated the immorality of the Vietnam war to the war against black Americans at home, is not sufficient comprehension of this responsibility.

Who then will really be the judges of Dr. King's achievements and failures? Who will be in the position of power to say, "We are free, at last!" or, "We are still not free!" — when this nasty racism is solved; or at least is no longer an immediate daily problem for black Americans? The people who will judge this achievement and this failure are those people whose lives are touched most closely, most often, by that very racism. The blacks in the ghettoes of Harlem, Newark, Chicago, Watts and Detroit. And it is precisely these dwellers of the ghettoes, the urban ghettoes, who have repeatedly shown their disillusionment with Dr. King. It is not without great significance that Dr. King was absent from Newark, from Watts, from Detroit. It is not without significance that he, as a black man, cannot walk through the streets of Harlem, unescorted. On one visit to Harlem, he was actually wounded by a black man. That is an indication of the black disillusionment with this man who whites have nominated as the foremost "Negro" leader of our time.

Dr. King has done nothing to bring about a coalition between his white liberal supporters, his black middle-income group supporters, and the urban ghetto dwellers. (If such a coalition is not, by definition, impossible!) But the alienation that already existed, (after all, Malcolm X told it like it is; and so did Stokely Carmichael and now, Rap Brown — regardless of one's propensity for violence or honesty), this anachronism of Dr. King's white-partnership ideals, saw its greatest futility when Detroit and Newark and Harlem rebelled, during last summer. What was important in those rebellions, was not the amount of black lives lost, nor the amount of property lost. But within the terms of this article, the important factor was the absence of white people who themselves live in Detroit and Newark and Harlem (those people identifiable by color, with the white-partnership ideals Dr. King so emotionally advocates), those people who submerged their conscience and their morality to the immorality of silence, the immorality of non-commitment. It was the responsibility of Dr. King even as a "Negro" leader to see and to exploit the tactical advantages in those rebellions. It was not his responsibility, no matter what his feelings about rebellions are, to deplore them to white people. It would have been a better political tactic on his part to have remained — even non-violently — silent.

But after all, America is at war with itself. Rebellions and riots are aspects of the American syndrome of violence. It was the responsibility of liberal white, "right-thinking" whites, to demonstrate in numbers, in words, in tears, in sack cloth and ashes, in the streets, against the unwanted brutalities that were accompanying those rebellions. It is one thing to give monthly donations to the NAACP. It is one thing to be shot (if warned beforehand) caught stealing from a store. But it is another thing to watch American citizens — fellow Americans? — being slaughtered; and in spite of this silence, remain and regard yourself, as just, as moral. Unless of course, the belief is that the Negro *is not* a fellow American?

The idea of white-partnership, within the terms of the struggle, is unacceptable and irrelevant. One cannot pay too much attention to something called a "white backlash"; because for some black Americans, there has never been a cessation in the "white-frontlash." And a white backlash means simply, suppressed white hatred of blacks, being expressed vocally and physically in a climate of opportunity and acceptability. White-partnership in America is irrelevant and unacceptable because it is based on the concept of white liberalism. The term liberalism presupposes that the person to whom you're going to be liberal, is a person who is inferior in some ways that the liberal person is not; it implies a person who needs this liberalism; a person who cannot exist at a level higher than his previous level (before liberalism) and without "gifts" — gifts of more jobs, gifts of token school integration, and so on — these "gifts being the characteristics instituted by that liberalism." It is an insidious thought based upon the presumption that the person to whom this liberalism is directed cannot achieve this thing, this freedom, by himself. White people are white liberals vis-a-vis black people: never white liberals in the context of white-white relationships. White liberalism also determines the amount of liberalism to be given, that is to say, the amount of "freedom" to be *given;* and this act of charity slackens the pace of any real progress, just as it negates the dignity in a man fighting for his liberation, and accepting the *gift* of freedom.

Where do we go from here? – as a question posed, as a question of non-direction, it is precisely the answer to the stage of progress, the amount of freedom that Dr. King achieved for black people in 1964. And if Dr. King, in 1968, can be realistic about a society in which he was born, he can give the answer to his own question. And the answer will be: *Nowhere.* By *nowhere, is* meant destruction. It will not be the Black Panthers, and other nationalist-oriented forces, that will bring about this destruction. It will be American intransigence. It will be precisely what James Baldwin prophesied — *The Fire Next Time!* – what, in this respect he was more sensitive to seeing, more realistic in comprehending than Dr. King: that America will destroy herself from within, internally, like a cancer, if America remains intransigent to its racist attitudes and practices. The first signs of this internal rotting are seen in the white anti-draft protests and the government's reaction to them; in the hippies; in the drug-taking cult — all white, or mostly white factions. For after all, and other things being equal, it is these very white "revolutionaries" who may provide the white leadership of America in the twenty-first century. And can it be imagined what kind of country America will be, if these dissident factions remained dissident, *after* they have assumed power? And also, what will be their moral state, in the strict classical sense of that term, when they do assume power, even if they have changed; and have modified their "revolutionary" fervor in favor, through chronological age and through the custom of power, for bourgeois materialism? For these reasons, Dr. King's bewilderment does not even have to be measured against the harsher reality of black urban rebellions, which are sure in bloodier intensity, in 1968. White America will have to make up its mind whether to continue to program a palatable, but ineffectual medicine, such as tokenism; or take the harsher, coarser, but more purgative portion of self-examination. Until this is done, the bewilderment of Dr. King's present state of mind, will also become a national bewilderment — white America's bewilderment. And anything can happen if this state of moral apostasy continues too long.

1968

EXILE

George Lamming's brilliant analysis of his life in Britain as an immigrant during the 1950's bears the title *The Pleasures of Exile.* There is obvious irony in this title to his essay on cultural and social dislocation, made all the more significant because Lamming is addressing his disapproval of Britain's treatment of him, a black Briton, a black Barbadian. His disappointment is understandable. A mother, even an oppressive, heartless one, does not treat her children in this unredeeming, brutal manner and remain a mother. What is more, the child-victim can no longer embrace this former familial relationship without cynicism. The relationship ceases to be pleasurable, if it could ever have been described in that way.

For these reasons, I have always felt that "exile" cannot be a pleasure. But more importantly, I do not consider my life in Canada for the last thirty-eight years to be one of "exile." For I am not escaping from any form of political oppression or social persecution in Barbados. And even though our Barbadian social and class differences, and the way in which they apportion privilege and reward, might, at first glance, be termed oppressive and disadvantageous to some who suffer under its complicated application, still it cannot be said that the society from which I came propelled me because of its heinousness to seek social, cultural and political redress and refuge in Canada.

If it can be argued that the material benefits are greater here than they are in Barbados, I still do not qualify under the aegis of "exile." But these very material benefits must be evaluated fairly and compared with the standards that are Barbadian before I can argue that this society offers more benefits thandid Barbados.

I admit that, intellectually and politically, my presence here can be termed an "exile." And the term takes on an added currency of sophistication because I am an author, a Barbadian writer who lives in Canada. In blunt terms, reflecting Frantz Fanon's "psycho-existential complex" as a means of measuring black-white relations in a white society, a black writer working in a white environment — I am tempted to say in a white culture, but to do so is to ascribe to "white" and to "culture" a pre-eminence that is undeserved and that from my experience in Canada and my knowing Canada does not exist — applying Fanon's measurement, the term "exile" is inapplicable in my case.

The term "exile" when used in the case of the black writer living in a white society has the implication that the writer is better off in this environment, that this environment gives him objectivity, if not a greater grasp on his creative skill, and that were this environment, this "exile," not possible, were there not this extension of hospitality and the provision of a climate suitable for work and existence, the black writer would be lost, or dead, or stifled amidst the memories of his former inhospitable native climate. There is also an insidious implication in the term that suggests a banishment and a cultural surgery carried out on the psyche of the writer. And therein lies its other inference of required gratitude towards the country that has saved you from your former inhospitable state.

If the term could be applied, as it was, to Richard Wright and to James Baldwin, who sought refuge in Paris from the exigencies of racism in America, their country of birth, it was properly applied in their cases, since it is doubtful that either of them could, in the context of the forties and fifties, have had the leisure and the protection from that racism so necessary for them to develop their art. They had no protection from their government when as young writers they left that country. And it is possible that at this stage of their careers, had not the French government extended to them, both officially and privately, a climate suitable for the creation of works of fiction — and nonfiction — their artistic development might have been curtailed by the brutality of racism in America. At least, this is their word.

It must also be said that today in America, in spite of lingering racism, no black writers would in Baldwin's or Wright's terms seek to be "exiles" in a foreign country as a pre-condition of their creative development or of their objective or subjective critical judgment in America.

Gratitude, one of the aspects of "exile" in its most traditional sense, is exemplified by a silence of criticism of the country offering this "exile." It is debatable whether in Paris racism was not so pronounced as it had been in America. If this is the case, why did not either of them, Baldwin nor Wright, make comment on this subject? Perhaps they were deluded in feeling that French *'egalite'* was less abstract than it was, and could be applied to them. The fact is, they did not make this comment about French racism.

And they did not, and could not, because cognizant as they had to be of gratitude and guided by the principle of decency, they, as "beggars" could not be "choosers."

The "exile" is a beggar in the most sophisticated sense that he must know his place. And he himself contributes to whatever deprecation of his native culture, his mores, his native view is implied, which he is forced to evaluate through foreign eyes and using a foreign sensibility. He is, most of all, a man who lives in two cultures; and when one culture is underpinned by a language he does not speak, his existence during his "exile" becomes, at the very least, schizophrenic.

Denying, therefore, the characterization of my life in this country as that of an "exile," I have to say how I look upon my time in Canada, after I arrived in 1955. I would have to say first what was the purpose of coming here, what my expectations were and how the mere act of arrival transformed me. My purpose in coming was to attend university. It was not to become a writer, for in 1955 my ambitions were not literary, even though I had tried my hand at schoolboy poetic ventures. Had I retained any of that literary adventurousness, I would have followed other West Indians, such as George Lamming, Samuel Selvon, V. S. Naipaul and Aubrey Williams, to England. The choice would have been appropriate, as England was then, and perhaps still is, the Mother Country and any literary tradition to which we were exposed through our education was English. It is an aspect of the disappointment those writers feel in their social lives there that has caused so many of them to define their time in England during the 1950s as an "exile."

In spite of their contribution, now acknowledged to have been significant, the exigencies of English racism cut them out of any meaningful role they could have played as men. And, to varying extents, their lives became alienated from precisely that font of creativity and the possibility of objectivity in viewing their respective islands that their going to England had promised.

My expectations about Canada were not so traumatic in their rupture, precisely because I had wanted nothing more than a university education from the place of my choice. My choice was mine (though it was not the primary one). And my expectations, even though tinged by aspects of discrimination and racism, were never dulled because my intention was to return to Barbados after having crossed the Atlantic to read Law in England. And my demands were not entirely frustrated because I had made no commitment to Canada in so far as applying for any status other than that of student. There was, therefore, no bargain, no negotiation, no promise, no exacting of loyalty. As a matter of fact, I was, by definition of being a student, expected to make no transaction. Get your education and run back to where you came from: that was the unspoken individual and official relationship ingrained into us as students.

I have always insisted that my arrival in this country did not bring a shock of culture. We had known Canada, in our geography books, and through the importation of cod fish, potatoes, Canadian Healing Oil, apples at Christmas, sardines, canned salmon and the lady boats which trafficked in Caribbean waters. And Canadians had always considered the sun and blue water of Barbados to be a spa of rejuvenation. In those days, unless you lived close to the Marine Hotel, the bastion of segregation a tourists' eccentricities; unless your mother, aunt, uncle or brother was in the hotel business, those Canadians were hidden from us, and we were protected from their enjoyment of our sea and sun by a line of defined exclusion: them from us, but more importantly, us from them.

Barbados is older, though not richer, than Canada. And if the first veneer of awe and spectacle, wonder and envy at the bigness of things, buildings and streets, cars and houses, is worn off, even at that first meeting a critical spirit was able to see more quality in the older, more established society of Barbados than in the newness of Canada at that time, also a colony of the Mother Country. There was nothing spiritual, nothing culturally compelling to make one want to embrace Canada as a place of redemption. This is not to say that I may not be grateful for Canada as the place where physically and psychologically, I have written my novels. But they could have been written in Italy or in Germany. Ironically, they could not have been written in Barbados. So there is some decency in acknowledging this and in being grateful, but without the deeper spiritual gratitude of the "exile."

We have a true spirit of multiculturalism here. I can, as I have done, become a Canadian citizen. And in a real sense, I am regarded as a Canadian. Not so the predicament of emigrants living in England. Those from amongst us who went to England were never regarded as Englishmen, even black Englishmen, unless the term was used with political cynicism. How then could "exile" be considered seriously as a definition of my time spent either as a foreigner or as a writer? And it cannot, because I have retained the ethnic and cultural flavor of Barbados, and the winters here can do nothing to transform them through a drop in the enthusiasm of Barbadian-ness. But the impossibility of that is more subjective. It was my choice not to permit this freezing of my expectation, to have me swallowed up culturally during my long temporary sojourn here.

In the month of August, when Toronto is transformed into colors of the Caribbean and there is music and a new pulse to the activities of men and women, an incident I witnessed, simple in its social significance, perhaps, brought home to me that the time had come for me to consider seriously the extent to which my senses had been numbed by too long a stay in this city, Toronto, and in this country. A store was playing calypso music through its loudspeakers, spewing the refreshing, pulsating beat onto the street filled with people, filled with their own business. It was a reminder of Barbados. The music was. And it was beautiful. It was loud because the bus had stopped outside the door of the store. I could breathe some of that memory. And relive the long past. But a woman, not West Indian, said disapprovingly, "Why do they have to play *that* music?"

The rejection was not only euphemistic, it was not only that many animosities were barely buried in her voice, which came close to being hysterical; nor was it the dismissal of this aspect of my culture, used in this city to enrich merchants during the annual Caribana Parade season. It was a declaration of subordination to things which she wanted to be Canadian: an intrusion upon her more bland consciousness. She would have no jerk-seasoning in her chicken that night.

Her voice and her manner in the voice killed the music. But the beat had already been made indelible. And I yearned for the first time in thiry-eight years to hear that sound, that noise, that pounding of steel on steel, of wood on tightened skin, once more, more often in its native, disturbingly loud, jungled environment.

I packed my bags, in that deep spiritual way, and removed myself from further assaults upon my true culture, assaults made by a declaration whose impact was probably not known by the woman making it. But it was made. And intent, motive and cause were now irrelevant. If I had ever thought of "exile," of the cutting off from known and accustomed ways, it happened that beautiful bright afternoon in August.

1994

from A Passage Back Home

A Personal Reminiscence of Samuel Selvon

I cannot remember how old those Sundays were and if the sun had travelled already over the Observation Post in Clapham, and was running over Britton's Hill, down into the Garrison Pasture, before night caught it, to plunge for that day, into Gravesend Beach, and end the light of Sunday. I cannot remember what time it was, when I first heard, either his voice or the magnificent acquainted language of his stories, sent back to us from overseas; and I did not, like all of us, consider it strange or characteristic of our cultural status, that our words spoken amongst us, in fragments and with no force of appeal, would be golden and acceptable portraits of our lives, *because* they were coming to us on these Sunday nights, from overseas: on the BBC's radio programme, "Caribbean Voices."

My step-father, Police Constable Fitz Herbert Luke, controlled the "private set," as he probably controlled the irascible men he had to arrest, with a wrist-lock, making their movements conform to his own obsessive views of obedience and order and lawfulness. And even if he could not precisely define these characteristics he had learned in the Barbados Police Force (not yet "Royal"!), and in his own upbringing, I was not too small not to know that he meant those criminals were lacking in "Christian-mindedness." And this could be achieved only by listening to the sermons that came all day long, every Sunday, over the "private set," from the Andes Mountains. Luckily, we had passed that chapter that dealt with South American geography in the textbook written by Dudley Stampp, at Combermere School. I would be entranced as he was, sitting in the front house, with the cold glass of lemonade, in a color I still cannot describe, with the chipped ice and the peth of the limes, swirling in it, as I listened to the voice and the chastisements and the thunder that summoned Sodom and Gomorrah, that gripped all of us into shuddering submission to those strange voices, those strange arguments, those strange men who through this mechanical device, the "private set," were able to enter our houses and occupy our minds, and scold us into this Christian-mindedness. My step-father listened to these sermons on Sundays for more hours than I would spend any day at Combermere School.

But luckily for me, a message would come from the Married Women's Quarters, near the Garrison, from Captain Farmer, the Commissioner Police, that something was wrong, and that "Mr. Luke was wanted." There was one telephone in our neighborhood, the Yarde's; and one of the Yarde-boys would have to walk the message from the Front Road, which all the boys journeyed, to Flagstaff Road.

And I would rejoice. The "private set" would be mine, after all. My mother's own feeling that we had been remanded from the onslaught of these religious sermons, from ten o'clock until the last leghorn fowl was on her roost, came out like mild blasphemy. "Praise God! He out o' the house!" She would have had her eyes on the part of the dial which brought Auntie Kay from Trinidad's Golden Network, with its own version of blasphemy over the seas to the sensibilities of Barbadians washed in Sunday properness of behavior. "Playing tuk! And on a Sunday, to-boot?"; but it was the time of year when the new tunes were being tried by the talent of children; and we might be in for some musical wonder. But before the "tuk, and on a Sunday!" I would be permitted to roll the heavy knob of the ball-bearing tuning button along the waves of miles of the dial, passing countries in Latin America, moving over Holland (the "private set" was made in Holland!), through Europe's intractable languages, until by accident, I was plunged into the Mother Country. *Inglann!*

And a different kind of "tuk" would take possession of the air-waves. Caribbean Voices! And this is when I first heard the name, Samuel Selvon of Trinidad. It was, as Oliver Jackman would put it, a literary "federation" taking place. Our culture of Sundays, regular as our bowels on a first-Sunday, regimented as the dry-peas and rice and baked chicken, sweet potatoes, pear, lemonade and rum-punch, was Rediffusion's recorded church services of ponderous, sonorous sermons delivered by Inglish vicars whose language was not the language of our miseries, and could not determine nor define what was contained in our hearts. They did not even know our sins. Or would it be choirs from Westminster Abbey, with which we joined in, demonstrating our own arrogant belief that Barbadians sang Hymns Ancient and Modern more better than anybody born. Or a chanced taped version of the same hymns, delivered by the men in the neighborhood, at a Wake or a Sunday "service o'song." And of course, the interminable foreign-affairs chastisement coming from over the Andes Mountains, out of foreign mouths.

But to hear, all of a sudden about the breadfruit tree; the casaurinas; the names of flowers we had passed earlier that very Sunday, to and from Sin-Matthias or Sin-Barnabas, or even the Cathedral — those of us who travelled through the Pine, when it still had canes and was a plantation; through Government Hill, and saw them growing over the wall of the Convent — the Kiskides, Couva, Port of Spain, Gravesend Beach and "Trumper": to hear these symbols of words, greater than words; greater than our recognition of them in everyday life, all this was to make us feel "we was people, too."

I cannot say that I understood all, or even most, of what was being transmitted back to me. I cannot say that I understood each poem about Sin-Lucia, Barbados, Guyana and Trinidad, written by men of those "unknown" lands, who were so similar to me, and others who had passed these monuments in our respective neighborhoods: the casaurina, the blue seas, the Sea Wall. I could not receive this "literary tuk" with an easy appetite because I had not been trained with tools that were Barbadian, to criticize it, or what is worse, to appreciate it. But I knew that something revolutionary, some "damn federation" was happening on those Sunday nights, when my mother and I leaned close to the magnificent speaker of the linen-clothed mouth of the "private set" in the front house.

Samuel Selvon of Trinidad was one voice I heard over the radio. His works had appeared earlier, I am sure, in the small, tidy, impressive and clairvoyant pages of *Bim Literary Quarterly*, assembled against greatest odds, money and energy, by Mr. Frank Collymore, who taught me English more successfully than he could French, at Combermere School. But apart from that, apart from the privileged peeping into those pages, illustrated sometimes by gargoyles and monsters and "colly-beases," we would know of his existence in a more magnified, romantic way, in the weekly injections of "Caribbean Voices."

My little world of no more than thirty houses on either side of Flagstaff Road, stretching from the Corner where the Kendal Hill bus stopped, to the top of the hill leading down into the Saturday iniquity, as my mother would say, of Club Morgan, a club which catered to the tastes of white people only, and foreigners, and with a view of the commanding sea and ocean, over which earlier Samuel Selvon, along with George Lamming and Derek Walcott, A.N. Forde and others had crossed in this new revolutionary and reversed "Middle Passage." There were the thirty or so houses perched on foundations of precarious blocks of coral stone mined by men from the same neighborhood, with their sleepy windows adorned with rich window blinds of gold and silver, white and pink; this world which before these "voices," were littled in their Inglanned sensibilities regarding self, regarding dignity, regarding blackness and the variations of that blackness — lightness considered beyond the meaning of 'lectricity — regarding nationality and nationhood, regarding the new raging men, Cox and Adams; Barrow and Walcott; Mapp and Allder; Mottley and Talma, and others, many others; my world received the injection of those "voices" which in turn made sense of the diagnosis and the bitter medicine of ex-colonialism that these great men were ranting about, on the political flatforms, and in rum shops throughout the island which was no longer small.

The dramatization of ex-colonialism and the building of a new sensibility, nationalism in its best sense; the disabusing of our minds from the position we had been schooled in: that we had no culture; that we had no models from amongst us, all this was vouchsafed in the language of Samuel Selvon . . .

The Lonely Londoners is my favorite among Sam's books. In it I can smell the perspiration of the laboring West Indians. Can feel their resentment to their treatment at the hands of the "Mother." Can follow them through the dark, cold, dreary and debilitating alleys on the way to their ambitions: a Barrister-at-law, a supervisor on London's Transport, a qualified teacher. And I can hear their pain. And most of all, sense their nostalgia, and their ambivalence about the wisdom of leaving Bridgetown or Port of Spain for Inglann. Sam gave me the blue print to that "exile," an "exile" not always so pleasurable as George Lamming contended it to be in his personal brilliant commentary, *The Pleasure of Exile,* which dealt with his own life in Inglann.

When I arrived there, armed with a Nagra taperecorder and a huge per diem account, I was both prepared and unprepared for the blight I was to live with and in, during those two weeks in Inglann's "summer."

But the *TLS* had extolled beforehand, the excellence of this renaissance of writing, this West Indian literary force that dared to demonstrate the working-out of the "new wine" in Inglann's backyards. George Lamming was at the height of his fame. V.S. Naipaul had just begun to court the Inglish and massage them into believing in his own nihilistic attitude. Jan Carew, living in a large house somewhere near Wimbledon, clothed in the huge skins of animals slaughtered or found dead, somewhere on the Steppes of Europe or the Latin American Pampas of boar-hunting, seal-hunting, or mink-hunting; and flitting from London to Moscow, and back many times, before the term "jet-setter" was invented and thrown into our lexicon. Andrew Salkey, whom I have christened "Handrew" in memory of his Jamaican Creole roots, buried amongst shelves and shelves of books reaching to the heavens in his prodigious study. Michael Anthony whose hands were caloused, and made harder, not from the solitary pounding on his manual typewriter, but from the laborer's job he held, for years, to put bread and butter on his table for wife and child. James Berry who persevered with poetry. And a man, later to be famous and notorious, for reasons that were not merely literary or political, Michael DeFreitas from Trinidad, later to be made more notorious even, by his countryman in the novel, *Guerrillas*; Michael DeFreitas later to be known as Michael X; later to assume a name more in keeping with his new religion, occasioned they say, through his meeting with Malcolm X, later himself to be known as Michael Abdul Malik. And in the company of my life-long friend and "brother," more "brother" and more friend, Henry Moe, in Inglann to do Law at Durham University and teach part-time, at nights; to meet these men I made the journey to some suburban district outside London.

I do not remember the name of the place. I do not remember whether we went by train, or by bus. I do not remember how long it took us to get there. I do not remember the disagreeable, disgusting, denigrating surroundings. Laborers, and those not in unions, must have lived there. It was "summer." But it was like winter. The houses were built from the same blueprint. There was no eye for beauty, no eye for individualism in the construction of this street of "brauhaus" deprivation . . .

Sam had captured even the smell of London's winter in his brilliant novel, *The Lonely Londoners*. And he had done something else. He had stripped them of the alienating hyphenation so common these days in the way we describe ourselves as minority ethnic groups living in a land other than our own. He christened them *"Londoners."* Not black Londoners. Not Trinidadian-Londoners. Not Black West Indians in London. Just Londoners. And he left it to the other tribes inhabiting that inhospitable landscape, to like it, or lump it. This distinction of definition is significant: for it describes not only the disposition of those brave men and women to the reversed direction of the "journey," but more than that, it expresses the ethno-cultural philosophy of the man. Never once, during countless meetings, from 1965 until two years ago when we met at Brock University in St. Catharines, Canada, have I heard, even in jest, a word of implicit racialism come from this man's lips. And in hundreds of letters we exchanged between London and Toranno; and later on, between Calgary, Alberta and Toranno, there is no trace of enmity caused by his encounters with racism (and he had many), that colored his behavior, his life, or his writing.

The house in which Sam lived at this time, was an ordinary house. Not outstanding in any of its dimensions. A house in which the Inglish put its under-class to live. It must have been the fatigue and exhaustion from the journey undertaken by Henry Moe and me that caused me to regret having taken this trip.

I remember he was wearing a sweater. And smoking. There might have been whiskey. But his circumstances tell me that whiskey could possibly not have been served. I do not remember eating lunch, or being offered any. The starkness of his surroundings and environment was not what I had imagined from his lively fiction in his short stories. This home was more in keeping with the lugubriousness of the life Edgar Mittelholzer wrote about in his autobiography. I could imagine the heavy strains of Wagner, which Edgar liked and listened to without taking a breath. I could imagine the locus of many of Charles Dickens' novels, except that this encounter was in the suburbs. I could imagine the garret and the woolened writer in darkness, no food, and the romantic prop of bottles of red wine, and burning candles drooping from a Chianti bottle whose mouth and basketted sides are drenched in dried tallowed sculptures. Not so this house.

But there was dignity. And humanness. Sam had lots of that. The dignity of simplicity. His words exemplified that. I sat with him, in this minimalized surroundings, there was no music, no oil paintings, and we talked about London and Inglann for hours; and we talked not too successfully about his work and its place in the sphere of the "new-wined" renaissance of West Indian letters. And his self-effacing nature was the ethic, the nature and the essence of the interview.

"Well, boy, I don't know, yuh know. I write my thing, and thing and thing . . . " We talked about Notting Hill and the recent riots that had erupted in the area; and Michael DeFreitas' name came into the conversation, as it should, because at this time, it was said that Michael was the "strong-arm" man for Rachmann, a rich Jewish gentleman who owned most of the dwellings in Notting Hill ghetto, and which he rented out to West Indians who had felt the pinch of prejudice against their renting rooms, basements, flats in the homes of the more genteel Inglish. And Michael and Rachmann both got bad names for their philanthropy and their extortion.

It was the day before, when I was in the basement of the CBC's studios in London, wondering aloud how I would meet this man, Michael DeFreitas, whose "reputation" had spanned the Atlantic and had reached me in Toranno, and which mentioned a Canadian woman with whom he was living in London, at the time. I expressed my desire to interview him, and the woman, another freelance broadcaster sitting beside me in the Editing Room, said, with the understatement the Inglish are famous for, "I could arrange it, Austin. I live with Michael." My puritanism, fostered in Barbados, led me to conclude that she was his room-mate; that they were living in the same flat; that she was paying her share of the rent, and he, his. But when I arrived at the imposing Georgian building, splendid in its appointments, I could not but conclude that the arrangement was a spousal one. He did not make any bones about it. And neither did she. I realized then, that there had been too much literary euphemism in the *Maclean's* magazine article that I had read as research, weeks before in Toranno.

And I think I asked Sam about his colleagues. Especially Naipaul, who had just made a mark for himself in world literature, if we may describe his success, in those terms. *House for Mr. Biswas,* perhaps his best novel, had just been published to great acclaim. But there was a problem. Was Naipaul really the son-of-a-bitch that Handrew had hinted at? It was Handrew, after all, who had introduced Naipaul to his publishers André Deutsch. And it was Naipaul, with the large publisher's cheque against advanced royalties, who could no longer remember Handrew's address on Moscow Road, London. Was all the rumor I was hearing, true? Were the recriminations about V.S. Naipaul, his nihilistic attitude towards black people, spread by his former friends, justified? I was convinced of his tremendous technical ability with the novel. I had not been able to separate this genius with structure, from the contents of his non-fiction, in particular, *The Middle Passage*. And years later, when he gave us the big book on his return to India, with the motto of Indian personality, *"The Indian defecates everywhere. He defecates on the street, in his temples . . . "* I asked Sam what he felt about *An Area of Darkness*, in which this nihilistic brand of satire appeared. I was expecting a personal commentary from a fellow Trinidadian. Something, though not so spiteful as the censure I had met, when the same question had been asked of other West Indian writers, the young nationalist intellectuals, and university students who did not necessarily read nor study Naipaul in their English curriculums — but something spicy. Perhaps, I was waiting to hear the latest personal gossip, to be able to bury this outstanding, money-making fellow author. Perhaps, it was too, nothing but plain envy and jealousy. For none of us had had Naipaul's wide and international attention. Not even George Lamming. Not Eddie Brathwaithe. And not, most certainly at that time, Derek Walcott.

I sat back, rubbing my two palms together, sipping the rum — or was it beer served too warm, which I do not like — waiting for the avalanche of what I felt would be justified disapprobrium.

Sam sipped his drink. Took a pull on the cigarette which was always in his mouth. And he said, in his voice that was so comforting in its soothing quality, like the voice of a dramatic actor who loves comedy; in a voice like the clown's, and the best of classical clowns, filled with wisdom beneath the humor; Sam said, *"Boy, Vidia is Vidia, yuh know. Vidia does-do his thing and thing, and that is Vidia. I ain't know nothing, eh, boy. I does-do my thing, and Vidia does-do his thing. Is so, yuh know, boy.*

There was no enmity, no jealousy, no recrimination. There was no hint of wanting to be in Vidia's shoes, and share in the enormous advances and prize money he had been having; no regret that he was not on the BBC television shows which lionized his countrymen; no word of censure against the recognition given to Naipaul, in such large measure that it was felt in Inglann at the time, that Vidia was the only author worth noticing.

It taught me the essence about Sam, this great man, "no longer whinnying with us," as Dylan Thomas would have couched the words of his panegyric, had he too been alive, and had he not succumbed to the record-breaking transitory fame of drinking scotches. "I think this is a record," Dylan is supposed to have said, when he drank others under the table, and himself, into the lamented coffin. *"Do not go gentle into that good night."* It could have been said about Sam's passing in Trinidad on the 17th of April, as it was said about the passing of Dylan's own father.

"Do not go gentle in that good night." For it was night, when Henry Moe and I left this un-named suburb in London's bowels, to trace our journey back to London itself, with the affect Sam had upon me, churning in violent conflict in my mind . . .

That year, 1965, was the year of rising discontent in Amurca, which had taken over from Inglann all the power of ideas, strategies of 20th century abolitionism, and had begun to create a literature of greater excitement, if of lesser content and structure. We were all looking towards the *Amerika* of black nationalism, and of black cultural nationalism, for guidance. I, on this side of the Atlantic, found greater political and cultural identity with the black Amurcans than even with Sam Selvon, living in an Inglann which had coughed up the traumatic surprise of the Notting Hill Riots. The Notting Hill Riots were not so believable as the summers-long bashing of black people with high-powered hoses, police billy-clubs, and with pure, raw, brutal violence. And I had embraced the more reasonable position of the nationalists, that violence ought to be fought with violence, although for all of us nationalist adherents, we did not contemplate, nor did we have a strategy to bring about this redemptive violence of retribution by physical means. It was pure talk. Tough talk. Black power talk. The scent of blood on this side of the Atlantic was more inducive, than the smear left by a wound in a thousand Notting Hills. And Sam's "Londoners" were, in spite of their significance in the body of West Indian literature, nothing more than men trying to find something to eat; men trying to find a job; men trying to fit into the Inglish landscape with a minimum of social and personal dislocation. They were not men bent upon a dividing-up of Inglann into a black one and white one. They had no such right of citizenship. And they were not contemplating at that time, a revisionist slant of history in the same way as the Amurcan blacks were. As a matter of fact, with the questionable leadership of Michael DeFreitas, they were themselves seeking political-intellectual leadership from Stokeley Carmichael, Rap Brown, and Malcolm X, who was still with the Muslims in Amurca, and was still the protege of the Honorable Elijah Muhammad . . .

Sam was one of the heroes embraced by the Inglish. The Inglish however, using tactics reminiscent of their political philosophy of warfare and former colonialism, selected some, (some would say, one, writer), and made him the representative of the entire body of writing coming from the pens of these literary and "lonely Londoners": Edward Brathwaithe, the poet; James Berry, the poet; Andrew Salkey, poet, novelist and children's story writer; Jan Carew, poet and novelist; Wilson Harris, novelist; Edgar Mittelholzer, the novelist; Peter Kempadoo, the novelist and herbalist; George Lamming, the poet and novelist; V.S. Naipaul, novelist and social commentator; E.R. Brathwaithe, the novelist; Michael Anthony, the novelist; Wallace Collins, the novelist — all these lived in Inglann at the same time. Their literal output in words, is phenomenal. And it spanned, for the main part of it, just ten years..

And then, the catastrophe of selectivity, the Inglish disposition for abandoning, happened. Inglann suddenly discovered Africa. And Heinemann and other publishers, acting in the same mode of political imperialism, decided there was more profits to be made from African literature, than they could get from that created by these West Indians.

This remembering of times, these journeys are not intended to be a critique of the comparative virtues of African literature (in English translation) as against West Indian literature. And I do not want to raise those emotional debates at this time: at this time of loss, and of joy for the contribution made by my friend, Sam; and for the tragedy of his early passing. But I shall say, that as in other times of similar choice made by an imperialist mentality, the supersession of African literature, with very few examples, was a decision to be praised more for its political and economical rewards, than for its purely literary and critical and intellectual argument.

The time was coming, when through systematic neglect (books not being reviewed — except Vidia's), these "lonely Londoners" had to choose the routes of another journey, another immigration, and look to the New World, even although they themselves had originated from there . . . They turned their attention to Canada and to Amurca . . . The "Londoners" were leaving. Not because they had outgrown the landscape; not because there was nothing more, nothing so important as when they had first arrived, to write about; but they were leaving because they had to do so: forced by the new iciness of hospitality; by the blatant expressions of disrespect in the House of Commons; by the repudiation of "citizenship" which during the Empire of old, was extended to anyone who lived in the lands, colonies, dominions, beyond the seas . . . Sam too, had at least contemplated that there were better places than the London of his loneliness. In *The Lonely Londoners*, the discussion of the choice of a better place, is couched in the peculiar ambivalence of the man who finds himself living in the home of another man, not certain of his welcome, not certain of his own choice to be a visitor, wondering if time and circumstance and condition are tougher than the realism of readjustment, of taking the long journey, another Middle Passage, another working out of the peripatetic nature of those of us, who had been wrenched from home and made to travel to the home of others, no home but that made into something resembling one, through the creative talent of our own improvisation:

"I would advise you to hustle a passage back home to Trinidad today," Moses say, "but I know you would never want to do that. So what I will tell you is this: take it easy. It had a time when I was first here, when it only had a few West Indians in London, and things used to go good enough. These days, spades all over the place, and every shipload is big news, and the English people don't like the boys coming to England to work and live."

"Why is that?" Galahad ask.

"Well, as far as I could figure, they frighten that we get job in front of them, though that does never happen. The other thing is that they just don't like black people, and don't ask me why, because that is a question that bigger brains than mine trying to find out from way back."

"Things as bad over here as in America?" Galahad ask.

"That is a point the boys always debating," Moses say. "Some say yes, and some say no. The thing is, in America they don't like you, and they tell you so straight, so that you know how you stand. Over here is the old English diplomacy: 'thank you sir', and 'how do you do' and that sort of thing. In America you see a sign telling you to keep off, but over here you

don't see any, but when you go in the hotel or the restaurant they will politely tell you to haul — or else give you the cold treatment."

"I know fellars like you," Galahad say in turn. "You all live in a place for some time and think you know all about it, and when any green fellars turn up you try to frighten them. If things bad like that, how come you still holding on in Brit'n . . . "

And we went.

It was CARIFESTA I, the first such assemblage of men and women to a Caribbean Festival of the Arts. It was initiated by Forbes Burnham, Prime Minister, and held in Georgetown, British Guiana, soon to be brought into the family of new nations, wrought from colonialism, into the early twentieth century tide of independence. British Guiana would become the Co-operative Republic of Guyana, taking back its real name, from the Amerindian roots, "Guyana." We were being invited back "home," to look, to see, and to return from our wanderings, from peopling unnatural diasporas, from being subjected to the "look," and told to "haul our arse outta the white people' countries!"

In the months leading up to Carifesta, the letters from Sam, who was still buried in the snow in London, still taking that natural journey from kitchen to out-door toilet through the piled whiteness surrounding him, became longer and more like a voice on the overseas long-distance telephone, rich in its language, richer in its hope and excitement. "I go see you in Burnham country!" one letter said. "I go be there! Jesus Christ, boy, this is fête!"

We were *all* invited. And all of us caught at the change: to be relieved of the uncertain hazards of being the writer, the painter, the sculptor, the jazz musician; exchanging this treacherous existence for a place in the sun, where we could recall all the memories that immigration and the systems of racism had been corroding from our skin, from our mind, from our very healthiness. "Is fête, papa!"

All of us were invited: and all of us went down, *except* Vidia Naipaul. I think he was the only important absentee. It probably had something to do with a book he had written recently, in which Vidia had exposed himself for the first time as a man who hated his native West Indies and had no love for black West Indians; and I am sure that he did not have any great affection for Forbes Burnham. And Burnham felt the same way about Vidia.

But George Lamming, Sam and Handrew, with others, came from London. And George was thundering in the rich deep tones reminiscent of Dylan Thomas, in his Inglish accent acquired naturally, after all his years living there and mingling with the Inglish intelligentsia; and Handrew too, was Inglish in this regard. But Sam retained the speech of Trinidad, as if he had never left there, as if the Inglish temperance of and climate had been triflingly ineffectual.

It has always intrigued me, to see how this thing about the acquisition of speech and culture and dialects native to the country of immigration or of "exile" as Lamming had defined the term, affect certain of us, who take on almost every other aspect and nuance of its psychological function. Vidia could not be distinguished from his Oxford accent. He probably came to it, just as naturally as he had adopted other aspects of British sensibilities and moralities, in his attitude towards darker-skinned peoples. And I suppose too, it is part of the adopting of the culture, the "language" as Frantz Fanon calls it, from the very people who had formerly colonized you, that you grow accustomed to that colonization, and in turn make it a part of your own life and demeanor. It became therefore, something working in the blood and in the veins; a kind of dermatological transfusion of the blood and the senses and the morality.

But Guyana at this time was not the place for such cultural recriminations; no place for the discussions of differences begun in Inglann and taken with us, to the "new world" of Burnham's cultural nationalism. Some of us were skeptical of the direction, even then, in which he was taking the young country; and some of us, especially the Guyanese, had cause for pride and for feelings of superiority, that it was Guyana, a kind of despised society in the eyes of certain other West Indian islands, who had shown this direction and this light. It was, all in all, a time of great rejoicing.

Not least of this, was the way in which we were treated by the Government of Guyana. We were treated like kings. Burnham later on, got the reputation of himself behaving like a king, in the midst of the relative poverty of Guyanese society. But we were treated like lords: in a way that very few of us had known in the former years of our lives . . .

A small white car, new off the conveyor belt, with licence plates that began with GUY, for Guyana, meaning it was an official car; and which we christened "Guy-cars," with a chauffeur, was assigned to each of the important writers and artists. It soon became a sign of status, to be able to sit beside your own chauffeur and be taken all over the city of Georgetown, with the entire urban population aware that you were a very important person, a VIP; to be taken to all the events, which took up all day and most of the night; and if you were not inclined to imbibe more of the unrelenting display and presentation of art and culture from the entire West Indies, then you could "parade" in this car, and go downtown in Georgetown, and sit all day in one of the remarkable restaurants which served the best curried prawns in the world. And the chauffeur would sit in the car and wait until you had satiated your starved appetite for this "goodness of life," this "fête."

We were housed in a "village" dug out of the swamp-like land, previously uninhabited and because of the size of the mosquitoes, who seemed to have a predilection for artists, uninhabitable; wooden houses with shower and kitchen and bedroom and living room, and built with an eye to the practical nature of architecture in a land that is below sea-level, that is to say, built on stilts. Some of the more important VIP's, had bungalows in a section of the new suburban developments; with maids.

We glorified only in the facilities, and did not ascribe any influence or importance to them, in any other manner. And we were all glad to be away from our works in progress, away from the tenuous life of the artist, away from the drabness of Inglann, Germany, Amurca, Toranno, and other places where we had laid our beds and were, to a man, unable, or unwilling to lie in them, with contentment.

The mosquitoes were not amused. And they demonstrated their resentment at the sudden alteration in status, by swarming us, and just before their escape, leaving the evidence of their sullen disapproval. Sam and I would compare the size of marks left by their stings, and more than one, we showed each other the amount of blood in a killed mosquito, if we were swift enough to have brought about that extremity. "Oh God, Copper! Is mosquito in your arse, boy!"

One afternoon, near his "house," with the GUY-car parked beneath, in the space demarcated by the "stilts" on which the house had to be built, we were regaled by a section of the Trinidad contingent, a steel orchestra. They were living in the house next door. For years and years, in Canada, the only steel-pan music I was able to hear was on record, and by the time the record reached me, through the mercies of a loving mother to her son, a student, the tune was old. Perhaps, two years out of date. But on this heavy, humid afternoon, with rum and soda in hand, feeling the unrelenting heat of Guyana's weather, but rejoicing that it was not winter, I listened to the poetry of the steel band orchestra, and for the first time, during my fifteen years in Toranno (at the time), I realized the enormous cultural richness I had left behind, in order to embrace the transitory and illusive "experience" of living in North America.

The first notes told me we had all made a profound mistake by choosing materialism, better-paying jobs, higher education which has really not served us in the way such training is supposed to do; seeking the distance that is claimed contributes to objectivity when writing about our homelands, and the mere fact of being away for such extended periods from the very roots of our being. The steel pan music underscored this cultural racism.

It was a sensation I had never known. For in Barbados, we are more in tune with the lugubrium of *Hymns Ancient and Modern*; we do not have the lilt and the sense of enjoyment that is so necessary to the production of calypso; do not really regard *that* creative production as any worthwhile cause of celebration. We listened to it, from afar. We could, in certain company, admit to its appreciative quality. But we could not produce it. And we therefore envied the Trinidadian's expertise in making it.

I cannot remember the tune the orchestra was rehearsing, but the emotional impact has remained with me since that afternoon.

"Pan in your arse!" Sam said. It was as if he had chosen this moment, to tell me for the first time, that his writing the language of Trinidad, and the cause of his writing that language, was the creative catalyst of the steel-pan orchestra; that it was, like his handling of the language, a mirrored improvement upon the music, the source of his creativity. And now that I write these lines, I am astonished that I have not made this point before: that Sam's understanding of the "language" was caused by the keenness of his ear and sensibilities and the profound knowledge, like an inner apprehension not available to the majority, of this music and what it means. "Pan in your arse, Copper!" It was the *first* time that he had made any comment on music — of any kind. And sometimes, I wondered whether he did not, like me, have to have some kind of music on the radio or the record player, while he was writing his books, as a means of shutting himself out from the rest of the world, as a means of contributing some essential other force to his work. "*That* is pan! Copper, it have pan like that, in Barbados?"

There was no need to answer his deliberative question.

I could feel the intensity of the regret that in his London, there was no such playing of the discarded oil drums, from which the Trinidadians, with their amazing ability to improvise, had made possible; that he could not wake up, go through his day in the suburban house, and work while hearing this music, and then in the evenings, when the "elders" meet to relax and chat about the workings of the day, to be able to hear this kind of music which he would have known, day in and day out, during his residence back home in Trinidad.

I could feel the pride he was making me accept and see the superiority (which I readily accepted) of this aspect of the culture from which he had come. I could feel the unspeakable ways in which he had retained this music in his language, when he wrote about those Trinidadians in London, who carried, and were able to carry, only a memory of the tune, the memory of the pan, the memory of the *sound*. For the sound is everything.

"Is classics in your arse, now Copper! Beethoven! Chaikofsky! Brahms!" he said. I recognized the Beethoven. Sam had never before made any comment on music; had never, like the rest of us, when travelling in a group, expressed any enthusiasm to visit a jazz club; had shown no particular interest in the music played in the homes of our mutual friends. Had never asked to have a piece played.

This was his way of telling, in plain blunt terms, and I was proud to have apprehended his meaning and intention, that he was once more within the lap of the culture and the people from whom he had come. And it was this appreciation and this oneness with the landscape, that was the fuel to his tremendous facility in reproducing the essence of West Indianness. He did it with humor, some say. He made us laugh, as he showed us the impossible situations of immigration with which we all have had to live, and endure, without protest. For protest in the Fifties and Sixties was not characteristic of West Indian immigrants, in any part of the world where we found ourselves inhabiting our respective diasporas.

I do not find anything funny in his stories, or in the message he gives in his significant body of work. I do not have to, like the white liberal, feel that he is making the immigrant's ambivalent experience acceptable or palatable, by using the technique of humor. This is no laughing matter. If we do laugh, we laugh for different reasons. Perhaps, because of the similarity in experience. Not because it is a joke.

How can you laugh at the inhospitable treatment of us at the hands of the Canadians, the British, and the Americans? And what logic is imposed upon our naturally-smart minds, suggesting that the disapproval of this treatment can best be understood by our "colonizers," if we cloak or clothe our respective protests, disagreements, resentments in a manner to make people laugh? Are we then, not minimalizing the tragedy? I have always rejected that view advanced by reviewers and critics of our work, Sam's and mine, that it is comic; or tragi-comic. Some say that I have made palatable the miseries of West Indians living in Canada, and their confrontation with the Canadian "mainstream," meaning nothing less than the Canadian version of racism, when I couch my resentment, or my presentation of it, in "comical terms." "Comic terms" goes further than saying that the "confrontation" is couched in humor.

Sam was never able to deal with this. He called it, when he was pushed to define it, and which he resented having to do, "intellectual gymnastics . . . "

Sam knew that I knew "Odo" Burnham personally. And this afternoon, at the residence of the Trinidad and Tobago High Commissioner to Guyana, there was a reception; and we were there with voracious appetites for the delicious food Trinidadians are notorious for serving at their functions. We were there, dressed suitably: Sam in a shirt jack, and I, still in my African mode, in a new Kente cloth outfit, given to me by an African friend with whom I had been at University. We positioned ourselves strategically near the entrance. We had heard that "Odo" Burnham was attending. And we had heard that in *his* new mode, he would either be arriving on horse back, or with ten motorcycle outriders. We wanted to be the first to hear the "sirens," and see the outriders, and perhaps get the chance to shake the hand of the great man.

The crowd was massive, as most receptions in Georgetown were in those hectic, romantic and superlative times. Everything done, either by government or private organizations, was the *very* best. The curried shrimps and prawns served with Demerara rice, was the best in the world. The women of Georgetown were the most beautiful in the West Indies, if not in the world. The feeling of belonging, the way in which Guyanese related to country and to the new nationalism was the best expression of cultural homogeneity I had seen in the world. We were at the entrance, Sam and I, in the outdoors, with the breeze relieving the oppressive humidity of Georgetown, for one second at a time. That relief from the humidity was enhanced by the sips we took of the rum punch in our hands.

And then the "sirens!"

"Oh God-oh God!" Sam said. "Sirens in your arse, Copper! Odo *come*, boy!"

The humidity lifted, the air was fresh and the skies the most rich azure, with the trees blowing more gently as if demonstrating their own genuflection, at the arrival of the President of the Co-Operative Republic of Guyana.

The whirring of the "sirens" did not have the same piercing effect they have in London and Toranno, or in New York, when they mean that another black man is being arrested, or a black man has been killed. Here, in our new land, in our new importance, this was the shrill voice of power.

There was only one outrider. Perhaps, the President, in a show of uncharacteristic modesty, was aware that in his midst, there were artists, easy to criticize their host if his behavior showed too great a gulf between their unaccustomed gracious circumstances and the trappings of his new, democratically-earned powers and influence. But it was power, nevertheless. And there was an outrider. And behind the motorcycle, a rich-black, polished limousine whose windows were tinted with the merest hint of the need for the man inside, to be private; and in that privacy a hint of the power of invisibility. It was a Bentley. We had seen Bentleys almost every day of our lives back home in the hot islands, when inside them, and totally invisible, was the Inglish governor. His influence over our lives was, however, not too invisible and abstract.

But with this new ruler, this new President, Comrade Odo, to his friends, it could not be like those strange white men who cared nothing for us, who were sent out, like other Inglish men all over the Empire, to rule for King and country over us and over their dominions on which the sun, less powerful in its scope, could not set. With this Comrade, we could imagine none of that distance, none of that doubt about his sincerity, none of that imposition of customs, habits and morality foreign to us all. Here was our new leader.

He dismounted the car. There was a hush. It lasted for a few seconds. Then he was seen. He had come completely out of the tinted hiding place. And a roar went up. He was sparkling in custom-made shirt-jack suit of white linen, adding a powerful beautiful blackness to his naturally black skin. He stood for a moment. A moment in which he wanted us to admire him. And he moved off slowly, stopping often to shake each hand extended to him. And at the same time, savoring the moment of grandness.

He came towards us. Sam smiled. "Oh God! Look the boy! Look the Comrade! Look Odo!"

"Comrade Sam," he said, and shook his hand.

"Comrade Clarke?" It was not that he could not believe it was me, standing before him, dressed "like a little African." His tone and slight surprise were directed at my Kente cloth. "How are you, Comrade?" He was remembering: I had interviewed him a few years earlier for a radio programme for the Canadian Broadcasting Corporation, during the time the British had suspended the British Guiana constitution, when he had, in a political move that turned out to be brilliant, parted company with Dr. Cheddi Jagan, then the Premier of British Guiana. The British, and the Amurcans, did not approve of Dr. Jagan's Marxist leanings. Burnham knew this. He left Dr. Jagan's Cabinet, and prepared to take all the apples in the new harvest of political power.

But here he was, standing before Sam and me, his face glistening from the sun and from the aftershave lotion, beautiful, black, and self-assured; and enjoying the turn in his fortunes, as much, if not more than any of us present was able to do.

And he moved along the receiving line that had formed hastily and on the spur of the moment.

"Why you didn't ask him to look after the boys?" Sam said, referring to an earlier drop of a word by me, that the Comrade liked his Johnnie Walker Black; that he and I, during that interview in 1964 had sipped the bottle empty in his office, as he outlined for me, and the Canadian radio audience why he had to leave Dr. Jagan; why he thought the British corporations should be nationalized; why the people of British Guiana were suffering, and would, under his regime, end that suffering; and why he should, and would, win the elections. And here he was now, the winner. The savior of his people.

It was a proud moment. I felt I had taken some part in this emancipation; and had, through the great exposure to the Canadian and Amurcan audiences, contributed to his election victory.

"Man, Copper," Sam said, not forgetting the power of influence and connection, "ask the Comrade to organize the fellars. Ask the Comrade to send 'round a case o'Johnnie Walker *Black*!"

Sam knew the chef at the Trinidadian High Commission, and he used *his* influence to get each silver salver of delicious food come to us first, before it made its rounds to the other guests, many of whom were, in terms of power and politics, much more distinguished than us. I was glad for Sam's connections: the salvers disappeared in the twinkling of an eye, and the passing of a hand.

I told Sam about the interview in 1964: remembering some details, and through the rum punch, embellishing others, but never misrepresenting the gist of our talk in the humid office, in Georgetown, that afternoon when the temperature must have been one hundred in the shade of the broad avenue of the main street.

The Comrade was dressed then in a suit that highlighted his regal bearing, even though he was sitting down; and it was made from a material like silk, and was custom tailored. He smoked Kent cigarettes. His hair was trimmed close to the skull. There was no mistaking then, five years before this "fête" for West Indian artists, that the man I was interviewing, who talked easily and with assurance, would some day lead his country into independence from Britain. He was obviously intelligent; and he was handsome, as the women of Guyana were able to attest to; and without doubt, ambitious. But he was ambitious not only in a manner of political greed, but because of the classical education he had received, along with his legal training. Because of the preparation that that education and profession had made upon his character, he had to be ambitious.

It was as if he knew, before anyone else; and that he wanted me to know too. The British had just suspended the constitution. The country was in chaos. The moral fracture that this political intervention had brought, was symbolized in the term, *appanjat!* It summarized the divisions in the native populations of African and

Indian, that the British disregard of national aspirations had brought about. And though, *appanjat* is an Indian word, it was not necessarily the Indians who were to be blamed for the racial chaos into which Guyana had sunk, as a result of the British action.

Dr. Cheddi Jagan, an Indian, had been stripped in 1964 of his power, by the British, because they disliked his Marxist leanings. And this is how Comrade Burnham found himself poised to take over power, in the elections which some say were rigged deliberately by the CIA, whose tool they also said, Burnham was. I do not know.

But the telling memory, above and beyond the intriguing jockeying for power, and the recriminations thrown almost every night on the political platforms of Guyana, by both adversaries, my lasting memory is of the suit and the cigarettes, and the Johnnie Walker Black.

Sam brought me back to this reality. "Tell the Comrade to organize we, eh, Copper?"

I got my chance as he was coming back out, with his entourage. "Comrade," I said, "the boys would like to know . . . " And he understood. And asked me to call his secretary in the morning; and Sam became skeptical, that a head of government and of state would, in these circumstances have the time to remember even telling his secretary that one amongst hundreds of visiting artists would be calling his office in the morning. "Old talk!" Sam said, and went back to the delicious food being shuttled from the chef in the kitchen, by the waiters, to us, still standing by the entrance. The other writers wondered why we did not want to mingle with them and dignitaries and promote inter-regional artistic solidarity, which was the purpose of this first Carifesta. And we did not tell them why.

But I said that I had not ventured from Jamaica to live in London as an immigrant, could only read about, sympathize with, and have an intellectual outlook on. I was somewhat spared this harsh but reasonable judgement, because they had heard about my political activities in Toranno during the early Sixties; had listened to my interviews of leading civil rights personages, and had given me some kind of lukewarm absolution. Still, it was not quite like Inglann and London, where the "fellars really catch' their arse." And Sam, in those discussions and arguments, would have added, *"Royally!"*

And I can imagine how the talk would center on racial responsibility; on Notting Hill riots; on the insensitivity of the police; on Vidia Naipaul; on Michael DeFreitas; later to re-name himself Michael Abdul Malik, and back again, like in a pecking order; and about those present, even though they were black and West Indian, but who could have no moral justification for offering an opinion about this time, when it seemed to them in London, and to us in Toranno and Amurca, that the blackness of your skin might spell your death. And not in bed.

In those days, both in London and in Toranno (certainly in cities in Amurca), it was considered a badge of being "relevant," of being able to utter an opinion about civil rights, if you had at least marched in one demonstration. And demonstrations took place almost every day. You had to have some accountability; and your station in life, if you were black, had nothing to do with your political position on the subject of civil rights. And this seemed to me to be justifiable, for others were, perhaps with some naivety and idealism, marching and demonstrating, and were being either shot down with high-power hoses or with real bullets. You just could not stand by and watch the parade, and glory in the aesthetic virtues of the parade, and compliment yourself that it had contributed to your own personal safety. You had to show your wounds. And in many cases those wounds were measured in your unsuitability to enter the United States of America, because you were regarded as a security risk, were too radical and were an extremist; were regarded as unemployable; and had your photograph and a file written on you in the files of the FBI, the CIA, MI-5; and in Canada, the RCMP. As some of the Amurcan brothers put it, "Motherfucker, you can't talk if you didn't *walk*, Jack!" . . .

The GUY-cars formed themselves into some kind of entourage, like at a wedding; and on either side of the road, not known by most of us, except by Jan and Aubrey Williams, the royal palms were like guards of honor, witnessing this journey from the houses we had left in the marked-out housing development, leaving house in the charge of the unrelenting mosquitoes, fed fatter in the short time between the argument and the departure, and wondered our way to the Comrade's hacienda.

I had called the secretary. Promptly, and with no pause of hesitation and recognition, she said, "Oh yes! Comrade Burnham told me to expect your call!" She gave us the time. The day. And the place. And Sam and I assumed that only the two of us would have the Comrade to ourselves; that the case of Johnnie Walker Black which I had gathered the guts to ask for, would be put into the boot of the GUY-car, and after a respectful time had passed, Sam and I would take the journey back, through the blackened streets with the royal palms no longer visible, to face the mosquitoes, in a long night of spirited talk.

But as we turned out from our compound, we saw the line of other GUY-cars going in the same direction; and we determined quickly, that others were going to the Comrade's home, on this beautiful Sunday afternoon.

We could only take credit that we had initiated it. And could not really resent the extra company. Foremost in our minds, however, was the threat of having to divide the case of scotch into more than two. We wanted our case of Johnnie Walker Black to be placed by a guard, with no one noticing, into the boot, and locked; and we could then endure the interruption of other writers who did not have the guts or the connections, or the privilege of having arranged this meeting.

It was, this arrangement made by the Comrade to have as many of the writers accompany us, without our knowledge, a master stroke of the political acumen of the man who called me Comrade Clarke.

Sam and I had considered how rude it would be, under the changed circumstances, to sit for a few minutes in this multitude of writers with whom we were becoming bored, then take our booty, and return to face even the dreadful, blood-sucking mosquitoes. What could they do, against the strength and medicinal quality of the Johnnie Walker Black? And how could a few dozen West Indian writers, compared with Guyana's mosquitoes, be a more unbearable intrusion upon our plans? "Oh God, Copper! You come through, boy!" Sam said, acknowledging even in spite of the unwelcomed crowd, that I was a man, even in Guyana, of my word. "You good, Copper!" I accepted his praise. But was alarmed by the multitude of writers and artists.

Is it not amazing, that we, I moreso than Sam, (for he was a gentleman of great patience and humanity,) would disapprove of the company of our colleagues, when the acknowledged intention of this first Carifesta, was to cement the ties that existed between us, and which required only the bringing together of us, on a neutral ground, leaving us amongst ourselves to work out the ingredients, the mortar and the straw, to build a new society which for years, we had talked about; had known of its significance both to the islands and to our own personal and artistic development? And now, on this Sunday afternoon, not many hours after we had stood in the huge Park, under the stars which hardly shone, in the presence of thousands, and had witnessed the taking down of the Union Jack which had been our symbol of decency and of degradation, and had gloried in the efforts of one man, the Comrade. We took part in the pride that must have surged through his body like new blood, like "new wine," on that independence night. Here now, are the two of us, resenting the presence of others, because we thought we had a selfish monopoly upon his time and attention.

As I thought of it, it was not amazing in the least, that the Comrade had thought that more could be accomplished, more experienced, more that was important said, if as many of the artists as possible were present at this "at home," this Sunday afternoon.

Just as the heat in the islands melts anxiety and anger and resentment, by the time we had counted enough royal palms, passed fields whose growth and greenness we had both forgotten, passed Indians near the edges of fields even greener, and Africans bearing a new ancestral pride in their posture and in their own hearts, we had had our arrogance dissipated, and were glad and honored, (for such it was) to have been invited at all. We understood then that it really was beyond the official obligation of invitations, to be asked to the home of the President of the Co-operative Republic of Guyana.

From my first disadvantaged meeting with the Comrade, I was aware of his remarkable intelligence. I had stood one night when it rained, for three hours in Bourda Pasture, known before this only for its dramatic inter-island cricket matches between Barbados and British Guiana, one of thousands, who seemed to be leaning on invisible sticks, to the magnet of his words, in a speech he gave, which had not repetition of ideas or even of phrases. "Jesus Christ," a man beside me said, "that man could *talk!*"

He held each of us within the palm of his eloquence, that night at Bourda, within the fist of his power, within the promise of national political improvement and progress. It mattered little that I was standing in the darkness, punctuated only by the weak bulb on the platform, not in my own island, but in a foreign place. Only the cosmetics were foreign. The thirst for words, of which all West Indians pride themselves in understanding and in using, with similar vigor; the tense expectation that something dramatic, something tragically important, a kind of political miracle was about to happen, and that we were seeing on this night, some aspects of this remarkable re-ordering of things, was the factor which bound us together, one people, African and Indian, on a Bourda night. I filled my heart with the power of place and of belonging. Never before since 1955 when I landed in Montreal on my way to Toranno to attend Trinity College, had I been in such an awe-inspiring, terrifying circumstance, made all the more terrifying because I had not known it in Toronto, was not there in Barbados when it happened on the Garrison Savannah, and never before was able to conceive even this possibility when I could, in spite of the ravages of racism in Canada, breathe in this holy air of independence. I could not fantasize that this time would come when I could be identified with the man making the speech, with the people listening, with the land on which I stood, on which the speaker stood, *his land*, and not fear the accustomed sting of the high-powered water hoses, the sheriff's cattle prod, the policeman's night stick in the pit of my back.

I saw then, his intelligence, and his political intrigue. The control his words have over the people. The political climax of that Bourda speech, came a few nights before this Sunday afternoon travelling within the honor guard of royal palms, the night when the Union Jack was lowered. And even in my rejoicing, I could feel the pulse and the sentiments of those who were more at peace and felt easier with the permanency of the Union Jack. But that night, when the sun went down, it was not there.

I saw then, too, his ability to manipulate; the trickiness in the man; the cleverness. Yes, *cleverness* is the better term. It takes the potential out of the depth of tricks and games; and elevates it to what it is, and was: his ability to use his brains, for politics, for psychology, for human affairs, in such a way that when he had made his conclusion and decision, lesser brains had not yet conquered the proposition. He was a clever man. And this cleverness would be demonstrated on this Sunday afternoon, in the huge verandah of his home.

Too many had heard about the invitation. There was a slight scramble for chairs. You wanted to catch each word that this powerful, romantic man, at the height of celebration, would say. Perhaps, some time afterwards, when we had returned to our various "disaporas," in the cold basement or in the unventilated attic, we might remember a phrase and use the writer's tack and *craft*, and craftiness, and put the words of that phrase in the mouth of a character, and claim that it is original. Perhaps, it was the physical environment, or the atmosphere, the men and women present that could be used as background to some story, to give the natural cultural flavor of truth to the setting. For many of us had not seen the islands in which we were born, for many many years. And too, to be in the presence of Martin Carter, in my view, more a politician than a poet and Cabinet Minister, to wait for what pearl of beauty that might fall out of his mouth, as he drank generously his favorite *Russian Bear Rum*. It was an experience to crave: what we did with it afterwards, would depend upon the force with which the occasion struck us; and whether we were not too deeply steeped in the marvellous "darrou" being served with a Guyanese generosity not many of us had known . . .

Sam and I were among the first to arrive. It was not only the case of the early bird getting the most nourishing nectar from this afternoon's festivities, but also that we were in a position to observe the political maneuvering of writers who normally eschew such behavior. But this was a new republic. And a new powerful head of that republic. And we all wallowed in the new ritual of address, and called ourselves, "Comrade."

"Comrade Copper!" Sam said to me, with a glass of Johnnie Walker Black in his hand; and smiled; and said with his smile, that this was "fête," which indeed it was.

"Comrade Sam," I said, "connections, man!"

And Comrade "Odo" moved amongst us, dressed in his custom-made shirt-jack suit, which I remember was white; and he assisted the butlers in serving us, and himself brought chairs from the sitting room, and other rooms as the crowd swelled, into the large verandah. There were more artists than space. It seemed that every delegation, back at the compound, seeing the place become empty, had gradually and deliberately felt that there was a plague of mosquitoes; that the mosquitoes were taking over; and that the Sabbath afternoon was no absolution holy and sacred enough to cause these unchristian pests from contributing to the decimation itself. So, they joined the caravan.

And from the insides of the large hacienda, I saw the wife of the Comrade, and then heard her voice, and then saw the beautiful body from which the voice had come. And then I heard a man's voice, which caused my scotch to taste like one of those strong, unpalatable teas that Barbadian mothers boil thick as tar, and serve with the same manner as prison guards, because it is good for the bowels, and is a purge. I heard the word, "slave!" The word was out of place in this atmosphere, in this gathering, in this new freedom of Guyana. And with the shock of the word, and all that it means and could mean, was the greater shock of whom had used it. It came from the mouth of Comrade "Odo."

Where in this gathering of the best creative minds in the West Indies, was the victim to whom this disparagement was addressed? Who amongst the guests, both foreign and Guyanese, could earn the enmity of the gracious, happy, effervescent host, to warrant, and be reminded of that kind of past?

"Slave." The word was uttered again.

It was used in the singular; so only one amongst us was being reminded of a condition, which for the life of this Carifesta festival had been so foreign a sentiment and an attitude, that its usage here, might be interpreted as a playful gesture. Among friends, we may take such liberties. In Guyana in these times, with no proclaimed virtue in women's rights and in feminism, the word even could not be excused. And when it was realized that this was the name used by the Comrade to address his wife, not in private (and he would not necessarily have the moral right to do this), but in the company of strangers in his home; guests, if you like, it brought an unredeeming taste to the richness of the scotch, and to the gaiety of the afternoon. I do not know . . .

I waited to see whether there would be an expression of objection. A look. A glare. A cutting of the eye. Even a flounce. But who dare look, or glare, or cut her eye, or flounce, in the face of the most powerful head of state (on this Sunday afternoon) the most powerful in the whole West Indies? Who would not be wise enough to pretend that the word was not used, and ignore it, and wait for a better, more private moment, perhaps in the bedroom when it is occupied by only the two of them, and bring this public remonstrance to his attention, now that he was no longer president, but simply a man; man in need of his natural needs?

But could she, even with her natural prudence, fail to realize that his natural need, which she could, in other circumstances, seek to withhold, could not now, in this time of power, be kept back from his demand of pleasure?

She said nothing that Sunday afternoon. Not in our presence. And she did nothing with her face, to suggest that she was putting down his "licks," for a time when there would be equality between them, and she could demonstrate her woman's superiority or advantage, in the withholding of her gifts? She said nothing.

I could say nothing. I could do nothing. I am aware of the power of such men. It can be used, in pleasure, for pleasure, and to demonstrate who possesses it. Often, it is used only because it *can* be used. She, as the wife of the most powerful man in Guyana, certainly must have known this better than I.

"Oh God!" Sam said, making a stronger point even than the thoughts passing through my head. He too, had heard. And had understood. Perhaps, even more deeply than I had. "Oh God, Copper!" And he wiped out any further analysis of the matter, which only a few of us, seated near the drama, had overheard. And of course, we would not dare mention it. Not *now*.

For *rum* is our demon. And our culture. Rum defines us, and puts us into categories according not only to our social status and our tastes, it also liberates us. And when the demon rum works miracles with our vocabulary and liberates our tongues, it makes fools of us.

This developed as the afternoon grew long, as the royal palms, and fruit trees in the garden of the property could no longer be seen.

A West Indian argument among writers developed. And soon the argument left the restricted precincts of the literary, and took on, as most do, the broader aspect of politics.

Martin Carter, with cigarette in one hand, and "darrou" in the next, felt it politically prudent, as a poet and as a former Cabinet Minister, to illustrate to the Comrade, and to some other Guyanese politicians, the mistakes the Comrade had made. And Martin enumerated the compounding of those mistakes by the Comrade, because he had been insensitive to advice made by the poet-politician. It raged like the effect of too many rums can rage in the brain and in the body. I began to see the words used turn into blows of violence; for they had reached beyond the pale of words used as blows in argument and logic. They were now being used as instruments of suicide. Or death. Certainly, social and political suicide.

But as West Indian arguments do not wear themselves out, and end in resolution; but are kept in the heart and the mind, for further serializing; as they do not end in violence, as a rule; and are not put down, with enmity and vindication, "for another time," this Sunday afternoon argument, nothing more than "old talk," petered out into the slapping of backs, and comments of "Man, you talking a lotta rass!" And in smiles. And in renewed, strengthened friendships. For these men had been at school together; had gone to foreign lands together, and when they had returned, the other characteristic of the culture of rum, automatically came into play, and they carried on from where they had left off. Friends behave this way. And rum has a way of working as the cement in these friendships.

I did not understand his bond at the time, not at this time, not in this August company. I had been isolated from the very root and meaning of my culture for too long. The effect of the argument and the rum might be stressed beyond the point of its significance. But still, the *taste* was left.

I am justified in this feeling. Taste is identifiable with rum. Taste is symbiotic with rum.

The taste of rum, in this tricky atmosphere, misunderstood by me at first as merely "old talk," was comprehended by another, as something much more palpable; and even if it were mere "old talk," the same prudence of the wife, must be engaged in this "talk," in this game, and it must be recognized with whom you are playing the game. For game it had now become. It could be nothing more.

There was still a need for chairs. There is something peculiar about West Indian parties: seats. Everyone, feeling status is related to a seat, a bench, a chair, a stool, must be seated. It probably comes from deep in our African psyche, and which we cannot now explain. But it is serious. "Bring a seat for the man, man!" Or, in the language of rum: "Man, draw up a pew, and fire one, man! Oh Jesus Christ! yuh can't stannup, all the time!"

Seats were still being needed. And the Comrade left the verandah and went into the sitting room, perhaps, into his private study. And it could have been the study, because of the ceremonial importance that would be placed upon the seat he selected.

He came back out, with a beautifully carved stool. Its sinews, the grains that ran through its deep, rich sacred wood, mahogany or *lignum vitae,* were like the muscles of some African beast, rippling and demonstrating, to the lower order about to be prey and dinner, sheer power and murderous physique. It was an ornament. And an extra-ordinarily carved piece of sculpture.

In his hands, it looked like a sacred object. Something the god and witch doctors would touch, and pray over to bring rain, or victory or damnation. He held it in this manner. And he placed it in the middle of the group, now parted in the middle, to allow him passage, and to allow room for seeing it. And then, his words. Spoken in a voice of the guide who takes you through jungles or through museums, or even through sacred, frightening caves that contain buried treasure.

"Comrades," he said, moving his eyes over each of us, "Comrades, this stool was given to me by an African chief. It is a stool of status. And power. Paramount power." We all could see that; or if not, imagine through our writers' sense, that magic and supernational power could easily be invested into this rich object. *"Let me see which one o' you is going to sit on it?"*

I could hear the breathing surrounding me. I could see Martin Carter move off, and get another rum. I could hear the wind in the royal palms, and the movement of animals in the farm which was on the property. I could hear the boots of the policemen guarding us, as the knobs of nails put into the soles by the shoemaker crashed against the pebbles in the driveway. I could hear the water in the sea of Georgetown that is really no sea at all, crash against the Sea Wall. And I could hear, in a moment beyond the boundary of this "game," a gate, made with less artifice than this stool, out of raw, rough-hit iron or steel, shut.

No one, with rum and Johnnie Walker Black in the vein; no one in this soaked Sunday afternoon, moved to sit on the stool.

The stool remained where it had been placed. Neglected, scorned, reduced to the workmanship of a carpenter who is not too selective with the size of chisel or plane with which he hews his wood. The stool was no longer, in our eyes, an object of ancestral magnificence. It had become a simple, ordinary piece of thing: but powerful still, like a pair of handcuffs. It did not, in spite of this reduction in value, with no one aspiring to conquer it, with no one wanting to acknowledge its metaphor, lose its symbolism.

And when, not a single one of us made a movement to approach it, or tried to fool the others of his demonic attempt, and made even a shuffle in its powerful direction and closeness, the Comrade himself sat on it . . .

It was quite the GUY-Car going back to the mosquitoes in the compound. I could not say that the beauty of the royal palms, or the vista of the country lane was taking up our attention. The night was black. And silent itself. I do not remember crickets. I do not remember any sound, other than that of the driver, fussing with a change from second to third gear; and the noise of the car itself. Once there was a different noise. It was Sam striking a "friction" against the sulphur on the large box of wooden matches, made in Guyana. And then the sound of the flare, and then the intake of breath, like a swimmer coming from after a long time below the water for air. And then the brakes. We were safe. We were happening in the renewed company of the mosquitoes, waiting for us, like lovers.

"Something here for you, sirs!" the chauffeur said. And opened the boot of the car, and disclosed the case of Johnnie Walker Black.

"Oh God, boy! Comrade come through!" Sam said. "Copperplate, you hold me, boy!"

"The Comrade and me're good friends, man!"

And as we carried the case together, as we would lift a coffin with not too much weight, the mosquitoes sensing our disability, swarmed down like Spitfires to devour our blood. We knew they would become intoxicated . . . and drop dead from scotch poisoning; and we won't have to raise a stool in our hand to kill them . . .

While Vidia Naipaul Maintained his paramountcy over the new rage over African Literature, and was lionized by the Inglish with glowing reviews, Sam's letters and those from Handrew both still in London, told a depressing story of their books not being reviewed, as they expressed astonishment and admiration at the large reviews I was getting in those days, in Toranno, in the late seventies. Sam's anger was palpable. And it became more dramatic when he looked around and saw his friends, disappearing from his side, and being courted by the raging interest in Amurca. They deserted him through the Amurcan need for them to teach in black studies programmes. The transference of the West Indian writer's exalted place in London, of his creative production, was now placed firmly, and with some pronounced anger and skepticism by his black Amurcan counterparts, in all the major, or Ivy League colleges in the Eastern Seaboard of Amurca.

I was already at Yale. Jan Carew came to Rutgers, and then to Princeton. Ivan Van Sertima was at Rutgers. Handrew found a place at Hampshire College, in Massachusetts. Orlando Patterson went to Harvard. Eddie Braithwaithe would make sojourns to Columbia and other New York universities from the University of the West Indies (UWI), at Mona. One sculptor from Guyana, Philip Moore, went to Rutgers as artist-in-residence. George Lamming preferred visiting lectureships at universities located in the warmer South. And Sam left Inglann for Canada in 1978 and settled in Calgary, as writer-in-residence, at the University of Alberta. He held the longest tenure in this position among all of us; for a writer-in-residence usually is limited to one year. But year after year, for at least three times each month, I continued to receive letters from Sam, written in his careful small blue ball-point script under the letterhead of the English Department of Alberta. He seems to have been at the University of Alberta, unless, as a writer, with the instincts of a squirrel, he had buried extra sheets of the university's stationery, just in case!

Sam's new migration in the opposite direction was now completed.

His life is laid out, bare and with frankness, and a great deal of humor, on the pages of those letters. He talked about his adjustment to the cold of Calgary, to him more bitter and penetrating than had been his experience in London. And I felt that he too had retained, subconsciously, the air of superiority that Londoners, by birth, and by adoption, demonstrate when they come to live in the "colonies," as Canada is regarded by them.

His attitude was fresh and positive. I could see from his words that he was excited, at that relatively late age for a man seeking to reposition himself as a writer in a foreign country, foreign not only from the point of view of his lack of knowledge about the country, but this "foreignness" made even more exacerbated by the parochial disposition of the Canadian, and in particular the Western Canadians, towards literary interlopers. For that is what he was regarded as, in my opinion. And this criticism is borne out by the fact, that in all the time he spent in this country, Canada, from 1978 until 1994, only *one* novel of his was published, and that was a re-print, by a black publishing firm, Wallace Publishing. In the first year of its publication, I did not see *one* review of the novel, in any of the Toronto newspapers.

Still, as a mark of the man's charity and lack of vengeance about this monstrous disregard, he continued in his letters, to introduce me to British publishers, particularly those who specialize in the West Indies, and promote West Indian novelists. He did not care that my career was not in the doldrums: he was still concerned that I should have greater attention and readership. This sometimes embarrassed me, as I knew that he himself had been grossly neglected by the Canadian literary establishment. It was as if he had come to that understanding, having regarded the Canadians, for their having ignored him, as not worth the effort of greater public relations. For *that* is all it is, in this country, to a large extent . . .

1994

Public Enemies: Police Violence and Black Youth

How should I know this stranger, bearing my own color, in build and in apposition to the snow that covered our heads with its white thickness. How am I to know that this man, a railway porter on the Canadian National, had prepared the soil for my own intemperate arrival from Barbados?

How should I react to the man, old as my grandfather, bearing the weight of my own color, dressed in a white butler's jacket and black trousers seamed as sharp as a Gillette, and in the shine of whose shoes I could see, if I had been so disposed, my disappointment and embarrassment? This man, in this sparkling men's room, its four walls of polished white, squared tiles, dwarfed by two white porcelain urinals. In his silent blackness, this man, with a skin polished high as the marble, standing with an ironic dignity handing out white towels to me (no brother of his: or son).

I disappeared before he could extend his hand. I disappeared in order to obliterate the man, his status and his memory from touching and tainting my status. For in those days of 1955, without question, without doubt, a man of my color was presumed to be a porter.

How should I write about that man, whose color I share, and who worked and saved and worked some more because his wage was small; and because he was industrious, and could see the opportunity in this country,in this land of "opportunity", he had the audacity to purchase a car, and turn it into a taxicab, and park it outside Union Station, beside that very hotel with the white porcelain urinals. Waiting for the first visitor to hail "Taxi!" And when he jumped at the opportunity, he had his arms broken, and his knees battered. Blood was pouring from his face when he entered his kitchen, in a street that is now in Chinatown, after he was discharged from the Toronto General Hospital where the nurses and doctors were all white — no black could be a nurse back then — and had to explain to his wife, and terrified children, that he had failed. "They would not let me," he said.

What sins of these fathers, what virtues have these fathers handed down to their children of this generation, what assurances of dreams fulfilled have they put into the genes of the young present inhabitants of this black Toronto community, or neighborhood? For one hundred years, the relationship between the blacks and whites in our neighborhood of Toronto was mistaken for integration and for racial harmony, precisely because for all these years our fathers, our ancestors, swallowed their disappointments silently, and ate their pride with patience.

Not so the attitude of young blacks on the night of May 4th, 1992. Not so the intention of that demonstration, called to protest the "innocence" of policemen whom these young black men swore had shot a black youth in the back of his head, because he was black. Not so the animus of that black crowd with whom a few whites had mixed, accompanying them on their journey to protest this "verdict," made dramatic and international by the acquittal in Los Angeles of the policemen who beat Rodney King.

It was not the first time that American racism had taken root in Canada in the minds of black Canadians. It was not the first time that black Canadians assumed an African brotherhood and sisterhood as the basis of their sympathy with the brothers and sisters below the border, negating any difference between American racism and Canadian racism. It was not the first time that the definition of police brutality, its meaning to black people and in particular to young black men, was put into the context of white against black; of white men against young black men. There was now no possibility of localizing this police viciousness against black suspects; in the minds of the black youth in the black Diaspora, the situation was something bordering on elimination, black pogroms

It was, on the night of May 4th, as if war had been declared. It was as if the first hundred years of patience, caution, dialogue, fear, fear of reprisals, and negotiation had been thrown out with no existing possibility of understanding; and a new slate produced on which would be written the new creed: "All cops are racists."

The demonstration began "peacefully," if ever a demonstration against police brutality can be termed peaceful, for those who march, who hold placards, who sing "freedom" songs carry within themselves the anger and the violence that they claim was ignited by the history of the relationship between policemen and young black men.

There were soft edges to the animus unleashed that night. Not all policemen shoot and kill blacks. Not all black men, young and old, regard policemen as killers. But the fact that there is too much violence against young black men cannot be rationalized. In the past, we have tried to be generous and even reasonable in looking at this problem, but on that night, it was as if those who faced the police wanted to solve the problem right then and there, with no regard to arrest and detention, detention and beating, charge and conviction. The Fourth of May, their intemperance said, would be a final pitched battle.

There were some ironic aspects. Rioters taking up pools of horse droppings and pelting them at the police. Their irrepressible anger venting itself on passersby, display windows, shattered glass cases, and scattering their own "droppings," "trashing" these formerly peaceful streets. It was unbelievable that, in Toronto, there could be a demonstration so extreme, so radical, caused by a "bunch of black people." It was unbelievable that there could be *any* cause to bring down this racial vengeance and vindication upon a city that had turned a blind eye to this possibility.

Toronto had deluded itself into the comfortable belief that the strategy of the older generations of black people would remain the same. That we would bear, and smile at, our inability to make the larger society sensitive to our hurt which although borne silently, was nevertheless indelible and festering. It was silent inattention that gave voice and action to the night of May 4th.

No longer will the protest against injustice, police brutality, racial discrimination, and plain black frustration be couched in respectable, conservative duplicity. No longer will the victim be ashamed to voice his resentment of this victimization. And we will no longer find it prudent, as it used to be, to express this resentment in an ambivalent manner. Today, it is simply a matter of black and white. The lines are drawn.

No one has been looking at the past; no one has been reading the history; no one has understood the change upon the landscape of Toronto's multicultural society. No one has recognized that a sizeable proportion of young black men were born here, are Canadians, and therefore have a constitutional right more sacred than the moral accommodation that bound the "immigrant."

May 4th issued a warning: this generation will not be as patient as earlier ones. May 4th was a symptom of the silent, festering of the wound. There is no longer any sense of mutual understanding on the part of the two principals: the police and young black men. But, in spite of the danger that this symptom suggests, there is still enough goodwill, born of that patience and that inactive "history," to prevent that night in May from characterizing their relationship.

Although there is no heraldry but scant pages in books called history texts; although there is certainly no known heraldry to emboss and highlight the plaints and pains, the disadvantages ascribed to color; and even though there are no statues erected to remind us, and especially the young, of the perseverance, the success and the failure of the brave men and women who, a hundred years ago, had a clear understanding of the meaning of this country's underground railroad to freedom; our imagination can draw a picture of their resilient attempts to adjust to a climate of disadvantage: to make friends of strangers, to become neighbors and, most of all, to appreciate the kindness and hospitality of the "community" in which they found themselves.

These men and women had left a landscape of whips and murder and rape, and had *chosen* passage to a destination that could not replicate that degradation. From Africa, they were involuntary guests of America; here in the North, their presence, even though illegal, was nevertheless voluntary. This voluntariness must have been the point of their determination to succeed, and to fit into their strange and sometimes hostile environment. This voluntariness also marked them as respectable men and women, although poor. In the pages of our history, they were "pioneers," respectable members of their incipient community; hardworking, and Canadian.

I cannot gainsay the sweat that poured off their foreheads, or delude myself that they were well paid for their labor, since today, in 1992, and in spite of May 4th, the puzzling political cry of "equal opportunity in employment" means, in blunt terms, that black people still can't find good jobs.

From the minutes of secretaries, from faded photographs, we learn the history of founders of churches, founders of schools (in the sense that they had turned part of the cold kitchen or parlor into a school room), of firemen and lifeguards; trappers and scouts in the uncharted wilderness. We know that some, later on, became doctors, barristers-at-law and city politicians; one was a Mayor of Toronto; one was, in our day, Lieutenant-Governor; and one now a Chief Justice of the Federal Court; and one a university chancellor . . .

If we want to justify our "ministry" in this country, we may begin in the *Canadian Who's Who,* and continue in the pages of

Contrast (our first, now defunct, national black newspaper) and in *Share*. In this enumeration, however, lies a danger to which we ourselves are prey. The implication that the success of our entire community can be measured by the outstanding prowess of one or two. We compound that danger if we ascribe messianic heroism to these individual successes: in the same way as we feel, ambivalently, that such success and distinction separate the man and the woman so rewarded from the rest of us. By extension, we feel uncomfortable when the media and the establishment misrepresent our leadership and call it irresponsible; we shrug our shoulders and insist we have no leaders. "He? He isn't my leader! He don't represent me!" because he is radical, and has no profession, and is not as educated as we are.

It is our ingrained schizophrenia that, living in a society such as Canada, with its peculiar racism, we cannot accept prominence among the ranks, particularly as that prominence is bestowed by the media and the establishment. As members of the colonized, we cannot abide the emergence from anonymity of one who, to us, bears the psychic markings of the colonizer. It is as if we want to remain, each and every one of us, oppressed.

Whether in Africa, the West Indies, or Toronto, we have an effective way of reproving those who have succeeded: "Who he think he is?" And if the point is not made by that rhetorical question, we are quick to add a genealogy of deprivation and low class to our resentment: "But I know he when he used to walk 'bout here barefoot, his backside at the door."

It is possible that our Lieutenant-Governor understood this when, as he was adorned in vice-regal raiment, plumed and epauletted in Elizabethan finery to resemble a Lord of the Fleet, he insisted, "Call me Linc." How could he not have seen the contradiction in that insistence on the commonality of things, the democratization of high office? But he had come from a similar psychology. He reminded us of his mother's occupation, domestic servant, when she had first arrived; and by doing that, drew a line from the red plush carpet to the linoleum, slippery from Ajax cleanser, on which that woman's knees grew sore. He was establishing the connection, identifying "community" and neighborhood.

How many women, the mothers of those "rampaging" young blacks, are on welfare today? How many women are in kitchens today? How many women in factories? How many women on the street — selling their bodies and committing their bodies to the inhospitable pavement? How many women are in rags, and using rags, cleaning offices? Those from our part of the world, will they sit in Toronto and smile and shed a tear and touch their Bibles, as their sons and daughters repeat this litany of the underprivileged? How many of those children in the demonstrations of May 4th have rejected that litany?

Today, there is no way of measuring the depth of our disillusionment, the hatred we bare, the anger we foster. Since the night of May 4th, we now speak with a different voice, one of youthful disregard for my cautious and conditioned respectability, as they march on Yonge Street, on subways and in malls in the raiment and the rhetoric of the "heavy dude," "the black activist," the "follower of Malcolm X" (and he would turn in his grave at the philosophical misrepresentation of his political theology). Today there is no way we can tell the extent to which these hyphenated Canadians, who are rushing to the font of an African consciousness in the most simplistic and revivalist manner, will convert successfully to this new identity.

How can I embrace Africa after thirty-seven years in Canada? How can I be more Barbadian than Canadian when I have spent two-thirds of my life in Toronto? How do I resist the dermatology of Canadian culture imbued in me over all these years, and have the racial forwardness to regard myself as African? And why should I? Merely to give my protest a sharper context. Or more bluntly, to evade the wounding of being called "nigger," "colored," "Negro," "blasted Jamaican," or "West Indian?" Do I look more African than Canadian? If I permit this reasoning, then I am saying Canadians are white and Africans are black. And if one is black, one cannot have been born here, one cannot be Canadian.

Derek Walcott is one of our heroes from another discipline, equal in importance to being a first black Mayor, or a first black Lieutenant-Governor: a poet. For in our quiet, closest moments of self-flagellation, we have had among us, sustaining us, creators of great beauty and the best of art. Derek Walcott's works gave us our meaning. He was our historian. He was our guru. He was our spiritual advisor, our psychiatrist — if we would listen to him. He faced the insistent question of our schizophrenia, which we have always misunderstood and considered a negative disposition — proof that we are crazy, that we aren't "together," not "cool, man."

Walcott faced the question, and recognized that it is our schizophrenia, in fact, that gives us our most positive definition. And he could not have dreamed about the question, or dreamed about facing the question, without some reference to the tribe, to the community, to the apprehensions of the *arrivants* of that community:

> *A wind is ruffling the tawny pelt*
> *Of Africa . . .*
> *I who am poisoned with the blood of both,*
> *Where shall I turn, divided to the vein?*
> *I who have cursed*
> *The drunken officer of British rule, how choose*
> *Between this African and the English tongue I love?*
> *Betray them both, or give back what they give?*
> *How can I face this slaughter and be cool?*
> *How can I turn from Africa and live?*[1]

I shall not give the impression that Walcott's philosophy has been universally accepted by the adherents of black cultural nationalism. It was presented in harsher psychological terms by the intellectual, Frantz Fanon, who said that the colonized man must imitate the colonizer, and that the extent to which he is successful in this imitation, which is primarily dermatological, is inversely proportionate to his assuming the mores of the colonizer. I must admit that there was a time when I considered these sentiments to be tantamount to Uncle-Tomism, a cop out. But I have lived with the racist demons, tentative, suspicious, mutually uncreative, and sad since the beginning of my presence here. I was the first to advocate a black nationalism. But then, in the heat and hipness of the Civil Rights movement, I was faced with the schizophrenia of living on a landscape that I cursed and, denounced, until I realized that, with wife and children born here, I was in a very real sense Canadian, and no longer Barbadian, and, most certainly, not African.

I had faced the "slaughter." Yet I had seen no ruins, no portraits in college halls, in legislatures, in boardrooms, and no statutes that had my imprimatur on them. Nobody who was anybody looked like me, and still I was called upon, both by my own determination and by the society that neglected me, to allow this neglect to drive me mad; even while the society insisted that I respect the structures of its civilization.

I owed my living, in its barest days, and later in its success and acclaim, to this country. I had cashed in the return ticket to Barbados: I had made that emotional and psychological commitment to Canada. Although a non-violent man, I still would have taken up arms in defense of my new standard of life, my societal principles (never for Arnerica!), the guaranteeing of the survival and non-molestation of my community (in all these years, the same square mile, bounded by Bloor, Brunswick, Dupont, and Church): and did, in fact, hail the Toronto Maple Leafs, the Blue Jays, Toller Cranston, Bruce Kidd, and, yes, Ben Johnson and Angela Issajenko. I sang "O Canada," and resented the rowdyism on Yonge Street on Saturday nights. But I do not regard myself as an immigrant in that negative sense, that I have no security against which to ask for the loan of decency, of recognition as a man, that I have no night to be here.

I have been thinking of the enterprising taxicab owner, bloodied because of his presumption to be industrious; of the man distributing towels in the Towne Tavern, of the silent, frightened majority of men and women who bear the nobleness and degradation of my color, and I wonder how each of them addresses their loved ones.

Do they prate upon the incidents of racism without recess? Do they see themselves as victims, and behave as victims of this racism, without remembering and acknowledging that they are men and women? Do they give up? Do they cast a net of antagonism, at random, to catch all racists? If this were the case, if they saw themselves in this unredeemably negative disposition, and if this disposition became the definition of themselves by themselves, they would all be dead: by suicide or broken hearts.

They have not been pushed to this extremity. They have not, because they understand the sustaining factor of our continuing existence: they understand improvisation.

Improvisation is that ethic ingrained into us; that antenna that cautions; that "spirit" that warns; that emotionalism which, to us, is as important as, and equal to, intellectualism: the ethic that permits us passage through any minefield of racism. Think of the black slaves who emerged from the "underground," battered and weary, their flesh stinging from the cowhide, but exuberant, as they must have been, to rest, to take a breather from the immediacy of physical and emotional deprivation and brutality.

Think of the present *arrivants* from the West Indies, from other so-called Third World countries, bringing to us their various multicultural dispositions. In spite of their cultural peculiarities, they must kiss the ground to know they are here. It has to be. Otherwise, they would take the first Air Canada flight home. Their refusal to satisfy the question, "Why don't you go back home?" is in itself their declaration that there is no longer any home; and, also that they have not abrogated citizenship of this country, in spite of the ill-wishers.

For we have all asked ourselves the same question: "Why am I here? In all this cold? With no job? With the police on our arse?"

How clearly, then, was this pessimism grasped on the night of May 4th when the youths repudiated that definition of themselves as powerless citizens, and took into their hands with their anger the law they do not seem to respect. They acted differently from their fathers. And they demonstrated a new ethic. Their fathers, however, showed more patience and more hope.

I have been angry, willing and ready to picket, to burn, yes, burn baby burn, at every incident of a policeman shooting a black man. It had to be so. And my anger reaches the pitch of the irresponsibility of our black "leaders," messianic as they are, but human in their consternation that if this "brutality" is not abated, not checked, not controlled by a citizen's committee, by a simple use of statistics, in a few years, "all our young black men will be in the grave," or in prison. The single most puzzling attitude of young blacks today is that, in their protest, they do not have the same fear of death, of prison, or the police. Theirs is a new bone-bred anger.

The anger is justified. And the statistics, used wantonly and inappropriately, do point a finger at the alarming relation of crime to color and police executions to color. I must feel, however, that while some policemen are bastards, all are not, and cannot be; and I must feel also, that these young black men and women do not understand that ethic of improvisation, that patience of their forefathers.

It is precisely that improvisation that explains my presence upon this landscape today. Were it not so, either through the efficacy of slavery, or through the lack of creative response to the insurmountable circumstances and conditions of my existence in history, I would have been wiped out. "Offed." It is more than the saying, "He who fights and runs away, may live to fight another day." There is no guarantee that the fight will be dispatched in my favor. There is merely postponement, relief, a reprieve; or a direction to me to change tactics, to understand that I must not, should the first encounter go against me; that with knowledge and experience, I should be capable of engaging the battle from another flank. We must now face the question: what form will the second confrontation take? Will it be more violent than the first.? Will more stores be trashed? Will we face the police with their guns? Will there be blacks against whites? And who will be the allies of each?

This brings me to the present history. It is brutal. It is disappointing. It is negative. It is misunderstood. It is criminal. It is racist. It involves, at its most dramatic and symbolic foundation, our community. "Our" is the word of importance and significance. For even though I do not live in those neighborhoods of Jane and Finch, and in the suburbs which, when they were developed, were intended to be "safe places in which to bring up our children" and have now become battlefields for those very children; even though I am not on welfare; even though I do not rent a rent controlled apartment; even though I do not live in Ontario Housing; I am still connected to those who do.

I do not use the word "our" in an Africanated sense, in any sense of the rhetoric of hyphenation, or of myths about Africa. I want to include in this sense of the word, those of my color who were born here; for the problem today in Toronto is about color and no longer about culture or ethnicity. It is about being black; *noir,* as they say in another province. Or, in the proper anthropological and sociological sense, it is about the *"presence africaine."* Many of those born here feel that the attention given to recent *arrivants,* to their presence, their attitudes, their mannerisms, their extremism, and their radicalism, denies the rightful place and function of Canadian-born blacks, who ought to be approached for solutions to this collision of colors. There is the feeling, justified in principle and in other ways, that those born here have been overlooked in the media's concentration on homage to the most recent *arrivants.* And it cannot be disputed that we recent *arrivants,* with varying degrees of improper attitude and behavior, have refused to admit that, before we came, there was the man who was a porter on the Canadian National Railway, the man in the wash room of the Towne Tavern handing out thick, white towels, and the man who owned the taxicab who was beaten up for daring to be a businessman. They are all connected to me because they are human beings, even more than because they are black. And if I am implying that this racial collision is the history also of poor whites, or unfortunate whites, then they too are connected to me. Blood of a blood. As my mother said, "Blood more thicker than water."

I must, therefore, find and embrace some symbiotic relationship between myself, and those like me, and those who are, in the rhetoric of the "leaders," the targets of racist policemen. The targets of racist policemen are black. It is an axiomatic statement. Are the police racist? Not every policeman can be racist. But in the same way as we are touched by the powerful applications of stereotype, so too, in this ironic way, are all the police assumed racist. In a very real sense, when you are on my side of this confrontation, it does not matter whether all police are racist, or whether only 10 percent are; the target cannot enjoy the luxury of liberal consideration. Unless there are no white youths robbing stores, stealing cars, and taking drugs, then the unjustified, excessive force upon black suspects is racist behavior. It can't be anything but this.

But we have still to look at the question of black youths and black culpability. Are they indulging in this behavior, and expecting a silkgloved treatment, because they are black, and can therefore raise the hackles of a black protest? And if this protest is bellowed and placarded only because the suspect is black, and the demonstration of anger taken up without examining the facts of the case, then these messianic "leaders" are doing those suspects a profound disservice; and, in a more serious way, they are pitting the black community against the police in a monolithic confrontation.

This was made crystal clear on the evening of Monday May 4th, 1992, a date that will reoccur from now on in any serious dissertation of what is called, loosely and disadvantageously to blacks, "race relations." This term can only mean the confrontation born of the *presence africaine* it certainly cannot mean or imply that there is a relationship between the races, since "relations" is a positive and reciprocal interaction. I am not speaking about private, individual intercourse. I am speaking, rather, about the entire system, that institutional structure of unapproachable, unseen power.

The first reactions to the fourth of May, as reactions without the benefit of thought or reasonableness usually are, were offensive, crude, racist and, at the same time, naive. The *Toronto Sun*, a newspaper that may not be accused of racial reasonableness, blurted out in characteristic sensationalism, "Ugly," with an action photograph of a black man to illustrate the metaphor. When looters terrorized downtown Toronto, the *Sun* regarded this black outburst, this extemporaneous explosion of years and years of pent-up fury and disillusionment at the unchastised, brutal behavior of the police towards young black suspects, as, "Toronto loses its innocence." What innocence? In all the years I have lived in this city, I have never considered Toronto to be innocent. Not in its attitude towards black people. Not in its knowledge that that attitude was racist. Not in the "race relations" discussions and meetings. Not in the meetings we have been having with the politicians since the Sixties, when I marched with others to City Hall, to Queen's Park, to downtown Loblaws Stores to protest the treatment of blacks in this city and in this country. What does "innocence" mean? It has a connotation of purity of blissful unawareness. It has a connotation of being vulnerable to evil, vile forces. It has the connotation of inciting undeserved abuse; manipulation.

I have mentioned the *Toronto Sun,* and singled it out as the conveyor of the most irresponsible commentary on the events of May 4th. The *Toronto Star* said, "Hundreds riot after anti-racism protest," and with some reservation, that reaction was my own. The *Globe and Mail,* with characteristic temperance, echoed the sentiments of the *Star* and said, "Yonge Street trashed as justice protest turns into rampage." It seemed to me as if the *Sun* were waiting for the riot to happen, in order to justify its acknowledged attitude to the black community in Toronto. What innocence?

In the Sixties, precisely in March, 1963, *Esquire* magazine attached a white piece of paper to its cover, a rectangle bordered in pink, with these words: "*How America is preparing for THE SECOND CIVIL WAR — Black vs White, the Weapons . . . the Strategy . . . the Leaders.*" "Twenty-nine years later, in all innocence, the covers of *Saturday Night* and *Maclean's* magazines, which seemed to have been in peaceful slumber during that time, are as shocked as the *Sun.* They cannot, in all honesty, be shocked.

I first witnessed Toronto's "innocence" in the middle years of the Sixties, a time when I joined and led demonstrations to highlight discrimination in housing, in jobs, and in social intercourse. I answered the advertisement of a vacant flat; I went to the door; I rang the bell; the door opened; I was seen; the countenance changed; and the flat was no longer vacant. Just around the corner, I called the telephone number listed, and was told by the voice, the same voice, the voice I recognized at the slammed front door, "Oh, please come! The flat is not rented." It was a European voice.

Or I had presented myself, complete with qualifications, at an office downtown: advertising agency, insurance company, Imperial Oil, all of them, I was interviewed; there was a smile; there was some mention that, "Oh, what a beautiful place you come from! I've been there on holiday. But I can't understand why you would leave that place and come here! In all this cold." And the application was filed because "the moment there's a vacancy we'll call you." *Don 't call me, I'll call you.* Or, as happened in most cases, "You're overqualified for the job we're offering. The person we're looking for should have only Grade 13."

And once, after my spirits were raised by expectation, forgetting in my self-delusion the harsh lessons of job discrimination, I had my application "kept at the top of the file" of those on the short list; and years passed; and I became a writer; and my circle of friends widened; and one night in my own home, at a party, a young woman took me aside, and said, "Austin, do you remember the time you applied for that copywriter's job at the ad agency? Well, when you left, the director tore up your application and threw it in the garbage bin!" There was no protest from me. I was in my own living room, and she was my guest. There were no expletives, no assuring her that I knew it could have happened that way. There was no regret, for I was already successful in other areas of creative endeavor. But what I saw in that action of her former employer, my prospective employer, was the sadness of my not knowing what was being done to me, what *had been done* to my aspiration and ambition. I grieved my lack of knowledge of how decisions were made about me. It is the exclusion, repeated over and over, the accumulated segregation that festers and crystallizes into an attitude of distrust, to put it mildly. He who is now being lauded and recompensed, and made a chancellor of York University, Oscar Peterson, was barred from entering the Towne Tavern, because on his arm was a white woman. Why this "innocence?"

When I picketed all of the downtown Loblaws stores because its president had made a racial and derogatory remark during his trip to South Africa in the late Sixties, about the black South African "mamas" liking white bread, that demonstration was meant to point out to Mr. Garfield Weston that it was unacceptable for him to make that statement in South Africa, the bastion of apartheid, and have it go unnoticed here by his customers, consumers of his white bread sliced and packaged with a blonde girl on the wrapper. We wanted him to know that his racist remark on that dark continent was reprehensible here, even though, at that time, the number of South Africans living in Toronto and the surrounding area, was politically insignificant. What innocence? We who are disposed to forget and misunderstand the lessons of the past are sentenced to be choked and strangled by that very history.

The boil of contained animosity and anger on the Fourth of May was therefore no surprise to me, whether intellectual or political. The historical use of unjustified police force against suspected black youths, culminated in the acquittal of the policemen accused in the Lawson murder, soon after four Los Angeles policemen were set free in that other case of police brutality. It does not take a sociologist, an expert in "race relations," or a Premier's Committee — a committee headed, ironically, by a former leader of the Provincial NDP, who in all those years made no statement, took no moral position, did nothing to demonstrate that anything more than the usual band-aid treatment of a boil that has been festering in Toronto since 1958, was needed — to inquire into the cause of this "loss of innocence." We say that Canada and Toronto are not America and Los Angeles. We say, and have been saying until May 4th, that it cannot happen here. *It!* The innumerable blows delivered on the unprotected body of that black man in Los Angeles, caught in human motion and in slow motion, were felt by each and every black man and woman living in Toronto. In the same way, as we felt the remark made by Mr. Garfield Weston in South Africa, the bombing of those four black children in that church in Selma, or Montgomery, Atlanta, Mississippi — it doesn't matter in which town or city, in which state or country, the metaphor remains indelible, fixed, understood by us, and as stinging as if we ourselves had received those blows; as if our young, beautiful black bodies had been torn apart like a crushed watermelon.

It is not
it is not
it is not enough
to be pause, to be hole
to be void, to be silent

to be semicolon, to be semicolony;
fling me the stone
that will confound the world
find me the rage
and I will raze the colony
fill me with words
and I will blind your God.[2]

I have chosen to "fill with words;" but I was not always so moderate and agreeable to discussion. And because I have chosen that strategy to describe and understand "it," does not mean that I shall castigate out of hand those who have chosen another method for the expression of their rage.

This is not to say that I am insensitive to the breaking of the law. The law has its own way of dealing with those who are culpable. But I am not talking about the "looters," whether in Toronto or in Los Angeles. I am talking about something much more important; the immorality of silence.

The term was first created by James Baldwin. And since that time, the silence has remained, and has become crystallized in what is called a backlash. How many times? How many times am I to be harnessed by the intellectual responsibility of explaining the behavior of the colonized? How many times must I be saddled with this intellectual burden, I, slave, Negro, colored, black, colonized, forced to assume the moral responsibility for that pervasive immorality of silence, and explain one more time, with futile and inefficacious result, the intensity of the sting in the whip, the pain at the sight of bodies swinging from a tree, the marksmanship of the innumerable blows pelted into Rodney King's body? Why am I called on to explain what is now a part of the system's professionalism with television and videotape genius? Do I have to prove that perhaps the blows I saw delivered and repeated on every television set in the whole world were really a figment of imagination, a trick of superior American technology? That, in fact, what I was seeing was not what I saw, but a metaphor of law and order, a euphemism for justice?

How can I convince the black youth of Toronto, who are the peers and equals in color and age and aspiration and dashed ambition of all those shot by policemen, that their fate shall be different from Lawson's? What intellectual ammunition must I use to convince them that what they saw on the television that night in Los Angeles, when Rodney King was on the ground, bent into the shape of a helpless embryo, symbol of the helplessness of the *presence africaine* upon a landscape of white racism, does not reflect the image held of them here, miles and miles away? And what should I tell the Premier's Committee, the Mayor's Committee, the Legislature's Committee? Can I tell them that the blows delivered upon the black embryonic shape on that night broke ten ribs instead of eight? That the blows did not cripple Rodney King, but merely stunned him? And that the bullet fired by the policeman in Toronto entered Lawson's shoulder, and not his heart, and his mother's heart, and the hearts of all mothers, whether white or black (for there cannot continue to be this unnatural division of sorrow). And that each young black man wonders why a policeman in Toronto shoots a black suspect, whether he is in a stolen car, or in an alley with a knife? Is it my business to explain to our black youth, who will in turn educate these "race relations" committees, that they must not see and compare Los Angeles with Toronto? I shall not blaspheme the intelligence of these beautiful young black men.

Indeed, what "innocence" can Toronto claim to have lost, when for years I would meet a man or a woman on the street, and he or she would agree that, "It is worse here, these days, than it was in the Sixties."

When I was demonstrating through the streets of Toronto in the Sixties; when I was singing *We Shall Overcome;* when I was leading demonstrations with the late Rabbi Abraham Feinberg; when I was gladdened by the signing of the Civil Rights Bill; when I was convinced of the Just Society; when I had seen the mountaintop; when John Coltrane's tenor saxophone raged and Miles Davis's piercing trumpet, sharp as a surgeon's knife, was cutting out the cancer of racism; when Abby Lincoln, and Max Roach were screaming out *Freedom Now Suite;* when Nina Simone was singing *Mississippi Goddamn* (and meant every word of it!); when LeRoi Jones was calling for a "black world," a world not separate, but a world in which black has dignity; when all these things were happening, where were you? Where were you?

You were, in the midst of this frustration, this anger, this delusion and this hope, sitting on your mothers' laps, accompanying them to rallies at which *We Shall Overcome* was chanted. You were held by the warm hands of your fathers, as they stood on the brink, on the periphery (but were present, nevertheless), and listened to Bob Dylan, Buffy Saint-Marie, Roberta Flack, and Billie Holiday, as they, artists and historians, witnesses and mothers and fathers, grieved collectively for the pessimism that had overtaken our lives. Nobody would have shown shock and "innocence" if the entire country had gone up in flames.

And when James Baldwin said that the "fire next time" was the inevitable consequence if we continued to be "innocent" and wallow in the luxury of the "immorality of silence," we all thought that it was just a matter of time. And the persons to whom we were speaking, in our rage and in our anger, with little possibility of reprieve, are precisely these men the age of the Premier of Ontario and the chair of the Premier's Committee. We thought that we had dug the cancer from the minds of the younger generation, so that, in the Nineties, we could build the really just society. But it was not to have been our heritage. It was not to have been our reward. It was not to have been the apprehension of our warning.

Otherwise, the unspoken point is to vindicate and make conspicuous the host society's existing reservations regarding members of that targeted racial or ethnic group. If our society and our community were not tinged with racism; and, certainly, if unspoken conclusions were not made about the worthiness of racial and ethnic groups; then, as would happen in a society free of such racism, there may be some benefit to be gained from publishing statistics of crime based upon racial or ethnic origin. As there is, at present, no mutually creative and no mutually acknowledged relationship between whites and blacks in the general sense; and since the goodwill that exists is expressed in inter-personal relationships (my white neighbor may be my most trusted friend, and vice versa, because we *know* each other); the confrontation will continue on that tormenting level. We can no longer be guilty of the kind of "innocence" that allows us to think otherwise.

The hope for all of us lies in our apprehension of the fact that anti-social behavior is not a function of race or ethnicity. And the fact that even the victims of this aberrant racist attitude have not yet gone "back where they came from" must suggest to us that the temperament of the black youth is fashioned in a different and more suspicious cauldron of animosity than the circumstances that fashioned men and women of my generation. We were not born here. Many of the black youth we see today were. And those who are not Canadian have become accustomed to the privileges and rights that this country extends to every man, woman, and child who lives here.

Patience is not a characteristic of youth. Patience is also not manufactured with a specific color. And we may not ask a young black youth to be more patient in the face of his experience and close knowledge of this country's institutions, which exclude him from joining more often than they entreat him to share in the building and organization of his community.

So he is not going "back where he came from": whether it is the West Indies, Africa, or back into that cocoon of patient non-activism He cannot leave because there is no place to go. This is home. This is where he belongs. And I daresay that this insistence on Canada being home carries the implication, in spite of the Fourth of May, that things will improve. But it is more important that the young black men and women believe that they can make, and have already made, a singularly distinguished contribution to the culture and the mores of this community, a community from which they find themselves left out — left out of schools, left out of jobs, left out of decisions about themselves and their future, left out of promotions, left out of decision-making positions in the private and public institutions of this city.

What meaning do the young find in the words of "Strange Fruit" from the mouth of Billie Holiday? How can they convince themselves that this song, a blues, does not touch their existence in Toronto, many miles from its locus? If I repeat the words, will they not see its application to their lives?

Southern trees bear strange fruit
Black bodies hanging in the Southern breeze
Blood on the leaves
And blood at the root[3]

Why do we only instruct our young men and young women in the fact of racism? Why do we wait for the shattering and rape of our "innocence" which makes us silent co-conspirators, at least witnesses, and in some cases branches of those "southern trees bearing strange fruit."

I do not intend to be guilty of the same stupidity as others, a stupidity as oppressive as racism itself: I will admit that the same policemen we sometimes accuse of violent discrimination, make my life safe and secure in a city that is bordering on the American syndrome of ghettoized crime. In spite of the Fourth of May, this city is still *north* of the border of America and of that racism. I must lament my own unscientific but stark accumulation of statistics, from which I cannot hide, which show me that blacks are killing blacks; that young black men (and a few black women), perhaps too entranced by the materialism in this city, and less impressed by "learning to get ahead faster, and more bigger brains," as my mother would say, are expressing their frustration and disappointment in a violent, pseudo-macho manner. This black badness is not new, as the police and the community all know.

There was a time when a black person ran to the other end of the subway platform to say, "Hey, man! How long you here?" and hug. A time when you disappeared into your basement room in shame if you got a traffic ticket. A time when you dipped out of society if you "had a li'l problem with the police," because you had *let the race down.* But now. In the Nineties. In this sharp age. With designer clothes. Pumped-up sneakers. Ninja garments — the raiment of the Bad. The young are plastered on the front pages, and held in close-up for us to see the new, bad motherfuckers who ain't taking no shit from the man, from the police, from the system. In one sense, the young black men and women have repudiated the history of their fathers, which to them is a history of unmanliness, and their father's role in that history, which, they argue, has delayed better "race relations" and an end to institutional racism.

A terrible time. And you may ask Bev Folkes-Small. Or ask Headley. If the underground railroad were still chug-chug-chugging along, it would stop for you at the Don Jail, or let you off at the detention centre in the east, or in the west. And if you could hitch a ride as far as Kingston, you would see the way this new badness is reflected in the statistics — we can't hide from this, — in the proportion, in the number, in the presence of our young men and our young women.

"I didn't know we was so vi'lent, man!"

"Must be the climate. The cold temper'ture."

"You really think so?"

"It could be the education they getting."

"You mean, lack of it!"

"Could be. They want God. They should go-church."

So, we look at the question of the relationship of the police to black youth, from the point of view of black culpability. And we cringe as we look. And we have theories. And we protest. And we have investigations. And we protest. And we have seminars. And we protest. And we have Premiers' Committees. And we protest. We protest too much. But we have still to look at the question. I can offer no answer. I can offer no answer because the question being asked is the wrong question. In fact, it should not be asked, for it has been posed before. And the evidence upon which the question is based has been accumulating for a long time. For how long is the question going to be asked?

How long are we required to remain immigrants? Frightened black youth? How long before national identity becomes an aggressive determination, before our black leadership" changes from one that reacts to crisis, from one that is messianic, to one with a pervasive intention to build bridges? Bridges necessary, because we are not "going back where we come from." That is not a solution. That is not an alternative.

The porter on the train, the man in the washroom handing out fresh, white towels, and that man who owned the first "independent" taxicab have each left footprints in the snow. And like thousands of Canadian blacks, who have been maligned for their integrationist attitude by West Indians, with a more recent radicalism we must understand that they could not have made their bad experiences the focus of their lives.

If the experiment of multiculturalism fails here in Toronto, in spite of the Fourth of May and if the disillusionment of being "tarred" with this reflected "new badness" makes us insecure about our image in the broader community; if we do not realize that Canada is the last remaining place on Earth where we can live as men and women (the eccentricities of racism, notwithstanding); if we throw out the bathtub along with the soiled water, the sullied water; we would be soothing the egos of pessimists. I have not lost my optimism, even though, after May 4th, it may be more difficult for me to accept that my optimism is a natural characteristic of the disposition of racism here. And I must confess that I may be in the minority. I am aware of the anger. I am a part of that anger. I am aware of the despair. I am a part of that despair. The rage is mine. But I, armed with greater age (if not greater wisdom as a consequence), put my reliance upon the poets.

Let there be no love poems written
until love can exist freely and
cleanly. Let Black People understand
that they are the lovers and the sons
of lovers and warriors and sons
of warriors Are poems & poets &
all the loveliness here in the world
We want a black poem. And a
Black World.
Let the world be a Black Poem
And Let All Black People Speak
This Poem Silently or LOUD[4]

I am tempted to set this poem of LeRoi Jones (Amiri Baraka) as the homework exercise of those chosen to sit down with us, to solve this problem. To understand "it." And I am tempted to gear their "innocence" from the presumption that what is advocated here is not a black world, a segregated society. And I am tempted to leave the rest to their well-intentioned un-virgined souls.

The porter on the train, the man in the washroom of the Towne Tavern, and the man who dared to be a businessman have left their experiences in the snow of this city. They have all this "history," all these "answers." And as we were told on the Fourth of May, if these demands are left unheeded, what shall be left is Sodom and Gomorrah. But that possibility is still unrealistic.

There will be no fire next time, even though there have been bricks. For we have trodden in the wine press too long not to realize the sweetness of the grape here, not to acknowledge the labor of those who went before us, those who were killed, those who were emasculated; not to be pleased, however, that we, all of us, have lifted this place from what it was when we met it, to a new residence, and a renaissance. We live here. I live here. I ain't going nowhere.

1992

1"A Far Cry from Africa" from *Selected Poems by Derek Walcott* (Farrar, Straus & Giroux 1964.)
2 "Negus" from *Islands* by Edward Brathwaite (Oxford, 1969.)
3 From "Strange Fruit." Lyrics by Lewis Allen. Originally recorded by Billie Holiday for Commodore Records Co., Inc. 1939.
4"Black Art" from *Black Magic* by LeRoi Jones/Amiri Baraka (Bobbs-Merrill, 1969.)

Introduction to Nine Men Who Laughed

Canada is the home of most of the characters in these short stories. Canada is the reality, the individual and subjective predicament, the hardship. Canada is also the cause of their laughter.

Hardships exist in spite of the potentialities and known abilities of such men as these. They have all lived as students of some kind, in an established and nationally recognized Canadian institution of learning. But they have lived under a cloud of confusion. Under a smear of self-doubt. They have been educated in a system which holds no regard for their intelligence.

And all of them exist on the periphery of rewards, and suffer from unfair chastisements.

These men could also be in London, Paris, New York or Moscow. They happen to be in Toronto. And tragically, they forget or are made to forget that their former status, the aristocratic status they held at home, should be the stamp of their presence on the university and on this foreign landscape. Their presence in city squares, in museums and on the city streets of foreign metropolises is very often so resented that they forget their former status, and this forgetfulness turns into laughter, the only available weapon against resentment.

Sometimes the self-doubt of the men in this collection thickens into depressing introspection. But the depression of the immigrant exists only because he has been forced to accommodate himself to the concept, whether political or cultural, of being an immigrant. Agreeing to being defined only as an immigrant, he is accepting that he is "different." This accommodation becomes, in turn, an evil and devious assault upon personality and character, upon the immigrant's nature.

The men we meet could be aboriginals, maoris, colored, native peoples. They are the unnamed man in the story "Canadian Experience." The man in this story is "unchristened," nameless, because he has himself forgotten to exert his identity. And so he is reduced to laughing at his own misfortune. He has forgotten who he is.

All these men have forgotten, at that most critical point in their lives, the moment of their *contact* with hostility: discrimination in jobs and housing; being given a passing grade for an "A" examination; bad food (that is, foreign to their tastes and culture) and tasteless food; the misery that results from imitating a way of life they do not know. Because they have forgotten their first *contact,* they have become numbed into thinking that these facets of life in Toronto, aspects of the Canadian culture, now deserve laughter. But to laugh at this late stage is to commit suicide.

These stories were written as a means of escaping the physical and mental torment skeined by the prepossessiveness of the new culture. It was an attitude that became so much like ice water in the veins, that it ceased to be merely an attitude, but became the *person* who confronted me with her prepossessiveness, the woman, the system. The person was now a microcosm of all the words, bad conclusions and faulty definitions of "immigrant" and became a metaphor for arrogance.

She, the attitude, the system, knew my meaning. Knew the meaning of the women who are, in a metaphorical sense, me. And since she knew my meaning, the meaning of my writing and its importance, she assaulted me. It was an assault that was all the more reprehensible because it was based on personal knowledge. And the more so because its timing was deliberate, to catch me off balance.

In their hearts, these men have refused to accept the various categorizations and all the conclusions that can be drawn from the categorizations that define them as "immigrants." They know, even though they are silent, that that status implies certain debilitating and mediatizing pathologies. They cannot sleep with the system or with the attitude.

But they do accommodate. They succumb to the assault. And find no weapon but laughter — the weapon of fools. It seems to be the only effective means of warding off the evil spirits and the devious assaults upon one's personality. It is a quick-witted tool that enables one to set up a temporary distance between one and those assaults. When the men in these stories laugh, they are being disarming.

In Barbados, at Harrison College, where I was schooled and trained in the British system of values — a public school education—we were taught that only fools laughed. But we (the same men before we emigrated to Canada) were also marked out as members of a colonial elite, persons whose futures were assured, both in Barbados and elsewhere in the English-speaking world, whether we found ourselves amongst civilized or uncivilized peoples. We were confident. And had we remained in the comfortable, warm mud of the colonies, had we remained at "home," we would certainly not have had to suffer fools or laughter gladly.

This colonial past, which gave these men a privileged position, which gave them the perception needed to understand the realism of immigration, began to be regarded with ambivalence. And this ambivalence is further intensified each day these men spend in a country in which they were not born.

Their laughter is not mirthful. It is contemptuous. Even though in some cases, the immigrant finds that he must laugh at his predicament or at the mistakes he has made in that predicament, he may be doing this merely to defuse and lessen racial and cultural tension. But should he laugh only for these reasons, his laughter becomes demeaning criticism of his own worth.

Laughter in Barbados, and laughter in Canada, by these same men, is, as my mother would say, "a horse of a different colour."

The men who laugh in these stories are doing so because they represent the powerless and the colonized. They are not laughing because they are amused that a policeman beats them in cell or that they see a green hornet friend being beaten or even that they are discovered in a tricky situation of sexual infidelity. They are laughing because they have become accommodating to a hostile society, and their laughter is therefore a "tick," an idiosyncratic adaptation to the society.

They may even cheapen themselves with this kind of laughter. Like the laughter in the story "Canadian Experience," it is harmless to the system but fatal to him who laughs. It is a means of embracing a system which would rather have them laugh than protest. The system hopes that "immigrants" will always be laughing. For the absence of laughter is the forerunner of a refashioning of the attitudes and the ordering of the system itself, calculated to include the "immigrant" at the highest levels of creativity — both political and cultural. The system cannot accommodate this. So it encourages laughter and seduces the "immigrant."

When a character says, "This fucking system" or "This system makes me laugh" (out of frustration or, more realistically, because he has become lazy, too lazy to think clearly), he is not trying to reduce either the seriousness of the hurt inflicted upon him by the system or to make the system's racism less abrasive: he is confessing to his own inadequacy to take a strict moral position and destroy the system. Such men laugh because they are, perhaps, already morally dead.

Some say that life imitates art. For the "immigrant" in these stories there is no life and there is no art. There is no "life" because they do not live freely or with any semblance of mutual, creative relationships. The "immigrant" is merely *living.*

"How are things, man?"

"Living, man. I just here, living."

In that word "living" is all the criticism, all the realism, all the truth of being in a foreign place.

Such men are created in an environment, a circumstance of "tenseness," in a mood of reappraisal, of discovering oneself. They were written in search of a rhetoric. The author is trying to discover something which a former black student at Yale University called a "black aesthetic," a black way of seeing black things, a blackening of the consciousness.

These stories were written to destroy the definitions that *others* have used to portray so-called immigrants, black people. They are intended to rip away the film, the cataract of perception, in order to provide clear vision, even if what is seen is crueller, less palatable than the picture exhibited previously. They suggest a new way of seeing such men and their disposition.

The language of these stories is the language these men would use when they are by themselves, when they are with friends, when they are apart from strangers. It is more suitable and more appropriate than formal English, which is incapable, in this context, of translating the essence of the "black aesthetic." When these men speak, it is always with a strange and, at times, unnatural compassion or laughter. But in most cases, it is only the language that laughs. The propositions and the anger that the language describes — they do not laugh.

In the same way that I detest the use of the term "immigrant" to define the presence of such men upon the landscape of Toronto, so too do I eschew my own term "black aesthetic" if it suggests that this is a literature about black men. It would be suicidal to permit that categorization of these stories. The men are black only because they live in Toronto, in a society which has officially branded them "immigrants" from the West Indies. Their cultural ancestry is a greater force than their color or the branded status of "immigrant."

The language they use to perpetuate their "aesthetic" is full of improvisation. Improvisation is the single most essential quality they would have used in the islands to ensure victory over a formerly oppressive system or to prevent their lives from being shortened by that system. Improvisation made sure that they did not accede to complete human degradation.

The sociologists call that system slavery. In the context of this collection, we may call it "immigrant life." But I doubt very much whether such men, restricted though they are by their status of "immigrant," would define themselves or describe their lives in these negative terms. For to consider themselves "immigrants," to accept this as the paramount definition of their presence here, to consider themselves slaves, would be to commit the unlaughable and mortal sin of suicide.

1986

Books by Austin Clarke

Fiction

The Survivors of the Crossing
Amongst Thistles and Thorns
The Meeting Point
Storm of Fortune
The Bigger Light
When he was Free and Young
  and he Used to Wear Silks (Stories)
When Women Ruled (Stories)
The Prime Minister
Nine Men Who Laughed (Stories)
Proud Empires
In This City (Stories)
There Are No Elders (Stories)
The Origin of Waves

Non-Fiction

Growing Up Stupid Under the Union Jack
A Passage Back Home

Austin Clarke was born in Barbados in 1934. He came to Canada in 1955. In his early years, and as a student at Trinity College, University of Toronto, he signed himself as A. A. Chesterfield-Clarke. These were the years 1955 to 1958. Becoming a professional writer, he published for several years as Austin C. Clarke, and in recent years as Austin Clarke. He has published eight novels and some fifty short stories. He has lived largely in Toronto, where he entered his name for the mayoralty race in 1968; also returning regularly to Barbados; while assuming the posts of visiting professor in English and African American Literature or Writer-in-Residence at Yale (1968-1971); Brandeis (1970-1971); Williams College (1972-1973); Duke (1973-1974); University of Texas at Austin (1974-1975); Concordia (1977-1978); and the University of Western Ontario (1992). Since 1976, he has written a weekly humorous column, as 'Tom' Clarke, for the *Nation* newspaper in Barbados: some 1000 columns. He had been, in 1975, appointed Manager of the Caribbean Broadcasting Corporation, Barbados (CBC), but he left that position in 1976, becoming Cultural Attaché, Embassy of Barbados at Washington, D.C., for 1975-1976. He ran for the provincial Progressive Conservative Party in the election of 1977. In 1989, he was appointed as a member of the Federal Immigration and Refugee Board. He resigned from that position in 1994.

He has published in Canada, the United States, and England, and has been translated into all the major European languages.

Reflecting the tensions of language so central to Clarke's work, the Tom Clarke columns employ standard English spelling; all other texts employ an Americanized English, which is familiar to Canadian readers.